Pax

Also by John Harvey

The Plate Shop

Coup d'Etat

The Legend of Captain Space

The Subject of a Portrait

Victorian Novelists and their Illustrators

Men in Black

Clothes

The Story of Black

The Poetics of Sight

Stairs/Vathmedon (with Aris Georgiou)

Pax

John Harvey

Holland House

www.hhousebooks.com

Hardback ISBN: 978-1-910688-87-8

Cover design by Ken Dawson
Typeset by Polgarus Studio

Published in the UK

Holland House Books
Holland House
47 Greenham Road
Newbury, Berkshire RG14 7HY
United Kingdom

www.hhousebooks.com

For Julietta Louise and Eleni Chloe

'Thameside, 1629'

This picture, this etching he has made, recalls an event: a surprise meeting, a veiled disclosure.

The scene it shows plays in his head. Here's a river so wide it looks like a lake, with timber-ribbed houses at its edge. And here's the diplomat, sauntering by docks and jetties. Beside him poops and fo'c'sles sway, there are thickets of sails bound tight to their yards. These are not what amaze him. His eyes have screwed to a place where the currents disturb. Something rises there from the deep, and moves towards him. It's a water-snake. A seal's back. Now a long ridge shows. The humped shape swells, the diplomat steps back. Will a monster rear up – Leviathan, glaring with jagged eyes?

Now the apparition looks like nothing so much as a rowboat turned upside down. The oars break surface, emerging from leather sleeves that stick out, like a beetle's legs, from either side of the vessel. For a vessel it must be, though it is a ludicrous thing – he gives a yelp of laughter. The oars plash and splash, coming closer.

Others have joined him: beside him hulks a grizzled, hirsute man: with his mane, beard and flat-featured face he looks to have the head of a lion; another, in black, wears the steeple-crowned hat of a Puritan; and other various citizens come, in doublet and mantle.

The upside-down vessel bumps the timbers of the wharf. On its top there's something like a window-frame covered in leather, coated black with pitch. The boat rocks unsteadily, there are sounds from within. What beings from the undersea world will emerge? The leather creaks as it bends and the wooden frame lifts. A handsome head appears — a gentleman's head, with hazel moustachios though with thinning hair. But his face is pale, he gasps for breath. The diplomat stares, then bursts out,

'Sieur Peter Paul! What in the name of all the saints do you here?'

The gentleman looks round, blinking, panting. Though pale he is beaded with sweat. He cries out, 'Dudley!'

As he clambers up they see his lace and his reddish-gold doublet.

Shakily, for the vessel tips, he grabs a timber and climbs onto the landing stage. Is he faint? Dudley offers a hand to his elbow.

'You are well, Peter Paul?'

'I have heard— I have seen—' He takes a breath, 'Come, Cornelis,' and turns to help the next man emerge. This figure is stranger still. He too, it seems, wears his smarter clothes, though his deep-turquoise doublet is threadbare and patched. His face is ravaged with marks, stains, burns and scars which even interrupt his straggling beard. He stands, none the less, with proud assurance as the gentleman introduces him to the diplomat.

'Sir Dudley Carleton – Cornelis Jacobszoon Drebbel of Alkmaar.'

'Minheer Drebbel,' the diplomat exclaims, 'your fame is great. This is one of your engines?'

'My descending engine. The Sieur Rubens desired to see it.'

'Peter Paul!' Carleton says, 'I never thought to see our master painter go diving in the mud of Thames.'

Rubens is a better colour now. 'Nor is this my first "dive" there.'

'No?'

'I had a ludicrous mishap – but never mind.'

Drebbel is explaining, 'This is the latest of my engines. The great king, royal James, he deigned to travel in my first underwater boat. He marvelled much, though it was a simple thing. My improved engine hides a terrible power.'

He nods to Rubens, who for a moment looks stricken. They have turned to the vessel, from which other men clamber. They are stripped to the waist, sweat runs and joins on their wide flushed shoulders. They swing and work their arms and take great breaths.

'We should all breathe deep,' Drebbel says. 'The air in my engine is not of the freshest.'

Rubens nods. 'Cornelis makes air in a wondrous way.'

'I heat salts of urine inside a great flask, but when that is used up we breathe their gaseous excrement.'

'Indeed!' Dudley's eyes have sharpened.

Cornelis bows. 'You will excuse me. I must tend to the storing of my engine.' He steps back to the landing stage, and is busy with the men, who are shaking on shirts and jerkins.

'Peter Paul,' Carleton says, 'you are bent on seeing all the sights in this woebegone realm.'

'Cornelis is a fellow-countrymen. He has shown me... marvels. I have learned today that the future is a precipice.'

Carleton too grows grave. 'The present is a precipice where *you* tread, I think.'

'Have you heard more at Court? The reports I catch trouble me.'

'It is true, for sure, that perils beset you. You have a noble purpose, which some fear, and some hate. Great powers in Europe are ranged against you, and you have made a mighty enemy. He dwells across the sea, but he has long fingers, that reach even to where we stand.'

'The Cardinal? He loves great art. When I talked with him a few years since, he made to be my friend.'

'He is no friend now. Of all the cunning minds of Europe, his is the brain I should most fear to be shaping machinations against me.'

Rubens heaves a sigh, Carleton studies his face.

'All I will say is, beware, Peter Paul. *En garde!*'

Rubens nods and looks behind him. 'For certain I am followed. Whichever way I go.'

Perhaps Carleton gives the slightest nod in response.

Cornelis returns. 'Let us sit a moment, and refresh!' He motions to a ramshackle tavern nearby. 'Servitor, ho!'

They sit at a bench there, and presently bread, pickles, salt fish and ale are brought to them.

'I know this house, for I am fallen to keeping an inn myself, as the Sieur Rubens knows.'

Carleton exclaims, 'You keep an alehouse, Minheer Drebbel?'

'I am reduced to that. The new King does not favour my inventions, as the Emperor and royal James were wont to do. But so the world goes – now up, now down.'

'Cornelis has shown me many things,' Rubens says. 'I have seen his Blazing Glass, which makes fire far away, and his *perpetuum mobile* which never stops. Within his house I have seen him transformed into a jungle beast.'

'I would like to see that, I love a wonder.' Hearing of the jungle beast, Dudley Carleton looks round. His eye has rested for some time on a shock-head of grey hair near the wall of the inn. As the man lifts his face, Carleton sees it is the lion-head who came beside him on the river bank.

When they have eaten, Drebbel orders a clay pipe from the house, and asks whether they want one likewise. On their declining, and with their permission, he lights up from the tinder box he has in his breeches, and soon is half hidden in cloud.

As they sit, talk and smoke the larger clouds beyond the river break. The sun peeps through, like the eye of God stooping beneath the cloud's brim to watch them. People's clothes come out in bright colours, reds, greens, yellows, blues. A fiery light bathes the derricks and the warehouses while a thousand sparkles play on the lapping waters, and on the further boats, scudding before the breeze, flags, banners and pennants break into fresh colour.

Rubens gazes as though he drinks the change in the light. Carleton murmurs, 'My friend, you are smitten. I see you altogether changed from how you were a short while since.'

Rubens smiles. 'My mood has brightened. And look who is come.'

The others turn to see two girls approaching the inn. One has deeply dark hair and a crimson dress, the other is sandy haired and wears light green. Both have scarlet lips, and much kohl to their eyes.

'Peter Paul, do you know these ladies?'

'They know me.' Across the company Rubens bows to the girls – in a way, however, that does not invite them to join him. They curtsey low with gentle, mocking exaggeration, then one whispers to the other so both dissolve in laughter.

Rubens shakes his head. 'Mistress Bridget and Mistress Audrey. Do not look so stricken, friend Dudley. I am alone in a strange land.'

'But such! And to acknowledge them! And before the world! For shame, Peter Paul!'

Rubens shrugs. 'Maybe I am not a gentleman truly. I am, after all, one that works with his hands, as all at Court remind me.'

'As do I,' Cornelis chimes. 'The painter and the engineer – they admire our works but hold aloof from us.'

Rubens reaches into the pocket of his trunk-hose.

'These girls remind me. There is something I had brought to show you, Cornelis. I had searched for it long before I found it here.'

He pulls out an object wrapped round in cloths. It grows smaller as he removes the wrappings, which themselves grow finer, so the last but one is a scrap of velvet, and the last itself is silk.

'What do you say?'

He sets the object on the bench. Carleton is the first to speak.

'Sieur Rubens! Where did you find this?'

'Why, in an old shop not far from here. But is it not most fine? The Romans left it. It is a treasure from the ancient world.'

'I know not what to say. I am both amazed, and shocked to my roots. Wrap it close, I pray. This evening I shall write to my wife. I shall tell her we met, but I shall not tell her you showed me this.' Carleton turns, for some at neighbouring tables are blinking now and narrowing their eyes.

'Dudley, Dudley, the world is huge, yet a vision of the world is hid in this thing. A vision which in these holy days we have lost. Cornelis, you have not spoken.'

'Nay, but I am not appalled. I wonder, though, how the parts are fastened, or whether it all was cast in one.'

'There speaks the engineer.'

Carefully Rubens wraps the object again, but afterwards simply sits staring at it. A change is occurring: his face shows red streaks, his breaths sound like panting; when he looks up, his eyes are bloodshot. He stuffs the object in his pocket. 'There is something I have learned anew, which in truth I knew before.' He catches their eyes. 'Of those things that make or ruin a life, the greatest and most grievous is what passes in the bedchamber.'

Dudley and Drebbel exchange a glance, then Drebbel stands. 'I have business in the house.' He is quickly gone indoors.

Seeing Rubens still in a study, Carleton places a hand on his knee. 'Well, friend. You have seen the sights London offers.'

'I have. I have been in the theatre. The King hath let me to copy the mighty 'Triumph' canvases by Mantegna, of which he is so proud. I but pray he see not himself as Caesar, in some like procession yet to come through London...' He stops, then starts again. 'Dudley, I told you I heard something not good today. I have learned other bad lessons here. But a few days since, I made a discovery in this town that turned my world – in that word you used once – *widdershins*.'

'You speak of your mission? The Court? The Cardinal?'

'No, nothing of those. I speak of something altogether other.'

Carleton waits, while Rubens gets to his feet and says, 'I must make my way. I am awaited at the Gerbier house. I have handsome hosts, I must not delay them.'

He waves to Drebbel, speaking with someone by the door of the inn. 'Cornelis, I must bid you farewell. I thank you for all you have shown me today. I still am in a daze of astonishment.'

'It was my pleasure. You will remember me to the King of Spain?'

At that Rubens frowns, even glares. Still, they exchange farewells, and further thanks.

'Dudley, it was a delight that we met. Commend my devotions to Lady Anne.'

'I shall this day, when I write.'

They too make their parting salutes, yet Rubens lingers. For a moment he seems to woolgather. 'I do believe some among my works may even last one hundred years – before the oilpaint flake and the canvas fray.' He shrugs. 'Whether any in a future age will pause to learn my own true story, that is more than I may guess.'

'You speak of that thing you "discovered" here?'

'No! For none must know of that.'

They tip again to each other, and he is almost gone. Then he stamps his foot. '*Damn* Van Dyck! God rot his bones!'

Dudley's eyebrows rise. 'Yes? Indeed! Strong words, Peter Paul. No?'

Rubens turns an inflamed eye on him. He gives a growl, another shrug, then a friendly nod, and leaves.

As his not-slim form walks away down the river-bank the man with the lion-head rises and follows, walking close to the walls of buildings. The man with the black tall hat reappears, and at his own distance follows the first. A man in a buff jerkin comes out of the inn, and he too follows after.

All of which Dudley sees, murmuring, 'Friend Peter Paul – indeed, you have roused most dangerous powers. I half guess who these may be, and on whose orders they pursue you. I fear for the mission that brought you here. Nay, Peter Paul, more than that, I fear for you.'

One

The Envoy from Madrid

1

Bloodsmith gazes through his Thameside etching to that Thameside meeting of the artist, the inventor and the diplomat. The scene is described in the battered paperback on Bloodsmith's trestle, *Playing Chess with Kings*. But what did Rubens mean when he spoke of a discovery that made his world go 'widdershins'? The author of the book does not say, though he hints he may know forbidden things.

Bloodsmith wonders, So – do I play the detective? Can I drag to light a scandal not known before?

He picked up 'Thameside', slipping it in with the other prints. Lightly he shuffled them neatly together, and zipped the black portfolio shut.

He turned to go. His studio was in order, as he liked to leave it, the weird square room he had painted red, slope-ceilinged on four sides like the inside of a pyramid. Its walls were spattered with images: cartoons of historical figures, an army with pikes, a war-wounded man, blind and with no limbs; exploded buildings, the twin towers fuming; nudes, Renoir, Ingres, but especially Rubens, their pearly, yielding, puckered bodies delicately, nearly touch each other.

He stopped before the big canvas that leaned by the door. No Old Master this, but one of his own, where the naked woman runs forward in – what? a battle-group? fleeing or charging? Behind her, artillery cranes to the sky and tank-barrels wallow to a curving perspective. Soldiers in hard-hats turn bemused. But what will happen at the garrison gates? Will this naked woman dance straight through, or be stopped at gunpoint and asked for credentials? Is she an attacker – unwanted refugee? In the meantime she boldly dances, the lovely full-figured blonde nude woman, in her graceful swooping coil. Her figure shows through a haze of dust.

He has stopped; he studies. Not an easy look, either. He sniffs and the holes in his blunt nose dilate. The dancer, we see, has serious eyes, pale-blue, keen, even dangerous. But what does she know of what he thinks? What does he know of what she does? We only have a man and woman, gazing with eyes that meet and don't meet, a rueful gaze of hours or years.

His shoulders rise, stirring as though he had wings in his shirt, then fall as he breathes out in an endless emptying.

Enough, he snaps to.

'Oh sodding hell, Robyn!'

Gone. The closing door fans us, the lock has snicked shut, his crisp steps die.

Nor will time, or light, stand still. Late afternoon it must be outside, while the sun emerging from clouds causes the red wall, the nudes and the soldier-photos, and, above all, this painted dancer, lovely naked with piercing eyes, to slowly brighten in gathering goldenness.

~

Lugging his portfolio through the streets. Why didn't I bring the car? But the real question is different. How do you ask her, how do you say it?

At that thought he stops, on the crest of the railway bridge. I don't want *this* question, I want Rubens' secret. Yet the question cuts him like a scalpel left inside by a careless surgeon.

There has been a shower, slates catch the light. The wet rails shine, snaking to the west, while a train pulls softly to a halt at the station. The evening city at peace. Beside him traffic beats, stalled on the bridge, and cyclists nudge him, insinuating on the inside. The weight in his hand is the hope of his art, he can feel the colours shut there like heat.

But bite the bullet, Bloodsmith, you'll say, it must stop, Robyn. I won't have it! I know it's going on.

He resumes his march into the eye of the storm, lugging the black portfolio.

~

I see this picture of an ordered house, warm red brick in a stasis of health. At his gate he stops. What was clear on the bridge is stale by now, and he's tired, at the fag-end of the day. The question is still there, it has walked home beside him, inflating with each breath. If he turned he'd see it.

How does it look, a question of this order? Well, its body and head are fused together, but it has a big ear like an elephant's ear, and a single aching big dish-eye. A mouth of fangs runs from side to side of its gut – this question is hungry, it will eat man and woman. Also it is proboscid: its snout extends, quivering, tentacular, a moist, snuffing trunk.

So the question looks, as it stands beside you in the early evening. Surely the neighbours will be peeping to see it?

'Robyn!'

'Hello, love,' she calls, from the upstairs room she has turned to an office. At her friendly tone his structure shakes.

As he heads to the kitchen, he hears the question follow down the hall, with a swish on the panelling, and the muffled glump of its shapeless feet.

Some moments after, she clatters down.

'Hello, Stephen.' It's the woman from the picture, fair and pleasant-figured. She's handsome, straight-nosed, her warm-blond hair coiled loosely up. She stands by the window, while he has sloped down on a kitchen chair. Beyond her, in the garden - how lovely, the Judas-tree, the purple-pink blossoms, delicate-rich, sprout in clumps from its trunk... He thinks: I can't spoil this. But his voice inquires,

'How was your day?'

'Fine.'

'Did you go out?' A fair question; her photo-gallery is closed between shows.

'Yes, I went out.' She smiles as she speaks: a warm close private smile.

'Where did you go?'

She looks at him quickly. He meant the question to be light, but it made a heavy landing.

'Oh nowhere.'

'Where?'

'What do you mean, where? I went into town. I was thinking about sites, actually.'

'For the gallery?'

'What else?' She has talked of moving, re-locating.

'Did you find any?'

'No.'

She has ice-eyes now, he beats a retreat. Is that all it took, to shut me up, to throw me back? The air in the room has set, you could cut it with a saw in invisible cubes. Looking round, he sees the question: its head-body shows above a chair-back. It has grown more eyes, roving apprehensively.

He asks, 'Where's Sal?'

'Out, of course.'

'Out? She's always out.'

'So are you.'

'I've been working late.'

She studies him, arms folded. 'You work late a lot, Stephen.' The counter-attack.

'I'm here when she's here.'

'That's not the point. We've said this before. The point is that even when you're here, you're not here.'

'I don't know that I can be the heavy father.'

'You have to set limits. She wants you to.'

He nods, he knows it's true. Is it true for Robyn too? You must set limits to what happens in your marriage.

From the corner of his eye, he's aware of the question, sinking from sight behind the chair. It won't be asked tonight. And he's thinking, perhaps I'm wrong. Maybe it's all my imagination.

He gets up, they begin to make a meal.

'Do you want a drink?' His well-tried cop-out. Their Punt e Mes period.

'Not right now.'

They have laid down terms, of a sort, for the evening, cooking side by side. He looks out at the brilliant Judas-blossoms. She says bright-voiced, 'How's Rubens?'

It's a signal, let's not bicker now.

'I think I'm ready.'

'You're seeing Miles tomorrow?'

'Yes.'

'You haven't shown me the prints.'

'I've brought them home. I'd like to show you.'

'What, the night before. What if you need to change them?'

Change them? That's not what he wants to hear. He softly says 'I'm sorry.'

'Yes, you're a lamb, when you want me to look at your prints.'

'It's true.' What corruption - I was ready to rage, from my suspicions, now I lay out flannel so she likes my pictures.

'We'll look at them after the food,' he says demurely.

'We'll eat when Sally comes. Show me now.'

She smiles forcefully, nice-nosed, clear-faced. He smiles shyly.

They leave the kitchen, and their meal's components, and go to the living-room, where the pictures wait.

~

Kneeling on the floor, he opens carefully the large portfolio. A sheet of clear paper, with attractive deckle edges, says in coloured writing, 'Rubens in London'. Underneath is written faintly '2002 – ', leaving a space beyond the present year for the year when he will finish.

'They're big, Stephen.'

'They're the biggest etchings ever. Well . . . '

He spreads the large sheets of thick paper, so the colours fan across the floor. And *what* colours, he thinks – wonderful crimsons, turquoise, indigo, with subtle lilacs, deep terra cottas, indescribable sea-greens.

'Wow!'

'I've carried the colours to the edge of the prints.'

He shows her. On top of the etched image, an embossed square nest of lines in the centre, he has over-printed a screen-print, which runs off the edge of the paper on all sides.

He mumbles, 'Mixed media . . . '

She raises her brows but also nods. 'It's a rich effect.'

He relaxes, she will like these prints.

And the pictures? Picked out by strong colours, as if they had auras, we see men in doublets, or ribboned like Swiss Guards, ladies in cartwheel ruffs. He pulls out a dark print, nearly black in its midnight blues, where a balding man sits in a lemon candle-flicker.

'That's Rubens?'

'Yes – he was losing his hair, that's why he wears a hat in his pictures.'

'He's just sitting there.'

'He's at a standstill, after Isabella Brant's death. And she had been sad since their daughter Clara Serena died. Now he's lost both.'

The whole picture is tipped up close to us, so the window behind him seems to be at his elbow. In the dark behind him (are they his thoughts?) we half-see historic horrors, limbs tied to wheels and broken with clubs, men hung by their arms behind their backs, and bleeding bodies, chopped-off, in clouds of bandage.

'He's looking at death.'

'Is that why it's so dark?'

Only his large forehead, and the tip of his not long nose, are bright, where spots of the white paper show.

'The idea is, he's faced with death. Her death, and their daughter's, and death all round them. This was the start of the Thirty Years War, and no one knew if it ever would end. He sees death waiting to swallow everything. I think that's why he wanted to make his embassy.'

'To make love, not war.'

'To make peace instead of war. Look at his paintings – he *loved* the human body. It figures that he hated war, the attack on body, injury, mutilation. That he *wanted* peace.'

That has been his obsession: a series of prints, about the trip that Rubens made to England, when he came on behalf of the King of Spain to make peace between the war-powers of Europe. Surely it is a wonderful story that an artist, a painter, should strike bargains with kings. Be important in *that* way. Who could do it now?

'Rubens is very special. He didn't only paint plump girls.'

She says, 'It's a funny. Do you think he wanted to do good things, to make it up to Isabella?'

'To make up for what?'

'I don't know, Stephen. You may know. You said she'd just died. But he was alive and successful and famous. He'd made a lot of money painting her and other people. Who knows what he felt he owed her?'

They look at the print. 'What do you think of it?'

What more can one say? The etched lines have been bitten so deep, they are so gorged with ink, that the paper seems crusted with hardened blood.

Her verdict, then. 'I like the darks. I like his clothes. I like the velvety feel you've got.'

Still he catches an edge to her voice.

'And— '

'And it makes me wonder, Stephen, why it is you want to be making pictures of a painter whose wife had just died.'

'Oh but. Oh. That's not the point.'

'Isn't it?' She looks away, sad and tight-mouthed.

'Robyn.' He's thinking, how didn't I think of this? But how could he know she would read it like that? What is she hinting, that he wants her dead, that his love is dead?

They're both at a standstill. The plump balding head of grave-faced Rubens gazes seriously back at them.

'It doesn't matter, Stephen. Really.'

Doesn't matter? They're squatted beside the print, as by a well of tears.

'Robyn, we've gone astray.'

'Have we?' Her eyes seem more deep-set in her head; his own picture grows darker while he watches.

She shrugs, and helps him. 'It's good. Wonderful tones. And the face is good. Show me the next.'

By chance they both lean forward at once. Their heads bump, their shoulders touch. As they stay touched, a shadow lifts. They are back together, looking at pictures.

'Here Rubens goes to see his patron. She backs him in his embassy, she set it all up.'

His patron? Strange. For what we see, surrounded by deep violet blue, is the same sturdy artist standing before a throned woman in black, who looks something between a nun and a queen. Her face is so white and grim, she could be Death in person.

'His patron?'

This is the Infanta Isabella, ruler of Flanders and the King of Spain's aunt: she took the habit when her husband died.

'She is sending him to Madrid, before he goes to England. To get accredited by Philip IV.'

'I don't know that this is great, Stephen.'

He looks up, caught-out. And back at the print – surely these violet-purples are great, hitting against the magenta throne?

'But the Infanta was crucial. She gave him his intros. Without her he'd never get past the flunkeys.'

And after all this Robyn simply asks, as in innocent curiosity, 'Will you show this to Miles?'

The question floors him. Before his eyes, his picture goes dull: a stout man talking to a nun – who in the world will be impressed by that?

He's scratching his forehead, scoring the skin. Is there anything here that's fit to show? Bloody hell! What if they're all bad?

So, number three. Through its protection of tissue he sees it, black, gloomy, another dark hole. More weeks lost in ingenious waste. Ruefully he pulls back the tissue.

'Stephen!'

This one is bigger than the others, it's enormous, the etching-plate itself nearly as big as the folio paper. We see the same man, sturdy, richly and darkly dressed. But now he has arrived at a grander scene, the huge chamber of a Court, or of several Courts... there is something odd in the perspective, as though this nightmare palace somehow grows bigger into the distance, where by the laws of optics it should grow smaller. The black print-surface is turbulent, simmering, turning to different things as you look at it. We guess at galleries jammed with courtiers, a glittering mass in a shimmer of jewellery – though this also is a darkened Court, hung with black drapes, with the courtiers in black; their pale faces, with hollowed-out eyes, hover like white lanterns. In the shadows there are figures in pointed hoods. Torches, embrasures, places of fire – and the flames twist oddly, like figures burning. Curiously, in corners there are Dutch tiles, and what seem doors of inlaid wood. Elsewhere the thick-printed ink bubbles, shadowily effervescent with treasure: chests burst open, cornucopias of plate deluge the floor. Strange opulent court that is also severe, with hanging crucifixes, gigantic in torment, as though they were not effigies of our crucified Lord, but men returned to life by pain.

Robyn gazes at the glimmering surface. The thick blacks shine as if still wet; gingerly she touches, but the ink is dry. The print is gorgeous and a nightmare, a danse and a court macabre. It is a black Paradise, the court of Last Judgement of a cruel faith.

'This is Madrid, the Spanish Court. Rubens had to go there, to be accredited, and told what to do by the Count-Duke Olivarez. He was given a secret message from the King of Spain, to give to the King of England.'

'It's an all right print, Stephen. No really, it's a nightmare. It's very rich.'

'Thank you very much.'

They sit back, relaxed.

'So. You've got something to show Miles. That's good.'

'Also, Rubens made a discovery in England.' He wonders, will Robyn give him a clue? She is good at guessing secrets – and keeping them too.

'You'll tell me later. Now let's eat. We can't wait all night for Sally.'

They ferry in their food, and put on the news. Another TV dinner then. The television shows a wide modern block, with a bite from top to bottom out of its centre: you see the inside of rooms, bedding in shreds, it had been a residential block. The number of dead, dead families, is not yet established. Scattered black curves round the shallow crater are all that remain of the exploded vehicle.

They look in silence. An American official is saying, 'There will be no security till we take out the source.' The Secretary General briefly appears, patient and weary.

An idiot quiz succeeds the news. They switch off. What to say? Presently, kindly, Robyn says,

'I expect Miles will schedule a show.'

'I'm glad you think that. Shall we have that drink?'

'OK, OK. The question is, where's Sally?'

Sometimes she's so late, they've called the police. Or he's been out in the car, scouring the night streets. He's tired and nervous about his dealer, he doesn't want family stress tonight.

Abruptly they hear the front door open, not as if turned by a human hand, but burst by a force so it bangs on the wall. And before they have heard her steps in the hall, the living-room door is exploded inwards, jarring the armchair in which he sits, and giving his body whiplash injury.

'Hello!' a young fresh voice says casually.

They turn to their daughter – in tight slashed jeans, a maroon T-shirt, a leather jacket all rags and linings, below a flushed face with gelled hair like fireworks.

Robyn's eyes narrow, tracking for pot.

'Where have you been?'

'Oh I was round Paul's then we went to Puke's. Do you know Sam's going to have a baby? Sarah's poodle walks round on two legs.'

'Do you know what time it is?'

Robyn's shout follows her towards the kitchen, where they hear a clatter of china and cutlery. They hear the fridge door bang on the dryer. Already she is back, with a bowl of brimming cereal. She has switched on the television, turned up the volume, and sat on the floor eating and watching.

'You should see this.'

The screen shows the words *Unto Death*. He has vaguely heard of it – a post-Islamic satire on the West, making it big in the States. Its heroes are four half-comic Mujahadeen, on a secret mission to New York. They have shaved off their beards and hidden their turbans. Handsome Mohammed has met a Polish-Jewish girl, while Mustafa, the fat Mujahadeen, likes, or pretends to like, the pleasures of the West: cocktails, nightclubs, casinos, girls. He has always with him a mysterious green attaché case, which he sometimes nurses in his lap, crooning prayers softly to it as though it were his baby. Enigmatically he mentions 'the bites of God'.

Robyn will not be distracted. 'I said, do you know the time?'

Sally looks up flush-faced, prettily caught.

He lumbers into action. 'We said six on weekdays. Have you done your homework?'

'Oh, there wasn't any.'

'What do you mean, there wasn't any?' But Robyn has cut across him. 'Did you go to school?'

Spluttering chokemouth, a voice of cereal, 'Course I did.' She eats. She ignores the blazing television. 'Are those your prints, dad?'

Robyn says, 'Aren't they good?'

His daughter looks at them. 'The colours are brilliant!' She shuffles them quickly, darting to details. At the end she says, 'I don't know, dad. It's all a bit excited. I wouldn't call them mellow.'

'You mean they're not hip, they're not cool.'

'No, dad. Hip and cool are not mellow.'

He snorts, but she's already gone. They hear the freezer open, and a dull banging of frozen loaves, as she rummages for ice-cream.

'Stephen, I'm tired of it. You go and talk to her.'

He's to the kitchen.

'Did you go to school today?'

'I did. Really.'

21

Her gaze is frank and bright-eyed. He can't tell if she's lying, only Robyn can do that.

'Have you been smoking pot?'

'No I didn't, we only had rollies.'

Well, he can't tell. Is Sally lying to him? Is Robyn lying to him? Is he someone who lets his women lie to him?

He doesn't make an issue, and Sally has shot upstairs. In the living-room, Robyn has changed the channel back again.

'I want Newsnight.'

They sit in front of Newsnight. Watching it? The sombre words give them mental peace. He sits back. The questions about Robyn are far away now. They're all here, the family. And he must think about his dealer.

Huge din erupts overhead. A fine dust of plaster will be falling invisibly from the ceiling, a ghost-snow dislodged by his daughter's decibels. Through all the racket he sees Robyn dozing. Her face has gone discontented and pouting, her jaw thrust up and out.

'Let's go up.'

She stirs, they go. They call to their daughter, no answer comes. He looks in her room, and sees she's crashed. In the harsh light, in the shattering racket, she lies across the bed fully dressed and sound asleep, a young face pretty but with puppy-fat and flushed from – what? is it drink or pot that's making her sleep? He pulls a light cover across her leather jacket, and turns off the audio tower and the light.

He gets into bed where Robyn's asleep. He worries a little about Miles Hearn, then lapses in slumber.

~

He's awake. In the dark he hears distant lorries.

Robyn's breathing he can hardly hear. Is she awake? He moves his hand to touch her thigh.

'Robyn?'

'Yes.' She makes no move toward him.

They lie still.

For all his thoughts earlier, he's affectionate now. His arm moves up, round her shoulder. He approaches to kiss her ear.

'I don't want to make love, Stephen.'

He lies on his back. When does she want to?

The questions come. Where is his marriage? Is Robyn up to tricks? The question he has not asked is in the room with him. If he switched on his reading light quickly, he would catch its topmost goggle-eye as it dipped below the bed-end.

But he can't, at this moment, go that road again. His thoughts of themselves turn back to his projects. To his suite of prints, 'Rubens in London', when the famous painter came, as envoy of the King of Spain, to negotiate peace with England. For the Thirty Years War grinds slowly over them, like a stone wheel milling them small. Rubens would hate that, he was a love painter.

From Madrid Rubens has come north again, and waits at Dunkirk. The English man-of-war Adventure, detailed to carry him, looks like a wooden fort on the water. He has seen his chests loaded, and has boarded with his party, which includes his wife's brother, Hendrik Brant. Brant is a vague figure, let's not see him now. We only see the artist-peacemaker, mounted on the forecastle as the Adventure points to the Channel. Canvas snaps taut on the wind's pot-belly, he holds his big-brimmed hat to his head. A June sea, hard-blue, glittering and brisk.

Turning to look back and down from the forecastle, he finds he is steadily watched by a tawny man in a wine-coloured doublet, with hair and beard like a lion. The man stares so hard that Rubens gives a slight nod. The man's face makes no change, and then, before Rubens' eyes, he melts from sight while seamen and soldiers pass to and fro where he had been.

Turning forward Rubens breathes the sting of ozone, and blinks in the strengthening breeze. Dunkirk drops behind, for his mission is launched. King Charles I of England – they must meet face to face. Let wind and waves sing to his cargo of hopes, as they sing his companion, the painter Bloodsmith, wistfully dreaming of that setting sail, wearily, finally, to the depths of sleep.

2

Such a sky the train drives towards, sulphurous and apocalyptic, as if London, still behind his horizon, were a city of tearing alarm. Such a sky let it be that greeted Rubens near England. The dark island, mountainless, low in the waves. What do I know of England? Only that Antony had prospered here, he had started to make his fortune then quickly left, for Antwerp and Italy. Why did he not stay?

The ship's wood creaks as it hits choppy water, the canvas shivers and suddenly flaps. To Rubens's left the clouds lift, a white shaft slants to a lit-up tree, while a voice says softly in his ear, 'Peter Paul, there is a secret that waits for you here'.

What 'secret' could have waited for Rubens in London? He half-hears the words, 'They have played a trick on you.' But who? The kings, others? The King of Spain?

Looking round in the train, Bloodsmith sees headlines: blasted buildings, a vehicle bust open in metal petals, a dead girl's face laced with blood. The papers' readers are hidden safe inside the pages. Nor can he attend, for through a veil outside the city appears, spires, blocks, the rising towers on the Isle of Dogs; the Post Office tower stands alone like a target. He wonders, Did Osama plan the Twin Towers for the year 2000? Two against two, to take over the millennium, more than two thousand dead – only it all came in a year late.

They run in a tunnel, and in the train-window he sees his snub face. His hair is awry, loosely curling every which way. He thinks, God, I look like a tipsy Medusa. While Rubens had a distinguished head, smooth, urbane, at ease with the world . . .

And how did Rubens first see London? That moment is described in *Chess with Kings,* when Rubens steps from his coach at a high green hill on the Dover road. He sees woodsmoke rising from the up-and-down rooves, round theatres like butter-churns flying brave flags. By the fat snake of Thames lie the arsenals of Woolwich, he hears the chime of struck iron. An odd touch in the picture is the cloud of smoke Rubens sees, where the city breaks to woodland. In some way that smoke is not quite like smoke, more like smudged paint on a canvas – and it moves, so when Rubens looks again, it seems to swell in a different place. He rubs his eyes, shakes his head, climbing back into his coach.

Bloodsmith pockets *Chess with Kings*, for the train has stopped. He descends then into the bowels of the earth; death could be waiting here as well, bombs on the tube, smallpox spores. He thinks, it won't happen today, and sits back between shoulders, for at leisure in the rocking tube another moment from *Chess with Kings* comes.

Here is Rubens arriving at his host's house in London. He steps from his carriage, which still sways behind him on thick leather straps.

'Sieur Peter Paul . . . a delight, an honour . . . Sieur Hendrik Brant, you are welcome both.'

The Flemings stretch their limbs and bow, while their host, a hot-faced man with biting eyes, vibrates tensely where he stands. Balthazar Gerbier, ex-agent to the Duke of Buckingham, another painter-diplomat, he and Rubens know each other a little. But he is a lesser painter, and possibly provoked by Rubens's comfortable fame? For an instant Rubens feels again the unease which he felt approaching the coast. It crosses his mind, will this man have heard of my father's disgrace, know of the shame? Most likely not.

His unease disappears now their hostess appears, and dips her head sweetly. A fair young wife – Peter Paul, take care! Deborah Kip has an easy manner, unlike her nervy husband. The famous painter, tired as he may be and covered in dust, steps up to her with brightening eyes, with moistening lips beneath his auburn mustachios, and bows to kiss her plump white fingers.

'Sieur Peter, we would have you stay long in our house.'

'As I gladly would, sweet lady.'

The eyes of Balthazar quickly jump in his head. Jerkily he hurries his guests indoors, where his children stand in a line: there is a tall fair-haired girl in her teens, Elizabeth; a lively brown boy, George; and a little bright girl whose name Rubens marks, as she, Susan, daintily curtseys. Behind them hover a servant called Lionel, and a plump and dark-bright-eyed kitchen girl, Marilian.

So, a scene. Let the tensions begin. In the meantime the train has arrived at the stop for New Bond Street. The 1620s disappear in the hurrying street. He is surrounded by galleries: Pop, Op, surreal, all the decades in a lump. There are too many artists in the world.

At the glass door of Gallery Hearn he looks up. Above the long street of bright abstracts, and spindly iron statues, and old masters stood on easels in windows, clouds like boulders, white-edged as with fury, slide fast as if the city tumbles down a storm.

~

Miles Hearn did not care who heard his phone-calls. From the open door of his office his silk tones suaved, for Bloodsmith and the receptionist to hear. His voice had a pleasant crackle and tarried caressingly, rather as his hand would lingeringly hold the hand of a millionairess, whom he led, not too quickly, to a picture. Was it so that Rubens addressed his Infantas, deferring and wheedling towards the commission?

Bloodsmith recrossed his legs. He noticed the neat nose of the new receptionist, and the dainty zigzag in which she sat. Over her stood a tall bulbous figure, pirouetting on tip-toe, painted all round in bright coloured rings – a work by one of Hearn's sculptors. Behind it was a gigantic abstract with bold strikes of the palette-knife, chrome yellow, soft blue, on a dark-magenta field. He thought, what colours! People would buy that, rather than his prints. Yet it was not bought, it hung there on his last visit. And actually, who buys gigantic pictures? They end up, at best, in museums' big cellars. After all, there is hope for prints.

'Stephen! How are you? Wonderful to see you! How's Robyn? I'm so glad you came.'

A meaty hand ploughed the air towards him, drawing after it a black sleeve, a suit, a round face webbed with veins, the good life. Beneath eyebrows like hedges Hearn's eyes sparkled, as though moved to tears by the pleasure of seeing him.

'How are you, Miles?'

'Very well, actually.' Hearn raised his big brows and pondered a moment, as if surprised to be asked this, or surprised to be well. Then he asked how Sally was, and the Art School where Bloodsmith taught.

Not the best topic. 'Well, there are the cuts – we're concerned.'

'Of course you are... Well, but you're not there all the time. What is it? Two days a week?'

'It's more than that.'

'I expect it is. And of course, yes, you've got Attila to deal with.'

'Adrian Grieve?'

'He was called Attila at Cardiff. That was some streamlining!'

Bloodsmith frowned. 'He comes to see me tomorrow. I shall get it all ship-shape. He'd bloody better not pull the plug on the Print Room.'

'You'll be all right.'

'It's not all right being in his power. Some of us will get kicked out for sure.'

'You won't.' He said it lightly, simply in order to get on from the topic. While Bloodsmith thought, And I'm in your power – it's much the same. You may sell me at a good price or flog me off cheap.

As they chatted Hearn moved, smoothly as if on castors, to his sanctum, a tight triangular office fitted under the stairs. On the threshold they talked art market.

'Stephen, I would say it's keen— no, it's worse than keen. Prices are going down, it seems we go with housing.' He gave a sharp laugh, then mentioned the dealer in the gallery next door, who put his best young-British artist up for auction, and by proxies bid against himself. 'Cyrus buys them back again, to get the price back up! And you know what they do?' He named a famous house. 'They run the price up on him.'

'They make up bids?'

'Fifty five thousand . . . sixty thousand . . . ' Hearn imitated the auctioneer, discovering bids in the corners of the room.

Bloodsmith made a mouth.

'Stephen, they all do it. Auctioneers are auctioneers. It hurts Cyrus, of course, but he feels it's a price he has to pay.'

'Hard times, then.'

'Oh yes.'

They nodded together, reviewing galleries closed, dealers working from their home addresses, picture-transport firms shut down.

'Still, good works sell.' Hearn raised his thick brows. 'Especially if they're not too big, if they're not... enormous.'

For a moment their minds wandered, through fields of space and money: gallery cellars filling faster, as paintings get only bigger; the cost of controlling humidity and heat.

'The wall is big.'

'Ah, Stephen, yes. That's a different kind of big. That's big-time big.' He himself swelled then.

There is a wall in Brussels that will soon exist, on a building still all girders, a wall that wants a millennial style of mural, twice the size of Picasso's for Unesco. They just missed the millennium, but still there is a competition: what artist won't put in? The theme will be Peace of course, coming on the cusp of the next thousand years. This was how Bloodsmith had come to Rubens, thinking Brussels – Belgium – Flanders – Rubens the peace-maker, reconciling enemies. It was *the* Euro-subject. He saw the picture he would paint. In the centre will be Robyn, gigantic and nude and golden and lovely, painted in bold colour-blocks, but with a single flowing line down her side and butt and calf. She is Europa, the soft body of the Continent. Also she is Pax, the goddess of Peace, whom Rubens painted. The tiny jagged shapes round her, like insects with stings, are the armies of the nations: they swarm like dwarf children, squabbling for their share, to carve and divide the lovely body. Beside her sits a portly big-hatted man, dressed in gold-studded black, who we realize is painting her. We recognize him: Rubens. In the centre of war he paints the body.

That is his idea, the style bold, contemporary, the colours wonderful from miles away. His life and art come right in one. He has shown Miles a sketch of it, dabbed with strong colour.

'How is it coming? It would be good if I could see it soon.'

'Yes.' His words trail . . . 'I'll finish it soon.' He will not say, the huge canvas has little more than outlines. Robyn in the battle group was another try for Pax. But painting Peace is not so easy. Or painting Robyn is not easy, not as it used to be.

Hearn's blue eye rests on him, puzzled.

'I took a break. In the meantime I'm been doing the Rubens Suite.'

'Ah, the prints. I haven't seen those yet.'

'They're here – a delegation of them. They help me with the big design.'

'OK. Right. Let me see them.'

The tiny office contains a big desk, as wide as the portfolio that Bloodsmith opens. Gravely Miles Hearn stoops to lift off the tissue paper and examine each print, before resting it down on the portfolio's other side.

'Hm. What's this?' Hearn has found 'Madrid', the nightmare court.

'I've soaked myself in the history so much, I feel I've got a theatre in my head. It plays the scenes, then I pick a shot. I am obsessed, I know. As I draw I guess what the people will say.'

Hearn touches the paper's deckle edge. 'I like this. How had you thought we'd show it?'

'I thought loose, like this. In a big portfolio, like a loose-bound book.'

'With some words? A text?'

'Something – a commentary. I'll do that after, I can put two words together.'

'Hm. A livre d'artiste. No – a beau livre.' Hearn's fingers play near his mouth. His lips are his abacus, a sign that he is counting.

'And editions too, of the separate prints?'

'Some, maybe. Not all.'

'Right. Yes. Of course, we'd have them all up, round the walls, for the exhibition. So you can follow the story. Together with the sketches and, especially, the big oil sketch, for Rubens painting Robyn.'

Hearn looks at the next print. 'Good God! What's that?'

'That? Oh, I call that, "Olivarez kisses the Pisspot of the Future King of Spain". Really he had done that, in earlier years – it was a good career move. Helped him to become First Minister later.'

We see the man who was to be Rubens's boss, the great Count-Duke of Olivarez, on his knees in front of his prince. The fleshy lips protrude from beneath the broad, down-flattened nose, to wet the raised gorgeous vessel. Politics and hypocrisy, arts known to Rubens too.

Hearn gives a hissing laugh through his nose. 'Hm. Continuez! What on earth is this?'

'Oh, this is my Thirty Years War print. It had been going for ten years when Rubens travelled, and no one knew if the wars would ever stop.'

This huge print has a thousand figures drawn tiny but distinct, who, when you look close, do terrible things to each other. One man smashes another with a flail for threshing corn. Another, fallen on the ground, is stuck through with a hay-fork. Other men are hung upside down over fires. Another man is cut in half downwards to his waist by a soldier wielding a two-handed sword.

'Because people fight wars for various reasons, but what's common to wars is that they hurt and damage each other much more than victory in war requires.'

'Thank you, Stephen, I can see what they're doing. It's good you've done it in black and white.'

'Yes, I wanted it a bit like old engravings, but also bit like black-and-white news-photos. So it touches modern atrocities. There's a soldier in Sierra Leone cutting off a girl's hands, and an irregular in Bosnia going for a prisoner's eyes with a teaspoon—'

'Shut up, Stephen, if you want me take it. But what the devil is this?' He moves to the next print. 'Will you have the three musketeers as well?'

'You're right, that's Cardinal Richelieu. His spies watched Rubens cross France to England – maybe he wondered why Rubens was going there. For if England made peace with Spain, that was no good news for France. They're like America, Russia and China now. So here Richelieu talks to his agent, Furston, who must get over to England and find out more.'

'Yes, well, anyway, I like the red.'

For this giant red-purple print is filled like a blood-bath with the hulking, straddling figure of the Cardinal, whose crimson robes swell like the petals of a fleshy, gigantic rose. A leather riding boot with spurs shows below the hem of his gown. He wears a wide-brimmed hat like a soldier's, and dwarfs the lithe, canny figure he talks to, lean as a reed beside the red pool of Richelieu, who has a sharp-featured face, a bony nose, and steady, dry, heavy-lidded eyes.

'Rubens knew Richelieu, from his time in France. He would have known this trip was playing chess with Richelieu.'

Hearn holds the large print up to the window, so a deeper crimson flares through the Cardinal's red.

'I *love* this red.' With full, fleshy lips – a little like the Count-Duke of Olivarez – Miles pretends to kiss it, across the air. 'I'll say this one has *magnificence*.' He lays it down. 'Anyway... So, you have big players.'

'The biggest player is King Charles the First, when he and Rubens haggle. I haven't tried to do that yet. Of course, when Rubens got to the King, he did something outrageous.'

'Yes? I'm very glad he did that. Now tell me, Stephen – is there something else? Something more *intime*? When people think of Rubens, they think of nudes.'

'They're not all fat, by the way – not really.'

'And they're not too thin. Shall we say, like people used to, they are not too fat and not too thin?'

Bloodsmith shrugs. But it's still a question. Rubens loved the human body and he loved women's bodies. Will there be love-pictures in this series? Rubens in London sporting with nudes? Or something more tender, more love than sex? Will Rubens have a love-adventure in England?

Hearn nods and smiles with emphasis, but Bloodsmith moves on. 'There *is* something else. Rubens said he made a discovery in England that turned his whole world upside down.'

Hearn frowned. 'Where did he say that? In a letter to Peiresc?'

'No, it's from a letter some diplomat wrote to his wife. But it seems that Balthazar Gerbier, the man Rubens stayed with, *he* knew something that Rubens didn't.'

'Something personal? Even scandalous?'

Let it be so! Bloodsmith makes to look cryptic. 'You'd like to know?'

'In good time.' Hearn gives sly frown. 'Tell me, Stephen: which biographies are you using?'

'To be honest, the book which gives me the most is Jens Claeys.'

'*Chess with Kings*? But that's like fiction. Some of it *is* fiction.'

'Well, but it's by an art-critic who wrote on Rubens all his life. It's true he calls it a "history-poem", whatever that may be. But he *imagines* the events, he makes the people speak – and that helps me to dream up pictures.'

'Hans Gotthelf at the Warburg doesn't approve. You know what he said about Claeys on art. He called him a loose cannon in a china shop – he'd wreck the store along with the stock.'

'Professor Sir Hans . . . And what did Jens Claeys say about Gotthelf's Rubens?'

Hearn made a wall-face.

'He said – for the prince of painters, the prince of pedants.'

'Well, you need that too.'

'I don't disagree.'

Hearn snuffed. 'So, are you going to tell us what's in "the missing chapter"?'

'I might.'

For Jens Claeys died before his text was complete. Stars in the text mark a hiatus in the manuscript. The chapter-numbers suggest a whole chapter has gone. And it seems it was here that mysteries were solved, questions answered.

Hearn ponders. 'Do you think he chickened out? As to saying what he suspected?'

'He said, "If I told you all my thoughts – why, it's more than my life's worth". But it doesn't sound like Claeys to "chicken out". Maybe he was almost sure, but still was looking for the final clue.'

'Ah, Stephen! And you think you may find that clue?'

'I'm on the case.' He made his face enigmatic.

'Good luck!'

'Thanks. There's something else. You know that Rubens bought an *object* in London, something shocking, which he called "a fragment of the ancient world."'

'This is from Jens Claeys?'

'It's in Gotthelf and everyone else. This is real. It's a good scene, though, in *Chess with Kings*. I'll reckon to make something of it.'

'You'll keep it shocking, I hope. Now, who are these folk?' Hearn pulled out the next print.

'Oh, these are the Gerbiers. Rubens stayed in their home.'

Never mind "the big picture", here is a family sat down at a table. Again the perspective is exaggerated and steep, so the ultra-distinct figures, behind the tipped-up table with its platters and pewter cups, seem inches from our eye. 'Here are the Gerbier children, Elizabeth, George and little Susan. And here's Deborah Kip, Balthazar Gerbier's wife, whom Rubens likes at once. And here is Balthazar with his narrow eyes, which are edgy and sharp and a little like gloating. I want you to see he makes Rubens uneasy, while Rubens also puts Gerbier on edge – although they have to plot together how to make Ruben's plan work.'

'OK, it's nice to have this to set that against your torture-pictures. What I really like is the wall behind them.'

The wall, with its strange look of overlapping flaps, again is ultra-distinct and close.

'That's how you covered your walls in those days – if you had money. With small leather panels, embossed in gold. Often they were black, with the gold on top. But in Rubens' house they were red. Gerbier was a bit of a painter himself, maybe he would choose red too.'

'Good! Because I love this red-leather look. It's as rich as the Cardinal. Do you know, I think shall get this one for myself.'

Bloodsmith thinks wryly, Miles would like his own wall covered in gilt red leather. Really Miles loves furnishings best – still, that's the secret of his success as an art-monger, that's how he knows what people want on their walls.

'That's as far as I've got. Oh, and there's this one, from further ahead.'

He pulls out 'Thameside, 1629'and they both are silent, staring.

Hearn nods. 'So. . .'

'So.' He takes a deep breath. 'Will you have them?'

'Stephen,' Hearn says, loudly, broadly, stretching the moment. 'I'll take them in.' He picks up a black-bound large-leaf diary. 'Shall we talk dates?'

'What, for a show?'

'For the whole set. Provisionally. Just to have a rough idea.'

'Yes!' But he is not sure. When will he be finished? Though it's always good to have a deadline.

They hover among months, and agree a rough date. He thinks, I'll change it later if need be. Still he is not pleased when he sees Hearn place a large question-mark beside the date they have agreed.

Hearn quietly muses, 'People sometimes ask me what you're doing. It's good you've given me something to show them.'

He smiles, and Bloodsmith too. For Hearn loves to give people privileged glimpses, and that is what Bloodsmith wants him to do. *No, he's working on The Rubens Suite. Rubens in England, at war with War. Yes, I do have some proofs. I suppose I could show them to you. It's a grand livre, one buys the whole set of course. It's true, some prints will have separate editions. And these — these are one-offs — artist's proofs. Maybe I could let you have one of these now. It just might be an* investment.

Echoing Bloodsmith's greedy thoughts, Hearn says, 'I'll say I think they're the most important prints being made in England now.'

Well, and do you think that?

'I'll say they are a *portal* – into history, and into Rubens. People like a good *portal*.'

As he likes the word. They are wafting at leisure towards his own door.

'Something else you were doing, Stephen, a year or two back. Another project . . . The Fire Girl, I think you called it. You showed me some drawings. What came of that?'

So suavely the words slip by, it is almost shocking to see how Bloodsmith jumps, and how his face goes lost and strange.

'You thought I'd forgotten? I've kept a drawing you gave me then.'

Bloodsmith still is collecting himself. 'The Fire Girl Suite . . . I never finished it.'

'No?' Hearn studies his face. 'I've touched a nerve.'

'No, no. It's . . . I left it.'

'Well, well. But the big picture, Rubens and Europa – you *will* finish that, won't you?'

'I will, I will.' He must.

'Because I like the prints. I'm excited by the prints. But they will do better as pendants to the big painting. The road to Brussels, eh?'

'We must get the show on the road.'

'We must get the roadshow moving.'

They agree on that. From here on his career goes up, or nowhere.

'Lovely to see you, Stephen! Send me more prints as you do them.'

For an instant they stand framed in the shop-door. The polished toe of Miles momentarily dips to the pavement.

'Give my love to Robyn!'

Hearn goes back in. Bloodsmith is aware of him chatting immediately on other subjects to his receptionist, as he himself starts back up New Bond Street. A fat drop splatters him. He looks up, the sky is black. He hurries towards the underground, in a race with the sky.

But no downpour follows, he makes the station dry. At the steps to the underground he looks up at the churning vapours as Rubens maybe looked up at the sky, on that first late afternoon in London, walking with his host, Balthazar Gerbier, in his tulip-packed garden, with rose-scents round them also, and street-noise coming over the wall. Rubens eyes the black boding sky over England, as Gerbier explains the politics to him. True, the King has just shut down Parliament, but this may help Rubens, since the Puritans would never make peace with Spain. They weigh the odds, while Gerbier's eyes crinkle with shrewdness on shrewdness. Finally he asks, is there a private message which Rubens must give from one king to another? Rubens falls quiet; he must not say. Gerbier presses a little, then has to stop, for suddenly, with lightning and immediate thunder, the biding downpour starts like a sluice-gate opened over them. They are instantly soaked, so both men, the minor and the major painter, sprint like any caught vagrant for the house.

Indoors, they change clothes and meet by the fireside. Deborah and the children sit at a distance while the men talk loudly about the art scene in England – and Rubens' great pupil, Antony Van Dyck.

'He has risen most quickly,' Gerbier remarks. 'Already he leads the rout of painters in this land.'

Rubens can be generous. 'From the start he showed a mighty talent.'

'You trained him well, Peter Paul,' Gerbier remarks. 'For all now at Court seek a portrait from his hand.'

'Do they so?' Rubens says, a little shortly, and turns to tell the whole family of his own adventures in the Courts of Kings.

Antony. I gave him the best horse I had, when he set out for Italy. I gave him too much.

Retiring at last, he pauses by his window, which looks out on the street. For a moment he wonders, can that still figure, lit by the beacon on a pole at the corner, be the man from the *Adventure*, with hair and beard like a lion? There is the slightest change in the slant of the man's head, as if he sees now that Rubens sees him. It is no surprise therefore when Rubens next looks out, to find the street empty.

Still, making his way to bed, he looked abruptly round behind him. The far corner of the room was dark, and the shadows disturbed there as though a dust-devil had got into the room. But there was no draught.

As he advanced with his candle the form he had seen, like a column of shadow, dissolved.

Was he, was his mission, haunted? He lay down, and said his prayers, then murmured, 'But who would set a spy on me?'

~

Bloodsmith sat by the window on the mainline train home. He had finished his reread of Rubens' first day in London, and scanned the author-photo of Jens Claeys, big on the back of *Chess with Kings*. A 'rogue scholar' – too bad. We see a thickset, combative, pug bulldog face in a rage of grey hair. The eyes are black. From the sun-faded, creased jacket, still he glares. You can see that the glasses which he holds have been repaired with sellotape.

'But you give me pictures,' Bloodsmith thinks with affection, 'and your people *speak*.' As for the 'missing chapter', will he find the clue to that? *Was* it written, or still to write? The hidden intrigue, the back-alley into Rubens' heart.

Gazing from the window he saw rain in the distance: strands and skeins reached from brown clouds to the ground, they made shapes like vague fingers, a shadow hand. He was pleased with the day; he sat back relaxed. Hearn had the prints, he would do something with them. He pictured the 'livre d'artiste' – 'Rubens in London'. If you wanted, you could buy it in a box case, covered in a thick-textured fabric like an up-market form of sacking. Carefully you would lift the tissue paper, and turn the prints. Or spread them on a table. The text, the commentary, would be printed large in a handsome type. It would be luxury for the eye. And full of stuff, rich with meaning.

A little he planned the next prints in the list. 'Rubens meets the inventor Drebbel' – he has yet to picture this. Then 'Rubens and Thamesis' – that must make a splash. The meeting of Rubens with King Charles I – he still must find a title here.

Absently he scanned the newspaper headlines opposite: foreign ministers were recording their alarm. But he could not run war-passions now.

Again he looked outside. Ahead of the train the sky was darkening, into deep-sea depths, black-purple, unbelievable. Let it storm, let it thunder, he was pleased with his art.

But Hearn was right, there weren't only the prints. He must do the big picture, the big painting. Brussels, the wall... I'm not getting on with it. And everything must be there, in a brisk bold style. He must look at John Bellany's pictures again, the way he updates Titian, a sumptuous nude in a bright splash of paint – that's the way.

In the distance ahead he saw lightning flash. For seconds afterwards still he saw it, like a bent piece of pink wire, connecting the ground to the pale, lit-up clouds. He thought, it's years since I saw that. He's always indoors, head-down to his pictures, yet all the time the energies accumulate. Maybe he'll make a lightning-print for Rubens: the war-storm of cloud slowly wheeling over Europe, while Rubens works to cajole plump Peace. Like a wave a hill was building, at any moment it would turn into a tunnel. There was a shape on the crest. A tree? A person? Then the clouds behind it flared, lit up within, flabby puff-bags of lightning, and he snapped it clear, it was a scarecrow, an old-style scarecrow, clothes on crossed poles, its arms stretched wide, slanted forward against the gale which blew its tatters back.

Only for a second he saw it, for there followed another flash, and this time he saw the missile arrive. Perhaps he only put the sight together later, but he saw the root-shape of lightning strike towards him out of the sky, then take a jagged turn and reach the scarecrow, which at once burst, all of it, into fire, not as if set light to, but as if with the arrival of such too-big power, every particle and atom, of wood, cloth, whatever, at the same time exploded in incandescence, so the whole figure flashed up as a man of blinding light.

He blinked, dazzled. The scarecrow now was a burning man, with normal flames, a human cross; the arms were gone, it was a burning stick; they were in the tunnel, it had all gone out at once.

He sat back, scarred. His eyes wandered the closed carriage, but no one else showed signs of seeing anything. His head felt damaged – had a knowledge arrived?

It had. That big painting – Rubens and Pax, Robyn as Europa – I'm not going to paint it. I've been kidding myself, and kidding Miles Hearn. Really I stopped work a long time ago. The Goddess of Peace, who wants to see *her*? But that's not why I stopped. The reason I stopped is, it's a picture of Robyn. I can't paint Robyn now, not the way things are with us. That's why I go on with the Rubens prints, they're an escape, war issues in another age. I am running away from painting my wife, from facing the situation. I used to say, 'Robyn – you are my Rubens woman'.

Which situation? That my marriage is in breakdown? That my wife has a boyfriend? If she does. I still haven't put it to her. I dodge it for fear of what she will say. But that's no use. But I'm tired tonight. Tomorrow we'll talk, after I've seen Grieve. Will she come clean, though? Maybe we'll have a fight.

The thunder passed, and a low yellow strip of evening light showed a church and a factory in clear silhouette. Only then he thought, Miles mentioned the Fire Girl. A dream he had at that time came back: an old woman crouched by a fire in a cavern. 'What are you doing?' 'I am making the Fire Girl.' He captioned one print, 'An angel sang in the heart of the furnace.'

He murmured her real name… Mae, where are you?

Mundane alarms return. Adrian Grieve comes tomorrow, to see me in the Print Department. Will he shut it down? The cuts are coming. Attila the Hun. Will he hack us to pieces?

He sat facing the direction in which the train travelled, exhausted but wide awake.

3

But where was Grieve? Bloodsmith turned, at a loss, in the gothic-windowed room. Late on purpose? A power trick, let the staff wait. Waiting for the barbarian.

The Print Department looked in good health. The old presses, for etchings and lithographs, were grand in cast-iron. New silk-screen prints, pinned on the wall, dazzled in crimson and veridian where the fat shafts of sunlight caught them. Idly he cranked the aquatint box, and heard the soft sound of resin-dust whirling. In a large print on the wall, a Bernini figure emerged from a russet tide of pomegranites; he shook his head, smiling with pleasure to see it.

He made no more adjustments to where things were. The room must not be too tidy, or it would not look like a room where much happened. In some way he knew this visit was crucial, but what did Grieve – Attila – have on his savage agenda? Would he close down the Print Room? Or cut the graduates and have only the Degree Course? Or cut the Degree Course and have only Foundation? He was famous for meeting the severest budget; Adrian Grieve, he gives you grief.

'Stephen? May I come in?' From the door he lopes forward, a soft-stepping predator. 'Ah! The smell of acid!' A zestful inhalation, as he shakes Bloodsmith's hand – for he has a formality, and the light suit he wears seems new-cleaned always. He is a small man and keen-faced, with a tiny fine nose that would fit a princess. His fair hair flows in a graceful quiff, but is close-trimmed behind as though cut daily.

'I'm sorry I've not been here more often. It's been a busy year. You'll help me make up for lost time.' He smiles a quick smile, which disconcerts, it is so tight in his face, and his blue eyes seem at the same time to glare.

'You took me round the equipment before. I think you have everything?'

They begin to patrol – the small etching press, the large etching press. One of them is turned by a wheel of long spokes, with no outer rim. Bloodsmith firmly clasps a spoke.

'We've built it up.'

'And within budget too, I remember your saying. The lithographic press was, what? A hundred pounds!'

Bloodsmith is pleased he remembers, for it was a coup. They are standing by the machine, with its long sliding bed; gothic arches between its four legs.

'A garage in Tunbridge. Is that right?'

'That's right. It was all in pieces, greased and wrapped in plastic. And all of it was there. In perfect condition. Edinburgh, 1883. I'm always on the lookout for Nineteenth Century presses. They're wonderful! We made it good of course.' Bloodsmith pings his finger-nail on the shining copper tympan.

Keenly sharing, Grieve says, 'It's a beautiful piece. Roy did it?'

'I did it.' Bloodsmith strokes with love the supple leather, which he himself attached to the scraper-board.

'Do you use it?'

'For my own prints?' Does a razor, at this point, graze his skin? Using the College's equipment? 'I have my own studio, I'm sure I've told you. It's not far away, I do my work there.'

'Of course, I've heard of it. A weird room, something left over from a brewery or a maltings? I know your prints well, Stephen.' But does Grieve know them? And why must he speak with a stare? They come to an odd pause, in which he sees Grieve is nervous. What's going on? Grieve eyes him like an ill-willed girl.

'And you paint as well, I think?'

'Yes, I'm a painter, fallen among printmakers.'

'I don't know your paintings. You must show me one day.'

'Gladly.' But it's softly said, and Grieve has moved on.

'How do you feel about that?'

'Sorry, about what?'

'Oh, being an artist, getting time for your own work, and running the Print Department. It must be difficult doing both.' Here is the famous well-honed edge, removing a sliver of skin from Bloodsmith. Grieve eyes him intently.

'Maybe. I'm used to it. I'm sure the different things help each other. And I like the students' work.'

'Good – good – good!' Grieve nods, in his tense-quick way. 'It's very good when it works like that. Like in the old days, when the teachers in the art schools were really all artists. We both know that. And it's so difficult now to keep that arrangement, there's so much pressure for full-time not part-time.'

This, surely, is menacing. Is Bloodsmith's job on the line? Not that he completely depends on the money, but without it . . . It doesn't bear thinking of. Well, he will try flattery.

'*You* are able to combine the two, Adrian. I mean you both run this place, and you did Wuppertal. I saw it in the Art Newspaper – impressive.'

Does Grieve smile at this flattery ladled with a trowel? A trace, and yet his glare tautens. For it is a sore point, his art. He has specialized in exhibition-design – international exhibitions, trade fairs, showplaces – and though he enjoys a premier success, still the old-fashioned artist will say, is that art? Bloodsmith will say it, other days of the week. They are both uneasy.

To divert them, he points to a multi-coloured lino-cut. 'That's Imogen Wroth. She wants to try for Goldsmiths. She's got a chance.'

'Has she? Ah yes, Wroth. That's good. It's important to know that.' Why important?

'And that's Laurie Park – they call him "Lorry" Park. He's got something, I'm sure.'

'That's Park, is it? I've read your report on him.'

'I'm betting he'll make the Royal College.'

'Good, good.'

I'll take the barbarian by the horns. 'So, Adrian… How do you feel the Print Department is doing?'

And Attila, instead of answering, says 'Hm,' and turns his neat profile, as if seized by philosophy.

They both wait. On the wall etched heads in cobwebby fine-line, lino-cut heads in chunky lumps, lithographed heads with a crayony look, wait staring on the event.

Grieve turns on Bloodsmith his uncanny, ultra-light-blue eyes. 'I think the Department is doing well. I believe so. But you're obviously wondering what I have in mind. Well, we have to reorganize. Some things must go. "Cuts", as we say – we can't avoid them. I have to deal with the powers-that-be. It's a difficult remit.'

He has been so direct, Bloodsmith is thrown.

'I can only speak for this Department, but I think our record has been pretty good. Roy is excellent.'

'Roy is good. Your record is good.'

Grieve stops, looks down, looks Bloodsmith in the eye. Levelly he says, 'Of course, there are those who say you can get as rich effects with Photoshop now, as ever Hayter could with all his relief etching.'

'Not quite, I think.' He eyes Grieve hard and inwardly scoffs – can 'Photoshop' get the texture of intaglio plus rollers? But where are they now? A duel of eyes, will it be to the death??

Grieve blinks first. 'Show me everything, if you would.' A cold voice: is it a request or an order?

So between the shafts of sunlight they go, alternately half-closing and opening their eyes, past acid baths and ink rollers, heating trays and drying racks. Grieve likes to be tidy, he pauses to adjust the rows of burins and burnishers, and with pleasure crumples tightly the mound of rough scrim, waiting crisp and white beside the intaglio inks. And again gives Bloodsmith dry, drilling looks.

At the end he says 'Thank you. I have to look at all of the options, but— ' But he does not complete this but.

Bloodsmith waits. The axe is rotating above the Art School; it is controlled by the neat man before him. You hear the thrumm thrumm as the blade cuts the air.

A brief ice-glance then from Grieve, tight, sharp and quick as a dart in a pub. To himself Bloodsmith prays, take your tiny nose out of here. Truly they are opposite types.

Abruptly Grieve stands tall and holds out his hand.

'Thank you very much.' Almost you could feel he has clicked his heels, like a Prussian officer in a film.

'Any time. A pleasure, of course.' They shake.

At that moment, a student strolls in, smoking.

'Hi, Steve.' He ambles casually to the screen-prints.

'Roger.' Bloodsmith frowns. Where's respect? Can't the kid see, this is the Principal?

But Grieve has already gone, the door swings in his wake.

Cuts, cuts, cuts, they do not stop, the saw-teeth spin and whirr; branches will fall, trees too, departments, colleges, jobs (like his own), working to stunt the tree of art, till governments and administrators achieve their dream: the tiny chic bonzai of New British Art, a stunt today and forgotten tomorrow.

Should he fear? No worries but he worries. I'm at his mercy. The branch he sits on trembles and sways, as the tree itself shivers and prepares to crack apart.

~

He breaks from the Art School, time on his hands. Grieve's visit was all his work for that day. What do? Go to his studio? The visit has unsettled him. Against all his habits, he goes home. After all there is the question, which he has still to ask Robyn. He will do that today for sure.

He enters, saying more than calling 'Robyn'. She'd said she'd be at home today.

Silence. And Sally, of course, was not back.

He poured a glass of water and sat at the kitchen table . It was odd to come home and find the house empty, but then he never did come back at this time.

He moved through the rooms thinking, we made a nice house. The Art Deco lamp they had chosen together. In the living-room he switched on the television, but there was rubbish for kids, he switched it off.

He was back in the kitchen for more water when the thought occurred, Or is she seeing someone else right now? A friend; a lover?

A latch clicks, he's turned to the hall. There's Robyn in the doorframe, her head raised, sunlight and birdsong behind her.

She stopped short, startled. 'Stephen!'

'Hi.'

'You're home!'

'I guess.'

She gave an odd small gasp. 'You're never here at this time!'

'I am today.' Was she pleased – displeased?

'Good to see you.' It did not sound good. 'How was Grieve?'

'All right – he made me worry a bit.'

'Why?' Now she's listening, her blue eyes to his.

'He talked about reorganization. Really he wasn't clear . . . '

'Mm.' She seems unsure where she wants to be. She picks up her handbag again, then puts it down. He thinks, she's dithering. Robyn doesn't dither.

Abruptly he knows. She's expecting someone. She hasn't seen the man yet, he's coming round here. Here, to our own house, where they know it's safe.

He asks like innocence, 'Is someone coming round?'

'No one's coming round.' Her voice does innocence too.

Maybe then there *is* no lover. I'll clear it up once and for all.

'Robyn.'

'Yes.'

'Is something going on?'

'What do you mean?'

'Are you seeing someone?'

'What, like a lover?'

'Right.'

'No. Of course not.' It comes so curt and clear, almost he thinks, Why did I ask?

'There's nothing going on?'

'No!'

For this denial he is unready. Always, in his expectations, the question will make her falter, her eyes will fall – instead of which she is staring hard.

'Ask me again, Stephen. Ask me as many times as you like.' Forthright. Then shyly she looks across the room. Towards the phone?

As they stand, the phone rings. Her face has gone keen, she knows who it is. Her hand snatches, to take the phone. But he has slipped across ahead of her, grabbing the handset.

'Bloodsmith.'

No answer, no clicks or buzzes: someone is there who will not speak. At once Bloodsmith knows. It's he, the lover, ringing Robyn at home at a time he thought safe. The wire from his own hand extends via cables into another hand in the room of sex. The man's helpless at hearing the husband answer, and not sure whether to slam the phone down, or make like a stranger who got the wrong number. But already it is too late for that.

He looks at Robyn, who is looking at him. Her eyes and mouth gape, as if she's staring at a road-crash.

He holds the interloper. He listens for a human sound, his ear crouched to the phone like a creature in wait.

Robyn has come to, she makes an obstinate mouth. He stands fixed; the other stays quiet; there the three of them rest.

Click, the phone has been put down. Well, he thinks, his nerve cracked first.

'Who was it, Stephen?' He catches her tremor.

'He didn't say.'

'I get calls like that. They're such a nuisance.'

'Yes?'

Then, while he watched, Robyn started to blush. Up her neck, her cheeks, the blotching red fire deepened and spread, it was a whole-body blush. He even thinks, poor Robyn – a fair complexion, she blushes easily.

'You're blushing, Robyn.'

'No way!' she says flatly. But at once her blush deepened, heated, crimsoned, irregularly, in patches, but growing and joining, as if an irritation, or fever, or radioactivity were heating inside her to the surface. Her eyes shone brighter, clearer blue – defiant.

It was he who turned away, to spare her.

'I must put these away,' she said. She must mean the things in her bag. She slipped quickly upstairs.

Leaving him thinking, that's clear enough. There *is* a lover. The question is, what'll I do? A gun'd be good. James Bond had a Walther PPK. What is a Walter PPK?

Soon Robyn tripped down and brightly made tea, like all was normal. So for a moment he wondered, *is* today evidence? What if that call were some private business which Robyn wants to keep quiet – who knows, medical? And not a lover.

Then again, how much proof do you need? One has a sixth sense, you know what is going on.

4

At last a day clear to himself in his studio. For work with metal plates he has bought, months ago, the sort of leather apron that steel-workers use. Strong good leather, he pinches it, loving its soft mobile suppleness.

But how can I make prints, now that I know? Around him his gravers, acids, a fresh cake of etching ground, from his battle-group canvas the dancing Robyn gazes: her face is brittle and opaque. So she denied it. And what if she didn't deny it? What if she says, Stephen, it's true, I am seeing someone, a Julian, a Jeremy, some crappo from the photo-world. I'm sorry, Stephen, I love him.

Love him? They are a modern couple, they know that people change and grow. But *love*? Can he handle that? I thought we were *married*, are we simply 'partners'? He's paused by a reproduction, taped to his board. 'Antony Van Dyck, Portrait of Isabella Brant' says the caption. Van Dyck was Rubens' pupil, Isabella Brant was Rubens' wife. There she sits, fair, calm and beautiful, holding a white rose and what looks like a black feather duster, though it must be a fan. Behind her is the grand arch of the Rubens-House. But she is not grandiose though she wears cloth of gold and a rich black mantle. She has a sensitive face, thoughtful eyes, a slight sweet smile. A true wife, for sure – painted with admiration by a grateful, respectful pupil of Rubens. Except, where is Rubens? You'd think he'd be there. There's a funny, foppish statue painted up on the wall behind her.

He turns from the picture. Something in it teases him, like a puzzle picture where a clue is hidden. He has noticed something, and cannot now catch what it was. It will come back to me.

In any event, Isabella, the true wife, died. While as to his own marriage—

He picks up the iron spike he uses for drypoint— by Christ, you could do a person damage with this. But he does no damage, he picks up a virgin steel plate. A moment he stands with eyes tight shut, then he opens and begins, scratching the spike hard into the steel, in a rippling groove razor-edged with metal scales.

Drypoint's good when you're doing bitter. He's thinking of Rubens on his afternoon rides – that was his exercise, in London as in Antwerp. But into what quarter has today's ride brought him? Downhill beside a shit-choked ditch his horse has led him through a narrowing alley, where the houses lean over him ever more crookedly. It's growing dark but we come to a square: torches, space, leering housefronts. But what grotesque picture's this? Rubens confronted by the beggars of London, wretches wading in the city's filth. The wounded of the wars, wagging their stumps. One man has had his nose sliced off: two upward slits show where it was. A stooping idiot makes zigzag runs, his lower lip drips. The damaged, maimed and hideous: night news from the blasted city. Rubens meets the human bodies least like those he paints.

But these are only the lower foreground. His subjects, behind them, in alleys and casements, in lamplit doors his spike scrapes open, are the lurid half-clad women. Pale faces, crimsoned lips, they loll their udders to the well-fed painter. The whores of London. They tower over the wrecked and wounded men. A skinny one slavers, insane with lust, answering to the idiot man. One's a girl with a big-eyed baby-face, false flowers twined in her lank blond hair. Young tender slender limbs – and a nudge of elbow, a cock of head, a twist of hip fair sir come hither. And one's a giantess, hugely fat, bulbs of lard like many breasts. Her vast hips breach her tearing skirt, her balloon tits flaunted by cups like panniers. Her cheeks white with zinc face-paint, with disks of rouge and black stars stuck there. Big with kohl her sidelong eye creases slyly at the corner.

He is hard at work, digging steel with iron. More clitoris here! I'll make the skirts see-through. Vulvas, vaginas, crotch and labia. Lower lips pout through the furbelow skirts.

He sits back, heavy-breathing. But why think of *whores* if Robyn is 'in love'? That's not good either. *If* she is… God knows where we are. He runs his finger on the savage sketch — and hisses, he has gashed his hand, after all, on the jagged burr his spike has dug. He sucks and spits, there are metal splinters in the wound. So I've drawn blood – about bloody time. Right. I'll stick on a plaster and go and have lunch.

~

But lunch was no good. His colleague Ollie could talk only about the great time in the sack he had with his new model, Sinead.

'And she gives me Intuitive Massage!'

'That must feel good.'

Ollie lifted the wide brown plate of his beard. 'Becky must never know.'

'No.'

A good time in the sack – heading back to his studio – *and* with Intuitive Massage. I could use a piece of that.

Back in the red studio he sits a little, digesting. He is drowsy, but wonders still – So, do I hunt out Robyn's lover? Never mind the Walther PPK. A duck-gun would be good, filled with tacks and rivets. Or I'll kick him out the door, and shoot him in the arse as he makes off down the road. A cannon, now, that would shred him. Though guns aren't me. Maybe I just clobber him? Rubens would. Because Rubens loved Peace but he also loved war scenes: confrontations, warriors brandishing. He had fights himself. Bloodsmith murmurs 'Lucas Vorsterman'.

Vorsterman was the great engraver of the time, he made copperplate engravings of Rubens' paintings, to sell mass-market – for Rubens was fly about money, publicity. And he and Rubens came to blows. Never mind world peace, never mind the whores, *that's* the print I should have in my Suite.

Still sitting, he pulls his sketch-pad over. Let's see how you are with your dukes, Peter Paul! Half in daydream, he flashes small cartoons like a film's story-board. *Chess with Kings* – of course – describes the scene: Lucas Vorsterman stoops forward in his own studio, with Rubens' painting leaned in front of him; a proof of the engraving lies flat on the bench. Rubens looms beside Vorsterman, comparing the two; his breathing has grown slow and hoarse, till he growls,

'Just look at that robe – it's grey, inert. Dead. In my painting it's crimson velvet. Can't you see the sheen it has? And there's no glitter, no lustre, in that copper jug. The whole plate's flat as a floorboard.'

The two apprentices nearby, inking plates and working the press, keep their heads down but freeze at their work, listening to the row.

But Vorsterman, too, is a master. His prints sell through all Europe.

'Are you blind, Peter Paul. Look at that texture! There's gleam! There's depth! I give you all the light and colour that copper, black ink and genius give.'

The short apprentice, hands jet-black with printing-ink, lifts his head to egg on his master.

'Genius! Are *you* the genius in this room? You'll get a new copper plate. Start again from scratch. Do I pay for prentice work? Get on with it, man.'

The tall apprentice, heaving the great crank of the printing press, yawns wide with amazement at this insult to the master.

'You're insane!' Vorsterman has stood. The plump cheek of Rubens is close beside him, in Rubens' fat self-righteous face. It's too good a target. Vorsterman's open, calloused right hand, strong from years of forcing knives through copper, swings an almighty ringing slap. Rubens reels a moment, mouth and eyes agape, then jerks his fist into Vorsterman's eye. He has another punch ready for Vorsterman's gut, but Vorsterman has kicked his leg from under him so he totters and stumbles down on the floor.

Vorsterman stands over him. 'Get up if you can.'

The tall and short apprentices gawp to see the prince of painters scrabble in the dust.

Rubens has crouched, getting breath, then panting in fury, glowering like a cornered dog. Abruptly he surges up flinging punches until he seems to have not two but four or seven fists. His hits are wild but some land, so Vorsterman has reeled back croaking. Rubens is big above him, but Vorsterman snatches a tool from the bench.

'You'll get this in your eye.' Vorsterman holds up his burin. It spikes through copper. Rubens' eye or cheek will be easy game.

His face a furnace, beside himself, Rubens can only gasp and pant. The burin pokes nearer, stab, stab.

'Out, Rubens! Out of here! Lug that daub with you! Get some hack to cut your prints, to engrave your rolling tubs of yard.'

'Vorsterman, you – are – finished.'

Rubens has no choice, however, but to retrieve his canvas, picking it up by the stretcher at its back, and sidle with it awkwardly out of the door. Where Vorsterman stands, hand on hips, to watch him go. An apprentice, with an indignant sanctimonious face, stands at either elbow.

That, or something like it, was Rubens at fisticuffs. He painted battles and rapes, he would know how to fight. It's part of the picture, I must have it in the Suite. He has got to his feet. Well, I must print this sodding drypoint. The pretty maids of London. Back to work then, mixing the thick paste of red ink he'll rub in, the dense muddy ink for intaglio printing. But that's a good red, between new blood and dry blood. With passion he forces it into the jagged steel grooves.

It is only as he works the ink deeper in that he realizes the colour itself is talking. Words rise towards him out of his picture, first a buzz then clear as megaphones, 'If they're doing it, I should kill them.' As he drags excess ink from the plate, with balls of screwed-up scrim, he sees that words have a special shape. Words reach back through life like letters in rock, getting hotter and darker as they go. But kill them? Crime passionel? He has never thought he could hurt Robyn ever. But this is a strange day, all doors open. He sees them before him, Robyn and the man, their limbs wound in one. They seem Siamese twins or some birth-abortion of two creatures fused.

As he turns the press-handles steadily down he sees what he will do.

They swim before him, the couple obscenely melted together. His hand becomes iron, and harder stuff than they are. He will reach inside their chest and clench the double palpitating heart so it bursts, a blood-bomb.

Or something like that. He unwinds the press, its plate slowly rises, till he can reach in and, very carefully, peel away the print he has made.

He holds it up. Good. That's the great thing with drypoint. Because the burr of the dug line caught extra ink, some of the lines are thick like fur. The whores, the cripples, plump Rubens gazing from his horse. It burns with grim vision.

Preparing to go, he glimpses himself in the mirror. He looks tired, but also agitated and odd. That's no surprise, with the work he has ahead of him.

At the door he pauses by an old portfolio furry with dust. The Fire-Girl Suite. She is there, Mae, sealed up close. There's no way back. He slams the door after him so it jigs in its frame.

If the people in the street were to look at him carefully, they would not see killing, for that is inside him. But the newstands knew what was in his mind: war preparing and battle groups forming. Nearly there now, the attic, the garden shed, hide if you can!

Quietly he has opened the door of his home.

'Stephen, is it you?' she calls from upstairs.

'Robyn— ' But his voice is voiceless, will she hear?

'Stephen?' she has called again.

The killer stands in the hall of the home. You will see him in the dimness if you look in that corner. Only wait, he won't move before you do.

'There you are. How are you?'

They stand confronted (she still on the stairs).

'Are you all right?'

He is on the brink... will he strike, will he speak? He is a jigsaw puzzle held by the ears, you see the space between the pieces. Till hoarsely, in a rush, he says, 'Robyn, can we go back – back to the painting we started? The big one for Brussels. I'm sorry we stopped.'

Slowly her face grows ever more serious. Quietly she says, 'Yes.'

He is still amazed at the unforeseen words which have jumped from his mouth. But he has no *real* evidence, after all, and the way ahead is abruptly clear. He wants no murders, that isn't him. He will ignore what he suspects. By force he will rebuild his house. He will work with love and art together. He will *paint* them back into their marriage. And if there *is* a lover, he will scare him off. Out of here, punk!

She says, 'It's been a bad day, I can see.'

'OK, yes. A bad day.'

He enters his home.

5

Man and woman will enter the cluttered red room, shy, conspiratorial, two on a verge. While he pokes utensils she will undress, shaking her head so her hair swings loose and settles on her pink-white shoulders. Her blouse, abruptly, she chucks in the man's face.

'Music!'

He's tuned to a pop channel.

Swaying, she'll withdraw her bra, and shuttle to either side of it held still in mid-air – then flick it away past her head in a sling-shot. Other clothes she'll cast to different ends of the room, while he will have tuned to a slower music, night-clubby, saxophonous, to which she will coil sultrily, her eyes in a tantalizing fix on his. While he dabs colours she plays different poses: Odalisques, Mata Haris, the Venuses of Titian.

So it was when Robyn first posed, or so now it seems in the drowsings of Bloodsmith as he surfaces slowly on the crest of the morning. But how will it go today, is the question. That dancing Robyn is very far gone.

He has only more trepidation, as he fully comes awake. It's a long time since he stopped work on that painting. *Can* they go back to it?

Robyn delays, fixing the washing-machine to wash.

'Let's go,' he's said several times.

The day itself is cold and blowy: the wind flaps and blusters, and snaps at the wrapped striding couple, the young-faced but weathered-faced tangled-haired man and the fair woman in the elegant top. The burdened cloud-cover thickens to bruise-black: it is dark for morning, and getting darker.

She pauses at his doorway. 'It's a long time since I've been here, Stephen.'

'Too long, no?'

From the roof-window grey light falls in the room. The backs of canvases show whitely.

'Here's Robyn.' He turns round a big canvas that was faced to the wall, where, lightly sketched in, we see Robyn reclining, and an artist in outline, in ruff and slashed doublet. Rubens, of course, painting Europa. Robyn's face is detailed, like a portrait sketch.

He gazes at the real Robyn, with her classical profile, gazing at Robyn in paint.

She doesn't speak.

'Robyn?'

He studies the crease he sees at her eye-corner: she is looking hard. The face in the painting seems nervous, and falling by the moment into ambiguity.

Finally she turns. 'I don't know.'

'No?'

'I don't know that this is me.'

'Oh.' His eyes have gone serious.

She doesn't offer more.

With a gravity, with no hint of dance, Robyn undresses, resting her clothes in a half-folded pile. It seems to be growing colder, as if outside the day still darkens. He aims the bars of his electric fire at the couch where she will sit.

It's a solemn-faced Robyn who now stands before him, with a don't-see-me tilt away of her body. Her full breasts breathe, in their carriages of muscle which hang from her collar-bones.

'Come,' he says, with an odd large gesture not usual to him, almost courtly, conducting her to a couch of state.

'You need your Muse,' she says.

'I do.'

With a movement of her hand to brush the velvet, she sits a little warily, perhaps even shyly.

'It's remarkable,' he exclaims. 'That's really good! You've gone back – exactly to the pose you were in.'

She seems pleased and smiles; perhaps it is an omen. So he won't need to do all his dodging and measuring, squinting at a brush-stem held at arm's length. When he first began the painting, he hung little weights on threads from above, to make a grid by which he could measure her. He doesn't need to do that again, but still he's got his fine adjustments.

'Can you put your foot there?'

'Where, there?''

'No, there. That's great.'

A moment he pauses: his head goes down, his eyes go unseeing. This is the turning point. So she has a lover? We'll disappear him with art. And after that – who knows? – with sex.

Also his ambition will be fulfilled for the big wall in Brussels. His Robyn his marriage his life his art, all come right like a masterpiece in one.

She knows from his breathing he is ready to begin. He is peering at her now with hard dry artist-eyes.

'Stephen— '

'Right. Yes. Music.'

He's over among his tumbled CDs. It's not a pop or jazz day, rather William Lawes: sweet notes of viols, with a melancholy, a strangeness.

She relaxes. 'Nice.'

On the wall, in a colour-supplement self-portrait, Rubens himself seems bland and pleased. And it is such music as might have beguiled the Flemish painter, of an evening in his English trip, sitting in the Gerbier house as the consort is composed. The company sits quietly, replete but with a lassitude, and as the haunting notes extend odd pieces of the past return. Rubens recovers evenings with Isabella, the boys hovering restlessly, as some of his apprentices play. The young Antony Van Dyck is with them, plying his bow, while his limpid pale eyes redden and return to Isabella, whose own eyes drop. A blush? A shy glance? And a nervous glance from Antony, to see if Rubens watches. Antony lives with them, in their house.

'Don't you want the lights on, Stephen? Can you see like this?'

'No, I like it. It's interesting.' Though the room is dim, there is a diffused pearly whiteness. The figure of Robyn is snow-white before him, except where he catches, in her shins, her stomach, the faint reflected gleam of the electric bars. Her body is a little slack with posing (a slackness he may later hide). A fair and fair-skinned woman, with a belly that has had a child, and a certain bloom and glow still to her. He notes the blue veins round the eyes of her breasts. Her breasts will be the lightest place in the picture. The next lightest is, what, her forehead?

But her head still has an obstinate jut, as if she is enduring an infliction.

'Robyn, what did you mean, the painting isn't you? It is you.'

From wherever her thoughts have been they return. 'I don't know. You can see her now, I can't. But she looks nice, the woman. She doesn't look stupid. She doesn't look weak.'

'So? What is it that isn't there?'

'I'm not sure. I suppose . . . It's too light and bright.'

'You mean she hasn't got a shadow side.'

'Yes. Yes, exactly.' Both of the women look at him now: the painted Robyn and Robyn – the woman without, and the woman with the shadow side.

'What do you mean?'

She gleams. 'The shadow side is made of secrets.'

She watches, waits, for him to speak. Perhaps if he asks his question again, everything private will be told, with pain, and brought to order.

They shine to each other.

The question, the question. But he asked two days ago, and she denied everything. And on the other hand, he knows the answer.

'What secrets do you mean?'

She frowns, looks down. 'You can't explain these things.'

She looks up, meets his eyes again. Obstinacy and fear debate in the air. Neither speaks.

The moment passes.

At a light pattering he looks up, and sees on the roof-lights grey-black splatterings: the rain has started. Light not heavy, but set to continue, adding an undernote to the plaiting skeins of music.

She, 'It has to do with wanting death.'

'What does?' He knows she means the shadow side. Its meaning is changing as the moments pass.

'Say, Robyn.' She doesn't say.

He paints.

With a sudden gust rain slaps the panes, there is a clash as a bin goes over outside. The sound calls his eyes up, to where rivulets of water run on the glass like crooked twigs.

Looking back, he sees, on Robyn's white skin, the faintest shadow of the coursing water: as though she sat behind a thin waterfall; or as though one could see time and life wash over her; or as if the plasma of her blood showed through transparent skin so you saw the slow streaming, which most of all is like a flowing sadness, as though in this cold wind-gusted room an unstoppable grieving were under way.

He places dim hue next to hue, as the sweet-sad notes come in rhythm with the rain. In the past also it is raining, outside the Gerbier house. The faces of the family are pensive and sombre, even little Susan's, gazing into the fire. The pattering on the panes is like pluckings on a lute, it makes Rubens think of rainy days in Flanders, the rain forever falling on the Scheldt and on the marshes, making his cloak heavy when he rides the soggy dyke. But when will King Charles of England summon him, so their talk gets down to business? Or may it be the king himself who plans to play a trick on him?

On the roof-window still the rain-tracks ripple, throwing their veinings on the floor and on Robyn. Bloodsmith is abstracted, gone out into eye, while his brush dips in cobalt and in crimson, which it stirs to a purple and touches to the canvas. In him too the sadness gathers, like a mineral in his head, like precipitating lead.

But how on earth do you paint the shadow side? How do you paint it in a face? But the answer's ready: you can paint a knowledge, in the eyes.

From those painted eyes he returns to Robyn's. Her face, inert, is gazing out but looking in with a mood of, what – deep hopelessness? He has not thought about Robyn's feelings or thought that, even if there is a lover, still she might be sad, rather than simply lost in sex-joy. She is far from him now, deep in a situation he doesn't know. They are far from each other. And down her face the shadows course, like a weeping inside her that is in him too, for the sadness, the sadness, of where they are now.

His painting's stopped, the music's stopped, there is only the drum of rain and sudden thresh of wind. At the base of the roof-window, he sees the top fronds of a thrashing tree, tossing like a blinded bear.

Looking back, he sees she's looking at him, with a look that questions, blue-eyed, intense, it is a look that undoes his art. It is a look that withdraws, when she sees him looking back.

Both slightly smile, the smile of the withdrawing eye.

He retreats behind his canvas. He's so still and quiet she presently asks,

'Have we finished, Stephen?'

From behind the canvas, 'We've finished for today'. In his hand his brush has stopped. The thought he had – that through art he could paint them together again, and make it good by making love – that thought is failing by the moment.

He has put his brush down, she stands up. They look at each other, but it is like gazing across a chasm, which slowly widens as they watch. Robyn gazes to him from the other edge of the abyss – and there is someone beside her, a shadow-figure. He strains to make out who it is.

The pattering of the rain has stopped, a white light grows in the room.

'Is that the time?' She comes to. 'God, I'd forgotten. I've got to see Hazel. There's the Sean Raven show – we said we'd set up the publicity today.'

Quietly she dresses. 'I'll see you at home.'

She comes close, and kisses him, but quickly, and she's gone.

And where? To Hazel – or, to someone else?

Probably, this afternoon, it's Hazel. He would have caught the vibration, if she had a rendez-vous.

Still the cogs in his head are turning. Sean Raven – so famous for his light-box photos. Robyn will host a show of his, they are in communication. Abruptly realization strikes. That phone-call the other day, when the caller wouldn't speak while Robyn blushed fiery red. The caller was Sean Raven. There is a ping in his head like a fruit machine scoring, and an inner voice says, 'Robyn's lover is Sean Raven.'

Is he? He must work on that. Play the private eye, hunt them down. He'll look out the phone bills at home, check for odd numbers, and ring them back. It'll be easy to find out Sean Raven's number. Will he snoop in Robyn's diary?

He is gazing at the abandoned painting. It is more unfinished than it was before. Nor will it be finished. Matters can't be repaired so easily. And the affair, if there is an affair – with Sean Raven, if it is Sean Raven – that won't just stop like turning off a switch.

He picks up the canvas from behind, by the wood, and carries it to lean with its face to the wall. He's dizzy, did he move too quickly? He sits, but nothing is still, like when you are drunk and the room heels over.

The room and he are still. Around him easels and trestle tables wait. His eye rests absently on the closed blue portfolio, the Fire-Girl Suite, where it leans in a corner near the door, faintly whitened with a frost of dust. Just one warm breath would melt that frost – or the touch of a dark hot hand.

That road is closed. But inside him walls and towers are falling. Slowly but unstoppably, like a man in automatic motion, he has risen and crossed the floor, and picked up that portfolio furry with dust. Coughing, he hauls it to the centre of the room, weighty and swollen as it is, tight-tied with grey picture-cord.

In the middle of the room he crouches down, to rest the portfolio on the floor. He unpicks the knot, and jerkily tugs back the zip.

And almost it explodes, it is so filled with drawings, sketches, print-proofs, they slide and flow and fall around him. He pushes them out in a big fan – where we see, over his shoulder, they all are pictures of the same person. In smudgy coal-hole charcoal scrub, in brisk-brushed thick-ribbed acrylic impasto, they all are a woman, the Fire Girl apparently, who is in no way similar to Robyn. She seems a Giacometti woman, tall and thin, spindly, dark-skinned, with a flaring frizz of hair and eyes with enormous whites, bright in her dark-skinned face.

And if we leave him for an hour, and return as afternoon gathers to dusk, it is only to find him still crouched by the drawings. Except that he no longer looks down. He has shifted his hams and crouches up, gazing to a point where a figure is forming. It rises slowly above the pictures, like a spirit conjured from a pool. It is no spirit, it is the woman herself, slender, dusky, tall. She stands in air, in the dimming light, more faint to us than a coil of smoke. But to him she's clear, he sees the large-lidded un-lustrous eyes that gaze down at him steadily, as they gaze up from each picture on the floor, in a calm long inspection… till his own eyes close, tight-shut as fists.

Can we draw closer? He seems so absorbed, he won't hear our approach, spectral as our footsteps are. Or perhaps he just catches the soft fall of these words, leading us closer to him. For he turns toward us, but though we see him, he does not see us. His glistening eyes cloud. His face is red-streaked, a face confounded. We catch his murmur, 'Where are you, Mae?'

And she, in her pictures, is all about him in the room. And, she is not there.

~

In the night he woke suddenly, as if he dropped out of bed. A change was occurring, like a clearing of traffic for the important car. Points were switching deep within him, for the sombre express to arrive. 'I don't love you Robyn. Mae is my woman. She always was, *she* is my Model.'

Beside him the warm steady breathing of Robyn evenly drew in and out.

6

Mae

Who is this Mae?

He first had seen her a year or two since, at a life-drawing session. It was an evening class, taken by Ollie, which he visited on and off to keep his hand in.

'Steve.'

'Ollie.'

At the door he had stopped, taking in the new model. Something about her made him think, what a weird business life-drawing is! Up on the dais, dark, lean, all angularities, she was like a sacrifice or an idol. The artists sat at their boards in concentric arcs, bobbing and bowing as if in worship; or they sat upright, scrutinizing, seeming to eat her with their eyes. She was naked, exposed to dissecting pencils, and seemed more naked because so thin. Was she nervous, oppressed? Her head was raised upright on the stalk of her neck. Her projecting jaw jutted grimly, the bulb of her nose had a sprightly lift.

He straddled a bench. Resting his drawing pad upright, he snapped his charcoal and started to draw.

There was quiet in the room. Ollie slid between the draughtsmen. There were stealthy words, then a quick decided scratching, as Ollie sat and the draughtsman stood.

'Yes, her arm goes down. But the angle that *we* see, from here, goes up. You're not drawing what you see.'

Then Ollie also sat, and started his own drawing. Normally there was a desultory chatter in the Life Room, as the draughtsmen completed a line before answering. This new strange model commanded their silence.

'Rest, Mae,' Ollie said. So he knew her name.

But it was only when she stood at the end of the session that Bloodsmith saw how striking she actually was. Up on the dais, she seemed preternaturally tall. She moved with dignity across the platform, and, solemn-faced, slipped on a dressing-gown. As she turned to step down, their eyes met. She registered his look seriously, with her heavy-lidded, large, not shining eyes. Then she made a slight frown, as if the fact that he was staring still, after the other artists had stopped, made him a puzzle to her.

While he was simply thinking: she's extraordinary, I have to paint her.

She had quickly changed and gone. He loitered as the students left.

'Who was she, Ollie?'

'Who? Oh, Mae. She's wonderful, isn't she? Bit of a Grace Jones.'

'Mae who?'

'Search me. She agreed to stand in. I didn't find her.'

'Will she be here next week?'

The blue eyes of Ollie focused on him: he registered he was showing too keen an interest.

The next week, the day of the life class arrived and Robyn said, 'Don't go tonight, Stephen. Let's see a movie.'

His mouth dropped, he was quite caught out.

'I did want to go tonight. I'm sorry.'

He went to the life class, but the regular model had come back. Ollie was vague as to who it was who suggested Mae to him.

That night, the next day, he was agitated as he seldom had been. Overnight he had grown certain that Mae was the person he needed to paint. When he started to ask if other people knew her, and met only dead ends, he felt a cruel trick was played on him. For years Robyn was his beautiful model, he worshipped at a blonde and golden shrine. Now the magnetism of the earth reversed, another and opposite model strode to him, alien, dark-skinned, a huntress. As she reached him, she disappeared.

Then he saw her in the street. He was idling by a shop, and when he looked ahead the pedestrians parted, like an ocean divided by God. Straight down this avenue she walked towards him, fast, as if to run him over. She wore a bright-red mac, tight-strapped at the waist. She gazed ahead and through him.

He thought, this is a miracle. Will I chicken out and waste it?

'Oh excuse me.'

To his amazement, he had spoken.

She stopped sharply, like a vehicle skidded to a halt.

'I'm sorry?' Again the knit brow of curiosity.

'I'm sorry. I surprised you, I didn't mean to. I drew you the other day. In the Art School. In the evening. I was wondering . . . if you would pose again. I mean if you would pose for me — if I could paint you. I know it's funny, asking like this. I'm an artist, I'm not being creepy. But... oh, I think you're wonderful.'

But if she was startled, and then had a curious listening look, in the end she gave a sudden bright wide smile of teeth.

'I haven't modelled for years,' she said. 'Except the other night . . . '

She waited, looking at him cheerfully: her eyes after all had a lustre. He thought, it may happen.

'I'd pay the proper rate,' he said. Everything must be right.

She made a mouth, he didn't know what it meant.

'Will you?'

'I've no idea.'

'Of course . . . I'm sorry . . . all out of the blue. Can I get you— a coffee?'

'What? No! I must go.'

'But... Can I ring you – when you've had time – discussed it?'

She turned side-on to him, thinking. He saw her curves play against each other.

'Would I come to the Art School?'

'I've got my own studio. I'd rather do it there.' He thought, Do I sound straight, or tacky?

Time hung. Pedestrians eddied about them. There was a friction from elderly big-built ladies, brushing closer than they needed to, and inhaling heavily as they passed.

'I'll come to your studio – we can talk.'

Was this yes, or not quite yes?

'When can you come?'

'I can't say now. I must rush. Can you ring?' She gave a number.

'I'll look forward— '

But 'Goodbye!' she said, and held out her hand. He was not ready for shaking hands; but it was proper and businesslike. The hand was thin, long-fingered, firm. They shook and she had gone.

At the corner she turned quickly, and abruptly flashed her wide big smile.

The rest of the day he could not work. The broken bits of him, eye, hand, foot, sprang little wings and flew round the town.

At home Robyn said, 'You're in a good mood, Stephen. What's got into you?'

At that point a crack opened. 'Oh, my work went well today.' He could not say, I have found a new model. Robyn was his model, and this person was different in all ways from Robyn. She was his secret, there would be desecration if he told other people.

~

When he rang, she answered straight away,

'No, I will come. Anyway, I'll come and see. But I haven't posed for ever so long. Where is your studio?'

Her voice had a dip or trip of breath, as if she were nervous too.

They fixed a time. He said, 'I'll look forward to then.'

'See you,' she said, and rang off.

On the appointed day he waited, so excited he was unable to visualize her. What pose shall I ask for? His thoughts ran off like mercury. It was not good outside, the roof-window showed the colour of slate.

'She'll never come in this weather.'

There came hesitant taps on the door. Of course she had come, it was never in doubt. Lean as a spindle, dripping rain from her tight-tied coat, she stood, diffident, in his door-frame.

'You're very wet. I'm sorry.'

'It's not your fault.'

When she took off the scarf, her hair burst big. They were speechless in shyness. The room was dark – had he brought her to Bluebeard's cave? He turned on his strip-lights, which blinked then shone. In the harsh light she hugged herself coldly, standing vertical and pulled-in, like a javelin stuck in the ground.

'I'll make some coffee, that's all I do hot. Stand in front of these.' He snaked towards her the two small electric-bar fires he kept to warm up chilly models. She took off her coat. She scanned his prints and drawings, many of which were of Robyn.

'Is that your wife?'

'That's Robyn.'

She went and looked close. 'I think I like the lithographs best.' As she bent, he noticed how the sinews of her neck stood clear.

'Perhaps you're right.'

'But that's not right.'

He went, carrying cups, to see. 'You're really exposed with drypoint,' he murmured.

'I think it's because that line is dead straight. It makes her arm go flat.' She pointed.

'Uh. You're absolutely right.' Already she had turned the tables on him.

'You paint?' he said. 'You make prints?'

'I've been meaning to start again. Somehow I stopped – you know, family.'

'That's a pity. Where did you go?'

'Norwich.'

'Right you are. And you pose? You model for evening classes?'

'At Norwich I used to pose. It was extra money, I needed it. I liked to do it. And it didn't stop me doing my pictures. I posed in the evenings, when I was tired. I was exhausted. I used to fall asleep. I was famous for falling asleep while posing. But I kept the pose.'

'You kept the pose because you're an artist.'

'It's curious, because I'm a shy person, but I wasn't shy when I was posing.'

He wondered, will she fall asleep here? The situation was changing by the moment.

She made a bony triangle, sitting on his kitchen chair. She had her heels up on a rail, and her knees and elbows out akimbo, as she sipped from the cup which she held in both hands. She was like a stick-insect angled to drink.

She reflected, 'Yes, I stopped my pictures. If I want to start again, I will.'

He blinked, this was all a different attitude from any he could take.

'What do you want me to do?'

'Oh. Just sit there.'

'What, on this chair?'

'I'll try to draw you there.'

While the rest of her body did not move, her long arm unfolded, to rest her coffee-cup on the wood floor. She folded her arms back in her lap. He was suddenly disappointed. For all her experience posing, she sat like a good girl, as if in a school photo. She could not have posed like that at Norwich.

'Can you sit less straight?'

'I'm comfortable like this.'

'Are you? OK.'

'I know what you mean. It's years, really, since I did this.'

He became absorbed in her figure, seated so slenderly erect. He thought of Christianity and missionaries, evangelical campaigns in the heart of the continent.

'Where are you from?' he asked.

'Ipswich.'

'Ipswich?'

She observed his surprise. 'My mother went there when she married my father.'

'She wasn't from Ipswich.'

'She was from Bermuda. She's a physiotherapist.'

'Right. But your father's from Ipswich.'

'No, my father was from the States, he was working at an American base. But I don't remember seeing him. They split almost at once.'

'Yes.' He drew. Musingly he said, 'I suppose you sound Ipswich. You don't sound . . . ' His words trailed off uncertainly.

'What don't I sound? I don't sound African? I don't sound American? I don't sound Bermudan? But I don't like the Bermuda sound, it's not got a lilt, like Jamaica. I expect you mean, I don't sound Brixton.'

'I'm sorry, I'm sorry.' His head sank over his drawing.

'Inside I feel like anyone else here. I suppose that's Ipswich. In London, it would have been different. Because I was the only person like me there. And my mother, of course. But I would forget, at school, it's funny... then I would get reminded, going home.'

'You mean, the other kids.'

'Of course.'

'The buggers!'

He was wondering, is the space between her eyes wider or narrower than the eye itself?

'What does your husband do?'

'He's a manager in a printing firm. He's good on art.'

Somehow this did not please Bloodsmith.

'He's very kind to me.' She spoke as though he did her a favour, marrying her.

Their questions have petered out. She seems now scarcely at all to breathe, seated in the chair like someone held for questioning. He has become nothing but a hand with an eye attached. There is the sharp scratch of charcoal on cartridge paper. They are becoming one in the relation of drawing.

Until she says, 'What time is it?'

They've arrived there, unknowing.

She came and looked over his shoulder. 'I was sitting stiffly. I'll ease up.'

'Thank you for coming.' He made to pay.

'Don't pay me, I don't want your money.'

'Let me. It'll go funny otherwise. And it's so little.'

'No, I'm sorry. I won't. I can't. I want to come because I'm flattered you asked me. I don't want to be your employee.'

Dressed, she looked suddenly prim.

'Do you want me again?' There was something brusque in the way she said it.

'Of course. Please. Are you willing?'

'I'll come some more times.'

They arranged a date.

'See you!' she said brightly, going.

'See you.'

He sat, feeling exhausted, as on a long drive when you don't feel weary till the car stops at last, then all the tiredness comes at once.

~

He had a colleague in the Art School, Annabelle Hobbes, who published paperbacks on the male gaze and nudes, and on the West, Race and Power. When he passed her in the corridors, he wondered warily, What would your take be, on where I'm going? Was he entering a danger zone? Maybe, but I want to paint Mae *so* much...

Soon they came to real posing, the nude.

'Do you mind?' he asked anxiously.

'It must be said, it's what models do.'

He had put up a screen, for her to undress and dress behind, and a kimono for times of rest.

'Where do you want me?'

The silk kimono clung close on her, as if her skin rubbed up an electricity.

'Oh – just stand. Stand comfortably.'

She opened the kimono and stepped outside it. She seemed not nervous. There was both a shyness, and a pride in her stance. And a tension, a chastity, he saw that clearly: as if she were a woman from another galaxy entirely, where matter was different and the atoms all turned in the other direction. If he and she touched, they would explode.

They began. She talked about her son, Gavin, who gave her mock embraces that hurt, like fighting. 'Perhaps he wants more from me.'

'I should think you're a very loving mother.'

Her brow knit at this, as though his words came too easy.

'Perhaps I'm not really. Perhaps I'm not very giving. What are you drawing?'

'I'm doing your collar-bones. I love the way they curve together.'

'I've got no meat.'

'That's not true. But I love the way your collar-bones curve, they're like bits of a violin. They're like phrases in music, you know, answering back to each other.'

'Thank you.'

'What does Geoffrey say about Gavin?'

'Oh, Geoffrey's never there.' Fathers never are.

'What's Geoffrey like?'

'Geoffrey,' she said, 'Geoffrey . . . ' Her face was gently wistful, 'Geoffrey was always different, right from the start. Because my other boy-friends, the white ones, they treated me like... I don't know, like a mascot of something. Geoffrey was never like that. And you can imagine how things were with his family. Geoffrey was very kind to me.'

Her wide quiet smile had a lovely tenderness – to see it, he hurt.

'Let's rest.'

'Oooh!' She was stiff. Her legs, from knee to foot, were deeply darkened, where the blood had collected from her standing so long. She stretched and rubbed herself.

'We'll call it a day.'

They agreed the next date.

'Had a busy day, Stephen?'

Robyn met him in the hall.

'Yes, a busy day.' He made a meal of being weary.

'Were you at the Art School?' Was she on his track?

'No, I was in the studio.'

She watched him.

The awkward pause, tonight, was longer than previous times.

He asked, 'Where did you decide to put the second dark-room?'

'I haven't decided,' she said shortly. Perhaps it was obvious his interest was false.

He thought, this is only going to get more difficult.

'I'll fix a Punt e Mes,' he said.

~

In their following sessions he still postponed painting Mae and continued to draw his way up and down her. He loved riding her form in charcoal, tracing where her shoulder blades stirred, swooping down the long curve of her back and curling round the sweet clear bulb of her bottom. No other body, not even Robyn's, had he explored in this close-up way. Somewhere behind his shoulder the piercing spectacles of Annabelle Hobbes hovered, watching what he did with eyes of ideology. He could not stop. Mae was too special, and simply too different from everyone else.

'Will you stand with one arm up, like the Statue of Liberty?'

He dragged an easel up beside her, and tied a rolled-up towel to the top of it, so her arm could be supported. He sat and stared at this naked Liberty: more than ever she was a Giacometti woman. The twist of her hand made the torch, her long fingers the flames. Her crinkling hair was again a fire. Her large eyes looked down at him – was she gazing like a prisoner, from within the pose he inflicted on her? But he thought, No, I shall make Mae the *Statue of Liberty*!

'Let's not do it, if it isn't comfortable.'

'It's a good pose.' She stretched taller, 'Be quick!'

'I will, I want to. Because you're the flame. You are to me.'

In the event, she held the pose. She seemed a person who was happy vertical, as if she were of the flamingo family and could sleep, if she wanted, on one leg. Or she was like a single stem of pampas, with a feathery bush at the crown?

'Tell me about your mother.'

She described their solitary life in Ipswich, in the home of the abandoned foreign woman, who was also lean and muscular though not as tall, with a dexterity in her fingers, which could reach into limbs and massage them whole. Perhaps the sternness came from her.

'What is she? I mean, what does she believe?'

'She's a Baptist. Her father was a Minister, and his Father too.'

'Have you been baptized?'

'I've been through Jordan.'

She described the long tank in the church in Ipswich, the tepid adventure of immersion.

'Do you believe?' he asked.

'Yes. You don't?'

He shook his head. 'I may have done once, a long time ago.'

She talked more of her mother, also of her mother's depression.

'I was the man about the house.'

He saw this house and life without men. Really it was a story of parthenogenesis, as if the mother alone had budded this daughter, who was identical to her and marched through life single. He knew Mae was married but he could not imagine it.

He finished Liberty and they both were pleased, as if Africa and History joined them here. As the sessions continued, he felt they grew closer, even they were becoming alike; as if he could quickly grow tall and thin, as if his pigmentation could change to hers.

Between sessions he wondered more how would Robyn take it, if she knew? She could not be pleased, for she was his model. He had once wanted to paint her for ever. He had thought himself an artist like Bonnard, who could paint the same woman with only more vision and love as time passed. Could all of that change? It would uproot his world.

And yes, of course, it could or must change. Artists change their models – for Heaven's sake! Look at Ollie, he finds a new model each year. And screws her too. And Becky weathers it. I wonder, does she make it up to herself?

He was getting more absent-minded at home.

'Where is your mind, Stephen? I don't know why I bother to talk.'

'I'm sorry— it's a problem in my work.'

'You've got a big problem in your work, now, I think.'

'Right.' He nodded evasively.

Still he said nothing. He had not told Robyn, and he would not tell her. Of *this* new model he must not speak. He had become double, but it had to be.

~

The next time Mae came, he was silent and sombre. He asked Mae to take a lying-down pose, and she stretched on a rug while he squatted low on the floor to draw her. To either side of them the elements of his electric fires glowed. He told himself, I won't be stopped from painting Mae, and he meant, by Robyn, or by the thought of Robyn.

The still air of the room was warm. He scanned his drawing. He had tried to draw her resting on the floor, but on his paper she seemed to lift and hover. With her large eyelids closed, she could look dead as much as alive.

As he watched, her breathing grew calmer, till he realized she had gone to sleep as she used to when she posed at art school. He watched in a slow amazement. There was something trusting in the way she lay naked on his floor. Stealthily he sketched, he must not wake her.

Her sleep made a space. His drawing paused on the thought, what is happening here? He sat over Mae's naked unconscious body. He thought I'm like a book-jacket for Annabelle Hobbes. Although, who's the slave here? I am a slave to my sight of Mae.

Still it was an obsession, kept secret from everyone. Was he hiding the sex-motive, and what really he wanted? At the root of his genitals an ache began.

In her sleep she rearranged her body. He glimpsed bright iris between the fringes of her lids, then her eyes were completely closed again. He sketched those closed eyes – then, looking up, saw they had opened... 'You slept.'

'I used to do that.'

'Do you want to move?'

'I'm happy,' she said. 'It's warm and nice here.'

'I'm happy too.'

Her breathing slowed further, she sank into deeper sleep. Her breasts, as she lay on her back, hardly showed. Beneath the waxy domes of her eyelids a slight bulge shifted, as her gaze, in her sleep, turned this way and that. He was watching that part of her life continue, which she never knew when she was awake.

He had rested his pad on the floor. No, this was not only Art. He was bending nearer to her, he felt the flare from the electric bar on his cheeks. It would be so easy, to lay his quiet body beside her long body. The way she lay invited him.

The air was heating, the light dimmed from above. The blood-colour of his walls deepened, their red light advanced and lay upon everything. Out in the world a magnetic storm raged, the polarities were under attack and would switch. His feeling and relation with Mae were changing. If only he could wait, the rights and wrongs of the world would reverse.

There was a check in her breathing, her eyes blinked open. For a moment she seemed startled, then said, 'Hello.'

'Hello there.' The red light sank back into the wall.

'I've really slept,' she said with wonder. As she woke, day returned to the room. 'I trust you completely.'

He smiled, he hurt, he did not want that trust.

'May I move?'

'Of course.'

She stretched and sat up, rubbing her neck.

'It's late again.' She stood.

'Are you stiff?'

'No. That was nice.' She yawned her mouth amazingly wide, and her eyes, nearly closed by yawning, sparkled amiably to him. He had never before seen this large pink yawn. Again she stretched her arms, which seemed as she uncoiled them to have no end, but to grow on outwards like the reaching limbs of a tree.

~

75

But it was only during the following day that the meaning of this session came home. He was in the Art School, teaching Design for Printmaking. As every year, he told the students to take three letters of the alphabet, any three, and make out of them an attractive design.

'How's that, Steve?' they asked.

'It's pretty.' He nodded complacently, because, as every year, the designs were 'nice' but also boring.

'Now take those three letter, and make the *ugliest* design you can.'

They gaped their mouths, he quietly smiled. He knew their 'ugly' designs would be more alive by far, especially if they added 'ugly' colours.

The students had their heads down then. He stood among them but he was not there, he bent beside the sleeping Mae, when all at once the seizure came. It seemed each cell in his skin stood up, tiny flames ran over him. He had stopped breathing, he half closed his eyes. I desire this strange person *absolutely*. Yet he had no erection: instead, in his genitals, came a stabbing pain. Probably he stood still, but he felt he reeled, he rocked, his breathing was a panting, as the desire-storm, desire-tsunami, or love-burst, if it was, swept through him. I *must* have her— It seemed almost he wanted to be her.

He came to, and saw the head-down students had noticed nothing at all. For the rest of the day, he was only half in any room he was supposed to be in. The question was, how had he not known he felt like this about her the very first moment he saw her? Except that it seemed, now, that always he felt like this for her. He could not go back to the earlier him.

One thing was clear. The next time she came, nothing could be as it had been before. But what then could happen?

~

As the day arrived when she would next come, he moved his easel and implements back and forth. His brain repeated, I know she likes me. But what if it all goes terribly wrong? I'm not Ollie. But he could not stop now.

'Hello!' Her smile was its brightest ever.

She wore her red mac: he thought, that's a good sign, red is sexy. She must see how nervous he was. She must hear it in his voice, which was hoarse and breathy. Yet she seemed to notice nothing.

'Has Gavin been good?'

'He has, yes.' She spoke from behind the screen, and reappeared in the kimono.

He must make his move before she posed, but she had already got down on the floor. The wings of her pelvis showed through her skin, he saw the line where her rib-cage ended.

He could do nothing else, but start to draw: his hand shook.

She said, 'Could you move this cushion? I'll lose the pose, if I do it.'

He got up. She had invited him. He was full of shyness, but it would all come right.

He bent down.

'Like that?'

'Thanks.' She re-settled her head.

'Good.' As his hand left the cushion, it stroked her hair: the crinkly texture was more tough and wiry than he expected. His fingers continued, and caressed her cheek, which also felt not as he expected, but as if her skin had a slight velvety nap.

Her eyes gazed solemnly up at his. He thought, you are so beautiful.

Gently she raised her hand, and took his by the wrist.

'Don't spoil it, Stephen.'

She said it with such sweet appeal, his resolution melted.

'I don't want that. Please. I've been so happy here.'

His hand retreated, her fingers relaxed. Then he thought, You are too wonderful, I can't let you go. His hand moved back, and clasped. And at once her fingers closed on his wrist, hard, those slender, dark-backed, spider fingers.

'I'm sorry,' he murmured.

She sat up on the floor, gazing ahead with a serious frown.

He murmured, 'I shouldn't have done that. I'm sorry. Let's go on.'

And after all she looked up brightly, with nothing but a friendly look, which was however also firm.

'I'm sorry, Stephen.' She was getting up. 'I must go. I don't want to hurt you, or give you problems.'

'Don't go. Or if you go today, come back another day. Let's forget it. I shouldn't have, I wish I hadn't. I won't do that again. We must go on. We must.' He would say anything. All that mattered, was that she kept on coming.

She stood and he stood by her, looking as serious as she did.

'OK. Yes. Let's go on.' She said it clearly. It was a decision, a rule. She got down on the floor again.

So things were clear, then: they were married, they would be good. This was not a problem to her, because she liked him in one way and not in another. But how can I go on? he thought. This is impossible. It will become unbearable. And also, I cannot stop.

~

So the sessions continued. At home Robyn had ceased to ask awkward or leading questions. She did her business for the family in a closed, grim way, and he did not ask, he did not want to know, what she thought. He made it clear he was busy, and got tired, sorting the replacement of a press for the Print Room, the prices, the haggling with different suppliers. And Robyn was busy – and preoccupied too – with the final preparations for her photo-gallery's very first show.

The pictures of Mae multiplied, and when he was alone in his studio, he sat with her pictures round him. Her large, level, low-lustre eyes gazed steadily from all sides on his face. The questions built. What obsession is this? I go on drawing a woman who does not want me, and it's not for art though I pretend that it is. It's turning into... an addiction. I go on seeing her when mainly it hurts me, but that hurt is precious, it's my fix. I'm strangling the desire at the core of me.

Nor do thoughts stay still, so he presently said, Or – will I try to *seduce* her through art? Don't take No for an answer. I will speak so kindly, so understandingly, she *has* to change. I shall *make* her like me, I shall become the Casanova of the canvas.

So my life becomes doubly double. I hide what I really want from Mae, which makes me creepy, while I hide from Robyn all knowledge of Mae. And I used to be, pretty much, a straightarrow guy. But I can't stop now. And the road ahead? Nothing at all, or an affair, or what? The end of my marriage? But he could not think that.

No, the future was unthinkable. Well, he had not reached the future yet.

So Mae still came, and he began a wide-angle canvas of her. In this painting she lies flat, outstretched, like a woman crucified laid down on the ground – unless you read her wide lean arms as stretching open in acclamation. Or rather she floats, on a plane of colour, that seems made of films of green and turquoise. The floor has been removed from under her. Her head is turned to us: the whites of her eyes seem slightly yellow, and her deep colour deepens to black round her eyes. When he works on this painting, there is scarcely movement in the room at all, only the light from the roof-window wheeling, as the turbulent sky disturbs. It's a picture of Mae and the shadow beneath her, which may be the past. Her past or The Past.

During a rest she stands beside him. 'I like this picture.' They are together, contemplating it.

He says, 'For this one, we're coming to the finishing touches.'

'I'd better get down again.'

He dabs his brush between long looks. She lies quite still in the studio's calm, in the painting she rests in the peace of air, she hovers in space between sky and ground as if she hovered between life and death.

When he next looks up, her eyes gaze to him with a different look – hugely, blackly glowing. Unchanging. His heart ceases to beat. Is everything possible after all?

He looks down to draw, then regrets it. Her gaze is different, afterwards. Then it's time she must go. Standing by the shut door, he wonders more, where is this heading? His life is on edge, but on what edge? A climax, a crash, a new world or no world.

~

It came out of nowhere.

'We'll have to stop soon.'

'What? Why?'

'We're moving to the States. Geoffrey has been head-hunted, it's all happened suddenly.'

'Oh.' He was stricken.

'It's an absolute shock. For us – for me – for Gavin, of course. Even for Geoffrey. Everything's turned over. It'll uproot us all.' Her voice had slowed, while her eyes, meeting his, grew serious, even solemn. 'I can't ask him to turn this down.'

'Of course,' he said, understandingly. He was thinking, crazily, I have to stop this. He could not stop it.

'We haven't gone yet. We'll finish the picture.' She smiled. 'I shall miss our sessions.'

'I don't want to think about tomorrow.'

She gazed at him in a thoughtful way she had, with her head lowered. Her dome of forehead projected as though she would butt him.

'Perhaps it is a good thing, Stephen. We would have had to stop these sessions, and it might have been painful, making the stop. I think I've caused you pain as it is. Perhaps it's for the best this way.'

He would not admit this.

In the remaining days he felt at times that his head would fall off. At home Robyn would glance his way as if she wondered if his brain were well.

All too soon, Mae's last day was here.

He said, 'I've so liked painting you.'

'And I've loved modelling for you.'

He registered that she'd said 'loved'.

She asked, 'Will you give me a picture?'

'I was going to, of course.'

He had it ready-framed. It was the sketch from their first day, of her sipping coffee.

She put on her coat, and tied her scarf as on the first day, so her head was like a sweet pudding above her slender neck. He wondered, how was it he did not snatch her?

At the door she turned to him. 'Thank you for drawing me – thank you for wanting to.'

Abruptly the question, which he had never asked, came to him. Does Geoffrey know you've been coming here? Did you tell him; or did you not tell him? At this moment it seemed clear: if she had kept these visits secret, then the future was open.

It was too late to ask.

'See you, Stephen.' She kissed him firmly, quickly, on the cheek.

Already she was gone, stepping crisply away. From his doorway he watched her straight-sided African figure, being walked away by her long legs.

At the corner she turned back, smiled, and vanished.

That night he dreamed of Mae. He was in a cavern where an aged woman crouched by a fire of sticks. She was wizened and crooked, but still he recognized she was Mae's mother.

'What are you doing?' He watched her blow a thread of spittle in the centre of the fire.

'I am making the Fire Girl.' As she spoke, the fizzing stuff within the flames unfolded in a minute slender shape, which grew taller swiftly, shimmering like a ballerina, till Mae, full-size, stepped out of the fire.

Though he knew her, he asked, 'Who are you?'

'Don't you know? My name is Fire.'

They embraced and her kiss was searing fire.

'How do we get out of here?' he asked.

'No problem!' she said. She launched up and forwards in a slow-motion leap. The cavern broke apart, they stood by the shore of a bright-lit sea.

'Mae,' he called out. He was awake in the dark. For a moment the bed, the room, the house, were sliding and tipping over.

'Stephen?' Robyn murmured, blearily.

'It's OK,' he whispered, although it was not.

~

She did not write or send cards: they had said goodbye, that was it, it was best. Still he turned his dream into a print, many prints, and he drew her still, from before and behind, from near and far. At first he was afraid his line would go astray, now he no longer saw her in front of him. He need not have worried, his head and eyes were brim-full of her, he could draw her from all sides and inside out.

Some drawings and prints he showed to Hearn, and photos of the paintings. Hearn's eye brightened, there were gender and racial politics here. But there was also pain, and maybe confusion of purpose in Bloodsmith. The Firegirl Suite stalled.

At last he collected his pictures of Mae, and packed them tight in his biggest portfolio. He tied it round and tight with twine, and rested it against the wall. His studio then was a red dead room— except for those moments when all at once he freezes. His shirt rests lightly, as if the hairs on his back have lifted. She is in the room. If he turned fast enough, he would catch her in the opposite corner, where she stands watching in silence for ever. When he imagines her watching, he gives her dark wings.

At home he gave no explanation for his period of aberration, of absence. He tried to make things normal, to be there again for Robyn and Sally. And slowly the home life did repair, like a gash or a wound that cannot help healing. Though there was not the closeness there had been before. Nor did he paint Robyn, he did not paint anyone.

He was able to be absorbed, and together with Robyn, in the last, hectic preparations for the opening of Print Positive. It was good to have so much to do, and they hung the first photo-exhibition together. They worked as one in the social whirlwind of the opening night, when the Mayor and journalists and the Arts Council came. Sally recorded the local telly's report, and when they played it at home they saw themselves swapping glances, excited and radiant. The Mae time was falling into the past.

In the following months he was truly busy, refitting the Print Room at the Art School. But in some way he seethed – he was blocked inside and sour. His imagination fastened on accessories of war. Photos, reports. The teenage, handless girl in Sierra Leone, now holding up her healed stumps. How could the 'soldier' who did that, do that? Or the refugee camp in the Middle East where the buildings were bulldozed by heavy military plant, then run over yet further again and again so the old people who could not leave their house were compounded in crushed concrete and married to the dust of it and became – this was the point – unidentifiable.

Only slowly the question rose in his mind, whether there was a connection between this appetite for pictures of pain, and a frustration, something stymied, at the root of him. He planned a series of prints that would be startling in colour and painful to look at, showing the atrocities and evils of war. If one could be the new Goya, show contemporary terriblenesses . . . Except how could he? War horrors were abroad. He knew them from news reports, got images from newsreels, war photos, sick shots in films. For him they were second-hand, remote. Nothing *he* had seen. How could he be a war-artist, or an anti-war artist, if he had never been to war? Where would he go, in life or art? Where had he come? Where was he?

~

He always had clever hands, with Meccano as well as with pencils and brushes. One love, when he went to Art School, was an ancient motor-bike he bought, a Triumph. His dream then was to be an Artist on a Harley. With passion he thundered up the Black Country, seeking out old foundries, blast-furnace towers of burning rust, which he turned into pictures with an art like clotted soot. When he had to, he stripped down the motor-bike's engine, oversaw the re-boring, and piled small coins on the bump on the cylinder to bank up the compression. Print-making – tuning and cranking presses while working with steel, stone and acid – brought these interests all in one. It was the marriage of engineering and art, though his Degree subject was Fine Art: that is, painting.

Also he used the motor-bike to take girl-artists for runs. Almost at once, on the pillion, there was one girl-artist only, radiant and stunning.

This was Robyn. She liked old foundries less, though she took black-gothic photos of them. Mostly then, on vacs, they bombed among beauty-spots from end to end of Europe, camping and making good-looking art, swimming nude in hidden coves, taking great photos of each other.

Marriage, a job and house, then Sally came. They seemed well settled. He did not have the need his colleague Ollie did, to seduce a new model annually. He and Robyn agreed, Ollie was the old-style Male – and old-style Artist. They were not old-style. Robyn was independent, she would star in her own career, they would draw a line before they had more kids. They shared the parenting and House stuff, and planned to get an allotment. They did not do drugs, though the Art School was a sink of drugs. Nor would they screw around, and as to painting the female nude, well Bloodsmith would paint Robyn. He would paint her honest nakedness with serious respect. You would see in her clear eyes she had as much brain as an artist. Bonnard, after all, painted mainly Madame Bonnard and even Renoir painted, mainly, Mme Renoir.

This all worked and they were pleased with their life, till Mae appeared. Appeared – then disappeared, leaving him in a strange confusion. So he came to his new-Goya pictures, of war and against war. He could draw grievous injury, and the machines men made for injuring. And still the problem was, that this was all in theory. Also there was something forced in his being so black and negative.

One day, after calling on Miles Hearn in London, he dawdled in the National Gallery, in the room at the back where the Rubenses are. Miles had mentioned the big wall in Brussels: they wanted a Euro-mural on the theme of making peace, something with history, and millennial too. As he studied Rubens, the cogs in his brain began to turn. He was in front of the big canvas at the end of the room, where Mars is pushed away from the banquet of Peace.

On the train-trip home, all at once he saw it, his Euro-mural: big in the centre, a fair woman reclines; she is Europa, she is Europe, she looks like a Rubens woman but you see she is Robyn, with scenes of history round her; also she is Peace. She must be painted with a Rubens-like love for the body – could he find that? He must find that.

But, going back to painting Robyn? *Was* that what he wanted? In the next days and weeks he read up on Rubens, till the idea for the picture came complete. Rubens would be in the foreground, you would see him at work, painting the picture of Robyn-Europa. The mural would be a memorial too, to the artist-peacemaker who had lived in Belgium. In his own way he would work for peace, as Rubens did.

Then, in a second-hand book-shop, he found Jens Claeys' book, *Playing Chess with Kings,* translated from the Flemish. 'Illuminating', 'provocative', 'it intrigues', the quotes proclaimed. The translation looked bad, but he was hooked none the less. Obviously Jens Claeys had an artist inside him: he made you see Rubens, and the things Rubens saw. And clearly he loved to tantalize. The author was described on the back jacket as an art-critic and controversialist.

From *Chess with Kings* he moved to meticulous histories, and the monographs of Hans Gotthelf. Reading these books, his print-series was born. 'Rubens in London' – a story in pictures, a revival of long-lost Narrative Art. It would be a pendant to the enormous mural. Steadily he came to feel more inspired, as if Rubens himself and all his world were sailing to meet him in a gilded caravel. Banners and pennants waved from the mast-head. It was laden with women of cream and roses, whose brocaded bodices held up high their white pushed-together breasts. Oh rich lovely vessel with Rubens in the poop (his easel set beside the tiller) wearing a broad-brimmed hat at an angle, with a flourish in the dance of his painting hand. Wavelets caress the vessel's sides, while nereids with milk-charged breasts, suave bellies, their plump legs turning to serpentine fish-tails, disport in the transparent sea.

Robyn must be his Rubens woman. And Robyn was pleased when he asked her to pose. She lay on the couch where Mae had lain, and where, before Mae, she had been.

A year or so after Mae had left, he thought he glimpsed her red mac, her dark head, far off in the crowd. For a second only. Had they come back? He kept a weather eye open after that, against the chance that he saw her again. He never did. He must accept she was gone, and not make dreams.

He continued painting Robyn, and his absorption in her tender limbs and torso returned. He was pleased with the small sketch and started the big sketch. Yet the big sketch did not take fire. He let himself be sidetracked, and spent more time on the Rubens prints. They showed Rubens fighting war with art, which brought him back to his war ideas. He was glad of that.

Robyn was distant. Even in the studio, there was a barrier. And Print Positive was succeeding, so often she simply could not come.

During his long mental absence with Mae, a gap had widened between Robyn and him, which did not close. He was nearly sure she knew nothing about Mae, though sometimes he wondered, could she have let herself into this studio? If she was suspicious, if he had been careless with the key . . . Was it possible she had seen the drawings?

When he started to wonder if she was seeing another man, he had to wonder too, did I help this to happen? Am *I* responsible? It was especially bitter then that nothing had happened with Mae.

Yet perhaps it was not true that nothing had happened.

~

And this is that Mae whom our painter Bloodsmith has so suddenly decided was always the only true model, woman, lover for him.

7

It seemed impossible, later, to say just when he changed from not thinking of Mae to thinking about her every moment of the day. Was it actual love, or a frantic fantasy? A mania? A delusion?

Not that he would forget the unending day on which this sudden need possessed him – when he pulled her portfolio from its corner of dust, and spread her pictures all over his floor. Through his drawings she came to him, growing more real through images and air. 'Mae, I want you back.'

He was caught in inner replay of all the tapes he had of her. He saw her stand he saw her sit, he saw her turn and smile back, he saw and heard her 'See you!' See you! He remembered the time he thought he saw her, far off, in town. *Could* they be back? Most likely she was thousands of miles away.

Never mind, he would ring her house. Strangers would answer – perhaps he would get a forwarding address. A contact number in the States; though what good would that be? There was no phone in his studio, he would ring from the Art School. What if he couldn't see her? Still she was his fate, this Giacometti woman. She was not a Rubens woman at all. Still he would think of her and tell Rubens' story too.

He looked through his Rubens notes for today. He had his next subject, 'Rubens meets the inventor Drebbel'. A remarkable encounter! Well, it must wait. He knew the phone he would go to, the kiosk was tucked under the Art School stairs.

'*Do* be there, Mae,' he said like a prayer, as he let his door bang behind him.

~

As he picks up the handset, he knows he won't find her. Or, by bad chance, will Geoffrey answer? As he himself answered when Robyn's 'friend' rang. But no, they are the other side of the world.

Even so, he chills with nervousness. Ollie wouldn't be nervous like this. The dialing tone continues.

He hears Mae's voice, with its guarded lift, 'Hello?'

'Mae? Hello. It's Stephen.'

'Stephen? Stephen! How are you?'

'I'm fine of course. You're back, then?'

'Back? Oh, from the States. Mm. We're back for good.'

There was a pause.

'It didn't work out?'

She was brusque. 'It went wrong – I don't want to say.' Then she was bright, 'How *are* you, Stephen? How are your pictures? How's Sally?'

He said. When he stopped, she simply waited. Her silence asked, 'Why are you ringing me now?'

'It's just – I was wondering – whether you might be willing – to pose for me again. I've an idea, a concept . . .'

He let his voice peter out.

She said nothing. He decided he would wait.

But why wait so long? Was he hearing her breathing? Was she weighing pros and cons?

When she finally spoke her voice was so faint he hardly heard it.

'You want me to pose for you again?'

'I want that *very* much. *If* you will. *As* we did.'

Again the silence stretched. Was she filled with doubts? Why had he let so much time go by? He prayed, 'Mae, *say* you'll come.'

Hesitantly her low voice said, 'I liked posing for you.'

Thank you, God, he murmured. Then simply waited. Hesitantly she said,

'I could come on Wednesday.'

'Please,' he said. They agreed twelve noon, she would have had a snack.

'Oh I'm looking forward to that very much.' He thought, will she say 'Me too'?

Her pause returned. Then, quite seriously, she said, 'Me too.'

'See you.'

But she did not say 'See you' back to him.

He emerges from the phone-booth stunned. It was all easier, quicker than he foresaw, like the impossible coming to pass. One thing is clear, something has changed. Or everything has changed. Mae has changed. Her silence, her quietness… did it mean they had a future after all? He is unsteady on his feet. Students, in the lobby, thrash past him. Turning, in a whirl, for a moment he sees her. Life-size in front of him. Her great eyes, her dark skin, towering slender in her scarlet mac. An apparition.

Had his eye tripped, for a second, on some lookalike student? Who cares? He clings to the hallucination. 'It just shows', he thinks, 'that's how much I have wanted to see her. All this time. I hid it from myself absolutely.'

But, next Wednesday – is that like putting it off, far off?

Never mind. They will meet at noon. High noon.

~

But what does someone's silence mean? That everything is possible; or nothing at all. He can't believe that. He mustn't build castles in the air, but hope wells up like a crazy geyser. He thought she was in the States, but she is here, and she will come. Things have changed, that can only be good.

Back in his studio he has the afternoon clear. But what to draw? This is no time for oils or acrylic, for the etching needle. No, water colours. He takes his old, small tin case of them. His small brush skips on the granular paper, sketching a portly balding man: Rubens again? But this is Rubens in sashes and ribbons, poised on one toe with one arm in the air. Is he dancing, cutting capers? Can this be – a man in love? We cannot tell if he is at court, or amid breeze and birdsong; but his fringes fly, almost the plump man dances on air, with his hat now added at the end of his arm, its feather the final flick of his flourish. Beside him a new figure starts to form, brown-skinned, tall and slim as a spindle. Strange, she is nothing like a Rubens woman.

While in Bloodsmith's head a voice will verbalize: Critics debate what it was, in that year, which changed the spectrum of 'Rubens in London' from its underwater blues and angry reds to primary colours, a rainbow palette. And to jump from the large-scale, heavy-worked etchings to light bright pieces, mostly sugar-lift aquatints, which have the look of quick-dashed watercolours. Such is the character of that series within a series, which later came to be known as 'Rubens and the Indian Maid'. An amour that history has not recorded. Was this the intrigue that turned his world widdershins? A thread, a knot, in 'the missing chapter'?

New subjects arrive, like sycamore propellers dropped from the wind. In a new big water-colour the painter escorts a dark-skinned passenger in a boat-trip through the higher reaches of the Thames. An oarsman rows and a flautist plays, but we hardly see them. Ah, the deep-sea blue of summer rivers, smooth as a mirror as far as the willows, which hang both above and below the surface.

From gold-stitched cushions in the gilded bows, the lady leans gazing into the depths. Rubens admires her small, fine-boned face, as she trails one finger in the coolness. Over her the stout painter bends, proffering a chalice of cherries like rubies, like drops of blood. He has a courtesy in his address, the shyness of a younger man, which chimes with the flute-notes we do not hear, in time with the plash of oars in water, which likewise we do not see.

8

At home, he is dumb, not there at all. Occasionally he hears Robyn's voice, asking above the sewing machine's thrum, 'What are you doing, Sally?'

'I'm taking in these jeans. Mum, can you hold that bit.'

'Sally, these aren't yours. They're a woman's jeans!'

'They're Pippa's mum's.'

'You're taking in Pippa's mum's jeans!'

'Why not? I can do it. I'm good at it.'

'But you hate Pippa.'

'I do hate her. She's a dickhead. She called me a dog.'

'Sally, love, you shouldn't do her favours.'

Sally's voice goes leaden with exasperation. 'I'm not doing her bloody favours, mum. She's giving me ten pounds.'

Their voices sink, he falls to watching Robyn. A slow reaction is occurring, as if he saw her far off through a powerful telescope. There is a minute mole at the corner of her mouth – has he really not seen it before?

The two women have their heads together, Robyn feeding halves of jean to Sally. Their likeness shows.

They have stood, holding the jeans between them.

'What do you think, Stephen? Hasn't she done it well? It looks professional!'

'It's great. You've got clever hands, Sally, and a clever eye.'

Sally is modest and pleased.

'Stephen, put this away, will you?'

'Sure.'

As he lugs the heavy sewing machine to its niche under the stairs, he thinks: how strange, we speak as though everything were normal here, when something enormous is lying in wait in that near and far place we call the future.

Of Robyn's supposed affair he sees no sign. The thought crosses his mind, And what if there is no lover? What if it is all my paranoia, what if I'm making it up? While it's me who's hoping to cheat. I'm lying already.

But something has been going on. And as to Mae – I can't stop now.

When he turns on the television, it is to see the American Secretary of State softly saying, with his friendly boy-face, that for rogue-states the countdown has begun.

~

Still there is nearly a week till Wednesday. Time hangs in his studio. Back to Rubens then. The looming big subject is Rubens' meeting with King Charles, but that's further down the road. Before then comes the day when Rubens meets the inventor Cornelis Drebbel. Perhaps the strangest person that he ever met in England – and a fellow-countryman after all.

How did they meet? Rubens was staying with the Gerbiers then, so Bloodsmith will begin in the Gerbiers' home. He must catch the scene in thumbnail sketches, between glances at the details in *Chess with Kings*. Here's the big room, the Hall, of their home. It will open directly onto the street. Deborah Kip is sitting with her needle and tambour, while little Susan plays. Nearby, in another carved wooden armchair, sits Rubens. He's got his sketch-pad, not so different from mine, though not Whatman paper, of course. He's trying ideas, big subjects: Peace, or Strife, the Spirits of Nations. But in the sketching stage he's happy sitting here, in desultory talk.

No, not so peaceful. Quick touches of the pencil's point make broken glass spread on the floor. The cat has knocked a wine-glass off the table, while being chased by Susan.

'Cattie! Cattie!' Crash!

'Susan!' from Deborah. But Susan stares back in truculent defiance. It was the cat, not me!

Discipline then. Deborah will say to Rubens, 'Sieur Peter, have you seen the Spaniard?'

'Even now,' let Rubens answer, gravely, 'for his boat is but docked at London Tower. He showed me the great sack he hath brought.'

'And wherefore hath he this sack, Sieur Peter?'

'Why, to gather the bad children of England. He will take them where the King of Spain will eat them.'

A quick sketch then of Susan's face, showing terror-in-doubt, since she knows it's a story. She has run into her mother's arms, which hold her hard. How to catch a child's face? The big eyes, plump cheeks, a wobble in the lips.

'But Susan is not one of those children, Sieur Peter?'

'Our Susan is one of the good children of England.'

We glimpse Susan, hugging Deborah hard, while Rubens has stood and touches lightly her gold hair. Is peace restored?

'Cattie!'

For the cat has leapt onto the window seat, and Susan, now a good girl, runs to join him. She grabs up the cat like one of her dolls, to show it the street outside.

'Have a care how you hold him,' Rubens calls, 'he'll scratch.'

In any case the cat has loped away, while Susan has turned back from the window, her face transformed: all her blood drained away, tears bulbing in her eye-corners; her lips now, maybe, yellow grey.

'You said he wouldn't come!'

'But who is come, Susan?' (from Deborah)

'The Spaniard!'

Susan has run now to the alcove across the room, where she keeps her dolls behind a curtain.

Cut then to the window, through which Rubens and Deborah together will gaze, where, between the gates of mansions, the strangest figure will make his way. In quick different sketches we see the same man. Does he limp? Or totter in a kind of zigzag? He is strongly built but his face is ravaged… with stains, burns, are they scars? His features work oddly. He has a battered felt hat and a large grey cloak, but beneath them a doublet of brilliant crimson – torn, however, and stitched and patched, like the cloak. A clay pipe sticks up in the band of his hat.

Deborah murmuring, 'But I have seen this man before – with Balthazar.'

Over to the alcove, where Deborah and Rubens pull back the curtain, to find Susan squatting on the floor, her face besmirched with tears, all her dolls gathered in her shivering arms.

'Don't be frightened, my Susan. This is not the Spaniard.'

In the meantime a cane raps on the street-door, which the servant Lionel hurries to open.

Let Rubens have asked, 'Who is this man?'

Deborah, pausingly, 'His name is . . . Cornelis Dribble.'

'Cornelis Dribble!' Susan cries, in instant mood-change. *'That's* a foolish name.'

'For a foolish man,' the stranger says, for he is upon them. 'Lady Deborah Kip, I bid a good day to you, and to Sir Balthazar also, if he be here.' As he bows, with a flourish of his battered hat, they see a painfully damaged scalp, where long fair hair grows in patches. A rank stink of tobacco swells about him, which Bloodsmith renders with zig-zag lines.

'Minheer Dribble, you are welcome to this house.'

He bows to her, and, more, to Rubens.

'And have I the honour to behold that great master, the Sieur Rubens?'

Rubens bows. 'Peter Paul Janszoon Rubens of Antwerp. I am honoured likewise, for may you not be the famed alchemist, Minheer Cornelis Drebbel?'

'Chemist, rather, nay, engineer. Cornelis Jacobszoon Drebbel of Alkmaar – I could say, of London, I have dwelt here so long.'

They bow again, and Drebbel hands his hat to Lionel, who otherwise is busy sweeping glass from the floor.

'But such a red, Minheer Drebbel!' Rubens means Drebbel's doublet. 'I must call that the King of Crimsons.'

'Patched and stitched though it be. Pray call me Cornelis. The secret is in the mordant I use; which secret I shall impart, knowing you for the Prince of Painters. In my dying I use the salts of tin – which none have done before – to raise my reds to scarlet, crimson, what you will.'

'I have never seen such a red in fabrics.'

Drebbel smiles. He sips from the glass of wine, which Lionel, on Deborah's instruction, has brought him. Presently he will proclaim to them all, 'You see me fallen from that high estate, when I served both royal James in England and his magnificence the Emperor Rudolph in Prague. Then my name was known to the ends of Europe. I have sunk now to be the keeper of an ale-house – to which, notwithstanding, I purpose to invite you all. To show you the wonders of my art, as Sir Balthazar once asked of me.' He will turn now to them, one by one. 'To you, Lady Deborah, I shall show my clavichord, that is made to play by the rays of the sun. And to you, Peter Paul, my *perpetuum mobile*, the engine I made that works for ever.'

'I have heard of that, and yearn to see it.'

To Susan now, 'To you, little mistress, I shall show the portable oven I have made, in which the eggs of fowls may be brought to be chicks, and the chicks raised to be fowls again'. And to George, who that moment bursts into the room, 'To you, my hasty cavalier, I shall show the greatest wonder of all. Before your eyes I shall turn myself to a tree, and after into a jungle beast. *For I am a famous sorcerer!*' With these words he stands tall, and spreads his arms and cloak wide, so he towers darkly above them.

While the family chatter to each other amazed, he quietly draws close to Rubens,

'But also, Sieur Peter, there is a further matter of which I would speak to you. I have in the making a device, which will touch the peace and war of nations. That is I believe your concern in these days?'

Rubens will slightly incline his head.

'I would have you to see it when at last it is ready.' His eyes wait on Rubens' words.

'I would welcome that.'

'I shall send for you when the day is come – but privily.' He sighs. 'Between ourselves I believe that it will be the Terror and the Angel of the seas.'

'I wonder the more.'

'I am glad of that.' Drebbel gives a kind of contented snort. 'Do you smoke tobacco, friend Peter Paul?'

'I love it not. Truth to tell, it made me spew.'

'Truly? Ach! You cause me grief. I can love no man who loves not tobacco, it is the New World's greatest gift.'

He motions to the pipe, in the band of his hat, and takes the hat from Lionel's hand. To the room at large he presently says, 'Lady Deborah, I must be on my way. Another day I shall wait upon Sir Balthazar, and propose to him that you come to my house. Until that time I am your abject servant. And yours, sweet mistress.' He bows low as a flattering courtier to Susan. 'And yours, young knight.' He gives a manly salute to George. 'Peter Paul, it was an honour, but much more, a surpassing pleasure.'

'For me, Cornelis, a pleasure – but more, a wonder. I wish you good fortune with all my heart.'

'I thank you; I am in need of that.'

As Drebbel leaves, Susan mutters to George. 'He never can turn himself into a tree!' But though her voice is indignant, her eyes are big like lamps. 'Nor a "jungle beast" – it cannot be.'

By the window Bloodsmith sketches the backs of their heads, watching a cloaked and hatted figure make a zigzag progress up the street. At the corner with the highway they see a lean horse, tied to a post, which forever fidgets and shuffles its hooves. It is as patched and irregular as the inventor who owns it, and turns round several times while Drebbel hops with it, mounting. When he is astride, he turns to wave his hat with a courtly flourish before being jerked forwards, so he nearly falls off backwards, as his steed lurches at once into a canter. Perhaps it is itself a *perpetuum mobile,* for in an instant it has swept him far away.

Bloodsmith scans his sketches, which run over several sheets, like a strip cartoon where the frames overlap. But the point on which he will pause, working it up into a busy print, is the moment when Drebbel spreads his cloak wide as bat-wings, proclaiming to them all, 'I am a famous sorcerer.'

9

Wednesday's here. He crouches in wait for her, in his sombre red room. Will she come after all? And if she does, will anything happen today? No, today must only be art.

Time passes, no Mae. She has thought better of it.

There is a tap at his door, hardly any sound at all.

She stands in his doorway. I'd forgotten she's so young-faced. He registers her bright dark skin – he has slightly faded it in his memory (I shouldn't have done that). She wears the bright-red mac he knows.

'Hello, Stephen.' There is a zest in her smile, as if her whole body is flexed with smiling. He doesn't remember her being so cheerful.

'It's lovely to see you.' He is aware of his size, big like a boney bear, towering in his lair. 'Let me hang— ' He makes to take the red mac.

'It's not very warm in here, I'll keep it for now. Thanks.'

'You'll have coffee?' She barely nods, while he turns full on his electric bars. The fable of the sun and wind . . . She has moved on, patrolling the room she used to know.

'It's hardly changed. Some pictures are different.'

He is pouring the coffee when the impulse takes him – declare yourself outright. Don't pussyfoot. No sly tricks. It will be the big gamble; he may lose everything.

'Before you pose, Mae, there's something I should say.'

'Yes?' She turns in bright inquiry.

'Mae, I want to paint you because I like you very much. I mean in all ways, not just as a model. I always did, I see it now.'

There, it's said. Her face grows so deeply grave that he panics. She had been so cheerful, now everything's sunk.

'Forget I said that. Let's just do art. Really.'

'Forget you said it? But it's nice that you said it. Thank you for saying it.' All unexpectedly her brightness swings back.

Still they stand, at an impasse.

'I keep taking out the pictures I made of you, and looking at them.'

She turns away — with an odd noise like a swallowed yelp. He sees the throb in her throat, and she has started to blink quickly. He takes her hand.

'I think about you all day long.'

For some moments that slender wrist rests in his fingers. He feels a pulse – is it his or hers? She takes her hand back, but then just looks at him seriously, earnestly, a slowly drilling look.

'Has something happened?' she asks.

'What?'

Involuntarily, he slightly nods. He will not say more. Her big eyes continue interrogating, dark and searching and not unkind.

He asks, 'How is Geoffrey?'

'Geoffrey? It's true, Geoffrey and I had a problem. But we've weathered it. We've come through.' Her face has set, even grimly. 'If you knew how things are with me, Stephen . . .' Her voice trails, she will not say more.

Coffee then. She takes the cooling cup, they sit on his kitchen chairs.

'Tell me about America.'

'I loved it, actually.' Happily she flies to early days in Manhattan. He sees her on Fifth Avenue, between striped chimneys gushing steam, while the Empire State behind her disappears in low cloud. When she moves to Chicago, he sees the endlessness of Lake Michigan, as though America itself were cut short at the lakeside.

'Your father could be there, I guess.'

'My father!' He is amazed by her rearing amazement.

'Didn't you say, he went to the States?'

'Who knows? I don't want to see him.' All her body says, why on earth do you bring him up? Why does he? 'He left my mother and he left me. I don't imagine he'd be pleased to see me. And I don't want to see him, he could be anyone, I doubt I'd feel anything, if I met him.'

He had forgotten her clear hard edge.

The coffee's gone, she has stood up.

'Shall I do the job I came here for?'

He stands. 'You must take off your coat for that.'

She hands it to him. To reveal a jacket like a man's, though femininely curved, and a pair of severe, ungiving jeans that make her legs like pipes. 'How would you like me?'

'Will you change?' He means: strip.

Dipping her head, lifting her big eyes, she says ever-so-sweetly, 'Let's not do nude today.'

'Of course . . .'

Dressed like this, she seems an adolescent who has shot up tall. They try postures on the chair, where he turns her shoulders to give her body a twist.

'Can you try and get more comfortable?'

She shifts, and a lean comes into her torso.

'Oh that's great, lots of angles.'

So there it is – we are back in her geometry. Back where we were, the play of angles in a matchstick woman. He can do it, even he loves to do it, and it is the sweetest torture.

But, to it, artist. He holds up a pencil, measuring lines with one eye closed. The room goes silent, except for a buzzing bar on his fire, an electrical discrepancy at hearing's edge.

At least he'll try to learn more. 'Did it happen in America?

'What?'

'What happened with Geoffrey? You said there was a problem . . . '

'I don't want to talk about it.' Her wide mouth, that curved so sweetly, sets grim as a sexton. 'What happened with you, Stephen?'

Immediately, he's tongue-tied.

She nods. 'You don't want to talk about it, either.'

She doesn't press. They are quiet, chewing on their private issues. He draws the attractive bell-curve which the skirt of her jacket makes.

'Stephen.'

He looks up.

'We should be careful not to make . . . a painful mistake.'

I'm dying to make that painful mistake.

Her look is serious. 'I understand. One wants to get even.'

You understand too much, he thinks. She is looking at him so searchingly, that she not he must be the artist.

He is thinking harder than he is used to. 'Whatever has happened – in your life, Mae – or with me – I think you know that always, from the very first second I saw you in the life class, always I was ready to fall for you absolutely. Utterly.'

'I saw that.'

'It was Geoffrey and America cut it short.'

'Yes.'

She seems to look inside herself. She looks up. 'You've stopped drawing.'

'I can't draw now.'

'Oh but you can, Stephen.' That's true, too. She looks happy again, as if serious things are way behind them.

'Hold that smile?'

'I can try. Won't it stop being a smile?'

'Right now it's a lovely smile. Let's see.'

And it holds, the smile, to a large extent. As he draws, he wonders, where does the benignity in it come from? Is it in the way her eyes slightly close? He studies her eyes, and starts other sketches when her expression changes.

'Rest.'

They must pause. Out of pose, she saunters in the studio.

'What are those pictures over there? I mean the historical-looking things.'

'I'm doing a series. Prints.'

'What series?'

'It's about Rubens.'

'The painter?'

'When he came to England, to play the diplomat.' He tells the story.

She nods, sifting through his source pictures. She pulls out Rubens's painting of the Three Graces.

'Look at the way they're touching each other. That's lovely.'

Touching, yes. He touches her elbow. At least she does not jump. But naturally, delicately, she moves on and away, leaving his hand gently falling through air.

'Who's this red man?' She points to one of his proofs.

'That's Cardinal Richelieu. He was Rubens' big enemy – at a distance.'

She peers close into the print. 'That is a wonderful red. *Is* that the red that Cardinals wear? The eyes are good. Shrewd.' She ponders, stepping back. 'And red is blood. More wars are coming to us, I think.'

He can only shrug.

'And who is that lady?' She has moved to his board of reproductions, and pauses by a famous image.

'That – oh, that's Mrs Rubens – Isabella Brant.'

'By Rubens?'

'Actually no, it's by Van Dyck. He was a protégé of Rubens, he lived with them for a time.'

'It's nice. You can see he liked her.'

'That, at least. But there's something funny. Where is Rubens himself? Normally then you either painted a married couple together in one portrait, or you painted two portraits to hang side by side. But Rubens isn't there, and there's no other portrait. Also we don't know if it was painted from life, or when Van Dyck lived somewhere else.'

'Is that cloth of gold she's wearing?'

'It looks… and she's wearing black on top of it. But it was she who died, not Rubens.'

'The statue on the wall is funny.'

'It's foppish, isn't it? Dandified. The way he sticks out his thigh and elbow.' He flashes a mock-gay posture, mincing, wagging a lewd elbow.

'Is it a man or a woman?'

They stoop together close to the nearly-naked statue. It hovers like an imp beside Isabella's shoulder; it stands beside her head as if it were a thought she had.

She wonders, 'Is it a dagger he's holding?' In its right hand the statue holds high a long and thin something. 'Who is it a statue of?'

'I'm not sure. Rubens liked to put statues here and there on his property. I'll look it up.'

The thought at that moment comes clear in his head: the statue is the clue I noticed before, hidden in this picture. A clue to Rubens' secret? But how could it be a 'clue'? It is not clear to him now why he thought it *was* a clue.

She has moved to the large reproduction, pinned beside Isabella Brant.

'*That's* a Rubens?'

He nods.

'Strange.'

She is solemn in gazing. And it is strange, this canvas in which four bearded, well-fleshed nearly-naked men lounge with their girls. A swarthy-skinned man has his arm round a white-skinned brunette. One girl is a blonde. In the foreground, his back to us, a white-skinned grey-beard with a muscular body supports the back of a black African woman. She has a fine-featured face, turned to gaze directly to us. Reflected light gleams in the black iris of her eyes, and in the pearls round her neck, in the silver jewellery in her hair. A blood ruby glows on her jet-black brow. Her eyes seize our eyes from the dead centre of the painting. Only she has jewellery.

Softly he murmurs, 'No race prejudice there.'

Mae, her brow knit, seems fixed in gazing. 'What's going on?'

'It's called "The Four Continents". The bearded men are river-gods – the Danube, the Nile, the Ganges, the River Plate. The women are the geniuses of Europe, Africa, Asia, America. *She* is Africa, he is the Nile, holding his urn pouring out the water. There was peace a few years between Holland and Spain. Rubens painted it then. It's his picture of the Greater Peace, a love-in of the world under one big tent. That's Rubens.'

'Hm.' She nods to the black woman. 'That river-god thinks that she's all his.' Frowning.

'She's not looking at him, she's looking at us. Maybe she knows the gods are done.'

Their eyes fall to the foreground, at the bottom of the picture, where the tiger of Asia snarls at Africa's gaping, long-fanged crocodile. She makes a tilt of her head towards the beasts.

He shrugs. 'There *is* violence. Should he leave it out?'

She lingers moments, then crisply turns. 'Tea-break's over.' A moment her eyes gleam, amazing, enigmatic. Then she steps behind his Indian screen.

He is surprised by that. Time passes, she does not emerge at once. Is it possible? All he can do is wait, keeping silent against his prayer. Presumably it would be an issue, having to unpeel those lock-tight jeans.

She comes out. Yes, she is naked. Smiling, roguish. Provocative – but also shy. She crosses her arms in front of her. Oh, but her beauty, her not large but lovely breasts. He's ravished, breathless, wonderstruck. So, he has seen her undressed before – but everything is new and different today.

Quietly, nicely, he says, 'Thank you.'

Once more her great eyes, their brilliant black shine. But as they look she grows more shy. Diffident, even demure in her nakedness. He thinks, like a new bride. Their train is on another line, from any they have travelled before. They will love today. No?

No. Crisply, businesslike, she says, 'To work.' She is the artist's model, she disposes her limbs along the chaise longue in a way that suits. She is at rest and facing him.

He must think, patience! Her pose is just right. Except, 'Could you give your hand – a small twist? Yes.'

Because there is beauty even in the human wrist if it turns a little like a slender waist.

So for now, Art. He will give his all to that. Drawing with love because seeing with love. Is this art-love or person-love? Both, as it was for Rubens too. Whatever their skin-colour? Rubens loved blondes, but would not be the prisoner of blondes.

He is reaching for his brush and water-colours when she says, 'Geoffrey had a thing.'

'Sorry?'

'You asked what happened in America. Geoffrey had a thing.'

'Yes?'

'A thing with a manager. I expect she was impressive.'

'I'm sorry.' What else to say?

'I was on to it. He said he didn't, then he said he did. Then he told me all about it. Everything. I wish he didn't, because that made him feel better but it was terrible for me.'

Crouched behind his picture, he thought – ah Geoffrey, *your* copybook's blotted.

'I suppose I must say, he's worked to make up for it. He tells me really I am the one he truly loves. Do you know, he opened an account, and put new money in it, all in my name and just for me. I *wish* he hadn't done that. I haven't spent it.'

She sits gazing just in front of her as if the air at that point is tied in a knot, while he sees, like a light switched on, that the thing that happened, which made everything different, was not just that Geoffrey had an affair but that he gave her money afterwards to make it all right.

She looks up. 'It's funny, isn't it? Whatever happens, things are never the same after. You can't go back to where you were. And in a way it was my fault.'

'How was that?' He is at once indignant for her.

'I think I was very boring for Geoffrey.'

'Boring?'

'No, I think I was. Because deep down I had been so grateful to Geoffrey – I mean, for marrying me – me being me.'

'That's not fair to you.'

'That's true. Also that grateful me, well, it wasn't quite the real me. It was a pretend person I put on all the time. You said a long time ago that I sit like a good girl. I've done a lot of that. It's easy to do that, if you're me.'

Still her smile, after she says this, is bright, even ambiguous. Good-girl/bad-girl?

She leans back with languor. 'Draw, paint, whatever you want.'

His brush-tip touches water-colour to Whatman's. He looks, dabs, smiles sometimes, and dabs again, the absorbed artist.

The quiet of the studio.

She says, 'I missed our sessions.'

His eye and brush pause.

'I missed them. Afterwards, in America. I'd think back, and they seemed a beautiful time. I was happy, lying here, posing. Is that vanity? You were nice to me.'

'I loved drawing you, painting you. You're very – particular.'

'I'm a one-off?'

'Exactly.'

She smiles contentedly.

He paints, she is still, the room is warm. He wonders, will she fall asleep like she used to? All their sessions from the past have drawn up beside them; it seems time can work like a concertina.

The quietness deepens. His breathing and hers have come in sync. His brush-tip lightly caresses the paper, as his sight-tip traces her upper arm. Perhaps a mouse at this moment peeps from the wainscot, a spider from its web peers with eight eyes at the art-work. Peace.

Outside it will be late afternoon, a yellow glow filters down from the roof-light. On Mae's dark body the rich light falls, and hangs through the studio in a gold-rust glimmer. It must be late. Very soon they will stop, she will have to go.

She looks up, their eyes meet in a look not of art. She is still as if trapped or tied, so her eyes are her only words. He rests his glass palette down and crosses the room.

As he bends, her face rises. She turns so her mouth meets his firmly. Between kisses he sees her face sway in close-up, her brows up high. Her eyes, nearly shut, show huge lids marked with veins. In a confiding voice she says, 'I do like you, Stephen.'

'Mae, I—'

She smiles, 'Let me put something on.' She takes the kimono.

He smiles too, that they dress to love. They kiss, he laughs, 'Put more clothes on.' She doesn't, they kiss and embrace. The impossible is happening.

His hand will rove, his caresses advance, and hers as well, so his own clothes begin to undo.

'Stop, Stephen.'

She is sitting up, her wraps half on half off.

'I can't. I'm sorry.' She makes a sound between a cough and a sob.

'It's just— I had a picture of Geoffrey getting into his car this morning.'

He embraces her tenderly, kisses her softly.

'It's OK, Mae. It's OK.'

She sits huddled in a quiver that is almost like sobbing. He kisses her lightly.

Abruptly she gets up, takes her clothes from behind the screen. In front of him she puts them on. She's dressed. She holds her coat in her hand.

'I'm sorry, Stephen. I can't. This isn't me. I don't want to.'

So the whole love-castle, that had grown so quickly, up to the clouds, collapses on the studio floor.

The red mac is on.

'I won't come again.'

'I heard you.' He squats clenched, she waits. His eyes come up. 'Can we say a day, *when* you won't come?'

'What?' She stares as though his words were gobbledegook.

'Let's say a day. Just in case you forgot something, and had to come back. For who knows what reason. And then, when you don't come on *that* day, *then* I'll know for sure you're not coming again.'

She frowns like thunder, then says, 'OK. Same time next week. Wednesday, that is. Is that clear enough? But I won't come. And when I don't... you'll know I won't.'

'Done!' he says.

But what has he done? Bought time? Stretched the agony? Or simply made an opportunity to wait in suspense, only to lose everything in the end?

'Goodbye, Stephen.' Cold and crisp.

Was she on the point of tears? But already the door's shut, she's gone.

~

Thoughts in a shadowed and blood-coloured room.

Not making love because she thought of Geoffrey: does that mean we won't ever make love? That while my wife is an unfaithful wife, my girl-friend is a faithful wife? But then, do I know if Robyn resisted, or whether she was so in love she couldn't?

Thoughts in leaving the room of art.

Geoffrey. The husband. And I'm a husband. Do I want to do to another man, what Robyn and her friend have done to me? It can't be helped, I stumble around in a daze of Mae.

Thoughts upon a teeming highway. Matters have moved on so fast. We're really on the brink of love. Will we really just stop on the edge and go home?

Thoughts on leaving the big streets. So for Robyn too I'm different now. Just like her I keep a secret close. We're far apart, yet the household goes on.

A bike beside him jumped up on one wheel, then came down with a bounce till the kid on it yanked it up again. Thank God Sally has no clue yet!

His house is in sight, outlined on the corner. He said a prayer, to God no less — Let me make adulterous love with Mae!

Treading the front path, does he hear a sound? He looks either way, to see (as usual) not a soul. As he fumbles his key, he hears the sound again, the sound which is like nothing so much as a woman crying. It couldn't be Robyn, she's never like that. Is it a fantasy rising from conscience? In the split of a second he is in the house, listening to a silence so thick, it takes him some moments to summon voice. He calls hesitantly, 'Robyn?'

He looks up the stairs, and out to the Judas Tree. The emptiness listens. Absence is sentience. He and his home are stalking each other. He hears quietest steps, with pauses between. Someone is abroad upstairs.

'Stephen?' she says uncertainly.

'Yes, I'm back.'

'I wasn't sure— I thought I heard— '

'I did call. You were in your study?'

'I had the door shut.'

'Robyn... you're all right?'

'No, I'm fine. I was just busy.'

Still they have not had a sight of each other. But, with delays, she will come downstairs. He meantime has gone on to the kitchen to give her time, should she need time.

He has put the kettle on – from what ancient impulse? They are not tea-drinkers. He is pottering as she comes in the kitchen.

She says lightly, 'Thank God you're not a photographer, Stephen. They're bigger prima donnas than painters, that's for sure. The trouble I've had, setting up the Sean Raven show.'

'This is the big one?'

'Sean Raven is big.'

'And photography's big. Good luck with it, Robyn!' Nor will he think about Sean Raven now. He looks up smiling, to see Robyn smiling, wanly. Her eyes maybe have a redness, but already she is rubbing them, 'I'm going to need glasses. I can't take that screen, not for hours on end.'

Still she looks more worried than that.

'What is it?'

'Oh.' Her eyes are wide. 'I was surfing. I got among the "new weapons systems", and how the war's a shop window. But of course the arms companies *would* want that! Buy *our* weapons, we have lasers that can make your eyeballs explode. We can cause your bones to run like water . . . '

Her voice breaks, though he wonders still: and is this the reason your eyes are so red? Red Robyn. Still his own eyes prick, in sympathy.

She sweeps her hair and sadness back. 'What tea are you making?'

'No, I'm still looking. Why does Sally buy so many teas?'

'Oh, she's a tea-buff! And they were all the-best-of-the-best when they were fresh.'

They choose a tea that claims to be aromatic and chocolatey. Neither of them troubles, in their long pauses, to explain why they are talking so gently and guardedly. One might imagine they were negotiating a chasm, which neither wished to peer into directly.

10

No Mae today, that's for sure. And his next Rubens subject is good for the upset he's just had. For something happened to Rubens on his way to his one-to-one with the King. An upset, a disaster. Maybe a baptism?

The King is at Greenwich, and has sent a royal galley to fetch the Sieur Rubens. Dabbing his water-colours, in sketch after sketch, Bloodsmith outlines the stages of the event (he will choose one sketch later to work up for the print), moving back and forth between touches of colour and the details Jens Claeys gives in *Chess with Kings*.

So first, in one stroke, there is a stretch of blue water. The dark shapes are boats, many of them, for this is the old Thames, twice as wide as it later became. Then that shimmer of crimson and blue in the centre, that's the King's galley, sent to fetch Rubens. A herald with a long horn stands in the bows, quietly joking with two men-at-arms, whose cuirasses glitter like new chrome on a car. At the back, in a fringed pavillion, the privileged passenger reclines, Sieur Peter Paul Rubens demure in his finest black satins and velvets, and with a wide and intricate lace collar. He is relaxed in conversation with my Lord Weston, a heavily-built man with a square doughy face and tiny mouth, a privy councillor to the King. Beside them a plump, rosy-faced man of God nods drowsily.

Lord Weston, maybe, is inquiring, 'But have you marked, Sieur Rubens, how you are followed in the street?'

'By no means. I have often thought, that I pass in this city and no man knows me.' He speaks a touch sadly; it is not so in Antwerp.

Weston's small mouth wryly crinkles. 'Be assured, Sieur Rubens, there are those who know you – and who track your movements also.'

'You mean the French? Some hireling of Richelieu's?'

'Of that make no doubt. But the Dutch also will have their "eye" upon you. Some in Parliament also, of the Puritan persuasion, they will not let you from their sight. There are other powers less clearly marked. Some, it may be, will not hide. Some you will never see.'

He gives an aged, worldly-wise smile, and lounges back in his wide furred gown.

'Indeed?' Rubens frowns. 'And do so many fear what I may achieve?'

'Fear? I know not how much they fear it. But they are on their guard. For let us say there were a truce between between Spain and England – then France and the Dutch would greatly fear, while many in our Parliament would froth at the mouth. All the world wonders what words they may be, which you carry from Spain for the ear of our King.'

Rubens muses. 'There is one I thought who watches me, a strange man, with a mane and beard like a lion. He was on the *Adventure*, when I crossed the sea.'

Weston's face goes blank like a wall. Rubens glances at the river bank, and starts when he sees smoke rise behind the nearby trees. It reminds him of the odd fire he saw from the Dover road. Has a blacksmith set up his forge in the heart of the woods? Again this smoke is not quite like smoke, it is more like cobwebs that hang and stir on the breeze.

Both men sink in reverie, so neither of them sees how the weather has changed. Some wet strokes of Bloodsmith's brush make clouds like flour-sacks, bowling ponderously overhead. The water is suddenly choppy. The little tassles on the canopy abruptly stream sideways, while the men at arms in the bows, caught off balance, clang together like metal buckets.

'I perceive you are no mariner,' Weston murmurs, since Rubens's face has gone grey-yellow.

''Tis but a gust.'

He speaks too soon, for that black cliff ahead is a cumbersome barge, oddly swung by the changes of current and wind. The rowers have their back to it, and as the barge heaves against the oars on that side, the shafts flick back, and those four oarsmen are laid flat on their backs, while their legs fly up and their slippers fly off. With their limbs all which ways they wriggle like a beetle laid on its back, so Rubens has half-opened his mouth to laugh when the prow of the galley strikes the barge, and the galley both rolls sideways and rides skywards. The men at arms clash together and fall, tumbling down the deck. For the split of a second my Lord Western is horizontal in mid-air like a flying log, with surprised eyebrows while his mouth seems frozen in a sententious utterance. The herald's long horn spins through wheeling clouds, as Rubens too is gently tipped over, his robes spreading into wings which cannot cushion his fall as he crashes spreadeagled, in a wide fat splash, and his mouth, in mid-gasp, gulps water.

Through the waters closing over him he can still see the sky, but he is choking as he sinks and taking more water. His clothing now hampers his limbs like lead. He is still going down while his lungs and head burst, and the prayer forms frantically in his head, 'Dear Lord God, forgive and do not forget me while my sins be burned in thy holy flames, including the great sin of my vanity in my art'.

A giant hand grabs him by the scruff of his neck. He vaguely paddles his limbs as the power lugs him upwards. Through the water again he sees wobbling clouds, the next minute he is in sunlit air. He is dragged, lugged, spluttering, while the men with scant reverence lay him flat on his front, and dig a knee between his shoulders and tug his arms back, as in torture he vomits suffocation from his lungs.

Nearby my lord Weston surges unsteadily up amid reeds, clasping a bull-rush and with duckweed, mud and tadpoles in his hair and his beard. Staggering from the weight of his water-logged gown, he stumbles under again then is back on his feet, a river-god from a painting by Rubens who has mixed too much wine with his water.

Along the bank, between flailing willows, shining men in sodden clothes are choking, cursing, calling,

'Fra Sebastian hath not been found.'

'Maybe he came ashore downstream?'

'He was God's, God hath him,' an oarsman gruffs, standing in the shallows.

Bloodsmith's brush-tip flecks splashed froth, completing his sketch for 'Rubens and Thamesis', a many-coloured etching. In the background looms or lurches the streaming weed-strewn trunk of Weston while in the further distance, but somehow up in the sky overhead, a tiny galley turns a somersault as it impacts on a wherry, with the oarsmen wagging microscopic legs like a woodlouse on its back.

All of these are dwarfed by the figure in the centre: Rubens himself, the well-fleshed man, on his hands and knees on the windswept river-bank; within his battered sodden collar his neck thickens like a giant blocked hose, his mouth spouts forward like a breaking trumpet, his eye-balls bulge in his tight-shut lids – as would those of any ship-wrecked man, retching up gob, bile and spew, choking his guts out snatching for air. This too was Rubens in England.

Bloodsmith stands from his trestle-table. Well, he has found his centre of interest. Sink or swim. As for me, do I swim – or am I sunk?

~

At home, he works not to show his distraction. Will his women, with their canny eyes, see his odd mood? *What's with you, dad?* But neither is interested. Sally is speed-eating; she has an agenda. Robyn eats with an absent-minded slowness – it's she, more than he, who is abstracted. Her eye-corners jump, tendrils of her hair quiver as if charged.

Sally's asking, 'Mum, can I use your computer for my homework?' when Robyn abruptly got up.

'I'm sorry. I don't know what I've been doing. I have to go out.'

'Go out, mum? In the middle of dinner.'

'No, there's a Directors' meeting. I'd clean forgotten. It's a special one. Because of changes they're making in Arts Council funding.'

With no more said, she has headed down the hall and left. The others blink.

'Mum's got a lot on now,' he said. 'There's her lottery bid, and this show coming up. The private view's very soon. Does mum talk about it – about Sean Raven?'

Sally looked blank, then stood. 'Well, I think mum said I could use her computer.'

'I didn't hear her say it.'

'She didn't say I couldn't'.

They quibbled, then Sally went up to the computer.

He was left thinking, *Has* Robyn gone to a Directors' meeting? He could find out easily. He could ring the Gallery, with some cooked-up question, and either Robyn would answer the phone, or he would know she was not there.

He went to the phone, and there stuck. I don't want to ring, I don't want to know. I don't want to think about what Robyn's doing. He went to the living-room and thought about Mae.

He was still in reverie when Sally came down. He heard leather crease stiffly as she put on her jacket.

She came in the room. 'It's all right, dad. I'm not going out.'

'No?'

'I'm just off round the corner to Nikki's. I'll be half an hour. I have to go and see them. They've had the water and gas turned off.'

'You did your homework, then.'

'Yes, I did.'

The door closed.

Had he dozed, or passed out? A fast car, a sports car, revved up the road, and stopped with decision a few doors away. Something in its noise took him by surprise. He heard car-doors, voices – was it Robyn? As the car drove off he heard, distinctly, Robyn shout, strongly, even with a sound like alarm. Was it a name she called? He heard nothing clear.

But perhaps it was all a mistake, no Robyn came. Minutes passed. Then he heard the clear clip of steps on the pavement, and the yielding of the Yale lock.

'Robyn?'

She came in the room with her head raised and her hair blown back, as if she had stepped in from a gale.

'It was a difficult meeting?'

She sat, looking serious. 'Yes, Stephen. It was difficult.'

'Do you want to talk about it?'

She did not say, and did not talk.

'Let me get you something, Robyn. Do you want water? Coffee?'

'Yes, please. Water.'

He took time running the water cold, and adding a slice of lemon. He made a water on the rocks.

When he returned, she was sitting bolt upright.

'It's some sort of ultimatum.'

The television showed the American President, his dot-eyes fixed it seemed on theirs. He said, 'Time has run out for the enemies of peace.'

Bloodsmith blinked. 'We've heard this before.'

'They're going in again, Stephen. The next thing we see will be the explosions.'

But he had not heard the start of the report. He passed the glass to Robyn.

'Thank you,' she smiled, 'it's a good water.'

She said more about impending war in the world, but his thoughts were elsewhere. For he knew now the name of the feeling he had hidden from, when he tied up his pictures of Mae in their portfolio. It was absolute, once-in-a-lifetime love.

As for Robyn, and her amours (or not), well, the private view in her photo-gallery was coming. He would see Sean Raven. Of course, Robyn's 'friend' might be someone else. Everyone she knew would be there. He would find out then if there had been a Directors' meeting. If not, then the big encounter was near.

11

When not trying to draw, he ruffled through the pages of *Chess with Kings*. He had still to work out just where in his series he would have Rubens' 'fragment of the ancient world'. Also he pondered the 'missing chapter'. What did Jens Claeys do with those pages? Did he burn them? Surely not. One day that chapter will be found . . .

Something which the editor of the paperback mentions is the name 'Saventhem', and it crops up in Jens Claeys' notes for his book. Saventhem (now Zaventem) is a village near Brussels. The name stands by itself, on different corners of pages in the notes, and is sometimes underlined. But there is no mention of Saventhem in the actual text of *Chess with Kings*. In an arch manner – so you guess he knows more than he says – the editor inquires if the village of Saventhem may have figured in 'the missing chapter'.

Bloodsmith sighs, and turns to his drawings again. Nothing takes a clear step to the front. Really he is in a state of suspended animation, waiting against the event which he says will not come, yet cannot dismiss.

Wednesday came and Mae did not. He sat then with the lights switched off, making a meal of being in the dumps. For it only grew clearer, as the minutes and quarter-hours added up, that of course she would not come. She had said. He needs his head examined.

What surprised him, with time, was the depth of his grief. As if he fell down a shaft which had no bottom. What has he been doing, with this insane love-delusion?

He had sunk so far, it needed for the door to be tapped harder. Tap tap. He lugged himself across the room, who the bloody hell is this?

And it is Mae. In her tight-wrapped mode, scarlet mac buckled, her head and hair packed tight in a scarf. She looked not well and almost grey-faced. Her eyes were sombre, searching, sad.

'Come in! I'm so glad you came.'

'I won't come in.'

Nor would she, she was planted there.

'I thought of ringing or writing, then I thought, that's a cop-out. Can we walk? I think we should use words, make a nice good-bye.'

A 'nice goodbye'? He's falling again. 'Let's walk.'

They began patrolling the nearby back-streets. He said with no conviction, 'We can go back just to painting.'

'It's obvious we can't.' Her voice was crisp enough. 'Anyway I don't want to.'

'I thought you liked being painted.'

'Like? I loved it.'

'So?' His arm hesitantly reached for her shoulder, got no purchase, and fell away.

'It doesn't work, Stephen, does it? We both know that.' She stopped and stood round to face him clearly. 'I don't want an affair, Stephen. What I want is a husband, and I have one. I can't handle the other. I don't like the lying. I can't do what you want, and then go to bed with Geoffrey. I don't know how you feel, about Robyn.'

'Robyn has her friends. Well . . . . . I suppose things are better with you and Geoffrey than they are with Robyn and me.'

They walked again, he led them up an alley of corners.

'I don't say they're perfect. But we manage. I can't put it all in a bad way again. Do you see? I don't *want* to rock my boat, not now.'

He must sadly nod – would he ruin their marriage?

'We will always be friends.'

'Friends?'

Her face went grim. 'Where is it we're walking?'

He did not answer. Deviously, he was leading them a back way to his studio. Round the next corner they saw it, the steep-roofed workshop, built against the converted maltings.

She made severe eyes like a teacher's.

'I'm not going in there.'

They stood glum.

He said, 'It's true I was in— a funny state. I love you, Mae. I have for years. It's true, now I knew it and now I didn't. That can happen. I love you, I love seeing you, I love painting you. And I want to *make* love to you. That just *is* what I want, whether I have it or not.'

From the rim of her scarf, free curls stood like flames round her head. 'It's not on, Stephen. Understand it.'

'I understand. I've got the message. Since you're here, come and have one cup of coffee. A goodbye coffee. I'll brew it with tears.' He nodded to his door.

'It's not a good idea.'

He unlocked the door. 'One bloody cup of coffee – you can do that.'

Clearly she called, 'I have to go,' and stood fixed to the spot.

'Mae, please please please come and drink with me one last wretched chipped old cup of instant coffee.'

He stood straight by the door like a sentry by his box.

Abruptly she came. 'I'd like some coffee.'

The room was gloomy, till he put on the light: then it was bleak.

She said, 'We made some pictures here.'

'Can I take your coat?'

She shook her head.

'Your scarf?'

'I'm not taking anything off, Stephen. And don't put on your electric fires.'

Yet she had lost her grave resolution. His heart bled to see her so cold, tied up tight like a vertical parcel. So we're back there, square one, hello.

He came with cups.

'Do at least sit. Please.'

She took the coffee and sat on a chair. Her face, that had looked strict, grew childlike-sweet, but also sad and tired and older.

He wondered what to say now.

Her heels are up on the front rung of the chair. It's the perched sort of sitting he knows.

'He can't complain, if you do what he did.'

She looks up frowning, all her grimness back at once.

'You mean Geoffrey?'

'Yes.'

'You mean one wants to get even?'

'That's what you said before. But perhaps it isn't just getting even. Perhaps you *need* new love from someone.'

Her face was wry. 'Needs? One wants it, maybe. Is it so easy?'

'I don't know.'

'Geoffrey has been nice to me, since then.'

He nods. How stupid, to bring in Geoffrey! Even more, they are sitting like mourners. But to stop short here and end like this... the sadness of it. Like a picture in his head he can see them both from far away, a man and woman on the Arctic tundra, sitting oddly on kitchen chairs. Behind them the aurora borealis spreads frost-curtains of pulsing light. But they don't see it, and the cold light dies, while the sadness thickens in a crystal fur all over them. She in her mac and he in his cords; they are both made of stone, like a Magritte dream. Before them is a flat sea sterile with salt – it is the sea of their tears, but as we look it goes dull with a crust that thickens to stone.

She's put down her cup and stood. 'I'll go.'

He's got up. So they are there, the end.

'Goodbye Stephen.' Her eyes, as she speaks, fill with tears.

To see it, his own eyes fill. He kisses her seriously, the goodbye kiss. She lets him kiss her, then lifts her face and kisses him. She bucks her head, and lifts her mouth and they kiss fully. He bends to kiss her more, she withdraws her head and buries then burrows her face in his chest.

She has pushed her hands to hold him to a distance. As again her eyes fill, while they bend to kiss, he thinks, we are the world's most weeping lovers. But her mouth is hot, and his on hers, their limbs have twined to a tightening knot.

From close-to, he sees her other-face: dark-flushed and glowing, her pupils dilated, her eyebrows soaring high.

As they kiss he unbelts and unbuttons her, till she is in underwear and he still in trousers -- let his corduroys be the rude flanks of the satyr! Kissing her front, he leads her to his cushions.

Till she breaks free, and strides off in bra and knickers.

'Stop it, Stephen. I don't want this.'

She has walked to the door, as though she would step outside as she is, her face gone cross like a petulant child's. 'I want to go home.'

'You're not going home. Not now. You're not.'

He brings her back to the cushions, not stopping from talking, 'I won't let you leave. I love you. I love you utterly. We've got here, and you're not going anywhere.'

Till they're down and naked, as he kisses the small breasts and small belly he knows, and the wings of pelvis and the buttocks he knows, and caresses each place he has painted, her shoulders and sides, while increasingly her long arms and lean legs clasp him, pulling him tighter to her. Her head rides proud on her high long neck.

~

They lie among cushions and cloths on the floor-boards. He licks the cavity of her armpit. It is as if his sight has passed into his hands or as if he now has eyes in his fingers, so his hands can see and smell as they touch.

He is raised on an elbow, studying while her eyes gaze up at his; she is half sitting, her face bright and bonny, not drowsy but chattering in happy bursts.

They have washed at his sink, and embraced again.

'I have to go now.'

Between embraces she's dressed, he too.

He wonders, will she eat? The question's from nowhere, it seems ridiculous: but he has biscuits and an old bottle of wine, iron rations against failing inspiration.

'A bite?'

They have eaten chattily, she's stood. 'Really I have to go. Oh, what's this?'

She has paused by a drawing.

'That – that's the big subject. Rubens meets King Charles of England.'

'They look as though they're sitting in a doll's house.'

'That's the Queen's House at Greenwich. Charles was doing it up, for Henrietta Maria to have her baby in. Of course I'm using different scales, the people big, and the house just a frame to them.'

'I see. Well, I hope I'll see.'

'I hope you will.'

As she put her coat on, he saw the change coming. Her face grew more serious as her buttons did up. Surely not another 'goodbye'.

They tread the few steps to his door, where she kisses him solemnly. With a dead-serious face and the big tears welling *yet* again, she says,

'Thank you very much. I'm glad we did it. Now it *is* goodbye. Goodbye.'

With a fling of tears, as if a gust shook her face, she's through the door and gone.

But this time he could not, he could not believe her.

12

Though Mae left in tears, his own love-happiness continued for the rest of the day to expand, as if what had happened needed time to come true wholly.

Rubens came to him at night. Nor was Rubens visible, nor did he speak, but still he was close and lent his sight.

In this strange state, which must be a dream though he felt wide awake, it was clear something wonderful had happened, both to Bloodsmith and to Rubens. Had Rubens lain with the Indian Maid? All that was clear was that Rubens was loved, and what this meant was that as his soul ascended, so the world grew bigger, as if he climbed in a jet and flew transatlantic to the home of his love. The iron plain of ocean slipped slowly beneath them, till the edge of the continent grew, and they and their plane became an eagle. In the south, they saw the jungles and peaks of New Spain, the armies of Mother Church and palaces rising. In pyramid cities, brown figures in feathers raised a blood-dripping stone. In the famed El Dorado, there were turrets and belfries laid with gold tiles. Then the eagle swooped north, over New France with its swamps and big river, and over New Holland, with its estuary-island that smoked with wealth, and so to New England in the northern-most region. They crossed a black pine-forest, undulating in waves like a petrified sea. They passed frozen lakes.

They were no longer alone. In some way the Fire Girl was with them also, showing them her world which was Asia and Africa as well as America. All of geography was expressed in her limbs, it was from her valleys that he saw these hills, and in her eyes that the continents lay. It seemed, with no change, they were now flying east, forest gave way to expanding grasslands, which reached as far as the rising sun. Beside a clear river the tepees of her people were pitched, and beyond stretched uncountable herds of bison. The sight of these herds in their peaceful grazing moved him with the sweetest, sharpest sadness; such plenty, such peace. A woman's voice said in his ear, 'The grassy plain, the herds of love, are given thee till the break of day.'

He came awake to these words, already grieving for the loss of his dream: for all that was given would be taken too. He yearned to be with Mae non-stop, to drive in cars and trains with her, to be with her at exhibitions and the cinema, especially to walk in open space, keeping up with her legs on the Sussex downs, side by side and not stopping from stepping. At the same time he felt gently for Robyn beside him. Whatever I do, I must not hurt Robyn, I must work things so there is no pain to her.

How with no form of pain to Robyn he could walk the Sussex downs with Mae, was not revealed. Simply he felt these different feelings, and discovered they were not at war. He had found an enormous space within him, where all discrepant wishes might ruminate, at peace in the morning sun.

He got up in early-morning happiness. It was bright sun outside and the birds busy twittering. All over the Judas Tree cobwebs glistened, and beyond it wet grass shone in the dawn.

He made a mega-kiloton coffee, which he sipped in peace, and later made more and took it to Robyn, and happily they talked about the day.

~

All that day still his blood seethed, as if he continued to make love with Mae: she breathes on him. His nostrils repeat a particular smell, that is fragrant and acrid together.

'I'm sorry, I missed that.' Coming to in the Print Room.

'OK, Steve.' Roger, a student, nods to his mates.

In the evening, as he left the Art School, he saw her. She waited across the street, standing rigid beneath a street-lamp.

She: 'I'm glad I caught you.'

They kissed a cold kiss.

'Do you mind if we talk?' He could see from her face that the catastrophe was on them.

The Art School was locking. But down a terrace they found a small park, and a bench in the park, half-swallowed by a menacing wave of hedge. Across the grass, an old person with a walking stick took their leave.

In this leafy privacy they embraced, but after kissing him she turned to keep her face free, and sat as if shivering inside his arms.

'How are you, Stephen?'

'I'm fine. I've somehow been in yesterday all of today. But you're not fine.'

'I feel terrible. It was terrible for me last night.'

'I'm sorry.' His embracing arm became a commiserating arm.

'I could hardly look at Geoffrey. I didn't know it would be like that. I felt dreadful. I don't know how I can see him tonight.'

He wondered, Shouldn't *I* feel worse? He wanted to feel all that she felt. All he could say was I'm sorry and I'm sorry, not for what they did, but for her feeling sorry. She talked, he listened, she resting in the arm that tenderly enclosed her. A blackbird hopped close, eyeing their invasion. Opposite, some leather jackets had arrived, with a plastic sack of beer-cans. He narrowed his eyes, peering to be sure Sally was not with them.

There was nothing to say that could make a change, but sitting there close was drawing them closer. A slight steady air-current streamed in their faces, and, behind them, threaded the hedge.

While they sat, the dusk arrived. Their breathing had come in harmony, they were sitting like a couple who had sat together years.

A girl's voice rose in a laughing shriek, and a youth rolled on the grass guffawing, pedalling air with his limbs like a dog.

She said, 'I feel so at peace with you.' Though this meeting began in agitation, he too had found a calm.

The air was cooling. With a sigh, she stood up. 'Thank you. I feel better.'

At the park gates they parted. She kissed him. 'See you.'

Walking home he began to sense the difficulties, building like tall structures round them. How could it be made to work?

Nor had they agreed when they would next meet.

~

He was listening and not listening.

'I like those, mum.'

'What do you think, Stephen?'

'Oh, what, the cherub brackets? I think they're great.'

He was repeating to himself, I must stay on the ball, when Robyn's voice reached him,

'Are you with me, Stephen?'

He looked at her, blank. Sally was rolling her eyes, and Robyn staring at him hard.

'We all use the bathroom, Stephen, you know.'

He nodded, and resumed his effort. But presently Robyn scooped up the prospectuses for different styles of wash-basin.

'I'm wasting my breath.' She switched on the television and sat back watching war games in sand.

'Please Robyn, I'm sorry. It was a bad day, I was thinking about Rubens.'

By persistence, by diligence, he won her back. He jump-started their conversation again, and this time kept himself on track. From the cherub brackets he moved to Robyn's Private View for the Sean Raven show which was set for the following evening.

13

Mae will come again, he's sure of that. It won't be today, nor tomorrow either. These things must be spaced, if they're going to work. Nor does he mind this space of time.

In the meantime, he has work to do. The great subject has waited too long but he's in the mood for it now. The one-to-one of Peter Paul Rubens with King Charles Stuart of England.

He has the general plan, of figures set within the shape of the Queen's House at Greenwich. But what moment to take? I need faces and postures. He drops his pencil and walks, he mouths and whispers like different people. Let them face each other down. From a monograph by Hans Gotthelf he knows the words they might have said, while *Chess with Kings* gives him the colour he needs. The pictures flicker, each dissolves in the next: he will turn himself into a one-man theatre, glancing alternately at their words and at his drawings.

The Queen's House has stood for decades and never been finished, and in 1629 it still has a thatched roof. Let Charles Stuart be busy in an unfinished room, bullying the joiners and stucco-stickers. With a slight nod, an offhand wave, he acknowledges the deep long bow of Rubens.

'Follow, Sieur Rubens. Before we s-sit, we w-w-will show you our w-w-works.'

Taken on a tour, Ruben hurries to keep up with this short, stubby-legged, stammering man, who walks with his body pitched headlong forward, while the secretaries trot; it is an un-regal progress. They arrive at a hall with rococo mouldings, surrounding areas of blank brown plaster. Charles announces to his panting retinue,

'We are of a mind to embellish these walls with p-p-pieces of p-p-painting by m-modern m-masters.' He looks at Rubens with his staring eyes, which have swollen, reddened, horny lids, like a man in need of spectacles.

Rubens bows, 'If your Majesty would consider a humble painter of Antwerp— '

Charles turns on him a fiery eye. 'Know this. We would have the subject be lofty and noble, and s-s-such as may engage an ab-b-bundance of l-l-ladies, since this is the Qu-qu-queen's House. And we would have the ladies be as b-b-beautiful as may be, and especially *svelte*.' The last word falls with peculiar emphasis, as bearing hard on the fat School of Antwerp.

'Your Majesty.' A deeper bow from Rubens, who has surveyed however the area of plaster to be covered. He has done a quick sum, as to how much he would paint himself (the figures for sure), and how much leave to his apprentices.

Charles also, he sees, is in a muse. 'We had thought,' he begins, 'for we want the very b-b-b-best of those who p-p-p-paint now, of y-your y-young m-man.'

'*My* young man, majesty?'

'Your b-b-b-best p-p-p-pupil – is he not a m-m-master now?'

'Oh, can you mean young Antony Van Dyck?'

Charles nods, his eyes stare hard.

'Why yes,' Rubens nods too, in quick consternation. 'Master Van Dyck is most competent. If I may say so, he has been well trained . . .'

But can it be? That King Charles wants paintings, not from his own hand, but from the young hand of Van Dyck? He is startled, aghast, can fashion so change? To be supplanted by a pupil!

But to the purpose, for he sees that Charles watches him with dry level eyes. For a moment he wonders, as he has with Gerbier, has this king heard of his father's great shame? Surely the Dutch royals keep all such things dark? Yet a king has a thousand ears and eyes; who can say what secret may finally reach him?

'C-c-come now to our c-c-cabinet.'

The attendants and secretaries Charles waves away, and sets suddenly off, in his paddling walk, so Rubens must trip quick in his slippers.

The closet they enter is finely appointed, with a rich carpet on a table that is wonderfully carved at the legs. From the window they see the red-brick walls of the old palace of Placentia, and beyond a wide-swinging bend of the Thames, with merchant ships and men-of-war, and tiny vessels like flies on the water. There is a noise of women's laughter from within the palace, and from under their window, quickly hushed, a burst of lewd levity between the gardeners.

Charles sits, and motions for Rubens to sit.

'So, sir artist. I believe there may be certain w-w-words which our c-c-c-ousin of Spain has bid you say.'

'That is so, most Christian majesty.'

Charles sits then upright and quite still, but with his head a little cocked.

Rubens clears his throat, his mouth and tongue fumble. But the words he has brought are tired of waiting and press to his lips.

'His Catholic Majesty has said I may say, "The Kingdom of Spain is willing that a Peace be agreed between Spain and England, and confirmed by an exchange of ambassadors." This message is given in secret, so that if my endeavours fail, no man should guess such words were said. For it is beneath the majesty of the realm of Spain to sue for peace with any power.'

Charles continues to wait, his ear still towards Rubens.

'Highness?' Rubens ventures. He has no more words.

The eye of Charles swings slowly to him, a trace supercilious, one brow raised high.

Rubens drops his eyes.

'Sieur Rubens, it is our b-belief that our c-c-cousin of Spain had more than this to say to m-m-me.'

Rubens knows what Charles is waiting for, and knows he must not mention it. Now, he thinks, my troubles come. He can only gaze before him, like a poor soul at a loss.

'Most elevated majesty— '

Charles makes a kind of grunting 'Humph.' His red-rimmed eyes are stark. Though Rubens cannot meet those eyes, he feels their heat.

Charles says to the air, with a sardonic edge. 'I need not say that his "C-c-catholic M-m-majesty" knows full well that before any peace be made with us, agreement must be m-m-made for the future of the C-c-county P-p-p-p-p-p-p-p-p-palatine, and of our l-l-lands and rights therein.'

What can Rubens say? He was told that Charles would ask for this, that he would bring in Germany – and that he must say nothing about it. And Charles of course will want a present, a sweet, to accompany Spain's request. Rubens has no present to give. All he may do is to speak only of the Peace, hoping that England may still want this, however annoyed Charles also is. But Rubens is not in a comfortable place, alone with a king whose look now is a freezing scorch, with the fixity of royal displeasure.

Think fast, Peter Paul. He must avert the wrath. 'Great British king – most sainted and gracious – you know most surely that I, a mere painter, am unfit for true diplomacy. I am but a stray bird that may carry one leaf. What further is to say of the County Palatine, and other questions there pertaining, must be said when the envoys are exchanged. *They* will have licence to speak of all things.'

Charles's eye stays hard. He gives again his grunting 'Humph'. But his anger is less, perhaps, than it was. One finger taps the table-top, then rises and falls in an offhand wave, which Rubens sees is his dismissal.

'Apostolic Majesty.' Rubens stands from the table, but then stays in that spot.

Charles glances curtly at him, as to say, We gave you leave to go.

'Illustrious serenity, may I tell my royal master you will consider what he has proposed?'

Charles seems at first too annoyed to speak. Then he sits back, eyeing Rubens. His fingers briefly drum the table. 'You may report to the C-c-count-D-d-duke that all m-m-matters of true m-m-moment that come unto our C-c-court are weighed not only by ourselves, but by our C-c-c-c-council also.'

Humbly Rubens bows his head. But does not leave, there is something further he is bidden to ask.

'Illustrious serenity.'

The King's eyes widen, as if to say, 'You still are here?'

'The royalty of Spain asks one thing, for that time in which we speak of peace.'

The King's wall-face has set in stone.

'That while both realms do treat of peace, England make no new alliance with France.'

From Charles, a slight intake of breath. Will fury break, that Rubens is so peremptory?

Charles does not move, he does not speak. There is no clue to what he thinks.

'Sieur Rubens.' His voice, at last, is quiet and clear. 'You may tell the C-c-c-count-Duke we c-c-c-consent to this.'

Rubens' own eyes widen. Legions of Heaven, he murmurs within, I thank you that he gives me this.

But Charles has not done. 'P-p-p-p-provided the same hold true for Spain, that no new bond be made with France.'

Reverently Rubens bows again. But where are they now? Has Charles given a promise, or only words? What may he do to make all sure?

The answer comes. But do I dare? To request of majesty such a thing? Charles seems not so furious now. Speak, Rubens! You are the prince of painters!

'Great prince, most glorious and Christian magnificence, one sole favour I would beg, that what you spoke as to alliance with France may be writ, in ink on paper.'

Now truly Charles sits back, his brows rise high, his eyes expand.

'*You*, S-s-sieur Rubens, you ask, and in our royal p-p-p-presence, if you may be given our w-w-word *in writing*?'

'Imperial and blest of Heaven, pardon pray my gross presumption, yet ever I have found it so, with princes of the church and yea with the princes of our Christian realms, that always it is the wiser course, and best for all, if what is said be set on paper.'

The jaw of King Charles has dropped. Papers there may be, but that they should be asked for, from a King, and to his face – and by a clod, a tradesman, by one that works with his hands for money. How ever did Spain send him this loon, this clown, this yokel from the swamps of Flanders, this simpleton who has no clue, what may be said to a Christian king?

Icily, he inquires, no stammer now, 'And did our brother king of Spain set down his words on paper?'

Even Rubens is surprised at the freezing rage in the royal eyes, which are hard like glass eyes now. He quails – My vanity! For anything he wants in writing, he must ask another day. To redeem himself he must betray himself. In deep chagrin he gravely murmurs,

'Most amplified and puissant greatness, forgive I beg the unlicked baseness of a low-born artisan.'

With solemnity, and dignity too, he bows extremely low, counts ten, then, slow as a tortoise, lifts his head.

Briefly Charles watches him, as though truly he were some reptile thing, then sits back in his chair. He shrugs. His eyebrows work. He quietly mutters eventually,

'You m-m-m-m-may retire.'

'Most Christian sovereign.' Rubens begins stepping backwards, while one hand lifts his gown behind him. If he should tumble in a heap, and in the presence of a King! He bows once more, steps back, and bows again. He feels for the door-frame, finds it, and withdraws.

A final sketch shows Rubens at the palace gate, his face a consternation. He has won those words the Count-Duke sought. He will speak of the skill with which he won them. But has he then spoiled everything, through not knowing when to shut his mouth – and ruined so the hope of nations?

Worse, has he acted so unwisely, that Charles will not now seek a portrait from his hand? Charles had shown him the blank plaster, in the Queen's House, to be covered with pictures. Is that another commission he has rashly thrown away? And what of Van Dyck? Can it truly be possible, that the king will prefer his pupil to himself?

Forget Van Dyck, that is not the issue now. Outside the palace gate, Rubens shakes his head bemused, then sombrely climbs down the steps to the quay, and the galley that will take him home.

As he settles himself in the pavilion at the stern, he notices an object on the further bank. Did he assume it was a tree, because it stayed so still? But there are no trees there, rather it is a man, a Puritan, perhaps, for he wears black and has a wide-brimmed, high-crowned hat. Though he does not pray, or sing some hymn, rather he stares, in a fixed way, at Rubens. As Rubens watches the man draws from his robe an object, which he then pulls longer. It is a seeing tube, a glass. Deliberately he raises it to his eye, aiming, exactly, at Rubens.

The man stays so as the galley casts loose, and begins its trip upstream. Rubens finds himself disquieted that the man so openly simply watches him. It is like an attack. No, it is an attack. Only when the galley turns a corner can Rubens lie back comfortably.

But nor can he be at ease even now, when he sees beyond tree-tops and roof-peaks a brown shade rising. It is not far off, and shaped like the canopy of a tree. It flickers with movement, so it seems not so much like smoke as like a swarm of gnats or wasps. Almost he hears their angry buzz.

But that sight too is hidden soon, and Rubens sighs, and rests.

Many though not all of these details are included in that house-shaped design, overprinted with royal colours, which Bloodsmith will title, 'Rubens asks King Charles of England if he may have it in writing'.

14

Not many guests had come when Bloodsmith arrived at Robyn's private view. Robyn, of course, had been there through the day. From the street he saw into the bright-lit room, saw people holding glasses, Robyn talking with animation, her new-cut hair looking silky and fine-drawn. He used to think, 'Robyn, you are a star!' He thought it now, in spite of himself – 'Robyn, you do this *very* well!' She wore a black dress, simple and elegant. But why black? It was not Robyn's colour. It made her look like Hamlet, come to see a Private View.

He came in the Gallery. Robyn mouthed 'Hello Stephen!', and returned at once to her conversation. He took a glass and circulated.

Half of the few there belonged to Robyn's Board of Directors, desultorily talking to each other. He looked round the gallery, with its white spaces and huge prints, and thought: it looks good! Both he and Sally had had their input.

Robyn was beside him. 'I like this one the best.'

She took him down a line of vast colour-transparencies set in light-boxes.

'Is he here then, your Sean Raven?'

'He's supposed to be, he isn't yet. No one's here. Not the Arts Council, not the local telly. Not even Sally.'

'That's no surprise.'

'Hello *Robyn*!' a long-jawed man in a sports jacket called, in a shockingly deep bass howl.

'Richard!' she called. 'Excuse me, Stephen!' She flashed the bright smile of social desertion, and slid off as if snatched by an invisible cable. Richard was the local limb of Arts Council funding. For a moment Bloodsmith wondered, could the lover be Richard? For Richard was tall, and fair, and straight-nosed; to look at them chat, you could think they were siblings. And the one thing they were not, was brother and sister. But no, that cutting, forced-down voice, he could not think it.

'Hello Stephen.'

'Paul.'

They fell into talk. Paul was a local arts grandee (bearded, of course), and thus on Robyn's Board of Directors. Allegedly he once wrote a best-selling book.

'How did the meeting go?' Bloodsmith asked.

'Meeting?'

'Wasn't there a Directors' Meeting – a week or so ago? Robyn didn't tell me the end result.'

Paul touched the buttons on a slender black wafer.

'No, it's quite definite, there's been no Director's Meeting for a month.'

'Maybe a Sub-Committee?'

'No, there's been nothing. I know there hasn't.'

'Stupid of me. I got it wrong.' They parted, heading to different photos.

So now I know. Robyn was lying when she said she was going to a Directors' Meeting. *That* is hard evidence.

After all it made little difference. Something secret is going on; but so it is with me. Now Mae's in my life, I've changed to blasé. He took a bottle of wine, and went round filling glasses. Robyn, he saw, looked pale and tense. She looked behind often, towards the door.

Through which Sally came, with a gaggle of chatterers. She gave eye-salutes to Robyn and to him, but she was with friends, she would not talk to parents. A bottle of wine was already in their hands as they gossiped in front of the photos while Sally cried, 'Oh no!'

He could hear they were discussing 'Unto Death', and the dilemma of fat Mustafa, seduced by the West, who has fallen for a pole-dancer. They move to the sinister green attaché cases, which each of the Mujahadeen significantly carries, and never seems to open.

'I know what they've got in them,' the strong voice of Sally calls.

'Yes?' they ask.

'They're dirty bombs.'

The others wonder – maybe dirty bombs are 'the Bites of God'?

The room was filling, then a vibration came. Sean Raven had arrived, a tall man in glasses with a sheep-like, gentle face. He had soft hands, a soft voice, an apologetic stoop. Bloodsmith looked him over, and knew at once: it isn't him.

The local paper came, a vigorous tight-haired woman in a windcheater. The local television came, with apparatuses strapped about their bodies. But still Robyn, he saw, was only more tight-drawn, and continued to look to the door as though there were a further person expected, whose arrival would change everyone's lights.

~

At home afterwards they stayed up late. Robyn was exhausted but also excited. All three agreed the Sean Raven Private View had been a success beyond their hopes.

In the centre of the night Bloodsmith dreamed he and Rubens met. He was still in the gallery where people milled and Robyn came and went, but he knew the portly man was Rubens from the smart shirt he wore, with wide black and magenta stripes. Beneath his white button-down collar, he wore a tie in which all the hues of the palette were mingled: it was extravagant, but worn with panache.

'Your servant, Sieur Bloodsmith.' There was a sparkle in the great painter's eye.

'Your servant, Sir Peter Paul.'

Rubens slightly bowed. 'I thank you. But I am not dubbed yet.'

The gallery in the meantime had expanded. Between people you saw the gilt edges of paintings beside black frames of photos, and other visitors again were strangely dressed. A man nearby wore, with his jeans, a sword. There was a pikemen dressed like the Pope's Swiss Guards. Especially he and Rubens watched the woman opposite who wore a white ruff with a red paisley dress. She was dark-skinned, fine-featured, with luminous eyes. Rubens' face had sharpened and lifted like a scenting dog.

'Ah, Sir Bloodsmith, I am much taken with that lady.'

'Indeed, Sieur Peter? I had thought you affected another order of beauty.'

Rubens focussed his grey eyes on Bloodsmith. 'Sieur Stephano, I would say this to you, people get me wrong. Most grossly would they crib and crab me, to plump blonde daughters of the dairyman. But I am a man of larger tastes. As of now, love's dart hurts from that strange maid' —Bloodsmith, at this point, saw the arrow, buried nearly up to its feathers in Rubens's bright tie and shirt— 'What know you of this lady?'

Bloodsmith found he knew everything. "Tis said that in the Indies she was a warrior princess, and there saved the life of an ensign of the King. They wed. Him the King hath late ennobled, saving your grace, Sieur Peter, for the many Spaniards he hath slain, in taking of their gold. But still all know him as Ancient Rawlings, and her they call the Indian Maid.'

'And do they so?" The plump fingers of the painter curled up one moustachio.

The lady now wore a different dress with a billowing flame-red skirt that swirled about her legs. As she strode across the room she kept her eyes on Bloodsmith; her brows were knit. Her dark face was like that of a pretty hawk, and different from Mae's, but he knew she was Mae none the less. He had never expected this – would he and Rubens be rivals for Mae?

He looked round, and saw Robyn talking, obliviously, with others.

'Sieur Peter, I have heard it said that in this realm of England, you have found something that you long had sought. Some antique thing.'

Rubens frowned. 'Not yet I fear. I have asked, I seek. I am on its track.'

'Nay, more. Even it is said, that within this town, you shall make most signal, no mighty, discoveries. Even such that shall change the turning of your world.'

Hoarsely Rubens murmured, perhaps to himself, 'Indeed I shall. I know not yet what they will be, but they will be the breaking of me.'

Bloodsmith was unprepared for the grief that broke in Rubens' face, which suddenly was older, thinner, balder; he had turned into an older, leaner man. He looked utterly stricken.

As was Bloodsmith. He woke in pitch dark with a blank sense of loss. Beside him the fragrant body of Robyn rested in the contentment of a successful Private View.

And Lady Rawlings? There had been a Lady Rawlings in the London Rubens knew. He had read a little about her in *Chess with Kings*. He would find out more.

15

Robyn's mother rang. Her father, Leo, had had some form of attack and she, Joyce, had trouble coping: Robyn would go for a fortnight at least to help. Robyn's assistants could mind the Sean Raven exhibition, which had settled – as exhibitions will – to a stillness broken mainly by the occasional shopper with time on their hands.

Within this period Geoffrey would be often away, and for days at a time. On days she felt free Mae came to his studio.

'Later we are going away,' she said.

'What? Where?'

'But that's not for three weeks or so.' When she went home to make Gavin's tea, Bloodsmith would go home to be there for Sally.

With Robyn away, his guilty awkwardness disappeared. Strange discovery, *how* much conscience depends on proximity, and on the odds of being found out. When the cat's away, the mice will play: it seemed as simple as that.

The amoral sun was keen to bless them. Daily, hot radiance poured through the roof-window, while by pulling cords he gave them fresh air.

Mae came one day in a cobalt dress, and with a burst of flowers. 'I bought us some anemones.'

'They're brilliant!'

From among his vessels for brushes and chemicals, she chose a red jug, and set the flowers on the bed of his press.

She said, 'You never bring flowers in here.'

'It hasn't been that sort of place.'

'And you don't play music now. Why's that? The equipment's here.'

'You're the music. No really. All I want is quietness and you.'

But they played his music now, and especially his most sweetly-melting love-numbers, 'La ci darem', the Spirits from Gluck's *Orpheus*, Handel's music of lost lovers re-found, on l'Isola Deserta.

Often she moved about his studio, possessing the space which was now hers as well. She would touch and move his pots of brushes, his tubes of paint, his drawers of tools. She would smooth the blankets on his etching press. She would rummage among his prints and drawings.

'I like your drawings.'

'Let me see your prints.'

'You will, you will.'

The next day she brought them. In each plate there were long, slightly curving, deep-etched lines, which arced through a void with decisive grace, like the tracks of unimaginable flying creatures.

'But they're *very* good. The way the curves play. You *shouldn't* have stopped.'

He lightly rubbed their surface, and bathed in their light and space and colour. They were a lovers' mutual admiration club, he could not stop saying how much he liked them. She had a way of digging her chin in her neck, when she smiled with pleasure at something said , a way of being modest and pleased at once. At times she roved the room in her underwear, which was nothing new to him, an artist and married, but still provoked him. Women's underwear, with its zigzag stitchings, it was the essence of intimacy.

We will find them on cushions in different parts of the floor. The room is warm from the electric bars, and they are neither naked nor clothed, but draped in some of his odd pieces of cloth. She has her chin on her knees, she is gazing into distance.

She says, 'This is something on the side.'

He goes quiet, it's not his phrase.

'But I don't see why it shouldn't go on for a long time.'

Abruptly he says, 'I wish we just declared ourselves. Just told everyone what we're doing, and got it in the open.'

She fires back, quick as a shot, 'To do that is the way to lose me.'

His bugbear is her directness, which will not let up. There is something to her, in all regards, that is keen and trimmed to the bone. Especially about Geoffrey she will be clear; there are ways in which she will not betray him. This loyalty hurts him, even in the simple phrase 'my husband'. The words privilege Geoffrey over any lover, for the husband will be always there, whatever they (either of them) do 'on the side'. On these occasions a distance opens, where he glimpses overhead a high big relationship: the marriage that Mae and Geoffrey keep, like twin chimneys of rock, a castle gate, that will endure whatever goes on in the dark.

Geoffrey's faults are not spared either. Nor their own faults. They talk of people giving up their space, and giving up space in their marriages too. That is how they help affairs to happen.

'That's what I did.' Her eyes will glow like lanterns at a road-works. 'I helped Geoffrey to be with her. People in marriages hurt themselves.'

Did I do that with Robyn, he wonders. But Mae has stood – 'Excuse me' – towering quickly over him. He will watch her step behind his screen, which he has stationed round the studio sink. This area is their private bathroom, where a plastic washing up bowl does duty for toilet and bidet and bath. For they live, this intermittent couple, in rudimentary circumstances.

He will hear tenderly the soft steady rattle of her pissing on the plastic, then the cataract-noise from the tap as she washes. The bowl is rinsed, she has put it down, with the hollow boumm of plastic on wood. She returns, her head dipped ruefully, from which her wide-set eyes look up, with the smile of someone caught out in privacies.

'Where is it you're going, then? This trip of yours, with Geoffrey.'

'The Gambia. West Africa.'

'Oh!' He is shaken. This is more than a holiday, travelling to the place her forebears came from.

'Well, don't look sad about it. I ought to want to go there. It's been planned a long time, I can't say no now.'

And he can't say, he is sad she should be going there with Geoffrey. If only she were going there with him! And what if it is a deep event, the Roots experience? What if it draws her and Geoffrey closer?

'I'll be back,' she says, with gleaming emphasis. She comes naked on all fours to where he is. 'So. What pose? Don't ask me to "recline" again. I don't like the way my belly puckers.'

'You choose.'

She frowns and makes a prognathic mouth. 'I don't know. I don't know why you're drawing me at all. I'm not a Rubens woman, I'm the opposite.'

'That's true.' He has his answer ready. 'But we don't live in Rubens' world.'

'No. We don't.' But her brow has knit, as if what he said was slick.

'A modern painter – might want someone lean – active – different –'

Different? Her eyes hang on the word.

'Do you think we should think a bit more, Stephen — about what's going on with us? You like me, I know, and I like that. And a bit you like me as – exotic. No?' She makes dangerous eyes. 'A black woman.'

Black? He is startled, she is black and not black. And a black woman – what's wrong with that? He is no racist! But her look is more serious than the words in his head. As if she is looking now past his eyes, so his own eyes must look inside him. Does she mean there is something else in how he likes her — some fetish thing?

But she has seen he is uncertain. 'I understand, Stephen – after my time with Geoffrey.'

Geoffrey? But he understands. She means after her time with another Englishman, their quirks.

'But you *are* exotic, for me. And I fell for you. *And* my pictures are love-pictures. Artists do that. Andrew Wyeth had his Helga. Bonnard painted his Marthe for ever.'

'There's a lot of "his" in this. But that is something men do. Owning women, owning their looks. Women don't do that with men.'

'Wanting to draw you doesn't mean I want to *own* you, Mae.'

'Are you sure of that, Stephen? It's true I like posing. But you could ask what the woman thinks sometimes, when the hours go by and she's stuck in the "pose". By the eye of a man who says "Don't you move". *Isn't* there a sort of slavery there?'

'Well. My God. I don't see it like that.'

'Isn't that the point?'

He has to pause, think, nod.

'Well. But it's also true I love you. I want you. And I want to paint and draw you.'

'That's a lot of *wanting* me.' But her voice crinkles, she is not severe. After all, there are two sides to *wanting*.

'Nor do I think I *own* your looks.'

'No? When they're in your pictures? It's *my* appearance, but if you had a show. Or if you sold them. Or if your dealer did...'

Selling Mae? A huge space yawns abruptly under their feet.

'I'll give them to you. Now. I'll write it down, they're yours.'

'Thank you.' A quizzical look. 'But then – a lot of me will be *your* me.'

'So I can't win.'

'And don't you forget it.' She half-smiles.

'You're saying there's a power-play in art.'

'You know there is. And in love. "You're all mine, dearest".'

'I'm in your power.'

She doesn't say no, but she has decided to ease up. She folds herself in a squatting position, her knees standing out like wings.

He has squatted the same way, deliberately, taking his pad and facing her.

It must be that outside the air has thinned further, for the light from the roof-window has brightened to gold. Her yellow coat hangs on a chair behind her, its colour fired to a yellow fury: and from this inferno she gazes to him. But even as he is dazzled, her eyes a trace narrow, the eyelids cupping softly round them, to make that veiled, tender gaze which he has come to know.

But he hasn't started, he has put his pad down.

'Draw, Stephen.'

'Not now.' He won't say why, but he has stuck on the words they have had. Issues hang in the air. He is uncertain, confounded.

'Just draw now.' Her steady eyes insist, he will draw her in a good way.

'Thank you.' It is like, she has given him permission.

Let it come, this picture, like a climax in love! In the heart of the conflagration, the slim figure squats, like a female Daniel studying us with curiosity from out of her kiln. Like a dark angel, examining from within her flame.

'Oh, by the way,' he nodded to the famous Van Dyck portrait, showing Rubens' wife Isabella, which was pinned on his board, 'I looked up that statue, who it's meant to be.'

He pointed at the mincing stone figure, placed up on the wall behind Isabella, standing right next to her head.

'And?'

'It isn't clear. What is clear is that the wall he stands on is the wall which joins the pompous gateway, which Rubens built in front of his house, which you can see on the right of the picture.'

'So it should be clear.'

'It should. Because Rubens did put two statues there – one of Hermes and one of Athena. That was how you showed your success. Hermes was trade and Athena was art. If you put them side by side, it was called a Hermathena. It said Art-Money – up-market success. But this statue isn't Hermes and it isn't Athena. Rubens' statues are completely different, they've got helmets and capes and wings and spears. In other words, this statue that Van Dyck painted was never there, actually. He chose to put it there.'

'So?'

'So – who are you?' He went and stooped close to the statue, then stepped back. 'Look at that forearm. Is that fat or muscle? The head's all blurred around the mouth. He will not tell us who he is.'

'Do you think he is Secrecy?'

'Secrecy? But he's nearly naked.'

'Well, a secret love, then? Guarded with a dagger. He could be a young man.'

They look again at the flaunting statue. It has something voluptuous and something grim... and the dagger.

'Did Cupid have a dagger?'

'He carried Love's Dart. It's often an arrow.'

'We're pricked,' she says, shining-eyed.

While he thinks, but this odd figure may be the clue of clues, to the secrets I have tried to chase. If only the 'lost chapter' was not lost! Or is he the reason that the chapter *was* lost? There is too much I do not know, like whatever it was that happened in the village of Saventhem.

~

Nor did they need to be confined to his studio. Next day he took the car which he and Robyn used mainly for the supermarket, and drove in. It was a clear bright day, not hot but with no wind at all.

'Let's not stay indoors,' he said when Mae came.

'Let's not!' she chimed with vigour.

He was exhilarated, driving with her beside him. The car was their relationship, forging onwards all roads open. He had left the town, and motorways and thoroughfares, slipping into country roads, and deep-sunk winding lanes where the trees closed over them, making a green tunnel shot through with glints of sun.

But where to go? Where, in England, do you find that wilderness where lovers can wander in nature, and love? Every field has hedges, maybe ditches, the woods are fenced in, everywhere belongs to someone who has locked the trespassers out. Casting for a place he paused in a layby, where another car had stopped. Inside it were a middle-aged man and woman, at a pause in a significant conversation. Somehow you could see each was married to someone else. This didn't please him, he drove on before Mae saw them too.

From the past, he remembered a wood where trees of all kinds ran up and down slopes. He remembered the farm track you took to get there. Today it had troughs of slopping mud waiting from old rains, but he was careful as they approached the dark-green crouching mass. He remembered the path to take, and between embraces he led the way, brushing past cow-parsley, skirting nettles, and holding undergrowth back for her to pass, till they came to the place he knew from past picnics. There the trees thinned, and the ferns and bracken flowed away downhill. Just under the trees there was a haze of bluebells, which spread away between birch-stems as though a cloud had come down and brought with it the colour of the sky itself.

'Mm. Mmmm.'

They kissed another long kiss, he spread his jacket on the ground and laid her top on top of it, so they made a place for love.

At leisure they stripped. Her ears were small and neat, his tongue-tip licked deep in the sweet salt pit. On his knees he kissed her bush, he found her lips. He burrows, love is a mole. Later she kissed inside his own ears.

He was huge with love. As she lay down and he entered not hurrying she rolled her head and closed her eyes. She said the phrase of phrases, 'I don't know what it is about you, Stephen. You're wonderful.'

After, he grabbed a hand of bluebells, and threaded them in her places of hair.

She was bright, full of words. 'I ought to say—'

When she had gone home the other night, Geoffrey saw she was different, and was crazy to make love with her. They made love.

'I didn't feel bad about it at all.' She stretched back.

'You had a good evening?'

She looked at him frankly, an atom roguish. 'It was wonderful.'

He didn't mind, he was amused, love is big.

She sat up, pensive, holding her knees. 'There'll be a reception when Geoffrey next comes back. I wish you could be there.'

'Where? At Geoffrey's reception?'

'Yes. I wish you could come as well. I wish it with all my heart.'

For a moment he rambled. He thought of threesomes. . . even foursomes, swap and double-swap... Mae and he and Robyn and Geoffrey . . . Could even that happen?

'I'll give you a picture.'

She got up, and headed for a tree across the clearing, from which a long low branch reached to touch another tree, making a bridge in air. With a few swings she was up on the slender, swaying branch. She held her arms out wide, so they made the wand of the tightrope walker. Gingerly, carefully, she laid foot before foot, slowly climbing upwards unsteadily out over greater space.

'A good shot?' she called, bright-faced.

He stood below and looked up, dazzled. He saw those lean limbs he knew so well – the extra length was in the forearms and calves, from ancestors on the equator who needed to lose their body-heat fast. She was a high slender wonder advancing with no fear. It was – *the* picture. It must be a painting, not a drawing or print. He was snapping the details, the angles that were different from what you would expect, till he had the exact geometry inside his head. Never mind sketches, he didn't need photos, he had filled his eyes and they would not forget. He would call it 'The Tightrope Walker' though you could see she walked on a tree. But you could not tell how high up she was, she could be over a precipice. It could be an allegory of forbidden love, the peril, the adventure.

The branch had begun to bend and wag. She wobbled, precarious — would she crash? But she and her wide arms swayed, found their balance, and precautiously stepped on.

'How'll you get down? You'll come back the same way?'

'No problem – man.'

She launched into space, jumping up as well as forward. For an instant she hung on the air, her arms spread wide. She was so slim she had no weight, she was a thistledown creature, at home on the wind. This was flying.

Still, coming down from such a height — will she break a leg, twist an ankle? On impact however she simple folded right down like a concertina, while her arms swung up then folded down round her. She stood up like a graceful Jack-in-a-box, then dipped again, as her arms opened like a greeting and her knees bent akimbo, in a ballerina's bow.

'OK?'

She was pleased, while he was dumbstruck. 'Super-OK. You did ballet?'

'I did lots of things once.'

Holding hands they wandered through ferns, which brushed their skin like a breath and left no rash. Occasionally they paused to kiss, long and slow. Half-smiling she said, 'You think this is us as Adam and Eve?' Her eyes glimmered, he was not sure he fathomed her.

Soon enough it was time to go. They dressed, kissed and made their way to the car, and began the drive back down the farm-track that brought them.

The land around here was high, lifted up like a plateau, so you saw bulging far-off fields of plough, tiny spinneys, a church-tower here a water-tower there, under a mid-afternoon sky that was clear and brilliant, with only one or two thread-thin low-down clouds. The unending space was huge and shining.

He was relaxed, saturated with love – and careless when he hit a deep trough of mud, which he had worked round cautiously as they came. He revved and let the gears into reverse, but the wheels only spun, and sank.

'Oh, bugger!'

He was more indignant than anything else, it was so much the wrong time for this. He revved again and the drive-wheels spun, splattering mud beside them all ways. As the car slightly sank it also swung round.

He got out. 'We're stuck.'

'I noticed.' She was quizzical, not desperate.

He went to the hedge and came back with bits of branch which he carefully wedged beneath the wheels, showing he knew what best to do. But when he tried the engine gingerly the spinning tyres chucked out his twigs.

He looked in the boot for anything useful but there was nothing but old shopping bags, jump-leads, a jack.

'No, we're *really* stuck.' He said it with a kind of amazement, looking round at the colossal radiant sky, a barn in the distance, a fence of pylons on the horizon. They were unbelievably far from help.

'We are,' she echoed, serious now.

He thought, what follows? If they walked and somewhere found a farmer, and got a tractor to retrieve the car, hours would have passed, it could be deep night. Geoffrey would be back from a trip, and wondering why she was gone many hours. And he himself was supposed to pick up Sally, to take her to basketball. And Robyn would ring, as she always did early evenings. All their secrets would come out.

Well, but something must be done.

'You drive,' he said, 'I'll push.'

'It's not my car.'

'Please try.'

She folded herself into the driving seat. He planted his shoes in sloppy earth and leaned down to push with all his strength on the bonnet.

'OK!'

He heaved and strained, his shoes slid then gripped, a little truly he shifted the car. Its engine revved, the gears grated and crashed, then it stalled with a shuddering bang.

'Try again.'

Gritting his teeth, frowning hard, he pushed with all his might. The car began to inch. He saw her face focused tiny in an almighty frown. The engine revved; then stalled again.

She disentangled herself from the car.

'It's not my car. I haven't got the hang.'

They scanned the empty landscape. They were utterly exposed, they could not be less hidden, though also they were miles from all eyes.

There they were then, stranded, on the cliff-edge of change. It was decided for them – not by them but by fate, or rather by chance. Exposure would follow, and consequences. Two marriages shot, and a new marriage born... or not. Was this the godsent opportunity? The question gaped like an abyss.

She said, 'You get in. I'll push.'

'What? No way.'

'Get in. I'll try.'

He got in, and turned the engine over.

'OK', she called.

Through the windscreen he saw her brilliant face, low down above the bonnet. Her projective jaw was set, her huge eyes were brilliant, fixed on his.

Gently as gossamer he let the engine engage. The car moved an inch, not downwards.

He called, 'It's moving.'

Her mouth broke wide in a huge grin of teeth. She leaned still lower and pushed, with all her lean spider-body of muscle taut and throbbing at full shove.

Gently as a whisper he let the gears touch again. There was a moment of clutch-slip, then the car reversed a centimetre. All his sensitivity was in the rubber ridges on the tyres, as they just began to get hold. Her dark-bright face, low over the bonnet like a rising sun, was brilliant with triumph and comedy.

The tyres took hold, the car backed from the mud. She stood tall, taller than ever before, and let her limbs swing, relaxed and laughing, while he climbed laughing out of the car. She had done it. He admired, they laughed ecstatic.

They got back in the car.

'But it's still in front of us.' She nodded to the dip of water.

'I'll take it at speed.'

He reversed further, then started forward. He must play his part, be king of the road. He quickly hit warp-speed, and when he reached the dip he swung the car over so it scratched on the hedge but was less in the water. There was a huge jolt and slithering, but already they were clear on the other side.

She laughed, remembering yesterday. 'Again! I got you moving again.'

He stopped and they embraced, a long, maybe their longest, kiss.

'Hey,' he said, as they were about to start. Caught in her tights, just over the knee, there was a tiny dark leaf-shape. They both gazed at it.

'It's inside,' she smiled. Later she would take it out.

They drove back to town, where he left her by her chosen bus-stop. She gave her long-armed wave, in the mirror he saw her.

So, after all, no apocalypse today. This was good – or bad? The question was too huge for now.

Driving, he saw her joyous face, brilliant, prognathic, with the smile of zest he would always see.

In his head as he drove some words jumped up. Was it a poem? He did pictures not poems.

Of love in the woods
The only sign
That tiny leaf
Inside her stocking.

16

Then Mae must stop coming; Geoffrey's short trips were done. She did not phone, and he could not phone her. Maybe there was a chance they would meet once before she left, but that was not sure.

He thought, this is how it is in the world of affairs. There's no solid foundation. Sudden cutoffs leave you hanging in space. I must – I want to – trust in Mae.

Also Robyn would still be away for days, nor did he know how things would be when she came home. Would she sense his betrayal? It was safest not to try to guess.

He must busy himself with other things. And like a person waiting at a turning in a lane, Rubens was there. Peter Paul, forgive me, I have been away. But nor could he sit down at once to make prints. How I can I draw anything? He had come to the crossroads of his life.

Yet it was as he sat brooding on Mae, on Robyn, on how he stood with them, that abruptly he saw, or glimpsed, rather, what that great discovery may have been, that Rubens made in England. He had thought it was some bad vision of how the big world worked. But maybe it was something closer to home. To do with marriages. To Dudley Carleton, beside the Thames, Rubens spoke of 'the bedchamber'. Had Rubens made a discovery like his own? Had he not seen what was under his nose? *Yes*, he said, though he had no proof. In Rubens' story too, was there a shadowy suspect figure: a Mystery Man crouched behind the bed-posts? Jens Claeys seemed to hint at that. If so, who was that man? Doubtless the 'missing chapter' revealed him. Maybe that man hailed from the village of Saventhem.

Things were not clear, he would get them clear. But as he looked through the prints he had made up to now he was disappointed. He thought, they're all about Rubens and King Charles. I don't go inside the man; I hardly glimpse his daily life. I must guess harder to picture his world. Pleasure gardens and inns, masques at Court, ladies and lords and street life too. Rubens' tête-á-têtes with Balthazar's Deborah. I'd better check the costume histories. When did ruffs give way to lace?

He makes a resolution. I'll give all next week to rereading Jens Claeys, with a glance at Gotthelf to stay safe in the facts. But right now I want a quick way in, a door I can go through inside Rubens. Inside the man, inside his sight. Before Robyn comes back, and the complications fall all over us.

He knows what door. He gets an off-peak ticket to London. Later he will go to see the Watergate, near the Thames. It stands beside where Rubens stayed. Then it was newly built and the old wide Thames lapped at its stones. If you touch the grainy limestone, you are touching 1626.

But now it is back to the National Gallery, and the red room with the Rubenses. A little he pauses by a Rubens portrait: Thomas Howard, Earl of Arundel. A dry, aquiline face. Not thin but reddening, from steak and good draughts of fortified wine. The seasoned eyelids lift from the wary, guarded eyes: such were the types that Rubens met. And Drebbel of course, though Rubens did not paint Drebbel. *Chess with Kings* has the scene, when Rubens and the Gerbiers went to see Drebbel, with all his inventions. Surely he will find a subject there!

But especially he stands again before that great painting which Rubens gave to King Charles: where Mars is pushed back from the banquet of Peace. That had been his starting point with Rubens. He drinks in the spread of it, the sumptuous reds, the dazzling cloth of gold of a dress. The warm soft glow of the bodies.

He steps closer, till his nose-tip is inches from the canvas. As an artist he must look inside the brush-strokes. The white-hairs on the underbelly of the leopard. The great shine in the black-lacquered armour of Mars. Behind the figures there are glimpses of landscape, dark trees lean in the wind, a wind-pushed cloudy sky – the sky of England then as now.

He is so close to the picture he could fall inside it. There comes a whirring in his head. Reflections in the varnish show something of the room behind him and, vaguely, a shadow-figure. Has someone larger than he is stepped up close behind him?

He glances round, there is no one there. And maybe he is woolgathering, for this figure he half-sees has white around the neck. But it cannot be that in some way the canvas may still return the reflection of the artist who once stood painting there. He thinks, God, I'm losing it. And yet it is hidden inside this picture, that knot where Rubens' story and mine run close. Marriage: the torch that boy carries means marriage. He murmurs, 'the torch of Hymen'. The labyrinth of the bedroom. But the picture jumbles, he sees nothing whole. I'm having a migraine, a disturbance of vision, flashing lights. Cardinal Richelieu had migraines. The details flicker, the tiny wings of the Cupid stir. The black cow-eye of the god Mars rolls. And, lower down to the right, a small bright girl stares back to him. She holds an apron white as snow. Her eyes ask, 'Who are *you?*' She is just like his daughter, Sally, when little. 'Get *down* from the picture, Sally!' he murmurs, the stern loving father. He wants that gone Sally back, she is so different now.

But Sally cannot come out. It is he who is falling in. His soul is tearing to split from this body. The threads of ectoplasm stretch and snap from each cell. His spirit, his sight, is taking off. It is falling, flowing, flying, pouring through the picture into its past. When he wakes – he must be blacking out – he will be nothing but eyes looking round him then. And how will he ever get back from there?

His hand has firm hold of the bashed paperback in his coat-pocket. It is as if Jens Claeys took his hand in his own, to guide him through the buried years.

'Come.'

'Do you need a chair... *sir?*' the attendant asks, without great concern. Then he too gazes into the painting, for the nest-headed man beside him stares still so fixedly that really it seems he is no longer here in the present at all.

Two

Balthazar's News

1

If his eyes locate Rubens in the 1620s, he will find that great artist marking time; still he awaits the decision of King Charles and his Council. Will they consent to his Peace, or will the Palatinate spoil it? On this period Jens Claeys comes into his own, with his picturesque details, his 'local colour', his sheer knowledge of 1629. From Claeys, and from Gotthelf and the other historians, we too may know, as well as Bloodsmith does, how events were for Rubens then.

He has spoken again with the King, and with the diplomat Dudley Carlton, whom he had known when Carleton was Ambassador to the Netherlands. Carleton has confirmed again that the King's Councillors, like the King himself, are much concerned for the Palatinate: if England accepts a part of the Palatinate, will she be renouncing the remainder of it? To Rubens it is strange that the Peace with Spain should hang on a haggling for German estates. He has other fears too, for it is rumoured the French are preparing to send a new ambassador to London. For certain the Cardinal will work to hurt him.

Rubens will more than once stop in the street. Is he followed? In the corner of his eye, the tip of a cloak flits out of sight. Are the Dutch spying on him? More likely the French, for the narrow eye of the Cardinal is said never to close. May it be just a passing cutpurse? Or, on some dim day, when few people are out, will he round a corner, and face... the assassin? Will he be a tall and silent ferocity, his face like the mask of a beast?

How to advance matters? Rubens has waited on Lord Weston, but

157

must not become tiresome. One day, standing in a nook of London Bridge gazing down the crowded spacious river, he sees there is something he may do. He will paint a picture – but such a picture! Large, with many figures, rich in colour. He will present it as a gift to King Charles, and pray that it helps to plead his cause, for his true eloquence is in his brush, not his words. Also it will show who is the greater painter: Van Dyck, or he who taught Van Dyck. Rubens muses, may this be his greatest painting? It has the greatest subject, the Peace of Nations in a world at war. With the force of Art may he *paint* these monarchs into Peace, and if that is a dream, still he will have made a noble work.

How will it look? In the background of the painting war must rage, you will see the fume rise from burning towers. The question is, who will he place in the foreground? Does he dare to show King Philip of Spain, the Count-Duke of Olivarez at his elbow, advancing to meet King Charles of England, with Lord Weston and others beside him? But what height may he give to short Charles, so he does not look a dwarf beside the Spaniards? Set him up on a hillock? No, better on horseback. You can be any height, and sit high on a horse. King Philip likewise. So, a mighty double equestrian portrait, with the attendant lords on foot, and their retinue also, in all their splendour. It can be magnificent!

But then – he turns his back on the teeming river – what if the parleys of the ministers take another course, so this scene does not fit? And will the Kings approve such portraits? Also, how may he show war to rage in the background, when the kings are making a Peace? The horses, true, can be mighty steeds, pawing the ground in their lust for battle: their heads toss high, their nostrils yawn, fire shines in their black eyes, their silk manes fling like a woman's hair. But can that be right for a scene of peace? He wants a battlefield, the flash of fire from bombard and cannon, the glitter of iron, torn blackened banners, so you hear the cries of the wounded and dying... in the distance at least.

Ah, the problems of the arts; of Art. He shakes his head, and starts back towards the Gerbiers' house. But he trusts his genius, an answer will come.

As it speedily did, for within two days he met a lady who gave some answer to the needs of his art, and of his desire too. His art works best always when hand in hand with Desire.

He had gone, in his keenest Spanish black, to a masque at Whitehall. He saw at once the lady was far from English. She was, he learned, native to a tribe in the Americas, but married now to an English officer. He had been ennobled but was still known to some as 'Ancient Rawlings'. Her colour reminded him of ladies of Spain, her hair too was black as the Spanish night. Her eyes were black with golden sparks. She was dark but fiery. In his mind he named her Phlogis, the Flame.

He saw to it that they were soon introduced. And she, as foreigner to foreigner, slipped at once into Italian, where he was more at home than in English.

'They tell me, Signor Rubens, you are both painter and diplomatist.'

Rubens bowed in acknowledgement, thinking still how dark as pitch was her hair.

'In these days, gracious lady, many of my art are diplomatists also. For our brush carries us from Dukes to Princes, and thence to Princes of the Church. Thus the great will say in our hearing things they wish others of the great to hear. We are the carrier-pigeons of the kings of the earth, and spies of the ministers of those kings.'

To his delight she laughed at once, and said with vigour, 'I care not much for the great of the earth. I have had the honour to be presented to a surfeit of them. I have been brought forth as a wonder.' For 'wonder' she used the word 'monstro'.

He said at once, 'Madam, you are a wonder to me. With a nobility of aspect I have seldom seen, and I have seen many. It would be an honour beyond all my deserving, should your great lord and yourself ever think my hand worthy to paint a portrait of your selves or of your family together.' For it was his policy always to strike when any iron was hot, and to miss no chance.

She laughed again loudly, seeing the liberty he took, then smiled, while her eyes burst with golden lights. 'I thank you, Signor Rubens. The honour would be great for us too, I believe. And for me, for I am no fair lady.'

'Nay, there are different kinds of fair. And you are the fairest that I see here.'

She dipped her head. 'Allow me to reflect upon your words. It may be I shall speak to my lord.'

He bowed, she nodded. They should not speak more, and turned to others who were drawing near.

Would she, and her kin, ever pose for him? Would he see her ever again at all? There was no knowing, but in the meantime he had his inspiration. It had come as he studied her, even as they spoke their courtesies. She was from the Americas, but she made him think of Spain. And he saw how he would paint her – not quite as herself, for no rumours should be started. She would become Hispania, the Genius of Spain. Forget kings and their pomposities; he would make the nations goddesses. Another mighty woman, but fair, would be Britannia. They would be warrior maidens, amazons, but their armour would be cast aside as they embraced in making peace. Their bodies must be young and full and ripe, ready to bear the fruit of peace. Far off, among hills, rose the smoke of battle, but they had turned their backs on that while a satyr, a figure of male vigour, brought forth a cornucopia, ready to flood the foreground with an abundance of peaches, pomegranites, quinces, pears.

He had his vision, the whole picture at once. He looked for the lady as they processed to the banquet. She sat with Ancient Rawlings far off in a high place. But several times her eyes rested briefly on his. It seemed to him then that no two people in that large gilded hall were as conscious of each other as he and she were. In some way, in art or in love or in both, they would meet again. He did not know how but life had taught him patience. Already she had many names in his mind, she was Hispania, and Phlogis the Flame, also she was the Indian Maid. He would not think of her as Lady Rawlings.

But now a new question confronted him. For who would be his inspiration for the beautiful ripe fair person of Britanna?

~

This great undertaking of his art hovered now at the front, now the back of his mind, as the activities of these days extended. Often he rose at four, and took mass with Hendrik Brant at the mansion of the Resident of Savoy. With Balthazar Gerbier he saw the paintings in the King's own collection, and began his copy of the King's Mantegna. He visited Lord Arundel, to admire his Greek sarcophagi. Otherwise, he and Hendrik Brant pass their time in the house of the Gerbiers. It is by their choice, for Balthazar had offered them separate quarters, but the Flemings, both, have preferred to live more at home, with a family. They do not interfere with the business of the house, though they are kind as they may be with the children and Deborah Kip.

'Sieur Peter,' little Susan cries, 'we are going in a week to the house of Master Dribble. Father has said.'

'To the house of Cornelis? Why, we shall all look forward to that.'

'But can he turn into a tree, and a beast? Can he make my dolls to live?'

'For sure he can do many things.'

'Bed, Susan,' Deborah says, and to Rubens, 'Please say nothing to excite her more.'

She shepherds them upstairs, while Susan busily reminds George and Elizabeth what Drebbel can, and cannot, do.

'No,' her voice rises, 'he cannot turn himself into a mouse. The cat would eat him.' The other must be teasing her.

In the hall, at the table, Rubens and Hendrik sit on in conversation with Balthazar. This is so every evening, and Balthazar is a hospitable host, though still it rankles that Rubens has so great a fame. A firelit scene then, chiaroscuro for Bloodsmith to cross-hatch with an etching needle. And again Rubens will catch that odd glint in Balthazar's eye that looks like ill-will, and a little like gloating, as if he knew something that gave him the advantage. He wonders again, can Balthazar have heard of his father's infamy, when he was attorney to the lame princess? Or is there something quite other, nearer home, that Balthazar knows about Rubens?

In one way or another, Balthazar will show his knowledge. He is expert in many arts, as he tells them, and in sciences too. He purposes to found an academy. So at his ease beside his hearth he will speak of Finance, and of the need of each nation to have its own national bank, free from the whims of lords and kings. When the Flemings blink he moves to Fortification, and asks them if they know the right spacing of bastions (he will say it is one hundred and four score paces). He will try them on Architecture, and ask them the height of a commodious stair (it will be four inches). He will turn to the taking of colonies, and say that the English have captured the mistaken part of the Americas, where gold may not be found.

'And have you heard, mes Sieurs, there is a new continent discovered of the Dutch, upon the southern side of the globe?'

It is too much for dazed Flemings, who prepare to retire, but Balthazar detains them, anxious to learn whether they, as good Catholics, know how far England has traveled down the road of heresy.

'For we have here not only Baptists and Anabaptists, but Se-Baptists also.'

'What is a "Se-Baptist"?' Hendrik asks.

'Why, one that tips water over his own head, and cries out, "Yea, I was born Johannes Smithers but lo, I baptize myself, 'If-Christ-had-not-died-for-me-so-were-I-damned Smithers." I venture he is soon known to all as "Damned Smithers"'.

The Flemings gaze.

'Others again preach that each man alive is or may be Jesus Christ, if but he knew it. Then there are those that preach naked as the day they were born— '

'In all weathers?' Hendrik queries.

'Why, more in the summer months, truly.'

'What may they preach?' Rubens asks.

'I thought you would ask, dear Peter Paul. They preach the true method of copulation, as practised by Adam and Eve in the Garden of Eden.'

'That is a brave heresy!' Rubens lit with delight. 'Balthazar, you have converted me.'

'Indeed?' Balthazar was not delighted. 'There was another who preached against all laws, both on earth and in Heaven above. He had the cholic, and cried aloud when his arse brake wind, "Let everything that hath breath praise the Lord!" The multitude laughed but joined his cry, till each did shout at his next fart, "Let all that hath breath praise the Lord!" Poor soul, he was not well and soon he died, but, sad to say, the people loved him. He was borne to his burial with clarion bursts of ribald noise, both from those who loved him dearly, and from some who loved him not.'

'I thank you for this homily on the heresies of England.' Rubens stood taller. 'We must rest now. Tomorrow we shall converse again.'

In his room he wrote short letters to his sons Albert and Nicholas; Balthazar would arrange for their posting to Antwerp. Then he said a prayer for poor Isabella, and briefly for Clara Serena, the daughter they had lost. He saw still the haunted, haunting sad eyes of his wife. Dear Lord, give her peace.

He had grieved, however, for many weeks now. So perhaps there could be no surprise that he dreamed that night of Phlogis the Flame, the Indian Maid. He woke abruptly in a pain of yearning, both for love of the heart, but also in an anguish of desire. Still he heard the breathy husk of her voice.

But Hispania – Phlogis – was far to seek. Maybe he never would see her again. Some afternoons, when he and Hendrik had lunched with wine, and when he did not care to ride, they took a turn in places of resort. Especially if we follow certain cartoons, which Bloodsmith later drew with caprice, we may see them saunter in old Spring Garden, where they meet two sprightly handsome girls who linger among the orange trees. One is deeply dark and one light and fair, so Rubens thinks of his painting. The dark girl wears brilliant carmine, sorting with her crimson lips. The sandy girl with the pale face wears a rustling taffeta of emerald green but she too has scarlet lips, and both have deep kohl about their eyes which gleam, dark brown and sapphire blue, like jewels in a cave. Their cartwheel ruffs are wreathed in beads, and each has on her forehead a jet-black ghibeline which stands out on a stalk before her temples.

The dark girl says, 'No, *you* broach them, Audrey.'

'Bridget, I ache. Do you accost the gentlemen.'

'Mm. I am put in fear by those alien mustachios. Are you Dutchmen, good sirs?'

'We are,' said Rubens, 'Two gentlemen of Flanders.'

'Two *gentlemen* of Flanders! We are in luck today, Audrey. And I thought them two barrels, two tuns of Flanders.'

'Come, ladies,' said Rubens, who liked them both, 'we shall pass together to a private place, and there we shall treat you to Flemish love. Shall we not, Hendrik?'

Hendrik shifted his weight from foot to foot.

'*Flemish* love? Do we do that, Audrey?'

'Bridget, I know not. Yet I fear we do.'

'But what may it be? Do you think it is like to Platonic love?'

'Ah, if it is like to Platonic love, we are no such common trash.'

'*Come*, ladies,' said Rubens, scooping both in his arms. 'Have you a room where we may repair?'

'Saving your honour, we have the back flap of a goodly cart over there.'

'Let us make away,' Brant said quickly, 'we cannot be seen to roll in a cart.'

'Do you not see they tease? And so shall I— Maybe, sly maids, we may find soft straw in the stable of that inn?'

'Did you hear the fellow, Audrey? Not the stable of an inn, good sir, a stable is a vile place.'

'A stable is noisome, truly, Bridget. Now, had he proposed a linen closet . . . '

'*Good* love may be made in a linen closet.'

'Or in the chamber where the wool is carded.'

'Oh, the carding chamber has a most soft floor.'

'Come, you rascals,' Rubens said, 'enough of your banter. I have coin today for you both and more. Lead us to a house where a room with a strong bed may be found.'

They took a turn then down Cockspur Street, while Hendrik voiced in Rubens' ear,

'Peter Paul, I misgive. I was ever shy of such houses.'

'Did not your father, after you were breeched, offer to guide you?'

'Nay, he did, and I said, "Leave it, daddy, I cannot bother to go." Our priest hath told me, there are some women grow teeth in their cunts. I fear they may ravage my cock and my balls. Most deeply too I fear the pox.'

'Worry not for the pox, I have with me protectors.'

'What are these "protectors"?'

'They are newly devised. I have brought them from Italy, the land of love.'

They came to a house in Whitcomb Street, where they entered a well-appointed saloon. In one corner two young blades in short capes were gaming with a young and an older woman, while a tall man nearby, lean as an eel, strummed on a lute as he stooped squinting to the cards then flexed his eyebrows to the older woman. Across half the room, for all to hear, a soldier in a big hat and boots like fire-buckets exchanged retorts with a blowsy girl as she leaned to drain the tankard of a customer then leaving. An aged woman all alone smoked a long clay pipe, munching on some inner debate and hawking loudly from time to time. A shaggy mastiff with melancholy eyes gnawed on an empty leather purse.

Brant fidgeted. 'Brother in law, let us hi from here. I am all of a tremble, and the house is low.'

'I have been in much lower than this, good Hendrik. For think of it, where may a painter find handsome maids, who will stand naked while he studies them for hours? Whom did Titian paint, under the name of Venus? My wayward friend Merisi in Rome, where did he find his Madonnas and Saint Ursulas? In the stews and nowhere else. There he loved to repair. But come, luscious maids, let us sit a moment. I must put heart in my brother in law here, and give spirit to us all for the sport of love.' Rubens sat, and motioned the others to sit. Hendrik frowned then sat down abruptly, scowling and blowing his cheeks. 'Courage, Hendrik. Think also, when I paint a crucifixion, to whom, after Jesus, do I give my best care?'

Hendrik's brow knit like a tangle of thread, till he held up a finger. 'I have it! St Peter.'

'Dear Hendrik, no. It is Mary Magdalene. Always I paint her with golden hair, and beauty, and pain and love in her eyes. When I may I place her next to Our Lord, so a thread of her hair will touch his foot. Enough, though.' He called. 'The servitor – the man, I say.'

'You pleasure – sire?' A lantern-jawed man bent down by his elbow.

'A jug of Flemish, if you please.'

The lantern-jawed scowled, grave as a sexton. 'We like not the wine of the papists here. We have Norwegian Black Bastard – and Amsterdam gin, a true Protestant drink.'

'You have Dutch Gin? But that is the best. Fetch forth the Jenever! We'll drink with John Calvin. And a kettle of oysters, if you please.'

Rubens plied Brant with the gin, and fed him the oysters which the girls gladly shared. And so they ascended the creaking stairs of the house, while the lean musician, observing, trilled after them in his high counter-tenor,

'It was a lover and his lass,
    With a hey, and a ho, and a hey nonny no.'

Hendrik stopped at the chamber door. 'There is but one bed!'

'But it is a great bed,' the girls replied. Truly it was a bed where two families could sleep.

'In a great bed, the pleasure may be great,' Rubens said. 'Hendrik, quick girls, let us make ready.'

'Pull down thy pumpkin breeches,' Bridget said.

'A moment,' Rubens said. 'For behold, I have with me two engines of love.' He pulled the sheathes from his breeches pocket. 'See, they are of the finest chamois, and most wonderfully closely stitched. They were fashioned in Genoa, for the Provost of the worshipful guild of the glove-makers. They are tied on with these ribbons so gay.'

The girls were far from pleased.

'Sir! I beg! We have no need of these. We both are clean girls. The Groom of the Chamber hath made trial of us, and approved us for the recreation of the guests of the Lord Chancellor.'

'Bridget hath given joy to the new envoy from Savoy, and a captain of horse of the Emperor's dragoons.'

'Audrey pleasured the Elector of Saxony his pastry-cook. He made a nectarine cobbler for her. And the Archimandrite of Crete hath called me his anchovy.'

Rubens would not be put off. 'Nay, you rogues, I use these engines always. They are for your protection also, in case I carry, unseen, the pox.'

With misgiving the girls fingered them.

''Tis true they are supple, we abhor waxed linen'.

'So, sir,' Bridget said, 'Let me buckle on your armour.'

Softly she loosened Rubens's trunk-hose, then her black eyes flared. '*Good* gentleman! Aud, give eye! We have the Maypole of Flanders here.'

'Merciful Heavens! We shall be rent. Be gentle with us, we pray, good sir.'

'Fear not, brave girls, I shall be both gentle and slow. I shall caress thee before I come in, so we share the pleasure you give, even in the innermost arbour of love. Pray open thy legs, for I shall venture a little with those arts I learned, in my time at the court of Vincenzo Gonzaga, the great Duke of Mantua.'

As Rubens bent low Hendrik turned away, but then looked sidelong.

'Sir, we are old hands, there needs no such making ready with us.'

'In truth our pleasure now is as much in coin as in love. We are grown to be hard girls, from our wondrous success in this town.'

'And not long since, you were just girls. You played as girls. Fear not, I shall give you coin this day that will make your privy place to tingle. And yet my pleasure will be greater, if we share it both and all. But Hendrik, what ails you? I see that still you are not happy.'

'Peter Paul, I dither.'

'You are still afeared?'

'Nay, worse, brother in law. My prick is down.'

'Alackaday! But these maids I am sure have a cure for that. Dusky Bridget, bright Audrey, desist from me a space, to help this woebegone gentleman here. Bestow him on thy fulness of carnal art.'

'Poor gentleman! Now lay you down.'

'Sweet sir, rest here.'

Gently they soothed Hendrik upon the mattress.

'Brother in law,' he weakly wailed, 'I know not what will come of this, neither in this world nor the next.'

'Be easy, Hendrik, they will help thy body and thy soul. Be gentle, girls.'

'Sir, we can be more than gentle. Pray turn and lie upon your front, dear sir. Aud, pray you knead his back while I do work on his great toe.'

'Aaaaaaa,' Hendrik Brant said faintly.

'Now turn again, sir. Let us work upon thy front.'

'Oh, I tickle!' Hendrik Brant began to yodel, 'Ho – ha ha – hooo!'

'Peace, good sir, we shall work elsewhere. Bridge, do you press and tug on the gentleman's ear-lobes, while I here fondle his cock and his balls.'

'Oo – ah,' began Hendrik Brant, 'Ah – ah – *uh* – oh – oh – oh – yea – hwoof! – angels in Paradise! – aaaaah.'

'Good sir, we are yours,' they said to Rubens. They kissed and caressed him as he did them, till at last he, who always loved fair maids, came home in the warm moist deeps of dark Bridget, then caressed Audrey too for her fruition.

Then they lay back, the four, upon the bed, and a little time passed, till Rubens said,

'Let us not haste away. There are other joys we all may share, and you keen maids the best of all. For I would have you to make love the one to the other, mounting slowly, and with patient joy, but once more to the peak of pleasure.'

'What sayst thou! Peter Paul, for shame!' Hendrik Brant sat bolt upright in the bed.

'Be easy, sir.'

'Be not troubled,' they said, 'We have done this many a day, when gentlemen with phantasy have come to the house. Close thy eyes, if thou wilt. But come to me, sweet Audrey, as the gentleman doth request.'

'Gentle Bridget.'

'There's good girls,' Rubens said, 'You are great beauties both, whether you know it or not, and more handsome than any the King's court can show. Are they not, Hendrik?'

But Hendrik had turned his head away while his eyes bulged behind their lids like eggs in a bag.

'Ope thy eyes,' Rubens said, 'Many pleasures abound in the Garden of Love. It will do no hurt to thy soul to know this. But slowly, girls, do not make haste. Let thy pleasures gently gather and ripen. I will have no forced squealings here.'

Sweetly the girls soothed the one the other, brushing lightly and twining arms. They touched each the other's breasts and touched and kissed each other privily. Their bellies and thighs slid together and parted.

'Sweetest Bridget'

'Gentlest Audrey'.

Till they came at last to their fullness. After, all four lay again on the bed. Rubens sighed in a deep still pool of contentment.

'Hendrik, dear friend. This scene we have witnessed — it puts heart into the picture I have in my dreams, of two great goddesses who meet to embrace. Not that they may go so far.' He laughed. 'But the light of desire must work within them. Thus it may work on others unguessed, making way through their eyes when they see my picture. Well, but let us refresh. I shall send for more oysters, and more Dutch gin.'

They spoke easily as they ate and drank, lounging athwart the great bed. Audrey rested her head on Rubens' belly, which caused him, when she laughed, to laugh as well, which in turn set Bridget to laugh.

'Come, let us make the square,' she said, 'As we did when we were girls.'

'This is children's play,' said Hendrik Brant.

'Easy, Hendrik, it will clear our lungs

Each laid their head on the belly of the next, so when the laugh returned it must catch in a chain, one on one, till they were helpless in the great beast of laughter that devoured them all. Bridget's laugh came with a husky roll and Audrey's with a high silvery chime. Rubens' laugh reverberated from the depths of his lungs, while Hendrik Brant's laugh came in barks, brays and hoots.

As the laugh subsided they sank to dozing, till the room heard only their slow breathings in and out, like small and large waves in a peaceful sea.

Through the casement as they rested, now the sun was low, a russet-gold light spread across the bed and warmed and deepened and softly sank.

Till dusk arrived, and they stirred. Then Rubens paid his dues – with more for a gratuity – and quietly they parted, at the street-door.

From the shadows of a doorway across the street, a tall figure in a hooded cape stepped forward and, discreetly, begin to follow the Flemings.

Nor was he the last, for from a further alley there emerged a stocky man with a cap. Last of all came a broad-faced man in brown. He had a wide, flat nose and hair and beard like lion. They followed, at their different distances, the far-off figure of the portly painter, and his lanky companion also — who had taken to walking with a certain swagger, as a gentleman now familiar with the *houses* of London Town.

~

In his room in the Gerbiers' Rubens worked with pen and chalk on his great design. Britannia still was unclear, but in the meantime he added two other figures. Beyond Hispania and Britannia he placed a further great woman, Minerva the Roman goddess of Wisdom, who was born fully armed from the hurting head of Jupiter. For though Hispania and Britannia had put their arms by, Minerva still wore shining steel – as she needed to, for she laboured to push the great war-god Mars back into the Temple of Janus, where he could for periods be confined. Mars must be a large and vigorous man, also armed, but quelled by her.

'Now my meaning is clear,' he thought, sitting back. 'King Charles will understand without more words. It is true wisdom to shut war away, so great nations may reap the harvest of Peace.' The harvest was already there, in the fruit the satyr was ready to pour.

He had his design. He must start on the sketch, in colours, in oils, before a day or more would be lost in the excursion to the inn of Cornelis Drebbel. From his large chest he took out the small chest, with drawers, and his leather-wrapped flask of oil. From the drawers he took his colours, his vermilion, a small measure of ultramarine.

As he pounded the pigment, and worked it with the oil from a dust to a paste, he found he was listening to the quiet of the house. On normal days, he was aware of trenchers scraped in the kitchen, and the thwap of sodden cloth from the laundry. But today was a fair day, both the servants and the children were out. His own man Joachim he had released to go, as he wished, with Hendrik's man Willem: he guessed they would both be helping the kitchen-maid Marilian at the fair. In some way he knew that one other person remained in the house. He listened for her sound.

He stopped painting and laid down his brushes. The silence called him.

Out on the landing, the planks stirred and cracked. He came downstairs, and in the shadows of an alcove, sitting on a linen-chest, he found Deborah Kip. She looked up, red-eyed.

'Sieur Peter.'

'Mistress Deborah, I am moved to see thee sad.'

She made to smile, but said in a smothered voice, 'Sieur Peter, my heart is still perplexed.'

In sympathy, he also sat on the chest.

'Will you tell me what's amiss?'

'Words, Sieur Peter.'

'You have had words with Balthazar?'

'He is a good husband. But, Sieur Peter... he is difficult.' Her tears had stopped. She sat on the chest, and he beside her. 'In our early days, we often had quarrels.'

'So do all newly-weds.'

'I have run from him and hid in the garden, and listened while he called for me to come unto him.'

'And you went to him?'

'I have let him wait. But yes, when I heard in his voice that he wanted me truly, then I have gone to him. And there is one thing I can say of my Balthazar, which I do not think many wives in London can say.'

'I guess what that is.'

'I know he is true to me.'

She gazed down before her: her small straight nose was delicate, her red lips were slightly pursed; her gold hair was done up in braids round her head, from which stray hairs caught the light like gold wire. By no means could he kiss that neck. He was startled again by the sweet sad pain of love.

'He is a man of foibles,' she said. 'He will ever have his nightshirt tightly fastened, and his nightcap tied below his chin.'

Rubens smiled at this picture of Balthazar at night (being himself a sanguine man, and sleeping naked when the season allowed).

'He sleeps not easy, especially in these days.'

'I guess that my friend might toss and turn.'

'Oh no, Sieur Peter, it is more than that. He is sorely troubled with bad dreams. One night he jumped clean over me, in making from the bed.'

'He still was asleep?'

'He woke only in the midst of the room, and I called out to him, for I saw him distracted.'

Rubens shook his head. 'I am deeply sorry my friend is not happy, and yet the more troubled to see you distressed.'

Rubens returned to his room, and to his coloured muds of paint. But his hearing stayed keen, and followed Deborah Kip as she moved in the house. He came to know, just by the sound, in which room she had paused.

Peter Paul, no. He must make no trouble here. But still he saw the thoughtful face of Deborah. So let her sweet face be Britannia's. There her beauty would find its home.

He looked up to those shadows that never were still, in the corner of the room. His glance sharpened. There was someone there and there was no one there. But the harder he stared, the more he saw only wood panels.

Then he heard a tiny voice. It was so quiet, so close to silence, it must come from many leagues away. Yet also the man's voice was distinct and clear, it spoke inside his head. It said only his name.

'Peter Paul'.

There was a tender fall, a shade of reproach. He knew that voice. It said no more.

~

The day came when they were to visit Cornelis Drebbel. As usual Rubens rose at first light, to make sure that at least some work was done. He had begun the oil sketch for the great painting he would give to King Charles. Immediately there were two figures to add, an architect with a set square and a woman with a lute – a Muse – to show the arts flourish when nations know peace.

'Sieur Peter?' George Gerbier tapped on the door. 'Would you have me read Lucan to you?'

'If you please, George. You read latin better than any I know.' For pocket money George would read as he painted.

'Sieur Peter.'

'George. You want to ask about Minheer Drebbel?'

'No. Sieur Peter, my father will not teach me to ride the Great Horse. And he was Master of Horse to the great Duke of Buckingham.'

'He teaches you Greek and Italian and Spanish. What more must he do? My own boys, my Albert and Nicholas, I shall not let them near the Great Horse till they are older far than you. Pray continue with the slaughter at the battle of Pharsalus.'

Susan ran in, to show the dress of black velvet she would wear. And to tell them that her sister, Elizabeth, was given a sonnet by a boy she knew, Neville.

'He wrote it himself! But Lizzie says no one must know.'

George shrugged to Rubens, 'The secret will be out, I think, before the coach is out of the yard.'

And in truth the Gerbiers, with Rubens and Hendrik, were barely packed into their coach when Balthazar leaned round severely.

'What is this I hear about a sonnet?'

All eyes in the tight coach turned to Elizabeth, who blushed instead of answering, and dipped her head so her golden hair fell in a curtain round her. Only the reddening tip of her nose was visible.

'Mistress Gerbier!' Balthazar's voice scraped. 'Keep a closer watch, pray, upon your daughters.'

Deborah quietly nodded, and Rubens saw that Elizabeth had shown her the sonnet. Pressed close together, mother and daughter exchanged trusting looks, so Rubens thought, I love these Gerbiers.

The laden coach rattled onward, with Lionel and Marilian up on the box with the coachman and Joachim and Willem on the bench at the back. The leather straps creaked and squealed continuously.

George bounced between the window on either side. 'I cannot wait. Oh, we shall see new-fangled things!'

'Patience, George,' Balthazar said, though all of them were breathless with expectation.

Glancing from the window, Rubens glimpsed momentarily, between gables and angular stands of chimneys, the cobweb smoke-cloud he had seen before. If it came from a fire, it burned in a different place again. The look of it now recalled the funeral veils a great lady might wear, disturbing by a draught. But what troubled him, in the instant he saw it, was that, yes, there was a presence within it. A denser shape; or shapelessness; what? A figure, a beast? A strange limb uncoiled.

In a flash it was gone, he could not catch it again. He was putting the odd sight together in his head, from what little trace the thing had left.

Their road wound beside the old Tower of London, then down towards the Thames.

Hendrick exclaimed, 'Is that one house or three?'

They had stopped by a building with windows of many shapes, its gables pointing in several directions, and three tall chimneys at different angles. Outside on benches sat dockers and sailors, boatmen and porters, fishermen and fishwives in harangue, while a spindly harassed potboy came and went. A few chicken pecked at the ground beneath the tables and a cock strutted, jerking its head sharply like an irascible constable. Two boney cats prowled but kept their distance from the chickens.

In the midst of them Cornelis sat by himself, bent over a glittering something.

'Welcome all, in good time you came.'

He was dressed almost smartly, in baggy trunk-hose of his famous red, and a slashed doublet of deep turquoise-black, but both with his trade-mark patches and stitches, and round brown-edged holes where acid had splashed.

Balthazar asked, 'How are you busied today?'

'I am putting to test a new Blazing Glass. Watch how it harvests the power of the sun.'

It was a round mirror that looked somehow hollow, held at each side in a three-legged stand. When he turned it to a wooden spoon on the bench, a blinding spot of light appeared, made a wisp of smoke then broke into flame. Drebbel shook the fire out, and showed them the charred black spot on the spoon.

'Consider,' he said, 'with such a glass, but of vast dimensions, I could burn a citadel to cinders. Or if I set a Great Glass on a London hill, I could cook all the food the poor could bring. Yet the aldermen say no, like frightened mice.'

Balthazar commiserated. Rubens said, 'The power of the sun is the power of a god.'

'It is the source of all.' Drebbel pointed up, and all of them gazed upwards, squinting and blinking and shading their eyes. 'With the lenses I fashion I have examined the sun. I find it is not one but seven globes, which constantly move round each other.'

The adults knit their brows and Balthazar, as their spokesman, said, 'We did not know this.'

'Indeed,' Drebbel said, with satisfaction.

Rubens touched his elbow, 'I am glad to find you active, though times are hard. I know not what I would do, if I were not busy.'

'I likewise,' Drebbel said. 'Nor are my skills without demand. I am newly engaged on a great labour of drainage, to empty the swamp between Cambridge and Lincoln. I lust to begin.'

'I am heartily glad.'

'My friends, pray enter.' Drebbel opened the inn door, into a place teeming with noise and smoke.

'We shall take the air a little longer out here.' Deborah took the heel of a loaf from a table, and broke it for the children to feed the fowl. Also Marilian had sat down with Joachim and Willem, and with Lionel and the coachman. Probably Joachim and Willem wished the others away, but the others liked her too. They would leave it to the quality to look at wonders.

Drebbel nodded, and went in with Rubens, Hendrik and Balthazar. Beside the great fireplace a tottering docker brandished a slopping tankard and sang, while the men and women round him either talked loudly, or banged out the chorus on the table-tops. Drebbel waved across the churning air to a stout handsome woman flushed in the face, with once-blond curls all over her head. She sat with two men, one of whom, but discreetly, fondled her breast. She raised to the visitors a small pewter cup, then elegantly sipped from it.

'Friends, I present my lady wife, Sophie Goltzius. She makes merry, as you see, with one or, for all I know, two of her lovers.'

Hendrik's jaw dropped as though it would fall through the floor, while Balthazar said, aghast, 'I am amazed.'

Drebbel said, 'But so it is. The last time she was brought to bed of a child, I had the two of them fighting here, "But I'm the father," "No, I'm the father". They did no hurt for both were blind drunk. But a moment before, they caroused together, for we are all free spirits here. But with the drink an anger rose, and so the twain made fools of themselves.'

Balthazar clasped Drebbel's arm. 'Dear friend, your anguish – and your wrath. I could not live with that. I honour... I worship your forebearance.'

'As I honour you and Lady Deborah Kip for the true good faithful life you lead. Yet not all of us find the same good road. For we are born in sin and live in sin, and what then is a man to do? It is true, I could burn up Sophie and her rout, with my greater Blazing Glass. And would I then be better off? Sophie keeps the accounts of the house. Also she is the daughter of Hendrik Goltzius, whose engravings all the world reveres. Long ago we knew delight. Now I have a sweet maid all my own, whom I love most truly. She hath a pointed and parsimonious nose— '

'Ah!' sighed Hendrik Brant, 'I would I knew her.'

Drebbel smiled indulgently. 'She answers my desires with joy. Therefore, let Sophie Goltzius play! Think how many true wives there be, whose husbands have seven, nay seventy, loves.' He gave a meaning look to Rubens. 'Here it is but the other way round. For always I am happy to do what never was done before. As an Anabaptist I forgive, as I myself I would be forgiven. So saith our Lord, who spent much time in inns, as I do. I truly believe, had He known tobacco, and the joy of it, He would have given the five thousand a pipe to smoke together with their dish of fish. Peter Paul, Balthazar, Hendrik – will you not smoke?'

He took four clay pipes from a rack, and offered them round, together with a fragrant flask. He filled a pipe for himself, lit it from a tinder box, and for a moment was lost to sight in clouds.

'I thank you, no,' said Rubens and Balthazar, while Hendrik carefully chose a pipe.

'Minheer Drebbel, I have longed to learn this subtle art. I would smoke as well as a roaring girl.'

'Dear Hendrik, you are a kindred spirit. But drink not too much fume at once. Alack, alack! Poor soul, I warned you. *Slowly* suck – but then, suck deep!'

With weeping eyes, choking, Hendrik tried.

'But I forget Lady Deborah. There she is at the door. A hundred, nay a thousand sorries. A glass of sweet Malmsey? Chrisostomos, quickly. And for your youngsters, look! I have set by on that shelf a great dish of marzipans. With gingerbreads and candied fruit. Little mistress, pray choose, nay, take one of each. Nay, two.'

He had cups of ale brought for the men and himself. 'But you came to see the marvels here.' He caught the children's eyes. 'Would you see a dragon in a water drop?'

He ushered them into a further room – except that Rubens saw Balthazar hang back in the doorway. He was shaking his head, and turning between the ebullient Sophie Goltzius and Rubens himself. When he looked at Rubens, his eyes shriveled, so Rubens thought, Peter Paul, take care. What if Balthazar sees in my Britannia, his Deborah?

'Forward, friend Balthazar.' He hurried him through the door, where the others were gathered. On a table near the window there was brass tube, up on three legs, with a glass plate and a mirror under it. Drebbel had the children look in, and they gasped and exclaimed. The adults peered afterwards, at the writhing worm and beetle-shapes.

'My first expertness was in grinding the stoppers to fit glass bottles. All my lenses grew from that. But Peter Paul, I believe that you desire to see my famous Perpetuum Mobile, which I was commanded to show to the Emperor Rudolph in Prague.'

'Indeed. My friend Peiresc has spoken of it.'

'It stands behind you.'

They turned, to see on a further table a wooden construction like a great clock. Within it was a globe of glass and all round the globe, like a thick outline, ran a thin glass tube. The tube made a perfect circle: in some way it was joined to the globe at the top. Within the tube lay a vivid red liquid, crimson as Drebbel's trunk-hose.

'But watch,' said Drebbel. 'Pray all be still.'

The room sank into silent motionlessness, except where Susan and George quietly shouldered past each other to the front. As they watched, the crimson liquid trembled, and moved just a little so that within the ring of glass it was higher on one side than the other.

'What is that red?' George Gerbier asked.

'I say it is salamander's blood. As you see, it lives. It sees the light and stirs itself. It prophesies. You see that dial affixed to the globe. When the red comes to that fine mark, I know a storm will come tomorrow.'

He tapped the glass tube sharply, and red liquid jerked forward. He said with drama, 'But no – a great tempest will break today!'

The others glanced to the windows, saw no cloud, and looked back with scepticism.

'It can tell the seasons of the year, therefore I call it my Clock Calendrical.'

Rubens took out a tablet and pencil. 'I shall draw its true likeness to send to Peiresc.'

Susan was frowning. 'It doesn't move *very* much.'

'That it moves of itself is the wonder,' said Drebbel. 'But come, little mistress. I had said I would show you my portable oven.'

He opened a small door to a yard at the back, where more chickens scrabbled in the dirt. A wooden shed with a tin chimney leant against the house. Inside it, in the half-light, they found a coop where young chickens, between down and feather, picked their way daintily in the half-light.

'And this is my oven, which never is either too hot or too cold.'

In the dim corner they saw a large metal box, from which a high-pitched cheeping came. Drebbel pulled out the metal drawer at the bottom of it, showing them a thin spread of charcoal, white with ash but glowing red.

'Come, little mistress.' He drew Susan towards a hatch near the top of the box. 'Do you see what's inside.'

Susan bent close to the window, and gasped. Drebbel opened the hatch.

'Do you feel how warm it is in here? And – ah! – we are lucky.'

In the straw on the shelf the yellow fluff-balls of tiny chicks jigged and cheeped. Reaching between them, Drebbel pulled out an egg, just as the small crack in it widened and a minute beak appeared. As he placed the egg in Susan's open palms, the shell broke apart and a bedraggled piece of fluff stood in her hands, glistening and cheeping.

'It's so *beautiful*,' crooned Elizabeth, stooping to the chick, while Susan could only gaze in her hand, paralysed with ecstasy. George poked his finger-tip for the chick to peck.

'We must put it back in the warm,' Drebbel said. He gave each of the children another chick to carry, and stood back to explain his oven to the grown-ups. From its side, near the firebox, a bulbous shape emerged, from which a rod rose and moved a rocking metal flap higher up. 'The air, heating, pushes the mercury which lifts the float which pushes the rod so the cap is closed and the fire dies back.'

As they watched the flap lifted tremulously then closed again, as though it were alive. The movements were slight, like the liquid in the Perpetuum Mobile.

'Well, well,' Drebbel said. They did not understand. Even so, the cock outside gave, at that moment, a tremendous crow.

'Let us put all the chicks back into the oven.'

As he closed the hatch Susan asked, '*When* will you turn into a tree?'

Drebbel slapped his forehead. 'Ah! I had forgot my transformation. Come back into the inn, I shall show you all.'

He led them then into a yet further room, hollering down a passage, 'Christostomos!' The spindly potboy quickly appeared.

This room was larger than the others, with benches set, and a wooden partition, from which a shape like a jug projected sideways. Drebbel had them sit, and stood before them. Chrisostomos closed the shutters so the room was dark, then went behind the wood partition. Evidently another shutter was opened, for abruptly light poured from the jug-shape, and lit up Drebbel for all to see. The light caught him stoking the fire in his pipe, so they saw him through coilings of lit-up smoke.

'Good friends,' he said, 'be not dismayed if you see me translated. Now you see me as a man, but I ask of you, what is a man? A man is many and different things. The which to prove, you shall see me change extraordinarily.'

As they watched, Drebbel, and the thin mist round him, slowly sank to a deepening green. In the moving smokes you saw leaves and twigs, stirring as if a light breeze touched them. Drebbel's skin, already scarred, grew ridged as tree-bark. Great branches sprang about his head. In a hollow booming voice he called,

'Behold! As in Ovid, I am metamorphosed. Our lives are but leaves upon an ancient tree.'

Susan's mouth and eyes gaped, but all were staring. As the smokes stirred the light changed again, heating towards a reddish gold. Where the smoke was thickest a savage head grew. The tiger came, a deep coppery colour between the stripes. Its whiskers and split upper lip joined the marks on Drebbel's face. Its glaring eyes were beast and man. As Drebbel stepped back the tiger-demon grew huge, amid the spiraling smokes.

In a great voice he cried, 'Beware the jungle-wrath in man!'

He flung his arms up high, his fingers claws, gave a hoarse roar, and made a short run forward. Susan shrieked, George and Elizabeth cried, and everyone gasped, and reeled or stood, while one of the benches fell back with a crash.

But already it was over. Drebbel and Chrisostomos were opening the shutters so sunlight poured in.

Drebbel bowed. 'I am your humble servant.'

They gathered round him in awe. Balthazar fingered the jug-shape that was set in the partition. 'Something I know was done with this.' Hendrik continued to shake his head, while Elizabeth discussed the event thoughtfully with Deborah, like a grown-up. Susan and George were both being tigers, roaring and clawing.

Rubens embraced Drebbel. 'Cornelis, I am transported. You made a vision.'

Drebbel was pleased. 'After my show, some refreshment maybe?'

He led them outside, and had a table cleared where they all could sit to a dish of chicken poached with quince and turnip, followed by fruit and hard cheese; there were eggs in a sugar syrup with orange zest, a speciality of Sophie Goltzius; ale or wine as the adults preferred and milk or small-beer for the children. Marilian and her admirers helped a little with the serving, then sat to the same dishes at another table. At certain moments Rubens quietly watched as the four men happily vied to please and amuse plump pretty black-eyed rosey-cheeked Marilian. His own Joachim, he noticed, sat with some tension, and every so often watched Willem especially.

When Hendrik and the Gerbiers were deep-involved in arguing how Drebbel's show was done, Drebbel nodded to Rubens and they slipped away.

'I told you, when I bid you come, that I had a further purpose here.'

Rubens looked up. 'I do not like that sky.'

Drebbel shrugged and led him down a muddy slope, so they stood by the dark lapping waters of Thames. Drebbel's tumbledown inn loomed above them, with the London's Tower a grim square behind it. Near them was a large wooden shed, of old odd boards wildly tacked, but with a great lock set in its door, which Drebbel unfastened.

'Behold, Peter Paul: the device that holds the future hostage.'

It was dark inside the shed, where a great shape crouched, with many arms. Rather, it was like a boat upside down, whose oars stuck on either side, from leather sleeves. The oars were strange, like the webbed foot of a duck.

Rubens blinked. 'How can this sail?'

'Peter Paul, this is my Descending Engine. The third, and greatest, that I have made. The others were shown some seasons since, both to royal James and to the people of London. But this is my last, and great, design.'

Rubens scratched his head, his brow was knit. He mumbled, 'This travels through the water?'

'Both through, and beneath. I pray one day you will join with me – that we make a voyage. I had thought it would be readied today, but there are things I must still make good.'

'Yes?'

'Peter Paul, I have, within this engine, inventions that may change the face of peace and war for ever.'

'For the better, I hope, if that may be. I must tell you I am afflicted with a great impatience, to learn what may follow from my meetings with the King. If I fail in my endeavour, I fear a terrible war – and war from end to end of Europe.'

'Then I pray you succeed. But one thing, I think, we both do know. There is no hurrying with kings.'

Rubens sighed. 'Show me these devices, which you say help peace as well as war.'

'In time I shall... when my Engine sails. You will, I think, be wonder-struck.'

'By all you do I am wonder-struck, so I ask, what may not mankind do? I find many future-men in you, together with a magician from the ancient days.'

'And showman too – some call me a fairground mountebank.'

'I too labour to make a show, to make a *noise* to the eye so all may look. The splendours follow afterwards. You might call my paintings, a mighty masque.'

'But in me you see art and failure met. I am scarred, and ragged, and patched and poor. I earn my bread by selling ale.'

Rubens gave a shrug. 'I have been more lucky. Yet, artist and engineer, we are both seen as "low" by people of condition. Because we are those *qui manducat laborem manuum suarum*. We work with their hands.' He made a face.

'Although we are men of genius, both!'

'And so we are!'

Rubens thought, then added, 'Unlike Lucas Vorsterman.'

'Lucas Vorsterman? Why, he is a great engraver. As great as Hendrik Goltzius, my master. For I engraved, before grinding glass. Is it true that you and Lucas came to blows, that you fought?'

'He learned his place, I think.'

'You will find he tells it otherwise.'

'What!'

'Nay more, he says an engraver may beat a painter any day of the week, because of the strength his right hand gains, in pressing daily through the copper plate.'

'Puh! Tis snail's-pace work, while the painter may land a lightning fist. And so I did. You should see the great black eye I gave him.'

'Ah! You hurt Lucas Vorsterman? I must avenge him. You know not, he is my bosom friend.'

'Let us not come to blows ourselves.'

'Unless we must. You will find my right hand strong as yours.'

'That I doubt. It does not look strong.'

'No? Be on your guard, Sieur Rubens.'

'En garde, Minheer, for I am ready.'

'Except, why fight?'

'Indeed. We shan't.'

'I revere your works.'

'So I do yours.'

'We are brothers, maybe, in invention.'

'And so I think.'

'As for what's to come, and my sad works, if it were not for my daughter, and my sons-in-law, I would fear that all must fall to nought. Something may follow, by their contriving.'

'Heartily I hope so, as I look to voyage in your Descending Engine.'

'I look to see you descend with me.'

As Drebbel closed the great lock on the boathouse, he said, 'My great dream is of raising a power in the sky, that could hover above us like a god. That truly could keep the peace of the world.'

'How might that be done?'

'I am not yet sure. But all smokes and steams and hot airs rise… if one could but catch and ride them… if I kept them hot with my Blazing Glass—'

'And who would be in command of it?'

Drebbel frowned. 'True. Both the Pope and the Emperor would lay claim.'

'Then the Protestant Princes would fetch it down, or the Turk, or the Muscovites. Or they would launch others. So you would have war in the skies above, as everywhere on the earth below.'

'That too will come to pass. If I had but the skill, I would fashion a chariot of the heavens. I would study the seven globes that make the sun, and voyage beyond the furthest star.'

Drebbel paused in reverie. Looking up, Rubens saw that the dark cloud overhead had formed a vast irregular disk, which slowly grew yet bigger in all directions. Lightning flashed inside it, lighting it up like a bladder of smoke, and beyond the chimneys more lightnings sparked. Long thunders answered them.

They climbed the slope to the house and rejoined their table, where everyone now gazed up at the sky. When the thunderstorm broke they hurried indoors, and afterwards, when the sky outside made a rainbow, Drebbel showed them his harpsichord. It tinkled faintly but prettily when the sun was let to fall on the globe and drum behind it.

All these scenes were sketched lightly by Bloodsmith, in the period following that visit to London, when he had felt faint – dislocated – even transported – in front of Rubens' great painting. For the visit to Drebbel two large designs competed in his head. In one, Drebbel stands before watchers on benches with both a tiger-head on his shoulders, and branches also spreading wide to the walls, at once a man and a great beast-tree-god within a turning dazzle of mists. In the other, Rubens and Drebbel stand at the door of a half-rotten boathouse, gazing with mingled misgiving and awe at a looming shape within the dark. It crouches with spreading arms like claws, like a giant crustacean caught from the deep; like a future waiting to fall on the world.

2

The day of Robyn's return arrived.

He was braced for difficulties, but even so was unprepared for the actual shock of meeting.

The station hung in a grey chill space; as the train stopped, a bouquet of faces blossomed from it. How could he find anyone in this multiple creature?

'Stephen! Hello!'

She came towards him smiling warmly.

'Stephen.'

She dumped her cases down, and watched bright-eyed as he came up. It seemed that in her time away all their difficulties had fallen from her.

He hardly knew her.

I see a handsome woman, yellow hair, blue eyes, who begins to build a plumpness on the flanks of her face.

He made haste to kiss her, but as a kiss it was a copout – she gave him a quick surprised look.

He's brisk with questions, 'How was the journey? Is Leo back to normal? Does he limp?'

'No, it's all come back, or it seems it has. Obviously it was a warning. He just *has* to go for walks – and stop eating all that butter and sugar.'

As they walk to the car, he holding her bag, he doesn't feel married, he is with a strange woman. It comes home that for two weeks plus he has lived, thought, breathed another person.

Driving home, he sneaked glances at the yellow-haired woman. Her white flesh was odd and foreign.

'The difficulty is that if something like that happens again, well, he's heavy, my father. If he fell down, I don't know if my mother could lift him. She's got to start driving the car again, she's really let it go. I said, *you* may have to drive him to the hospital.'

They walk, tired, into the familiar house.

'I'm so glad to be home!'

'Do you want some coffee... a bite... do you want a drink?'

'Oh, a drink,' she says, which he fixes.

Fortunately Sally's soon back: their chatting leaves Bloodsmith free to think. He has supposed he could live with Robyn as usual, and somehow fold in his love with Mae: that, as they say, he could have his cake and eat it. Such meals, he sees, are not so easy.

But the home looks good, the accumulated newspapers thrown away, victuals cramming the fridge. Sally and he have worked, dusting and clearing and changing the bed-linen, to make it look like the house of hygienophiles.

Robyn's tired, they are off to bed early.

'Oh, this feels good.' She stretches in the familiar bed.

'Come to bed, Stephen.' He has dawdled in the bathroom.

He comes and she works close to him, affectionate, happy, ready.

He only kissed her. She murmured, surprised and baffled, 'Stephen . . . '

They lay in awkwardness. He could not comply. She was tired, and soon asleep.

He lay awake in the dark, recognizing the chemical change in himself. There was a chasm between them. While he wondered also, what's with Robyn? Is the affair over, is the lover gone? Was there *not* a lover?

Then where are we?

~

In the event Mae did manage to come, that one time before she left. He had made his studio warm, clothes quickly slip off.

'I had to see you before I left,' she said. 'I *had* to.'

'But how long are you going for?'

She named the dates.

'But that's for ever.'

'I'll come back, Stephen.'

He remembered when she said she was leaving for America.

'I've got a very end-of-the-relationship feeling.'

As he watched, her eyes, increasingly, shone. 'Don't say sad things.' She reached and held both his hands, they kissed with a tightening clasp.

'Stephen, it doesn't matter if I'm away. We've got something real, that I haven't had before. We'll be here the same when I get back.'

Will we?

'Trust me, Stephen.' Her solemn eyes endorse her words.

'I trust you.' Of course he does. Or at least, of course he must. His mood lifts. He caresses her, gently as a breath.

'Ah! You've greased me.'

He looks again at his hands, spotted cobalt and crimson. Her belly is smeared where he has stroked her.

'Reflected lights,' he murmurs. 'I'm sorry.' But then, of a sudden, inspiration comes. Standing, he takes a battered box.

'Sally left these ages since.' The box lid says 'Face Paints'.

'What are you doing? No!'

'Please, Mae. A moment! A touch of make-up.'

He waits, his finger tipped with bright yellow. She too is waiting. With care, like an artist, he traces yellow curves on her collar-bones. He gives her a blue third eye in her forehead. A dot of turquoize on her nose-tip.

'I can't use acrylic, it would set on us like a plastic skin. And I can't use oils, we'd need endless turpentine.'

'Mmmp.' A kind of grunt. Then, 'My turn.'

Her finger hovers, she thinks. Then she spots him with polka-dots. Two paisley curlicues. He squints down his body.

'This is not war-paint.'

'We can still take sides.'

With a smirk she adds snakes and ladders, and plays noughts and crosses across his chest.

'Stephen.'

She stands straight before him, almost at attention, waiting to see what he will do.

'I want lift-off.'

He finger-paints stars on her, a comet, crescent moons. He adds a sun and Saturn with rings. On her dark skin the wet colours glisten fluorescently.

'Hail, Queen of Space!'

She darkly shines to him, a slender-elegant one-woman Universe. Then he sees the smile rising through her. Daintily she takes the red and squeezes out a luscious shining extrusion. Into the other hand she presses a coil of blue. She bangs them together, making a purple with red and blue glints. Then slaps it on his face in patches, making a comic black-face like a black-and-white minstrel. A white spot goes on his own blunt snub.

'OK?'

He takes it in, gazing into the mirror – and nods with slow emphasis, 'Spot on!' He goes behind her.

'What are you drawing?' – she can't see her own shoulder-blades.

'I've given you wings.'

'Like Red Bull?'

He cough-laughs, 'Very good! So spread them. Fly to me, Angel of Anglo-Afro-America! Fly to me, Bermuda and Ipswich in one!'

'Give me air-space, please.' She motions him back.

As she takes a step, she does dip down so her arms turn to wings, in a slow lovely wide-stretching flap from her ballet days. For a moment her finger-feathers brush the walls.

But the talking's stopped now they intertwine as the welling flood-tide of loving desire spreads tingling and electrifying through all their cells.

~

After the event all their hues are messed. He points to them side by side in his mirror. 'We look like two bruises.'

'How do we get out of this?'

'No, problem man. I'll bring the turps.' 'Turps' is a joke, he brings canisters of hand-wash and dish-washing liquid, which he will apply neat and wipe off with tissues and kitchen-towel. He is well equipped for colour spills. Working so, he wipes them into a state of polychrome slime – in which they embrace again, slippery as eels. Their limbs lose all bone and slide sinuous as tentacles. Her eyes, in her mauve slime-face, are enormous and both dark, and brilliant as search-lights.

To his sink and taps then, to water and lather. He is dabbing ever more carefully and gently. Their faces are very close, nose to nose.

They are close to clean, between rainbow sticky mountains of screwed-up kitchen-towel which he gathers in dustbin bags. Both have mauves and browns caught under their finger-nails.

'You'll need a shower at home. And women's creams.'

'Thank you.'

They dress, they stand. Solemnity descends again.

She says reflectively, 'We know each other very well.'

'We're close.'

With a sad slyness, she says: 'Well, we used the time we had.'

They hold each other hard and harder, as though the wind may soon get up, that will blow them apart or away.

'Bon voyage, love.'

'And you – good drawing, Stephen. Rubens there is waiting for you. Stay with him! He opens the big window that you need.'

'You're right, actually. Thinking Rubens does that for me.' His brows take their quizzical lift.

There, that's it, already she's gone. All round him the Rubens sketches wait, his notes and scrawls, his zinc plates with their protective film. But he can't go there, this second. He daudles, broods. Finally he packs up, to head for home. Not that things are good at all there. There is a new hard frost between Robyn and him, and hot danger brewing in Sally. Also he feels, more than before, the difference between making unfaithful love when your partner is away, and doing it when she is at home. As if he gleams with his adultery, Robyn will see it all over him as he steps through the door.

So is it from foresight that, turning into their street, he sees the grey-black disk of the war-cloud, wheeling low above his roof? In its cloud shapes you could make out weapons, artillery-pieces turning with lightnings inside his head. Or is it because, from several doors off, he hears their voices?

Women's voices: Robyn and Sally. When they quarrel, it's Armageddon.

From the path you can hear that an unseen door has banged to shatter. He can see the loosened lintel, and plaster powder on the carpet. Sally, you'll break the house in bits. Like an echo there followed a fainter bang – that's Sally's door.

He steps into a house of quiet. He hardly believes what he cannot hear. There is no rucked carpet, no broken object. Following instinct, he enters the living room. Robyn sits there breathing hard. Her moist eyes, bloodshot, are so pale-blue they are nearly white; they observe him enter her field of vision. Her yellow hair stands up like a head-dress.

'I'm not having this, Stephen. She shouts and swears at me, and she knows you'll let her get away with it. If you weren't so soft with her, she wouldn't do it.'

'What happened?'

'I don't know what it is, Stephen. But I can tell you're not sorry if she attacks me. You've got a grudge against me, I know. Then you steer things round, so it's Sally who hits me.'

'I'm sorry I wasn't here.'

She looks away, sniffing.

'What happened?'

'You'd think she hated me!'

He sits in the other armchair. It crosses his mind: Did I nurture this quarrel, being 'together' with Sally while Robyn was away?

'Tell me what happened.'

'She wants to go out.'

He makes blank eyes, waiting for more.

'She wants to go out with Abigail.'

Still he looks blank.

'I know one thing, Stephen, which you've forgotten. Abigail's mother was on heroin.'

He doesn't remember, all he can do is make a serious face, when a boisterous voice hollers in their ears 'Liar! You liar!'

The door already has hurtled open, which Sally has been listening at. She stands in its frame as if in lightnings.

Even Robyn, momentarily, is startled. He stands, he calls,

'Have you done your homework, Sal?'

She ignores him utterly. Talking through him, with abrasive sarcasm, she grinds, 'It's not Abigail's mum was on heroin, mum. It's Nessa's mum was on heroin. Abigail's mum had LSD *thirty bloody years ago.*'

Robyn does not argue; she looks abashed.

He'll take the initiative. 'You don't go anywhere till your homework's done.'

Robyn, behind him, 'Don't tell me you've done it, Sally. I know she hasn't, Stephen.'

Sally's posture has changed. One arm akimbo, she surveys them, head cocked to one side, her made-up eyes gawping total truculence. Her mouth protrudes at them as if she has in it a gob-stopper, which any second she'll launch in their face. Her t-shirt rides high, showing bare navel.

Robyn has taken over. 'If you've done your homework, show us the pages.'

Sally gazes in mockery. She works her mouth, as though she will blow a balloon of bubble-gum at them.

He says, 'You will go to your room this minute. You will go and do your homework. Later we will talk again.'

She shouts in whooping contempt-indignation, 'I haven't got any homework tonight. There wasn't any.'

Evidently his face shows uncertainty, for Robyn says sharply, 'Do you believe that, Stephen?'

Sally has turned on her. 'I'm lying, am I? What *you* said about Abigail's mum was a lie.'

'Don't talk to your mother like that.'

'Oh no, who's going to stop me? Not you for sure. Doi doi.'

'Sally, go up those stairs and do your homework before I bloody clobber you.'

Contemptuously, furiously, she roars in his face 'I haven't got any!'

In the meantime, Robyn has acted. She has crossed the room and slapped Sally's cheek.

From Sally a gasp, then she's run to attack Robyn.

'Get her off me, Stephen!'

But he's already doing that. He has hold of Sally, has her arms pinioned tight.

'Get off of me!' He has to use hard muscle to hold her. By now she has turned about, and faces him as she twists and hurls. Her face in front of him is round and blazing: the furnace of youth.

'Let – me – go!'

Will she head-butt him? Will she spit? He is taller than her and stronger, but he cannot hold her for ever, and he cannot afford to let go.

'You will apologize to your mother.'

'I'll apologize hell.'

'You'll sodding apologize!'

She is writhing and hurling harder and worse. Keeping hold is like trying to hold a bomb-casing closed in the instant the bomb explodes.

'I am not an animal. Let me go.'

He lets go, pushing so she falls on the sofa.

'Apologize!'

She looks up, frank-eyed. 'I am not your slave.'

He will try quietness. 'No. Even so, you will apologize.'

What will he do, if she doesn't apologize? Will she burst from the house and not come back all night, so they cruise the streets, or ring the police?

Yet quieter, with almost no voice at all. 'You will apologize, Sally. That is a fact. You will apologize to your mother before I count to three.'

Her rage is sliding to contempt.

'One.'

She scoffs, a ribald insulting grimace.

'Two.'

She speaks. 'You're pathetic. Absolutely pathetic.'

He's paused, they are approaching three. What will he do, if they arrive there?

Sally got up.

'All right then, sorry. There, I've said it. Is that wonderful? Is that great?'

It had worked, the count to three. It always did when she was little, and still she will not push to the final number. Perhaps what Robyn said was true, she wanted a limit she could not push past.

Not that it was a good apology; it was ugly, an apology for an apology.

'You'll apologize properly to your mother.'

'I've *said* I'm sorry, what do you want?'

He felt Robyn's hand on his arm: they could let that point go.

'You'll go upstairs now and get on with your homework.'

Whereupon at full volume she bawls deafening in both their faces, 'I haven't got any homework. No homework, there wasn't any. You don't believe anything I say. I have no homework tonight.'

Shouting she banged from the room, and ran clumping upstairs. After her door slammed, they heard her weeping loudly.

They looked at each other.

Robyn said, 'We still don't know. She could be lying.' She looked at him narrowly, in case he was weakening.

He nodded gloomily.

They sat. They listened, through the ceiling, to Sally's sobs.

Robyn said, 'I don't know what's at the bottom of this.'

He only looked glum, but he was thinking, children sense things. Does Sally read the state of this marriage? Is that why she's going off the rails?

He looked at Robyn, who sat preoccupied: handsome, tired, thoughtful, serious. And that's the good job Robyn is doing, she keeps the limits there for Sally.

There was quietness upstairs. Sally would be rolling her rollie.

Presently Robyn went and talked to her. He let Robyn go. It was Robyn especially with whom she quarreled, it was Robyn with whom she would make her peace.

Later Sally came down. Her face was still flushed and red in patches, though this scarcely showed beneath the new lipstick and mascara she had applied.

'I said she could go out, Stephen. Till ten.'

'What! After all that? You said she could go out?'

'It's all right, Stephen.'

'It's a mistake!'

'I've talked to her. I think it's all right.'

Sally was quiet now, subdued and good-mooded. She was friendly with both of them, there was a low-key but kindly mood in the house.

Sally left but returned in good time. The three of them sat a little in front of a film before they went upstairs.

It was only as sleep overwhelmed him, that he realized how far he had been carried this evenings from Mae. The question ran through his head, like a pattering of rodents in the attic above, 'Have I brought my life into confusion?'

~

Then Mae was gone, and it was not clear when or how any message could come from her. He was far from her now. And far also from Robyn, though they lived in the same house. In the home he made up for not loving by helping more with cooking, by washing up for most meals, and by taking out the vacuum cleaner and sucking dust everywhere. Also Robyn was busy in preparing her lottery bid, so Print Positive could move to better premises. Together they decided which consultant to engage, to prepare the Pre-Feasibility Study. Together they considered comparators, SWOT analyses and the calculation of an outline capital cost.

'Thank you, Stephen,' she often said. As to love, it seemed she had decided to wait until their tensions sank into the past. This could only mean that things would be yet more difficult when Mae came back. But Mae was not back. At times he wondered if ever she would be.

His solution then was to spend as much time as he could in his studio. He would come home late and tired, but kindly, so Robyn understood how busy he was.

And busy he was. His truest friend was Peter Paul Rubens. He dug yet further into the 1620s, and on his trestle tables new drawings spread. Carefully he rebuilt in his designs the mansion in which the Gerbiers lived. Even to the rooftop (and who is that clambering on the tiles up there? Can that be Rubens himself, manhandling a canvas?) In the garden he drew a small girl and her cat. A youngish woman bending to cut a tulip, or standing to gaze, beyond the garden, to the Thames, at the bustle of skiffs in a dazzle of light.

He asked himself, What is it I am after in these Rubens drawings? Mae said, Rubens opens the big window I need. And it's true, I'm trying to picture someone the opposite of me. Confident, good with other people, with large-hearted concerns, *and* gifted with enormous talent. Can anything of it rub off on me? Someone who gets life right by nature. But does he, though? Did he? What was *his* problem?

He returned to the roof-tiles, and the odd sight of Rubens clambering there. That shot, like the others, came of course from Jens Claeys. To Claeys he mouthed, Guide me, Jens! To Rubens he said, Peter Paul, you don't see me, but I see you. Once more I shall follow what paths you take. Who knows, if I look round quickly, I may catch the lion-face – or the puritan hat – who follows where you go everwhere.

3

Truly, one of those sheets has a title scrawled on it, 'Rubens on the Rooftops'. Peter Paul moves awkwardly on the Gerbiers' tiles, since this is where he will lean his glistening oil-sketch, which is all wet paint. This is how, in those days, the oil in oil-paintings was let to dry – through frank exposure to air and sun.

Now the painting is lodged, and Rubens has his feet up on the parapet. He can lounge at his ease. In the canvas beside him, in the picture within a picture, we glimpse the gleaming dark tower of Hispania. Also: a luminous and distinctly sweet-faced Britannia; a Minerva shining in fresh-lacquered ironware; a scowling Mars shunted into his cupboard.

If we step inside Bloodsmith's drawings and lean back with Rubens, we see swallows dipping close by the eaves. Before us the Thames winds away in its ampleness, ruffling and shimmering, busy with every form of boat. In small galleys oarsmen lean back in white shirts. Upstream the view is blocked by some bishop's mansion, downstream there is a fragrant shining haze, where woodsmoke rises from the packed rooves of Blackfriars. Rubens makes out the columns, legs, and stilts, which prop up the houses on the waterfront. Antony Van Dyck had rented rooms there, but he had not stayed; he was an uneasy man, shuffling fitfully between England, Italy, Flanders. Every few years, their paths nearly cross. Now Peter Paul is in England, Antony is back in Antwerp, as if the man wanted to keep out of his way. Why is that, Antony?

'Ah, Isabella!' Rubens murmurs. The painting Antony made of her comes to his mind. He had not thought of it for years, but in that painting Isabella was serious and beautiful. Antony had given it to both of them for a present. That was when Rubens saw he must act fast. For Antony lived with them in the house. In the evenings he had seen Antony gaze at Isabella, and Isabella shyly catch that gaze... and return it. Once she caught Rubens watching her, as her glance left Antony, and then her face turned crimson. She blinked, her eyes looked all ways. Antony, he saw, was watching them both, his eyes alarmed, his mouth dropped open.

He had seen enough. It must be stopped at once, before they all came to grief. For he, Rubens, could be decisive. Quickly he planned Antony's trip to Italy, then told him he was leaving, within a pair of days. With a purse and letters of introduction from Rubens he would travel freely, see all the great works, meet the true masters. It was the gift of a lifetime and Antony, he knew, could not refuse it. To sweeten the parting further, he made Antony a present of the best horse in his stable. Antony must think it a wonderful gift, though Rubens' private thought was, let the nag carry him quickly away.

On the day of the parting they all were uneasy, and Isabella, he saw, was unhappy and cross. She and Antony both had tears in their eyes, so much so that his own eyes watered. Also, he *was* sad to lose his best student, to lose the one young man of true genius, who had come as an apprentice. Had Antony stayed, he would have learned still more, so all who saw his paintings would see, as through a gauze, the genius of Rubens behind that of Antony.

Soon Antony was gone. Then Isabella was sour, and sharp, and morose. He left her to her sadness, she could be left to forget. What was good was that he had acted fast, and saved all three of them from misery and shame. You did well, Peter Paul! One day, glancing at Antony's portrait of Isabella, he attended to the statue on the wall behind her, and thought, 'That's odd'.

All of that was long ago now, and poor sad Isabella lay in her tomb. Would it not be good to meet Antony again, to meet as fellow-painters, fellow-masters in one art? He should not be jealous, he was the greater

Master still. Nor should it seem they did not want to meet.

He sighed. Let the past stay safe in the past. He stretched out at length to drink the hot sun with his eyes tightly closed, quietly scratching his back on the tiles. A further sigh came, as he thought of his sons, and his home in Antwerp. Then a deeper sigh still, as he turned once more to Phlogis, the Flame: to the Indian Maid. Was she nothing but a dream, and a will-o-the-wisp?

He half opened his eyes. Nor was he surprised to see, far away on the rim of the city's roofs, his old odd friend, the brown shadow that never was quite like smoke. It was not high now, but low and spread wide. Again there was movement in it, almost as though giant figures lay there and slowly shifted monster limbs.

He looked for a little. It was far away. Then he stirred himself, for over the roof-ridge there came a new wave of the racket, the clatter, the shouts and the neighs, from Charing Cross. Before him, below the parapet, all is quietness. Sitting forward, he gazes down into the garden, where rose trees run from the house to the Water-gate. By a tulip bed Deborah Kip strolls, carrying a shallow basket. Just as he looks, the shape of little Susan, like a tripping star, trots to join her, with the young cat loping at her heels. Then they both look up. From high on the parapet he waves and calls. Deborah lifts her whole arm and waves to him heartily, with a strength that seizes his heart. 'Sweet Deborah, but I do love thee.'

He returns to his room, and works on paper with black and red chalk, playing with the scheme of his painting. Should he introduce Hercules, at Minerva's left hand, to join her in the struggle to discipline Mars? He sketches the flowing bumps of Hercules's muscles, but in the end is not pleased.

He has gone downstairs, and found Deborah and Susan in the great hall.

'Sieur Peter, what do you say to this dish of Rose Tulips?' For Deborah Kip has an extraordinary habit: she will cut priceless tulips, and stand them in vessels here and there in the house.

'But what a wonderful Semper Augustus!' Rubens studies the

blooms: none are plain, all are striped scarlet on glistening white. 'There is not a flower that you should alter.'

He smelt Deborah's fragrance. Her soft skin gleamed where her cream-white breasts were pressed up by her bodice.

Peter Paul, discipline. 'What work are you about, beside the appointing of the flowers?'

'We have made Aurelia a new collar,' said Deborah.

'A new lace collar in the mode of the Court,' Susan added. 'Aurelia has been a good girl. Not like Pleasance.'

'What has Pleasance done?'

'She does not do as she is told.' Susan picked Pleasance up, and swung her round so she banged her wooden head on a chair.

'Susan!' Deborah cried, 'Poor Pleasance! She's hurting now!'

But Susan was stern as she sat the doll down.

Deborah asked, 'What have you painted this day, Sieur Peter?'

'It is but a *schetz*, as the Dutch say, in oil-paint, a trial of the design I have, for a painting on the subject of peace and war.'

'Ah, it is a great subject. And this is the picture you may give to the king.'

Rubens smiles, but also raises his brows. 'If I can but find my way. I am perplexed for the *disegno* of it.'

She kindly says, 'You will not wait long. But Susan and I going to market. Pray, Sieur Peter, will you walk with us?'

'Why, yes!'

They set out for the market, with Marilian and Lionel bringing baskets for the shopping.

The market stalls were not far off, spreading from Charing Cross into Hungerford Field. Deborah chose meats and vegetables, and when Susan stared at the butcher's wood block, Rubens said,

'But see – the red of blood is the colour of kings. It is the richest great colour that an artist may know.'

Susan caught his eye brightly. 'Do you like markets, Sieur Peter?'

'Indeed, I love all that a market may show.'

Deborah looked at him then. 'Do you, Sieur Peter?'

'Why yes. If I paint the Horn of Plenty, when I show the Fruits of Peace, then they must be real fruit. Quinces, melons, pomegranates, grapes. My painting must be a market stall, and painted with appetite too.'

Deborah laughed. 'Grapes and pomegranates we shall not find here.'

With pleasure Rubens savoured the apples and strawberries and melons and plums spread before him. There were quinces too.

'*And* I see a Horn of Plenty here. But do *you* like markets, Susan?'

'Yes, I like the pancakes, and I like to see the monkey play tricks, and the bear to dance.'

Presently they found the monkey, wearing a miniature cartwheel ruff. Its quick fingers touched Susan's shy, reaching fingers, which quickly drew back.

'And there's the bear.'

But the bear next door was a sorry sight, surly and mangy and torn at the jaw from when it bit at its chain. Its eyes were hollows of sadness, it shambled heavily on the spot.

'Let us not stay,' said Rubens.

'Not that way, Sieur Peter. There they make cocks and dogs to fight. Come away, Susan. Do not look.'

'You are right, mistress Deborah. Susan, take Aurelia and Pleasance far off. But I shall stay, a moment. I must note the rolling eye of a dog in fury, and the set of the teeth in the slavering jaw.'

'Sieur Peter!'

'Gentle Deborah, forgive me. I must see such things for when I paint a great hunt.'

He left, and was lost to sight in the raucous close-packed bawl of men.

Presently he caught up with them, with a pale face but shining eyes. To himself he exclaimed,

'But the wounds to those proud and cruel cocks — and the splendour of their green and red and gold!'

'You have seen what you desired, Sieur Peter?'

He made half a shrug. 'Still it is a wonder to me, the fury of the savagery that you find in beasts. Beasts do not make war like men, but when they do fight, then you see the killing fit that is on fire in the heart of Nature. That you may see in men as well, in their fury in war to maim and kill. He who paints the great god Mars must know this. Likewise he who plans a mission of peace.'

Deborah nodded, but her brow had knit. 'Look, Susan – the pancakes!'

The pancake-makers sat on stools in a row, each with a three-legged gridiron set over a small log fire. They made and tossed the pancakes, and stacked them on further stools beside them.

Rubens inhaled. 'But I smell something richer than pancakes. Let us follow our noses.'

Deborah nodded. 'It is an ox day.'

So they ate of the ox roasted that day on Hungerfield Field. The flayed body, black, brown and red, unevenly crusted, swung heavily round on the giant spit, dripping and running with blood and fat, some of which was collected in pans while the rest sizzled sparkling in the charcoal. The hot fat meat filled their mouths with taste, so they all took a further piece. Deborah wiped Susan's mouth with bread and with her kerchief, while Rubens drained an earthen beaker of beer.

Afterwards, in quiet digestion, they went to walk beside the nearby Thames. Deborah sent Lionel home with the baskets, but kept Marilian with them. It was pleasant to saunter beside the wide water, where the quality, and the clergy and soldiers, and rich and poor families without end, promenaded. The river was busy with boats of all sizes, elsewhere clouds of midges danced near the surface.

'But who is this comes?'

A ripple of attention swelled along the riverside. A flotilla of galleys was coming upstream. Already they had lanterns and torches lit, all redoubled and reflected in the water, so they looked like a sailing palace; a consort of lutes and viols played, and a bright music of voices that carried to the river-bank.

Susan held her dolls up high. 'See Aurelia, see Pleasance. It is the King returns, from Placentia to Whitehall.'

Deborah said lightly, 'Do you see him there? Your friend the king.'

Rubens smiled, but narrowed his eyes, searching. He did make out a very short man, in iridescent satin, who seemed to talk gaily, a short woman beside him. But he saw there were other short persons around them, so he could not be sure.

'The king,' he sighed. He felt – he could see – the huge distance there was between them now. And the king was far from thinking of him, or of his embassy. 'I know not when I shall have word from the Court. Also I have news that worries me greatly.'

Deborah looked her question.

''Tis said the Cardinal will send a new French Ambassador. This is Monsieur de Châteauneuf. Him I greatly fear. He has made embassies to many Courts, he knows their arts far better than I. He may offer the English some treasure, to make a new Peace with France, and not with Spain.'

Deborah's face was serious, but still she said, 'I know not if the English will be so easy.'

The beautiful flotilla passed on, and faded towards the rising dusk. He thought, that distant king may give me nothing, not even an order to paint his portrait.

''Tis time we were home,' Deborah said. 'Come, Susan.'

'I'm tired,' Susan said.

'Well, there's no carriage near.'

'Aurelia is tired, and Pleasance too. Carry me!'

'Come now, Susan.'

Susan looked at them, then sat down with her dolls on the flags.

'Get up off the ground, Susan – now!'

Susan arranged her dolls' skirts, so they sat neatly also.

'Susan, up. I shall lock you in sea-coal house as soon as we are home.'

Susan clutched Aurelia close and stuck out her jaw.

'I shall have Sieur Peter to send for the Spaniard, whom he knows so well.'

Susan's jaw trembled, her fluttering eyes swung between them. Still she sat with defiance.

'Mistress Susan,' Rubens said, 'It is true the King of Spain is much to be feared. But I see Aurelia is tired indeed, and Pleasance is so tired she has fallen upside down. So I shall carry them.'

He bent down then, and in order to lift the dolls he lifted up Susan, and placed her on his shoulders.

'So I used to carry our Clara Serena, when she was little, and we had to hurry.'

They started back the way they had come, beside the river, till Deborah, turning, said, 'Why, Sieur Peter!'

He could not answer. His face, between the young plump knees, shone.

'You have remembered your daughter,' Deborah gently said.

Rubens swallowed, and lifted Susan down. Then she held Deborah's hand, staring up at him.

When he could speak Rubens said huskily, 'But she came here.'

Deborah shook her head, not understanding. Nor could Rubens explain what had happened. It was not just that he remembered, he found his shoulders remembered. He was back in Antwerp beside the Scheldt, when, walking with Isabella, he had carried the exhausted Clara Serena. But it was not a memory. He knew he was in London too, but a miracle happened with time and space. For the child on his shoulders had changed. It was not Susan at this moment, it was Clara Serena. He knew this from the way the plump legs pinched, and the way she rocked and bounced like a rider urging his horse. Clara Serena had returned to him, and that was when the tears began without check. Her plump legs held him hard, and her very voice said inside his ear, 'Gee up!' Then she was gone, and he knew she was gone.

Deborah touched his elbow gently, and Susan, on the other side, took his hand.

When he had breath, he said, 'I grieved for her. But I did not grieve as Isabella did. She grieved without cease, while I was busy with my fame. Even, I grew impatient with her grieving. I am ashamed to say it. I did not do as I should.'

'Grieve now, Sieur Peter. It is for the best.'

Rubens faintly smiled. They continued on their way, with Deborah beside him and Susan holding his hand. His grief swelled then slowly calmed.

Gerbier was waiting at the door of the house.

'You have been long gone,' he said. One could think he was enraged, though he checked his anger. But his few words to Deborah were impatient, and Rubens felt his red eye blaze upon him.

At table Balthazar hardly spoke. He harshly demanded sauces and spices, while his glance shuttled between Deborah and Rubens.

To please him, after they ate, Rubens brought down his oil-sketch from the tiles, and set it in a chair, and asked with deference for Balthazar's opinion. Hendrik also turned bright eyes to Balthazar, as though he had a share in the production.

'I title it, "Hispania and Britannia hymn the Fruitful Peace of Nations". A mighty title, I think, for mighty figures. I dare to wonder, may it be my best work?'

Balthazar slowly raised a dry eye to him, then looked back at the oil-sketch. He screwed up his eyes at it. At the end he sighed, and sadly, gravely, shook his head. 'It is a pretty piece, friend Peter Paul, and may be painted with virtuosity. Yet... the Geniuses of the nations... I had expected a newer conceit than this.'

Rubens swallowed. He was startled, nettled. Quietly he murmured, 'Thank you, friend Balthazar. I shall think on this.' He looked round to the family, thinking they would see his art. Balthazar was a wizened stick, after all. But this was a mistake, for Deborah, Elizabeth and George were gazing at the picture with faces that were puzzled, uneasy, not happy. Susan already had turned to her dolls.

Shyly Deborah said, 'Sure, when finished, it will show all your powers.' There was too much kindness in her voice.

Elizabeth gazed at it unhappily, it seemed she was tongue-tied.

George glanced to his father, then boldly spoke, 'Sieur Peter, I think it is too allegorical.'

'I thank you all,' Rubens said, 'for telling me straight your true opinions. That is always the best.'

Hendrik Brant looked nonplussed and began to fidget. Clearly nothing would come from him.

Barely making pleasantries, Rubens picked up the canvas, and carried it to his room. There he set it on chair, and sat on his bed to study it. He thought, what do these Gerbiers know of art? I should have stayed in the mansion Balthazar had offered to us. Was there too much likeness to Deborah Kip, in the thoughtful sweetness he had given to Britannia? Balthazar could have taken if for a compliment.

The problem was that as he gazed at his painting, the figures, their meaning slowly changed. For what was its great Truth after all? Hispania, Britannia, what was new in making personifications? Players sometimes dressed as Nations when they danced in masques at Court, even in processions in the street. And trying to shut Mars up in a cupboard, where was nobility in that conceit?

His door burst open, Hendrik never would knock.

'Brother in law, you need a change of scene. Let us go out upon the town.'

'Dear Hendrik, I am out of humour.'

'I saw that downstairs, and I know the remedy. Let us away to Bridget and Audrey.'

'I like them, truly, yet I shall not tonight.'

Hendrik departed, shaking his head.

Rubens sat in the dumps. Beside the hurt to his work he had other concerns. The sight of King Charles, so far away, troubled him. When would he hear news?

By candle-light he started a letter to the Count-Duke, but his eyes were tired from staring at his painting, and he put the letter by. He sighed, and then he simply sat. Someone watched him as he sat. In that shadowy corner, when he glanced up once, he caught the figure standing there. It was draped in black but with a brilliant white ruff. It had a sallow, exhausted face, its veiled eyes cobwebbed with sadness.

He looked away, and when he glanced back to catch that figure, it had already disappeared. He shook his head. He prayed for the well-being of his sons, and lay down to wait for uneasy sleep.

He woke abruptly in the night. There were noises, footsteps, alarm and commotion. Outside his door, he heard Willem and Joachim mutter in Flemish. Was there a fire? Was a thief caught? He pulled on his furred gown, and hurried in the dark towards the candle-glow.

At the stairhead stood Balthazar, in his nightshirt, with his nightcap tightly tied as Deborah Kip had described. Deborah stood beside him, with a pretty cap on her head, from which fair hairs escaped. She held Balthazar's arm in the flickering lantern-light which Lionel, in his nightshirt, brought towards them. Balthazar looked round wide-eyed, while Deborah said softly to him

'Be peaceful, my sweet. Be calm, my love.'

'Be at rest, good friend,' Rubens said, coming to him from the other side.

Balthazar rubbed his eyes hard with his hands. He was awake now, and the gaze he threw at Rubens seemed ferocious. His mouth worked, his eyes danced, as if he burst with words that held all pain.

'Speak, friend,' Rubens said.

'Think on your wife,' Balthazar snapped, like a quick sharp dagger stuck in Rubens' chest.

Then he looked about him, from person to person. Elizabeth, George and Susan stood in the door of the children's room, side by side in their nightshirts, staring and making wide eyes to each other.

Balthazar shook his head.

'I have woke the house.'

Deborah stroked his wrist. 'Come to our bed, my own Balthazar. When I wake and am alone in the night, my heart is perplexed.'

Balthazar said to her, in a gentle voice Rubens had not heard him use before, 'Dearest Deborah, I have broke thy sleep.' Tenderly he smoothed the hairs which strayed from her cap.

He turned to Rubens. 'Pardon me, friend Peter Paul. I have been distracted.'

Cajolingly Deborah led him towards their chamber. 'Come, dear heart.'

By the light of the lantern, Rubens saw the couple at the end of the landing, beside their door. Deborah still held Balthazar, and his arm came round her waist. Rubens was surprised by the pain the sight gave him. Was it possible, for all the oddities of Balthazar, that Rubens still had to see in this couple marriage itself, such as he, with all his loves, had not quite enjoyed, even when Isabella lived.

The servants, and Hendrik Brant, had shuffled yawning away, but the children still were wide awake. Rubens went to them.

'Quiet now, Elizabeth, George, Susan. Your father needs rest, and so do we all. To bed now, sleepy heads.'

'I can't go there!' Susan said.

'Why not?'

'There's a hobgoblin under my bed.'

Elizabeth and George gave big shrugs to each other. 'Don't be tiresome, Susan.' 'Susan, what a story you are!'

'I'm *not* a story. Last night he jumped out and bit my backside.'

'*What* a fib!' George cried, gaping his eyes and mouth to Rubens.

'Listen to me, all of you. I *know* the Hobgoblin, and tomorrow, if you are good, I shall draw his picture for you, with all of you beside him. I shall draw him with his horns and tail, and with seven noses round his head. But if you want to see him, you must go to bed now. You too, Susan, and you George and you Elizabeth.'

He spoke kindly firmly. Susan narrowed her eyes but went, and George retired frowning. Elizabeth smiled gracefully, and gave a dainty curtsey.

'Good night, Sieur Peter.' Her fair hair was fine as gold, he saw the beauty she would have as a woman.

'Good night, Elizabeth. Good night to you, George. And good dreams, Susan. You sleep well now.'

Rubens returned to his room, but when he sat for a moment he felt a quick piercing hurt in his wrist: his painting hand. He had an enemy, also, inside his body. Not yet, not yet, he prayed, rubbing his hand as he lay back in the dark.

Also, in the dark, Bathazar's words came back. 'Think on your wife.' What had he meant? Balthazar had never met Isabella.

With this question Jen Claeys closes one of his chapters, while Bloodsmith sits back from sketching the scene. With an intake of breath – for the clues are falling into place.

4

More and more he will pause, one hand on his etching press, and murmur over, '*Still* I've heard nothing from her.'

Mae had said it would be difficult to write to him or ring him; in some way Geoffrey was on the alert. After a week of no contact, the light was changing. *Will* she come back?

Being alone in his studio is not good for his love. Of course her absence can't be forever. Still, she's with Geoffrey, all day and all night. No contact, that's the killer. She could have sent a card, at least.

So here we are, on yet another morning, alone in the studio. A large sheet of cartridge paper, which he's tried to flatten, lifts at either end like a scroll. What will he draw – Rubens with the Indian Maid? He looks across the room, at Rubens' painting of 'The Four Continents', at the blood ruby the African woman wears on her brow. Is it passion? Is it slavery? Some question stirs within that face, within the thoughts of Rubens behind the canvas. Why does she eyeball us so directly?

Kings and Cardinals, then? But they too are remote. Instead, he draws shadowy huddled faces. Which face is Rubens?

For matters are darkening in the Gerbier house. In these sidelong eyes we see Rubens aware of Balthazar's look, and Balthazar devoured when he thinks of his guest. There is a worm in his sight. Too often he has returned from his dealings to find Rubens and Deborah have been home all day. He can tell from their faces they have talked with each other. What else?

How will these issues come to a head? But the answer is waiting, for

Bloodsmith knows from his sources what the ancient part of the Roman world was which Rubens sought to find in London. Rubens must describe it to Balthazar, because Balthazar must help him find it. To what shops or markets should he go? Which learned antiquarian should he ask?

Balthazar's response will startle Rubens. The very description of the thing inflames him.

'Wings?'

'With wings – flying . . .'

Balthazar glowers, the room as we watch grows quickly darker. There are candles on the table now. Balthazar's face is working, swelling, his skin growing hard and red. But why should he be so consumed?

He mutters, 'There are some things, Peter Paul, you do not know. It is best by far you do not learn them.'

This is the scene then, flared by candles in a darkening room. It is starkly visualized in *Chess with Kings*, in a passage which glares with needle hints: Rubens sits, Balthazar may stand. But what especially this picture shows is one man anxious to hear something said, which the other man keeps secret.

'You will tell me, Balthazar, what it is you have heard.'

All of Rubens is open like an open ear, his hands open on the table, his eyes wide, even his lips apart. While Gerbier stands rigid, as though tied to a stake. His arms hug his side, his eyes glitter like gems.

'Say? I must not.'

'Say.'

'I will not.'

Even as he draws them, Bloodsmith is asking, which secret is this? Will this be the discovery that turned Rubens' world widdershins?

It isn't clear. All he has is the sharp drama of a secret *not* told. Any great mystery is still to be guessed.

Till the drawing is done, then he stands clear of it. Enough of secrets which I don't know. There is one thing I know, as clear as day. I want Mae and no one else. Why think dark thoughts? I need air, away from this dark hot red room.

He is through the door, and striding down the street. Damn and blast it, Mae, where have you gone? Find a way, dammit, to send me a sign.

But no sign has come. No sign will come. And there is no Mae, in this street today.

~

Next day, in his studio, turning over a page, he comes to that scene which is known as the strangest in *Chess with Kings*. Rubens, coming home at early evening from his afternoon ride, finds a part of London where the clustered houses, the shanties, dwellings, sheds and mansions all jammed together, are wholly lightless. No braziers, beacons or torches flare, no candles flicker in windows. There are no people, no horses, no dogs. Darkness itself seems solid – has the pestilence raged here? Rubens understands that he has come, all at once, to the very heart of that strange, smoke-like shadow he has glimpsed in different parts of the city. It is like the home of evil. But even so, after hesitating for many moments, Rubens says a prayer, up on his horse, and crosses himself. Then, with a light movement of his heels, he prods his horse to enter the dark, where soon their forms are lost to sight.

As to what Claeys meant by this darkness, we must assume his purpose is poetic, since he called his book a 'history-poem'. We are not meant to ask whether a real fire smoulders in the cellars of a warehouse where rotting material, burning slowly, makes the air foully thick so you choke to breathe it. The scene smacks more of an author's metaphor, touching a dark meaning which Rubens must find very soon. This seems the clearer when we recall that the manuscript of *Chess with Kings* interrupts at just this point. As the large stars in the printed volume indicate, the pages that once followed here must be those of the famous 'missing chapter'.

With or without that absence, the passage gives Bloodsmith another strong print: the small but bright-lit form of Rubens on horseback, braced before a vaguely tentacular darkness that wells out of and round the tumbledown houses that are piled in a heap up the plate's right-hand side. Rubens sees peril, but also is tense with readiness to enter it. The black darkness there is wonderfully deep, made with a combination of mezzotint (the metal surface savagely roughened with a rocker) and deep-bitten etched grooves, so the thick paper holds a gleaming richness of ink which, if you set aside its meaning of trouble, you would think as luxurious as black silk velvet, or as delicious as a beautifully caramelized treacle.

Even so, for all his print-maker's skill, Bloodsmith cannot catch the last words Rubens murmurs, at this break in *Chess with Kings* where, making out the giant presence inside the cloud, he says over to himself, 'But I know you.'

~

At home he was no use to Robyn.

'Let's have a nice evening,' she had said, in a voice that surprised him both with its sweetness, and with its hopelessness, as if she tapped at his closed window from outside in the cold, but the window was locked tight, the key thrown away, the glass impenetrable plate. No sound could thread that pane, and even the sight of her could scarcely arrive, while a cold wind of his devising swept across the bare plain at her, and night deepened so they lost all light, both on her side of the glass and his.

Till the hour came. 'How long will you punish me, Stephen?'

'I'm sorry . . . '

'Is it going to go on for ever?'

'What?'

'You know what. I don't think you have any love for me at all.'

'Robyn . . . ' he mumbled, he was still en route.

'You can't forgive, can you Stephen? There isn't any point in our trying to go on.'

So, in that instant, they had reached it: the precipice.

He switched off the television. 'What do you mean, punishing you?'

'What do you mean, what do I mean? I stopped. It's over. Can't you let it rest?'

He was still catching up. 'You stopped the affair you were having?' The stationary air in the room was heating.

Her eyes were not contrite, just level and direct.

'Yes'.

There it was, the big secret laid before him. Robyn's affair was real, as he always knew. Never mind Rubens' big secret, here was their own big secret. But he thought, do I want all this now? Even so he was trembling, as if a blow had landed from which cracks spread.

'I knew you knew, Stephen. It was hard going on, after that. I am sorry, my love.'

But he was still taking on board her 'Yes'— yes, I had an affair, after all the denials before. From that 'Yes' a process had begun, like an accident starting in a nuclear plant, as the fuel-rods heat towards meltdown. Though no danger showed in his unhappy face, as she took his hands and held them crooning, 'It's been a difficult time, my love.'

At which the overheating reactor paused, and for a moment felt ready to melt in sadness. Could it be that all he wanted was to hear loving words? Though he was Mae's man now, not Robyn's at all. But he clasped her hands that had clasped his.

When crash! the front door open flung. In one instant they heard the ticking of bike wheels, the tinny blerplonk of bike on plaster, robust steps and exclamations, but already the door of the room was knocked wide.

'What, are you two just sitting there? Oh gosh, an exciting evening. And you haven't got it on! I've been racing to get here.'

While they stared she strode between them. The television, in deference, sprang to life: it blazed, it blared. *Unto Death* is here.

They gazed at the back of Sally's head, from which stray hairs lifted and leaned towards the screen, which was only inches in front of her face, pouring pink and veridian light.

'You have to see this. Tonight they have the spaghetti fight. And they open one of the attaché cases. The papers said they would. Look, they're doing it now.'

On the screen fat Mustafa, and beautiful Mohammed, and Ahmed the gloomy Mujahadeen in glasses, lift the top of the green case towards the screen. We cannot see what's inside, though a lime-green glow from inside the case lights their noses from below. Slowly the camera zooms in closer, to a half-heard murmur at once like songs and multitudinous screams.

'Allah Akbar,' they say. They exchange grave looks, and as the singing/screaming dies they slowly close the case... to Sally's fury,

'*What* a cop out! They're not going to show us. But I know what it is.' She shouts at the screen, 'It's a bio-weapon, isn't it?'

They retreated to the kitchen, where he sat heavily on a chair. In the large picture window, with curtains undrawn, he saw a second Robyn standing by the work-surface. In that dim, low-lit frame she looked haggard and blanched. And he – the light snagged on his nose-end, otherwise his face was in shadow. He looked an old man.

So he saw them, in the ghost-room opposite, in the weak reflection of the tired bulb. Yet a question hung. 'Who was it, Robyn?'

Her fingers touched his shoulder. In the window he saw her face lift uncertainly. She did not answer.

It was not that he expected surprises: he knew it would be someone he did not know. She would have avoided family and friends. Nor would it be Sean Raven. It would be some suave creep who had slouched into her gallery, a Damian maybe. Who knows, an Antoine? It made no odds, he had their number.

'Robyn?' He looked up briefly and saw her real face on top of him, slim-featured, blue-eyed, fair. She stared at him in a ravaged way. He got to his feet, aware that another Bloodsmith stood up in the picture-window.

'Tell me, Robyn.'

'Let it go, Stephen.'

'I'd better know.'

In the window two people hovered, hung out in the branches of the Judas Tree; two wraiths who became figures he had recently drawn. They were not him and Robyn, they were Rubens and Gerbier. Beside the table. At that moment when Rubens pressed to be told what thing it was that Balthazar knew.

'Tell me, Robyn,' he silkily repeats.

From far off in the living room there came a comic frantic shouting amid a noise of breaking plates, while Sally bawled out, 'Wicked!' They must have reached the spaghetti-fight. And as the Islamic voices surge his heart thunders in divination.

'It *is* someone I know.'

Robyn does not deny this. It is clear to him now that she is surprised to find he does not know. This news will be extremely bad.

'Robyn,' Bloodsmith says. He knows it is the last time he will need to say it.

Robyn nods. 'It was Adrian.'

'I don't know an Adrian.' He looks his puzzlement, while Robyn gazes back.

In the radiation of this gaze, a switch or trigger trips, so the long-strained walls fall down at last. There is an Adrian that I know. A famous designer of Euro exhibitions. My boss, my employer, the head of my school. Adrian Grieve and no other.

Elsewhere the television breaks in new bedlam, as the voice of Sally soars to screeching, 'Oh no! I don't believe it!'

'Adrian Grieve. But you don't know him, Robyn. You've met him, what, twice? at the Art School.'

Gravely she affirms, 'But I did know him, Stephen.'

He has sat down again, all the wind taken from him. 'He came to the Gallery?'

'He did come to the Gallery.'

' "Adrian",' he grinds.

She only gazes, in assent and sympathy. 'It was very difficult. It was filled with difficulty.'

But he, will he weep, dash his head on the wall? That boy-man, squirt, that neurotic control-freak.

Outside, in the picture-window, Rubens is alone now. Gerbier has spoken, and gone. Leaving Rubens grey-faced, dejected, sat like a sack. He is digesting the news (whatever it was) which burrows and gnaws within his gut.

'I think he loved me, Stephen.'

Loved her? Grieve could love none other but Adrian.

She rests her hand again on his shoulder. 'Let it go now, Stephen. It's dead and gone. It came to as sad an end as ever you could want.'

He sees her unhappiness, her soul in her face, which is open and stripped, pink blotched as from weeping, her blue eyes wide and wild. He takes hold of her hand, shakes his head.

'Robyn.'

Yet, Adrian Grieve. He has still not connected properly. Oh, but this is worse news than ever he guessed.

'Stephen, I want our home to go on. I want to stay with you. I love you, my love.'

When he looks in the window he sees only the pair of them. Ironically Robyn looks, in the dark space, like a fair-haired angel at his elbow, stooping to take him in her care. Out there he sees her hand on his shoulder, as he feels, under his hand, the warm vertebra line of her knuckles. Should he be exploding with fury of envy or be striding off to his own love, Mae? May this be good news? It sets me free! But then, Mae, Mae, where are you, Mae?

Above the racket of television, the strong voice of Sally broke out in hilarity. Something over the top had been said, it kept her gasping with shock and joy for minutes.

After a period Robyn said, 'Come to bed with me, my love.'

In the dim room beyond, he saw the sad couple stand, then he lost sight of them as he himself turned away. But someone at his vantage-point, like another artist, would have seen that couple move down the hall, and turn at the stairs and ascend out of sight.

What then did he do, the jealous man now the lover of Mae, who in earlier days forged visions of wrath?

He made love to his wife. Only minutes before, he could not have thought it possible. Yet it seemed he wanted it and so did she. He held her, kissed her, fucked her. But what love was this? Was *this* understanding? Even, reconciliation? Or was fucking her like this a way of hitting her? Or was he excited, was this his turn-on, that she had fucked the other man? Was this his way to reclaim his property? He would erase and cancel the other man by fucking her blind and fucking her dumb. Was Robyn thinking comparable things? There would not be recriminations. There would not be fights. They would fuck themselves together again. Also with their mouths, they ate each other, to the top-volume heavy metal, and blurred explosions of audience-applause, and the raucous yells of Sally's laughter, coming up through the floorboards like earthquake shocks.

They lay back like corpses. They had nothing to say. At the moment when he lapsed into sleep, he felt the house slip, as the subsoil shifted.

He woke in the night, snap sudden alert. She was fucking with Grieve, his employer, his boss. He sat up sweatily steaming in bed, a knotted sheet-end tangled round him.

'Fucking... fucking!'

Robyn blinked confused awake.

'Fucking Grieve!' He said it with fury. It wasn't clear if he meant sex, or was cursing.

Robyn has raised herself, awake now.

'Grieve – I loathe the man. More than anyone I know. *And* he's my boss.'

'I'm sorry, Stephen. But that's not the point.'

'Isn't it?' he growled. He knew she was right.

'The point is, it happened. I am sorry for it, I'm sorry you're angry. But you could be more unhappy — that I didn't love you like you thought I did. You're much more angry than you're hurt. There's a lot of anger deep down in you, and I don't know that it's just about this.'

He heaved around, baulked. And she went on,

'Stephen, please. What happened is your fault, as well as mine.'

'What?'

'You've been away from me. Like all that time you were off every day, painting your "Fire Girl".'

He has to gawp. She has said the name, 'Fire-Girl.'

'You *saw* my drawings?'

'Drawings. Paintings. Prints. Of course I did!'

'You went in my studio.'

'Of *course* I did.'

'You took my keys?'

'What do you expect? You leave your keys everywhere.'

He's gasping, floored, like the tables are turned. Is she saying that all of it is his fault?

But what to say? Any mention of Mae is dangerous now. Will his own affair come out as well? It isn't just the tables are turned, the whole sodding issue's gone upside down.

'So I had another model. Artists do, don't they? That was art.'

'Art my arse! I saw those pictures.' She is sitting up in bed, red in the face. He is cowed by the force that is in her face.

'Well, but nothing happened then.' He mustn't say what happened later.

'Oh really?' She makes a sour face, and mutters something.

'What did you say?'

She must have said, 'The more fool you!'

'What!' he shouts.

He's shouted too loud, her head snaps back like whiplash-injury. She's quickly up and out of bed. As the door opened, he saw her silhouette, vague against the boiling greyness. Then he heard her moving through the rooms, turning light-switches, shutting doors.

He lay getting nowhere, the house was quiet. Finally he heard softest steps, mounting in stealth stair by stair.

The steps crept past, to Sally's room. Of course, she would spend the night there. He heard Sally's mumble; she slept rock-solid. She would not wake if Robyn jumped on the bed.

The house went quiet. He wouldn't sleep, that much was clear. He listened to the quiet outside the house, the distant rubbering noise of lorries: far off, a train passed through non-stop. His passion was at a distance now, like the beating of a gong, away in the forest of his lower soul.

He must after all have gone back to sleep, for he woke with her voice saying, nearby, to him, to him,

'You're not going to kill me, Stephen, if I get back into bed?'

Kill her? He was surprised at that. But of course, she had no idea what he had been at. For her he was just the hurting, jealous husband who must for now be let to rage.

'Come to bed, Robyn.'

'Sally's bed is too small.'

'It is.' He made room.

~

In the early hours he snapped wide awake. The secret that Balthazar kept – exactly now the mists will clear. The words walk into Bloodsmith's head as a guest comes through a door.

A 'waking dream'? He sees them both, set as before: Rubens sits, Balthazar stands. The candles waver.

In a swallowed, almost cringing voice, Rubens inquires,

'Master Gerbier, there is something you have heard that touches... my Isabella?'

'Do not press me, Peter Paul.'

'Nay, friend. I shall press until I hear.'

Gerbier deeply sighs. 'For sure, they are idle words.'

Slowly Rubens rises. 'You will tell me that, in her sadness, my Isabella found a friend?'

Balthazar's nose lumps forward like a fist clenched to hit you.

'And this friend is someone known to me? Both in this land and in Flanders.'

Balthazar's eyes glitter in his mask-face, while Rubens murmurs to himself, Not my best student, not the one man of genius who came in my care. Not my dear Antony, whom I loved as a painter and as a man.

Rubens sits, as slowly as he rose.

At last Gerbier hurries, 'It is but words. Van Dyck hath made this brag in his cups, speaking in a low hall with drabs. He was far from home. He thought no person of quality heard, but there were gentlemen there who heard.'

It is not clear, at first, if Rubens has heard. He nods absently, 'I remember the soft eyes of Master Van Dyck.'

He sits below the swollen face of Gerbier, whose thrusting eyes are hotly bright, as if within his sympathy he still has a zest to see the world's great painter brought down to the perplexity of any poor husband in this cheating whore of a world.

And after all was it only this, Rubens' discovery in England, that his pupil Van Dyck had fucked his wife? Bloodsmith should have seen this long ago. Did he need his own shock to make him see it? For where's the surprise? Everyone fucks everyone. This must have happened every day, when a Master had live-in apprentices.

Was *this* the secret in the 'missing chapter'?

So. The intuition he had, that his story and Rubens' would converge, comes true. It is as if he and Rubens were two locomotives (a big and a small one maybe) running on converging tracks to arrive together at one set of points, in a crash that throws them both on their backs, their boilers bursting in smoke, fire and steam while their wheels spin like helpless limbs.

5

In the morning they felt unslept. They crawled to breakfast, where Sally poured cereals. Then Sally went to school. They had huge things to talk about, but Robyn could not stay for long, a lottery consultant waited in her Gallery.

She left so he left. He had nowhere to go but his studio. What to say for yesterday? Robyn was in the wrong and he was in the wrong. And Robyn had been honest and he had not. But fucking Grieve! The truth is, really, I never loved Robyn. I said I did but it was all put on.

Hurriedly he unlocked the studio door, as though the oxygen he needed were shut in there. He pulled out the Mae pictures, then hardly looked at them. He took a board, and charcoal, and began to draw. It must be Mae. He would draw and stop and shut his eyes, and lift his head like a blind head listening. Mae, Mae, you are my love—

Mae would not come. No, he must draw screwing couples, humping, fucking, getting a leg over. And not just anyone, but Rubens himself – he pulled out his old drypoint, of Rubens with whores. But who will this whore be? A gross sow, a sweet maid? A nutbrown girl, the Indian Maid. Bridget and Audrey? No, Rubens' head will be filled to bursting with Isabella Robyn and Adrian Grieve Van Dyck. Panting and sweating then sighing with bliss. O Antony! O Adrian!

Nor could Rubens screw anyone now. There are marks like charcoal streaked on his face – well, they *are* charcoal, rubbed in with tears.

Isabella. Robyn. Mae. My marriage, my home. Confusion and love.

By the pools of acid I laid me down, by the rivers of acrylic I made lamentation.

For as soon as Gerbier spoke, Rubens will know just how it happened. It was in the afternoons, when he rode out to take air, clip-clopping along the river bank, complacent with success. The servants rested, the house was quiet. But Van Dyck and Isabella are awake. They know how long his ride will last, and presently they are alone in a room. What will not happen, when a man and woman are alone in a room?

Art and tears: what good are they? A man must act. All I do is sit and draw, while Grieve orders me this way and that when he isn't fucking my wife. Up Bloodsmith! Never mind what I've been at. Right or wrong, I'll slaughter Grieve. Because that's what matters, it's *who* she fucked. It should have been . . . It should not have been *him*!

What would Rubens do, when he found out the adulterer? Even though he himself is an adulterer. He has a sword, he'd get a cudgel. Revenge, revenge. He has abused my honour! Rubens will be up on a lusty horse, galloping in thunder over the cobbles.

He's out in the street, up the road to the Art School. People will see, here's a man possessed. When screeches— Christ shit! He's nearly run over by a careering bus. Teenage driver, demon-king of the road. Imagine it, running someone over, with all the passengers sat on your shoulder.

In his head now Rubens and the horse are confused. Has Rubens, sitting backwards, fallen under the horse? He is caught in the reins, while the horse's big member whacks and whops his cheeks and chops.

Bloodsmith shambles on. He'll fracture the atoms of Adrian Grieve. And Rubens is righted, he spurs on faster through jam-packed London's fume of urine.

Let the building grow clear before both these men! A red-brick fortress in the Twentieth Century, bobbing and lurching as it widens and towers. The pedestrians thin and the entrance shows clear, while three hundred and fifty years deep in the past a large part-timbered house grows tall, with pargeted walls, swaying like a drunkard between the horse's pricked-back ears.

Bloodsmith's through the main doors in a hectic lather, his coat cross-buttoned. Oddly, no one seems surprised at his look.

While Rubens has overshot the house, and leans back at full yank on the reins. As his head goes back his hat comes off, its wide brim riding the hurrying air.

'Whoa, curse you!' But the horse does not know Flemish. It rears up tall, paddling feet in the air.

Bloodsmith, sounding like hobnailed boots, is clanking up the grass-green iron stairs. The uncertainty only grows in his head, as to quite what he is going to *do*.

Let Rubens lose hold and tumble down in the dust!

He emerges on the landing of offices. He could enter any one of them, with a query, a point to make. But the dark maroon door at the end awaits him. He stops for a second, but there is no turning back.

Though Rubens turns back. Scrambling to his feet, his jerkin torn, he pats the horse's flanks and leads it towards the pargetted house.

Bloodsmith has reached the maroon-black door. Does he burst in, or knock? As he takes the door-handle, passion repossesses him. It is the fury, not he, that bangs open the door. Alas to find, as door hits desk, an empty office – except for Frieda, Grieve's secretary, looking up to see him, surprised. The two of them gaze then at the Babel tower of folders which is piled up high on a corner of the desk. Jarred by the impact, it gently rocks, then in very slow motion proceeds to tumble, folder after folder sliding one by one till the remainder crash together in one burst on the floor.

'Sorry,' Bloodsmith murmurs. Still he asks the question whose answer he knows, 'Is Adrian Grieve here?'

'He always lectures at Goldsmith's on Wednesdays.'

'Oh.'

'Shall I tell him you came?'

And he (the final humiliation) in a dingy voice, can only murmur, 'No don't bother. I'll catch him another time.'

He scrambles some of the folders up, and leaves.

While Rubens faces the pippin-faced goodwife, who frowns at his Flemish hoot.

'Why no good sir, you are come upon us in a mistaken year. It is not till 1635 that Sieur Van Dyck will settle in Blackfriars for good.'

At which Rubens slaps his bald brow and murmurs in front of her, 'I am an ass.'

The goodwife says tut as she shakes her head, watching the prince of painters lead his horse down the road, and bend in the dust to pick up his hat, which he bangs on his knee so a red cloud blurs it. Wearily he remounts his steed, to commence the slow ride back to Charing Cross.

As Bloodsmith emerges in the howling street, and starts to walk back the way he had come.

~

But where to go? He ends up at home again. The house is empty, he throws himself from room to room. Is it all his own fault, what happened with Robyn? Because of Mae? I fell in love with Mae. Where is she now? I've made a goat-fuck of my life.

Upstairs, he turned on the bath-water. When it was deep and hot he got in, and lay like an island. What did he intend, to wash his grief and shame away?

He wanted music. He got out dripping, turned the bedroom radio on and splashed back in.

To hear some guy talk about 'Simple Gifts'. The old Shaker dancing song, composed by Shaker Elder Joseph Brackett, of Gorham, Maine (1848). It has conquered the world.

'Tis the gift to be simple, 'tis the gift to be free

'Tis the gift to come down where we ought to be—'

The Shakers were celibate, they had no sex ever. They made beautiful furniture and were great with herbs. Young voices sing,

'And when we find ourselves in the place just right,

'Twill be in the valley of love and delight.'

What did Shakers know of love and delight? But as the song repeated, he joined in, loudly through the empty house.

'When true simplicity is gained—'

Those words undid him. He was the other end of the universe from whatever 'true simplicity' was.

'To bow and to bend we shan't be ashamed,'

Dancing in their meeting-house, the Shakers bow and curtsey. But his voice had broken. Whether it was the simply the lovely tune, or the example of the water lying all round him, he had started to cry. Cry? Like some kid, fetching up sobs that hurt his chest.

He stopped short. He'd heard a noise.

'Who's there?' he called. It would be an astonished burglar, that found him weeping in his bath.

Robyn's voice, 'Are you there, Stephen?' But had she heard him sing, or sob, or both?

'I'm having a bath.'

She did not answer. He had better not be crying, but trying to stop made the sobs resume. The radio sang,

'To turn, turn will be our delight,

'Till by turning, turning we come round right.'

The Shakers lift their arms to whirl like dervishes while Robyn climbs the stairs. She's turned the radio off. Well, the guy was finishing. He tried to hold his mouth closed tight. But the hurt strain anger spite deception guilt of months were piled upon him, and as she came in the room he broke out in a single choking sob.

She sat on the lavatory lid where he could see her. Her white face was exhausted.

'I'm sorry I've hurt you, Stephen.'

He tried to smile, but that effort failed, and then, in a new gust of grief, he said, 'I'm sorry I was cold, and gone.'

'Stephen, love.'

'Robyn.'

He stood up tall in the bath, a wet statue running with water and tears. She stood up to get towels, but before she had got them the streaming figure made of water had stepped from the bath, and he and the woman in dry clothes had touched, and kissed.

As they embraced there was further melting, as if the barriers, the grudge and jealous bitterness, were running away as the water ran. In spite of Mae, in spite of everything, rock-solid obstacles were softening, liquifying as if he washed back through years to a kind of love for Robyn he had forgotten he could feel. For so long they had been ugly to each other, but they could let the whole of that go. He hurt inside: the unimaginable was occurring.

Dabbing himself in the toga of a bath-towel, he led her into the bedroom, as she looked at him, wearily and warmly, also with a love from the past.

To the bedroom, to the bed. Their hands moving in reacquaintance, re-exploring the estranged zones. He kisses her soft milk-white belly, her full breasts and long thighs. Most softly and delicately he kisses her shoulders, as her hands trace lightly his back and arms, quietly feeling and reclaiming. This was the body he was at home in, from which for so long he had withdrawn. At this moment all of his action and soul was in the repossession of this softly glowing Robyn.

~

They float in calmness, on the surface of this anomalous week-day mid-day. His mind idles: is this real, or nostalgia for what we had? His feelings have followed a crazy graph. And is it from nostalgia that another purpose stirs, for something he has not done for months and for years?

If later we return they still are there. Go quietly past the door of this room, or if you pause, for the door is open, stay unwatched while you watch. They rest in stillness, the woman and man. She is leaned up on two pillows in bed. He is sat before her, on the wicker chair they keep in the bedroom, with a large cartridge pad set in his lap; his water-colour box, and a clouded glass of water, are on the dressing table beside him.

He studies with warm, with kindly eyes. the slim-featured woman with the lovely milk skin, lightly flushed at cheek and neck, who gazes back in drowsing contentment, with an extraordinary glow and ripeness, lit by the sunshot window beside her. A gold light that feels like stooks of corn. The lacey edging to her white silk bedjacket makes a delicate filigree against the peach-tinted light of her skin. Her eyelids descend relaxedly. Be careful, or the posture will give her a double chin. There is whiteness on whiteness and warmth in the whiteness; the attractive full body, the fertile body, of the mother of his child.

Is this how he will make good any damage? Or is he maybe seizing the chance to make studies for that reclining Robyn whom he wanted in the foreground of his mural design? We hear the swish of his brush on the granular paper, and the catch in his breathing when his colours flood. It is grown so still, that the soul of the cat whom once they had re-enters the room, and settles where the sunlight warms the carpet.

Almost the picture will paint itself, his brush dabs and glides with no guidance from him. Of course he has painted Robyn many times before, and all that past practice is with him now. There comes a tingling buzz in his head, a sensation he used to get as a child when his father explained how you make a drawing. He must not look round, for someone has come who would be startled by his looking. Perhaps it is his tiredness, an after-effect of emotional turmoil, but he feels something too-big swooping from all sides down upon him. A changing light wheels through the air, and his perspective slips as the room turns widdershins.

He blinked and there came a change in the colours, as if his eyes switched to a better-tuned channel. The red cover on the bed was a deeper vermilion, more satiny and sheeny, like a silk of royalty. Robyn's skin has grown more creamily white, with yellow lights and hotter pinks, and threads of blue vein he had not seen before. She has grown larger, more sumptuously languorous. The corners of her slender features find a more distinct focus.

He blinked and the strange effect became dazzling, as if, in another extreme dimension, a greater sun emerged from its veils. The room seemed different, with more wood in it, the bed a four-poster: the walls were hung with panels of leather, painted red and stamped with gold. He watched his hand move in scallops of curve, like a student watching the art-teacher's hand, as if two painters were in the room, at work side by side though unseen by each other.

'Welcome, *maître*,' he murmured. For a moment he knew that Rubens had joined him in the room.

Robyn sighed and stretched in the bed, growing only more golden, and ripe and soft and white and hot.

Slowly the effect diminished, the exaltation of his eye receded. The light he had seen was taking leave of the room. But he did not stop painting, as the glow sank down into the texture of things.

As Robyn shifted in bed, the wood frame creaked and the ghost-cat stirred.

'I want to read my *Guardian*.'

'Read it,' he said. 'I've done. Or, I'm stopping.'

He wiped the brush dry on Robyn's tissues; and sat back abstracted.

Critics will divide on this famous water-colour, a pendant to 'Rubens in London', which is anomalous in that series for its mimicry of the style of Rubens himself. As if it had been the artist's aim not to allude to the manner of his predecessor, but rather to produce a pastiche of his art, in which aim, too, he had unexpected success, as if for the period that he made this picture, the great artist stooped close to see through his eyes.

Bloodsmith himself got back into bed, showed Robyn the picture, and lay down with her and drowsed.

~

This loving clear picture he made of Robyn was not to be the start of a new suite or series. He was tied to the un-ceasing wheel, which rolled him on through opposite frenzies. Again he pictured Robyn and Grieve making love, and wanted Grieve dead and Robyn hurt. But how could this be, while he was the adulterous lover of Mae? Or was he that, for where was Mae? Was something developing between her and Geoffrey, on their safari through West Africa?

Thus began the unfolding of Chaos in his life. What was worst was that Robyn began to 'tell all'. As if, in retrospect, he could be her ally. True, he could have said 'Don't tell', but also he was curious to know. He would snout it up, with his teeth he'd fang it to the light.

He learned thus about her complaints of Adrian: they were lovers, but still she must prop up his ego, just as a good wife is supposed to do. She had had to remind him when her birthday was due. He had something in him of Peter Pan and wanted her to be like a mum.

In these days, at work, he caught no glimpse of Adrian Grieve. Was the man lying low? You can run, Grieve, but you cannot hide. And when I find you... then. Well, but what, then?

While still Robyn pressed on with her 'sharing'. At times he just nodded while the gale blew through him, Oh Mae it's you! You are all my love, you are the love of my life.

Though still he saw there was a question down the road, which grew by the day. For what *will* happen when Mae comes back? Robyn has told him everything about her affair. How easy is it going to be for me to go on as before with Mae? Somehow he was cheated, the tables were turned, in a way that put him, the victim, the betrayed man, in the wrong.

Or would he and Mae declare themselves? The true deep love was theirs. They could tell the world, and take off together. This was their chance.

Could they? Would Mae go for it? Did *he* want that? Where was Mae, dammit?

~

In the event the Bloodsmiths missed the world news event. Had they been up to see twenty-four hour news, they would have caught the jump to night-vision. Beyond the silhouettes of palms, minarets and blocks the green fizzing sky flared dazzling. Cut to the carriers and airfields, where planes queued to catapult skywards, their jets fluorescent as they banked to destinations deep in the target territory.

But they did not see it. The images entering in digital code died unseen inside the set. It was only later, in abbreviated newsreels, they caught up with the images of buildings and people turned in an instant to dusty mosaics. Of the screams in that distant city not even their dreams had caught an echo. It was only when the Today programme startled them in the morning that they hurried downstairs to watch in hot astonishment the replay of events that were hours old now.

'I knew it,' Robyn said. They were both of them shaken to inarticulate rage.

The coalition partners sounded almost humble, awed by the success of their controlled precision strikes. Strategic targets, military, administrative, economic, had been taken out simultaneously, and with really a quite small loss of life, since it had been done late at night.

The war – a real war – had begun. Even if the targeting, the dying, was the other side of the world.

6

Bloodsmith still chews on the revelation he had that night, about Van Dyck and Rubens' wife, Isabella. *Was* this the idea that Jens Claes had, that was 'more than his life was worth' to say? The problem is that, after the 'missing chapter', the story resumes when some weeks have passed, and Rubens has other preoccupations.

Bloodsmith, in his studio, pores over his notes from old accounts. It is clear that Rubens packed Van Dyck quickly off to Italy. Rubens gave him his best horse, to get there fast. It used to be a story that art-lovers told, how Isabella and Van Dyck were sweet on each other. Artists painted pictures of their tearful parting, while Rubens waited nearby with the horse.

There is, though, another limb of tradition. Delving in notes made a year or more since, Bloodsmith discovers how the village of Saventhem figures. When Rubens dispatched Van Dyck to Italy, Van Dyck did not, in fact, make haste away; he quickly left Antwerp, but then paused in the village of Saventham, near Brussels. He stayed there for weeks, though no one in the Rubens house knew that then.

In various accounts, he stayed to paint a portrait of a girl he met and liked there (named either Anna or Lisbeth), or he stayed to make a painting of St Martin for the church. Certainly, Van Dyck's painting of St Martin, dividing his cloak so as to share it with a beggar, can still be seen in the church of St Martin at Saventhem. Paintings of Anna or Lisbeth do not survive. In any case it is clear to Bloodsmith – and surely that idea was in Jens Claeys' mind? – that if Van Dyck found a reason to hover in Saventhem, and stayed there secretly for weeks when Rubens thought he was heading for Italy, there may have been a further reason. For either no one in the Rubens house knew Van Dyck was not far off, or, maybe, one person knew. If Isabella was that person, they surely found a way to send messages to each other? Even to meet, Isabella to the market while Van Dyck, in inconspicuous clothes, waited in an upstairs room. Did some scene of Isabella with Van Dyck make the body of the 'missing chapter'?

Filled with revelation, Bloodsmith snatches out a fine-art reproduction he bought. On the back it says, 'Anthony Van Dyck, "Rubens mourns the death of his wife"'. In this painting you see Rubens, with his thinning hair, kneeling by Isabella's coffin (we glimpse her pretty profile) while a child clasps his hand. But who is the figure who stands behind him, this handsome tall young man in scarlet hose. He holds a portfolio tightly filled. A fellow artist?

But is this a Van Dyck? It has a nineteenth-century smell. Still the sharp-faced young man holds him. Why is he there, so prominent? There is an enigma, a puzzle, here.

Back to Rubens. He not Van Dyck is the subject now, and Bloodsmith must guess the scene Claeys does not give. He can do that, he has the history in his bones by now. But what picture to make, or picture within a picture? For if Rubens learns that Antony and Isabella loved, what jealous anguish will not be his? If he finds branched horns stand on his head, which he never glimpsed in any mirror . . . Though Balthazar Gerbier saw them clear enough.

Isabella, if you betrayed me, I'll hang you from the butcher's hook.

What to do? Isabella is dead, no arraignment may reach her. The adulterer, if it happened, is in another country. Well, his children at least are his own, Antony has not left a cuckoo in his nest. Nor is any shame known in Antwerp, Madrid, Paris, unless the Cardinal's spies found it out. Though who cares what a painter suffers? Here's a ducat, Sieur Rubens, to take yourself off.

If he caught Antony some day in a closed alley in Antwerp, if he had with him his gentleman's sword, one downward cut would slit his torso open so Antony's popping sheep-eyes, looking down, saw his red-brown kidney, his glistening entrails, tumble with sluicing blood in the dust.

But for his marriage... The memory comes of a ripe gold cornfield seen once in Italy, rippling away to the southern sky. When next he passed the stalks and ears were black, with a white crust on them. Maggots crawled, flies swarmed, it stank.

I shall say no prayer for you when I retire, Isabella, as always I did every night of my life. No, I was not true to you, but I am a man with the male beast in me, while you played the chaste angel, the sweet maiden and goodwife. That was your cheat.

Peter Paul, he will say, as all his being comes together in words, You will think no more of Isabella Brant, than if she had never been.

Nor is Rubens alone, through these long waking nights, for the patient presence, who has hovered in his room, grows clearer now. It is a tall sad man, dressed in black and with a white ruff. He has a worn, lean, weary face. His eyes are hard to read because the darkness wraps him like a cloak. A tingling in the air becomes the words, 'My son.'

Jan Rubens is here. Always Jan Rubens was with him, beside him, behind him, like a shadow. No: Jan Rubens *is* his shadow.

For it has been the Curse of the Rubenses. Adultery, the sin that overwhelmed his parents, and now, in a different way, overwhelms him. The griefs of marriage. Their marriage, his marriage. Every marriage has a hidden corner, in which adultery waits.

And here Jens Claeys can help, after all. A scene from his first chapter comes to mind. Not that Rubens remember his father's trial for immorality, but he has heard how the troopers came to their house. His mother, Mary Pypelinx, defied them loudly, but still they came clanking indoors as his father shambled forward, flustered and panting, throwing a face of pretend-bewilderment to Maria Pypelinx.

To no avail. Already the soldiers had tramped off with him, while Maria Pypelinx sat near the door, gasping and shouting to the children, till weeping overwhelmed her.

Nor was it many hours before the children run amok through the house calling, 'Mamma, mamma, what is adultery?'

For that is the charge that has taken Jan to gaol. To a hidden trial and conviction. To be sentenced to a lightless dungeon in the catacombs of Dillenberg Castle.

His father the adulterer, the shame of the family. Nor has he pictured the moment when his father fell; but Jens Claeys has pictured it. At one point in the book, an image comes to Rubens, small and distinct, like the little scene you see when you look inside a camera obscura. Very clear but far off there is a close-curtained chamber with an armorial fireplace, and a busy fire. There are candles on the table, where a man bends to papers with his quill. He is smart in black with a neat white ruff, and darkly, softly handsome: Jan Rubens, attorney to the quality, proud of his degree from Sapienza University in Rome.

Behind him a woman in a fur-lined gown limps heavily back and forth. Anne of Saxony, the lame princess, wife to Prince William of Orange. Faint yet distinct, like the tiny voice Bloodsmith heard before, come her waspish words, 'He has me wait on people I was born to precede. The daughter of Duke Maurice!'

Clear but thin, Jan Rubens says suavely, 'I cannot think but that Prince William is a full and proper man.'

To which Ann snaps, in gross plattdeutsch, 'Prince William cannot get it up.'

She is close to Jan now, her gown falling open. She fondles his head, and Jan fawns. He rubs his cheek on the heel of her hand, wheeling languid eyes to her. Then Jan stands tall above her. They have enfolded each other in burning coils of desire. Ann loosens her fur-lined gown so it falls, while Jan unties the strings of her shift.

The figures have grown big and close. With furnace-eyes Ann watches Jan study her nakedness, and the hollow twist in her spine which makes her buttock, on one side, swing up in the air. She lifts her thin leg and clumps it towards him. The chimney begins an empty booming, and a gust of woodsmoke blows back in the room.

Leaving for another room, she winds her body forward in a slow corkscrew dance so her up-turned tail wags in his face. Behind her he stalks, the handsome dark man, ablaze with excitement yet in some way sheepish, the black hangdog shadow that treads at her heel.

Let this be Bloodsmith's picture within a picture. Of Peter Paul Rubens looking into the past, and seeing his father, Jan Rubens, as he steps into infamy.

~

Chess with Kings resumes, after the missing chapter, with another imagined moment of discovery. We are asked to believe that Balthazar said, standing at the foot of the staircase.

'Peter Paul, there is something you will be pleased to know.' You might wonder, was it triumph – or malice – that spark in his eye?

Rubens looked round startled. What new bad news was this?

'I have found it.'

Rubens could only frown.

'That thing you sought. Your "fragment of the ancient world".'

'Oh.' Rubens' mouth stayed open. Found, after all? But did he want it now? Truly our wishes come home at strange times.

Balthazar waited. His crooked smile inquired, 'Shall we go to see it?'

'Where may it be?'

'In a shop for curiosities. 'Tis but a pace.'

Rubens nodded. Balthazar waited. Does Rubens want to see it now? Or is it the last thing he wants to see?

And for Bloodsmith, do I want to draw it now? Or is it the last thing I want to draw? Will it pull me apart; or pull Rubens apart?

Rubens quietly says, 'Why yes, my friend.' He sighs. 'I thank you for your perseverance. Let us go to see this thing.'

Bloodsmith stood. Enough for today. His next subject will be that 'fragment of the ancient world.'

7

Arriving at the Art School, Bloodsmith paused in the empty custodian's office – the man would be doing his midday rounds. The television there was blazing and blaring, beside the changing shots of different gates and spaces: the screen had filled with the Prime Minister's face. His hair was softly fluffy as if blow-dried in the last half-hour, his eyes were slightly too wide-open, excited, engaged, his adrenalin pumping. He was speaking of the recent strikes, and of his grief for the loss of life, small though that was by normal war standards.

'Yet every human life is precious – invaluable – that is why at all costs we must seek peace. Even when peace must be enforced *by* force.'

He spoke of his passionate devotion to peace. It almost seemed he felt more alive among war-risks, and in gravely consigning unknown people to death, than he did in day-to-day politics.

'Ho, Mr Bloodsmith, I'm sorry for that.' The custodian heaved in with his bad leg, and at once changed channel to a football match replay. 'Oh, were you watching?' he heavily asked, without changing the channel back.

'I'd seen enough,' Bloodsmith remarked, and left for the Print Room. He wanted students, absorption in work. Tomorrow was the date Mae was due to be home, but the thought of her arrival filled him now with confusion. There was a dark space inside him.

When the next day came, he said, It's wonderful, Mae's back! I can't wait to see her! But he did wait. He put off ringing. He thought, it's early, they will still be unpacking. Geoffrey will be in the house for sure . . . .

At the end of the day when he had not rung, he thought, What's going on? Do I not want to see her? His huge emotions were hiding from him. Can love just desert you? But it isn't that. What it is, is Robyn. Can Robyn stop me having my affair, just by making a clean breast of hers? He fell into a kind of grinding anger. Can Robyn make me lose hold of Mae? I won't have it.

The next day opened with a torrential downpour. He drove to the Art School; today, everyone drove. He sat motionless in gridlock under the drumming tympanum, knowing in his bones this would be a bad day.

He joined a mass of wet plastic macs, flooding and muddying the lobby. What if he met Adrian Grieve among them?

'Après nous le deluge,' a colleague said.

He went to the Print Room. The morning passed like other mornings.

After lunch he went abruptly to the telephone kiosk beneath the green stairs. And what if it were Geoffrey who answered the phone? He would deal with that when he had to. As the dialing tone continued, he found he was looking through the open door of the Life Room. At the far end he saw the anatomy statue, who stood in a relaxed way, all flayed bare, his sinews scarlet and his cartilage ivory.

Mae answered. 'Stephen – hello.' Was her voice formal? A chill began somewhere.

'How are you? Was it good?'

There was quiet, then she said, 'I couldn't write or ring'. He understood: Geoffrey had come to be on the alert.

'How was Africa?'

'Africa? Africa. I don't know how I never went to Africa before.'

She described the British fort, on a small island in the mouth of the River Gambia, where the slaves were kept in transit.

'What made the most impression, was how cheap and mean and tiny it was. Black holes of Calcutta. They shoved and crammed them in, then lugged them out dead or alive when the next ship came. You couldn't keep animals like that now.'

'Criminal.'

What else to say? He heard her breathe in, then eventually out. She moved to the people living there today, and how they all said 'No problem!' though their life was made of problems. Also a compound they had visited, where an old man lived with three companionable wives.

He murmured ruefully, 'Maybe that's the answer to our problems.' Then he wished he hadn't spoken, since he felt the air between them thicken to ice.

'Stephen, I have to speak to you.' Not good, he thought.

Hesitantly she began, 'These weeks... in those places... Geoffrey and I were – very close. More than we have been for a very long time.'

What is strange is that though it seems now that he knew all the time she would say this, still the words bomb in like a kidney punch. Silence on the line. He knows what she is waiting for.

'You want us to stop.' He does not even say it with a question mark.

Silence still. Probably she is swallowing. Maybe her eyes shine. A tremor at her lips?

'Stephen. Thank you. Thank you for liking me so much. I'm sorry.'

That's it, then. Game over. Love nil. Rather, nil nil. The true zero sum.

'No, let me say "Thanks". Thank you for coming to me. Thank you for letting me love you.'

He hears her swallow. She says again, 'I'm sorry.'

'I understand,' he says. Will she say more? Does he want any more? 'I hope things go well,' he says. 'Really.' Then, 'Goodbye.' Enough is enough.

He's put the phone down. Did she say 'Bye'? But the line is dead now. Dead as a cadaver in a mortuary fridge.

Through the door of the Life Room he sees the lurid dissected man. He holds one hand out nonchalantly, from which tendons and skin hung down in ribbons. Hi, he murmurs, that's me.

But *was* that it? Just like that, over, finito! The real news is not here yet. It has hardly begun boring its way to his core.

On automatic pilot, he taught the afternoon. The numbness continued, so he began to be amazed that he accepted the end in this funny cold way. Mae, dropping me like that! An anger was brewing. Angry with Mae? He had never thought that could happen, but the charcoal of fury was reddening.

Time to go home. The low sun washed in lemon light the forecourt and the car park. The surfaces of the cars were rain-cleaned and shining, he felt an odd lightness. I won't go home. I'll drive off and away. The open road! A voice said, You're free! From women and from emotion. From all that demand. Dammit, he thought, I'll buy that Harley, second-hand if need be. Then I'm off. Robyn can have the house and car. I'll stay in touch with Sally. He smiled: clichés came easy.

Then the inescapable occurred. Adrian Grieve crossed his path. Literally so, for Bloodsmith was edging forward when Grieve stepped in front of his car. Little brisk trim soldier of a man, with that quiff for a plume. His head was down, his eyebrows lifted, he was arguing with someone inside his head. He did not know in what danger he stood. For in the instant he appeared at the edge of the windscreen, the thought broke clear in Bloodsmith's brain: I thank Thee, God, Thou hast given him unto me! Surely *this* was the lightning-strike, blinding and white? Down with the accelerator. His car would leap forward as if rising in air, and hit Grieve amidships, breaking his back. As he hit the ground his head would split, his body be mangled as the car dragged over him. Bloodsmith's thoughts raced while time slowed and stopped, and the words came lucid. Grieve, you're dead.

As if in slow-motion, Grieve bobbed to the windscreen's other side. For what Bloodsmith had done, in spite of the revelation, was that his foot, instead of spasming the accelerator, lightly touched upon the brake. Grieve passed between other cars, his crest of quiff shining like wire in the sun.

Bloodsmith huddled in a car that idled in neutral. A great day! I've lost my love, and let my enemy go. I should cleave his bloody skull! All he could feel was confusion and loss. I'm good for bloody nothing, not even sodding revenge.

~

So the two great questions that hung on Bloodsmith – How do I go on with my affair, now Robyn has told me all about hers? Why is it that I go on in this marriage, when it's clear that it's Mae I love? – dissolve to air and nothing now. The story's over. A happy end? Robyn had her affair, he'd had his. Might home life grow peaceful after all? Forgive and forget? Hardly that. For the whole story was his fault at bottom. It all began when he fell for Mae. But how can you be blamed for love? Now it had ended, and he would pay the price in grief. It served him right.

It was only in the following days that Mae's news reached his centre. The feeling that overwhelmed him then was not like sadness or even grief, but more like being sick unto death.

Robyn these days was patient and kindly; probably she believed he was 'digesting' her affair. And he was nice with her, depressed as he was, he did not make quarrels or jealous rants. In truth, he was not thinking much about Grieve, for when alone he saw Mae all the time. His head became a cinema, he saw her smile, he saw her turn. Or her sharp scent would start in his nostril, for a moment he inhaled her, then he saw the close-curled back of her head, as she left the room without looking back. In his studio he winced if his eye fell on the River Nile, the bearded white man, in Rubens 'Four Continents', with his hand gently holding the black African woman. The man is elderly because the Nile flows four thousand miles. Bloodsmith felt millennia old with grief.

As to the repair-work on their marriage, well, they had each other back, and the house felt like a tomb. He'd nothing to give Robyn. In each room of his life, the lights were out or going out. If he had thought ever that in order to rebuild his marriage with Robyn, he needed first to break from Mae— Well, that wasn't true. For actually, without Mae, nothing worked. He could not have both the marriage and the affair, yet he could not have either without the other.

They went on long walks out of doors. We have all seen them or been them, those couples that have a problem that treads with them invisibly. They need the open space, wide sky, the landscape where the furrows stretch over the horizon. The sharp wind blusters and nips their faces, under a low cloud-cover which boils frozenly overhead. That English landscape of long hedges and the soul, where the wandering couples need huge space because they are in a closed tight box. They need the mean wind because inside they burn and stifle, in the oven of the marriage under strain which they can't leave. Nettles, barbed-wire, stagnant ditches. Let the chill wind needle, he is walking at the bottom of the trench of the bereaved. He thinks, I'm in the same state Rubens was, with nothing to chew on but the cheat of his marriage, and his own infidelities locked up in the past.

At home he and Robyn watched, together with embedded reporters, the attempt to re-take a mutinous region. The terrain was difficult, the tanks fired their shells and all you saw was distant smoke. At some point he thought, I am watching and not watching. There is war between countries from opposite sides of the world. Rubens fought war and I thought I could. Really I'm switched off from it. Love affairs are blinkers, they close your sight to all else in the world.

Then the aerial attacks came in, so that across the smoky horizon there was the pretty sparkling of cluster bombs, so daintily like a Guy Fawkes sparkler that it was hard to picture, within the smoke, just how the shrapnel from the tiny bomblets dismembered, maimed and killed.

8

Still he made progress with his prints. Shouldn't heartbreak and despair disable him utterly? Maybe. But when he sat down to his trestle table, art came to his etching needle just the same.

As to Rubens, he has come to that moment when Rubens finds his 'fragment of the ancient world'. Bloodsmith did not know when he sat to make sketches for the plate that he would bring an apocalypse on his head.

In the main sketch, as later in the etching, the cross-hatched lines nest in close. They shed deep shadow through the ramshackle shop, where candles brighten a dim interior. The scene is described in *Chess with Kings*. The plump painter we recognize, and bulge-eyed Balthazar. Hendrick Brant hovers close with excited eyes. That crinkled, aproned man must be the shop-keeper. Little interest has Rubens in his bones and dried plants, his stuffed lizard with bat-wings stitched to its sides, for something else is on the crowded counter; it rests within a light so bright you would think the sunlight has just found it, snapping down from a high cracked shutter.

'Dear friend Balthazar,' Rubens whispers, 'I know not how to thank you. This is that very thing I sought, as I told my friend Peiresc.'

Grimly Balthazar shakes his head, while the shopkeeper murmurs, 'The learned have assured me, indeed it is a work of the Ancient Romans.'

'And so I believe,' Rubens says.

The tarnished dark-brown metal artefact is an erect lone phallus, with broad wings a-beat as it flies through the air.

243

'Brother-in-law!' Hendrick Brant bursts out – he has puffed as much as he can bear – 'What *can* you want with this work of Satan? It is beyond abomination!' To the battered artefact he says, 'O noisome cod! Thou lewd appendage!'

'Why so, dear Hendrick? To the Ancients, the member was a god.'

'The cursed pagans! You pay them too great heed, Peter Paul.'

'Maybe.' Rubens ponders. If he wants it, he must hide his interest. To Balthazar he says, 'You abhor it likewise?'

With accusing eyes Balthazar mutters, 'You are right, Sieur Rubens. I like it not.'

With a show of sadness Rubens turns away. 'Ah, but look here, Hendrick! This is most curious.' He points to a nearby piece. It appears to be a charred and blackened dead bird, ancient indeed but as big as a goose, whose feathers have a metallic gleam.

'Ah this, great lord.' The shopkeeper lifts it carefully. 'This is the original Phoenix! 'Twas fetched hither from ancient Memphis by a company of Magi.'

The scorched head stares harshly with its indignant yellow glass eye.

'The Phoenix itself!' Hendrick screws his face in disbelief, yet fetches up his purse. He starts to haggle – which allows Rubens to add in more casually the Roman piece.

'Balthazar, I am satisfied.'

Rubens looks replete, as he carries home the artefact, wrapped in precious cloths. Beside him Hendrick clutches the aboriginal Phoenix, holding it, in Bloodsmith's sketch, like a child with a giant toy. Balthazar shakes his head, and displays his shrug to the world at large.

'I shall show it to Cornelis,' Rubens tells him. 'He will wonder at the art of it, as I wonder at the thing itself. But the Ancients! They saw the world with golden eyes.'

Balthazar gives a dry gasp. 'You have found... a curiosity.'

A later sketch shows Rubens in his chamber alone, gazing in thought at the venerable object while shadows hug them close around. That is like Rubens, he thinks, to want to own, for his own especially, some ancient secret power thing.

So far then for the preparatory sketches. Now Bloodsmith is deep in the etching itself. The shop scene of course, with the men stooped round the luminous find. What rich cross-hatching! The darkness glimmers with light like the sheen in velvet. He has breathed the bitter vapour, as his acid bites the crossed lines deep. With his feather he has stroked away the bubbles which cluster where the acid eats. Finally he has cleaned off the etching ground, for it is time to print. The 'artist's proof'! He has lit a candle like one in the print and moves the metal plate over the tip of its flame. For the steel must be hot, so his viscous printing-ink will soften and run into the deep-etched grooves.

Bending low over the steel, he sees *through* the plate, to another image in his head. It is the greater phallus. Through the burning ferment of the night of desire the divinity flies on inexhaustible wings. Never mind ancient Rome. It is huge and majestic as Shiva's lingam in India. It seeks the bowl, the flower, of the feminine, the 'yoni'. And the petals of the yoni yearn and yawn for the phallus. They will meet and deep, deep will be the joy in their joining. The snag is that the phallus will find more than one yoni. And the yoni— she will welcome more than one phallus. Hence Armageddon.

Or are we on the ground, in some prehistoric city made of red mud, in Mesopotamia maybe, where the gigantic god-phallus, mounted on a juggernaut, is pushed on by multitudes while down a converging avenue comes the vast bowl big as a radio telescope of the yoni on its own great cart? Tambourines bang, drums beat, wild ululation fills the air, for the processions will collide where there is no space, while in the throbbing air above gather the sex-gods of the human race: Aphrodite, Shiva, Egyptian Min. A demon vision, joyous and terrible.

Hardly seeing his steel, bending over his flame, Bloodsmith is exalted. Without the phallus, there is no human race. The divinity of sex, all quails before it. As to Mae... when I think about it, I know she will come back to me. She has said No and Goodbye before, and always she comes back again. She will come because I want her so. Deep down she will find that she wants me.

But he had bent too close to his candle. It took a little time to hear the crackling, though he caught a sour, unfamiliar smell. Either the room, or his head, was hot. Looking up to his studio mirror, he saw himself looking back, with flames standing like blades from his head. He had set his hair on fire.

It was not a sudden blaze. The separate flames rose from his thatch in a crown, with black points of smoke that began at their ends. He knew the flare-up would follow next second. His head would blaze then shrivel, and be a charred skull. With an odd detached, inquisitive awe, he waited, staring, to watch his death. Come, thou Death, and make me blaze!

After all hair does not burn in that way. Already he was banging his head with his hands, brushing his fingers through the crop. He put the fire out, it was not so difficult. But he saw around him, and in the mirror he saw, a horizontal blade of smoke, hovering like a scythe just over his head. The smell in his nostrils was acrid and bad.

Sitting alone in his studio, he gave a sudden guffaw. After all, it was ludicrous; it served him right. He sat on, shaking his head, with sighs. Well, it was long since he had laughed at anything. Till he thought, So, I'm the Fire Boy. Where *is* my Fire-Girl? Then he went quite still, sitting bolt upright with his eyes closed tight. The words gathered in his head, with a cathedral clang.

'Mae – come back to me!' It was a spell, a command. It was an act of will.

He relaxed. She *will* come back, whatever havoc that makes of all our lives. I want that havoc.

As to what he would draw, in the days till she came? After all, he had a subject. He had 'Rubens' Underwater Voyage' , famous from the *tour de force* in Jens Claeys' *Playing Chess with Kings*.

He would sink his vision in that descent.

9

For it was in Rubens' darkest days in London – unhappy for his marriage, anxious for his mission, in troubled recollection of his father's tragedy – that the invitation came from Cornelis Drebbel, to travel with him in his Descending Engine. Which would give him the chance also to show to Cornelis his Roman 'fragment'.

Invitation or summons? The lanky youth Chrisostomos arrived one morning, saying simply that Rubens should come that day, alone. Displeased by the order, still Rubens followed Chrisostomos through unknown streets, in his pocket the Roman bronze. There was low cloud and the wind nipped. When they came beside the Thames the waters were turbid, and in some way the surly trudge of the river chimed with a weeping like bleeding inside him. Seeing the muddy slop at the water's edge he thought of drowned sailors, lost lives, sunk hopes. He too had nearly drowned. He remembered the slow grieving that overwhelmed Isabella. Faithless Isabella. In the moaning of the wind he heard her sighs. His own death might be not far off. There was a hurt in his joints that had grown as he came.

'I see you sad,' Drebbel called, as they arrived at a landing stage. 'But this was a night wind. My *perpetuum mobile* has prophesied that it will fall.'

It seemed Drebbel had travelled upstream to meet him, for the upside-down boat was there beside him, moored to a post. Its strange oars rested on the water.

'I am never sad,' Rubens said., 'and I joy to see your Engine.'

'With a stout-hearted crew.' Drebbel motioned to the menacing giants beside him.

'Your servant, sirs.' Rubens dipped his head.

'Yours, y'wuship.' They looked like men who had been told to admire him. His mood brightened.

'You are ready?' said Drebbel.

Rubens sighed, nodded. Pull yourself together, Peter Paul.

Drebbel balanced now on top of the boat. Carefully he lifted the leather-covered lid.

'They enter first.' He meant the oarsmen. 'Hey! Steady! Easy now!'

The vessel bucked so it almost tipped over, as the big men disappeared through the vent.

'Now I,' said Drebbel. He had climbed half-in. 'Your hand, mon Sieur.'

Reaching, he helped Rubens onto the tipping hull. Inside the boat there were steps going down. Drebbel pulled the lid shut, and screwed its clamps tight.

The space was so tight that Rubens bent nearly double. In the glow from the windows he saw the oarsmen settled on their benches. He nodded once more.

'Y'Wuship,' some muttered.

Most astonishing was to see, beneath the wooden bar on which each pressed his feet, water: lapping, greenish, cloudy. The platform where he stood stopped short. Drebbel saw him staring.

'Yes, that is the river. Thus sinking is easier.' He motioned to the two carved chairs beside them, and they sat. Rubens rubbed his cramped neck, and gazed through the distorting glass of the window. In the shelf before him a compass was set.

'Down,' Drebbel called.

Turning, Rubens saw the oarsmen bending over and pulling on cords, so they fetched up, as it seemed, baskets of rocks that had rested on the river-bed. The water-level outside the windows rose, the light grew dim. Rubens stifled, for a moment he felt the terror of his own near-drowning. Then the window showed only greenness. With calmer eyes he watched the wavering weeds, where a grey shape stirred. A trout? A pike?

Drebbel bent to a glass tube that stood up from the bench and held a silver liquid. When it reached a certain mark, Drebbel called to the oarsmen, then turned to Rubens.

'Now, Peter Paul, we voyage where few have voyaged before.'

A creaking sound came from the leather cuffs of the oars, as the trailing weeds fell away. A flat fish like an ugly face goggled at them momentarily. Drebbel pointed upwards, and Rubens saw the keel then the rudder of some ship. Minnows flicked by as they passed the thick hawser running down to the anchor. A water-snail had begun to climb up the window.

The dim light wheeled, the vessel turned.

'We must be sure to make headway upstream, lest the current sweep us away. We are passing the pier where Cherry Gardens is planned.'

Overhead they saw the bottoms of skiffs, splashing paddles. A galley passed quickly, its oars beating evenly – it could be the King. Ahead of them the river-bed was thick with objects. A wagon wheel stuck up from the weeds, tangled with fishing-nets. They saw a ladder, broken baskets and pots, bottles, a hay-rake, a rusting helmet. Was that a dead sheep? Clots of wool strung away from the reddened bones. And stranger things: a four-poster bed trailed weeds in lieu of curtains, its rotted posts sagging awry; a bulbous carved armchair lay flat on its back like a fat man who had tipped over laughing too hard; a carriage of the quality leaned over drunkenly, crusted with limpets, clouds of tiny black fish swarming through it.

'But how did that come there?'

'On its wheels, maybe? Some gang of fellows chucked it in. It floated a while and then it sank. The tides push, the currents pull – everything slowly comes about here.'

The river bed sank lower, they passed a wrecked caravel. Its masts had snapped or rotted off, many timbers were gone though the ribs remained. The tiller still stood. For all he knew it could be decades old.

Then there was only green darkness below them, and green-brown dimness in front. They hung in space, though still there was the creaking noise of the oars.

'But look – a prize!'

Drebbel pointed to a vast curved shape like a whale.

'The admiral's warship, nothing less. And now you will see my further device.'

From beside him Drebbel took a small keg, covered with pitch. A spool of twine was attached to it.

'Refreshment?' Rubens murmured.

'Oh yes!' Drebbel laughed. 'This is my latest water-petard.'

'A water-petard? You mean, a mortar? It bursts.'

'Indeed! It is packed in tight with saltpetre, and sealed as you see.' He indicated the water that lapped inside the boat. 'A diver may enter the river here, and attach the petard to the underside of a warship. Then he swims back, unwinding the twine which he hands to me. There is a flint-lock in the keg, which with one tug ignites. Kerbang! So the vessel sinks. The weight of its cannon drag it down.'

Drebbel's face shone greenly, his eyes had lit. 'Maybe too it sets off the powder kegs inside the ship. Then all is burst.'

'And those who can't swim... drown?'

Drebbel shrugged. 'War is war, Peter Paul. For just think, with this engine and my water-petards I could blow an armada to the skies. But think of the victory!'

'I did not know you were so bent on war.'

'No? War is one partition of my art.' His voice rose high. 'When Britain laid siege to La Rochelle, I was master of the fire-ships to the great Duke of Buckingham, him that royal James did love, but, sad to say, he died.'

'I am dismayed. I came here to make a Peace, as you do know, I think.'

'Most honoured friend... but that is why I show you this. With such a boat war has to cease. It is not seen. No vessel is safe. No invasion by sea may be set forth.'

'You mean if all have such a boat?'

'It must be so – and you may bring this thing to pass. For if the King of Spain learns of this boat, as he may, but with a word from you . . . And if England knows that Spain does know. And the French then want one for themselves. And the Dutch. And the Swedes. Maybe Muscovy. So all are careful where they tread. Or rather, where they swim.' He laughed again. 'For I have more inventions which may again ensure a Peace. I have fashioned another water-petard, where but a touch sets off the flintlock, and if you sow the sea with these, why then your sea becomes your rampart. Also I dream, when I see my boat dragged on the land, that if it were of iron, with wheels beneath and pushed by many, with bombards in the forward part, so might you smash a gate to splinters and trample the defenders down – who then, be sure, would sue for peace.'

Rubens sat tall, he had begun to be nettled. 'I came here to make a true peace. Not a peace of terror and fear.'

'Peter Paul.' Drebbel seated himself so they faced each other squarely. 'Let us no longer play with words. There is a truth that I must tell you.'

'Peter Paul' —the man was too familiar. Look at his rags.

'You are called the Prince of Painters, and I say No, you are the Emperor of Painters. But there is one thing you should know. There will be no Peace. This "mission" of yours, on which you set your heart. It will fail. With a bleeding soul I tell you this, and as the truest friend you have.'

Shock, annoyance, disbelief, rage; what word could fit his indignation?

Nor had Drebbel finished. He waited while his hurting words sank in. 'A little I hear, far off, from Court – for I was once Prince Henry's darling. And they say there that you will fail. In particular I have heard tell that the Cardinal sends a new envoy to London, who is charged to make certain that your efforts collapse. A seasoned diplomatist with the Devil's own skill. He is called de Châteauneuf. He is to be feared.'

Rubens kept his face stoney, since he had heard already of de Châteauneuf. Nor would he let Drebbel see his fears.

'But that apart, in grief I tell you, I know these kings and emperors. They are all deceit and falsity. They let you make your mission but to buy a little time, while their arsenals choke with new-made arms. Even now their forges flare, their smithies thunder. They cast new cannon, and plot campaigns.' His eyes were bright as diamonds, he leaned too close to Rubens' face. 'Do you think, if the King of Spain, or of England, or of France wanted a true Peace, he would let it be contrived half in secret by a painter? Nation cheats nation as men cheat women, women men. With all honour to your genius, still I tell you this. If they wanted a true Peace, they would send a Duke at least.'

To be insulted so, as though he, Peter Paul Rubens, were dirt, in rags, like Drebbel. A failure, a beggar.

'I say this not to humble you. And you will be rewarded – Arise, Sir Peter Paul! They will give you baubles set with jewels. But there will be no Peace.'

A trace Rubens was mollified, with the thought he would be honoured. Also, he saw that Drebbel was mad.

'And therefore I declare' —Drebbel raised an arm high— 'We must foresee new armaments. I say unto you, if you go home to the King of Spain, and say, Alas, I brought no Peace but I know the secret of the newest weapon, believe it, your glory will be beyond compare.'

Rubens was split, between laughing, scoffing, weeping. His hand made a fist. Yes, he believed he would be honoured... but for a mission that failed. That always, from the start, was going to fail. For though Drebbel was insane, his words had barbs. Within Rubens a tower— no a city fell, walls crumbled, roofs fell in, a temple crashed in smithereens.

Nor could he breathe. The air was stale in here, it was hot and stank. Drebbel's voice, in the distance, had grown kindly. 'Always there will be war, Peter Paul. Always countries will vie, and lie. Nation whores with nation, and what are you but the pimp of Spain?'

At those words fire broke, in his head, in his gut. He was rasping and panting. The panic grew, as when he was drowning in Thames. But also he was dizzy, fainting. Drebbel's voice sang high.

'In time, as I have told you, war will rage in the sky. With a Blazing Glass the size of the moon, in some way borne above the globe, you could burn a city, nay a country, to ash.'

Rubens snatched open the lace at his neck. He was caught in an oven. Drebbel's words filled the boat.

'There is also the hurt in the inventor's heart, when he makes a great weapon that none dare use.'

Rubens heard his own voice thickly ask, 'Are you man or demon?'

'Men invent. That will not stop.'

Rubens wondered, was he dying even now? Confusedly, outside his window, he saw the scenes that Drebble raised. A mortar-shattered vessel sank, and looking upwards he saw, through water, fire that raged in other ships. Masts burned, sails blazed, sailors on fire jumped into the threshing, body-filled sea. A giant cannon, complete with mountings, plunged down just in front of him. Then a soldier struggling to get his breastplate off; from one side of his head his cheek was blown away so you saw grinning jawbone, long teeth. From a man who had lost his arm at the socket blood poured to fill the sea like smoke. Like a muffled music he heard the screaming of uncountable voices, though how could that be under water, and through glass?

A voice said, 'Breathe in.'

Drebbel waved a flask in his face. Something came from it, that his lungs drank greedily. He began to feel drunk, light-headed, dazed.

Drebbel was saying, 'This is the spirituous essence of air, from which the gaseous carcass is gone. It is got by heating certain salts, and pumping them tight into a flask.'

Drebbel himself took breaths from the flask, and Rubens saw that the oarsmen also had flasks. The air about them was keen again. Rubens looked in his window, and after all there were no wrecks, no drowning sailors, no sunk cannon, no fire that blazed above the river.

Weakly Rubens said, 'May we make for shore?'

Drebbel nodded. 'We had better, I think. You have gone a strange colour, which I do not like. And my rowers are tired.'

He leaned round to call instructions, and the boat turned back. The oarsmen lifted the baskets they had hauled up before, and paid them out, with their load of rocks, towards the river bed. The river's surface then appeared at the top of their windows, and steadily moved down the glass. Rubens saw galleons at anchor. With full sails a caravel rocked merrily forward. Buildings appeared, a distant spire, gulls circled so you thought you heard their cry. Though the sky was white it was also bright. His lungs hurt to breathe that air.

The print of this scene, in 'Rubens in London', has something of a Jules Verne look. In a strange craft, with oarsmen shadowily hinted at within a bent perspective, Rubens and Drebbel sit in carved Jacobean chairs before a great window, which must be larger than the windows Drebbel made for his boat. Ruben's breeches pocket bulges with the Roman object he has brought to show to Cornelis. In the middle of the window is the surface of the river, where you see what Rubens saw: old sailing ships, rounded like plump birds, some with sails furled and others tripping forward before a lively breeze, or tacking hard against it. With wood-ribbed houses and hills beyond, and light and peace, a happy scene. And under the surface, in the lower half of the window, there is darkness, wreckage, dismembered skeletons. This riverbed is an endless battlefield, as when dusk comes down on the dying and the dead. Cannon and pikes rust, and the wounds to the dead, if you peer in close they are more than grisly, as in Bloodsmith's Thirty-Years-War print. It would be ghoulish to describe them, probably it is ghoulish in Bloodsmith to see them. Close to the window a ghastly face looks back at us with half its flesh torn from the bone.

Nor is the surface world simply happy, since a curious shape hovers, tilted , in the sky. It is elliptical, maybe it is a disk at an angle, like a gigantic coin. An alien mother-ship filled with threat? The not-so-secret weapon of a superpower? It scintillates in a disturbing way. So maybe it is a giant Blazing Glass, of the kind envisaged by Cornelis Drebbel, in some way raised over the globe, and able by warping the rays of the sun to guarantee peace, or to destroy it. To know more one must read the commentary on the prints, which is included if you buy them as a 'livre d'artiste'.

~

Mulling 'Rubens in London' (which is nearly all he has to do these mourning days) Bloodsmith finds a further subject. For how will he represent the climax of the schemings of Cardinal Richelieu, his biggest throw in the game, the dispatch to London of his most veteran diplomatist, M. de Châteauneuf? He is the *will* of the Cardinal in person, and dangerous as a snake.

Bloodsmith knows the scene he will take. The details here come from a paper by Hans Gotthelf. For it is on record that Rubens was deeply grieved when he first heard of the new envoy. But we also know that he took heart when he heard how the Ambassador was greeted. Of the carriages sent to meet him, the greater part were empty. Let this be the picture, 'M. de Châteauneuf and the Empty Carriages'.

We look down on the scene, over the crescent of carriages which have a menacing air, as if they were a species of crab-like creature. They surround the knot of newcomers, who have at their centre a man be-sashed splendidly, with bows at his knees. With their black windows the carriages resemble gilded hearses, as if the dead have come in state, to witness with grim intent the arrival of this new player on the board.

Doubtless M. de Châteauneuf greeted his few hosts with seasoned urbanity, and composed himself comfortably in the carriage reserved for him. He has his skills, he will not worry overmuch about the poor reception as he leads the hollow procession up the flank of Dover's cliffs. For he is on the road to London, there to engage in a war he will win, by grinding to dust the endeavours of the upstart, the clerk's son Peter Paul Rubens.

10

Although he told himself Mae would come back, she did not come. She did not ring, she sent no sign.

So – what would he do? In practice you cannot just do nothing. Would he stalk her? Hang round her house at night, squat in her garden, eyeing the first-floor bedroom window? Or would he lie in wait in the street? Tell her his outrage. Not that I could ever hurt Mae. But I can see, in the pictures I did of her, that there is a hardness in the way her jaw clamps. And those ruthless cheekbones, the Grace-Jones hard look, you can see the skull behind the up-nose. Only child of a single mother, she doesn't join to people as other people join to people.

Surely she'll ring, leave a message at the Art School.

Every day he goes to his pigeonhole, every day it is empty.

He shouldn't ring her, it would look like weakness. But already he's hunkered into the telephone canopy. Rrm rrm, the dialling tone; will no one answer?

A click on the phone and a man's voice.

He was shocked to the core. It must be Geoffrey.

'Yes? Hello?' An assured, practical, comfortable voice. He was caught out, shamed, but he must say something, not hang in silence as the other man had done when he himself had answered and as time extended knew it was the Lover.

From nowhere, in Bloodsmith, a Scottish croon trills, 'Is that the Glasgow Herald?'

'Wrong number,' Geoffrey said shortly. He hung up.

Bloodsmith quakes, he is deeply shocked. Only now, Geoffrey comes real.

He stands in the open shaking his head. Somehow, these months, it had been weirdly easy to think only of Mae, and never of Geoffrey. Of course it was Mae's business, not his, and Geoffrey had cheated Mae, let's not forget.

Still it crossed his mind, would he turn round some day, and find Geoffrey right behind him, with menaces? Was Geoffrey craggy, or soft from desk work? Probably Geoffrey worked out. He had better stay alert. Should he go to a gym? Do artists do that?

But the big question was Mae. Where is she? I can't ring her at home. What *do* I do?

There was nothing he could do.

~

The most enigmatic print in 'Rubens in London' looks as if it is made with pitch and phosphorus. We see two lit-up figures on the sheets of a bed. We are behind them, so we see the soles of his feet between her legs and feet, and beyond we see his buttocks, fat white colliding planets. The bed itself sits within the skeleton of a box, so we are not sure whether this framework is geometry or whether we are to think of an old four-poster bed. Dipping shadows like curtains festoon the lovers, but cannot hide them from the stark face that is close to us, filling the picture's right-hand side, hovering within a block of solid pitch-black. It could be a cut-off head, like the head of King Charles I as it dropped in the basket. A face pale and open with listening, the mouth dropped and the nostrils waking. It leans towards the bed as if seeing were hearing. Is this the head of a voyeur? Or is he a husband? Is he Rubens, uneasy as he hears his floorboards creak, or Rubens guessing at betrayal years after it happened? Or is the head a disguised picture of Bloodsmith, tormenting himself with thoughts of Robyn with Grieve? Or of Mae with Geoffrey, come to that. The woman is shaded, it is not clear how light her skin may be. Or (most likely this is it) the couple are Van Dyck and Isabella, in some tryst while Van Dyck lingered in the village of Saventhem.

It is hard to decide: is the picture ironic? Does it mock the lovers' stout thighs, their pouching buttocks? But then their fingers trace each other's faces with a gentleness, even with the swooning tenderness of (could it be?) all love.

A trick picture then. Of lovers in or out of wedlock, we cannot tell who is what. Maybe it hints at those different knots that lie in wait for any happy couple that steps from love's chapel into the decades of life.

~

Still their home life went on, in normality. He was decent in his behaviour, being quiet because depressed. He was there as Robyn quietly fretted, worrying for news of relocation.

On his way home at the end of each day Bloodsmith would visit his studio. He no longer expected that Mae would come there, but pausing at the place was a kind of keeping vigil. So it seemed like a day-dream when he stopped there one evening, and saw near his doorway a figure he knew.

It was dusk, she was hard to see. It was late, and not a time she would come. So she must be a spectre, an illusion of grief. Yet he saw her red raincoat, belted tight at the waist: her exploding wild head on the stem of her neck; her skinny ankles. He saw her at the moment she turned from the door – not in his direction, her head was down.

'Mae?' It had to be a question, it was so impossible she should be here.

As she looked round, a gust blew her hair up, so he saw the shine on her forehead and nose-tip.

'Stephen?'

Tightly locked hugging they pulled together, as though they were two halves of a person, who could be rejoined by holding.

'I knew you couldn't be here. But I had to visit someone this side of town. I kept starting to cry, all the time I was there. I *had* to come.'

She had become a flattened figure, like a paper cutout, in his arms. His fingers were in her tough hair, he breathed her distinctive scent.

'Come in.'

She stood at his elbow, solemnly vertical, waiting while he undid the lock. He heard her sniff. With a suave warmth of welcome, he bid her enter his red closed room.

'I couldn't go near the old places, Stephen. If I passed near the Art School, I started to cry. If I remembered posing, I started to cry. I saw a poster from the Art School somewhere – oh, miles away – and my eyes just ran like a tap.'

She was not crying now. Hardly they are through the door when he's swarmed all over her. She's grabbed his face, as if through her mouth she'd swallow his head. Their clothes are flung and they're on the floor, and feral love, the supple monster, towers in the studio and braces feline limbs to eat.

Now that their violence of embracing has finished they softly and lovingly touch each other, feeling like a blind man's touch for that secret catch, which if they graze it quietly enough will open the inmost love.

Evidently they have found that catch, for they slowly sink below the frame of my camera, while all I may do it is wish them, 'Good love!'

In sum, his Mae had come back to him. He was back with her.

~

Of course, at home, it was back to deception. The false face smiled, and false mouth spoke. Even about the worsening war he found he said easily the words Robyn wanted; after all, the war was the other side of the world. What especially he must do was be kind to Robyn, be more helpful, more concerned, than even a faithful husband would be. Such his intention . . . .

Before he next saw Mae, he made a canvas. Oh the pleasure of being practical, a carpenter with tools! In shirt-sleeves in his studio, with sawdust in his lungs and hair, he dug tongues and grooves in selected lengths of wood. He fitted them close and screwed them tight, and put in the cross-bars to hold them solid. Finally he had an enormous stretcher.

'This is the big one,' he said over, inhaling the smell of new-cut wood.

He pulled off the polythene from the tall white column of his roll of canvas. Carefully he unwound a length, watchful to keep it off the floor. With a Stanley knife he slit it down. He folded it up round the edge of the stretcher, and with his staple-gun tacked it to the wood, testing the tension, making sure it came even. Afterwards, carefully, he brushed it with size.

He leant it against the wall and stepped back. The coarse strong off-white stuff of the canvas was clean, satisfying, beautiful. For a time he simply ate it with eyesight, as if it contained every picture.

Thus it waited, when Mae next arrived. Before her eyes he clamped it solid to his largest easel.

'This will be the gigantic Mae!'

'That big, Stephen? Can I fill it? Do I lounge across it from side to side?'

'I want you standing, in the middle. Hovering in the centre, a presence.'

'There's a lot of space to spare. What will you put there?'

'I'll put... I'll put your background in.'

'What do you mean?'

'I don't know, the hidden history . . . ' He's dabbling paints, making small mounds on a sheet of glass.

'This is to be oils, is it?'

He nods. 'I've had enough of acrylic. I want lustre. Enough of matt looks. Now. Be still.'

She positions, while he inwardly murmurs, Mae, Mae, it's in your stance! He seeks again the elusive boundary, where you see her breasts begin. Her clasped hands hang at her crutch exactly. With her legs slightly parted, the lines of her limbs make a narrow star.

She hears the damp scrape of sticky bristles on canvas. He's paused, frozen, in a leaned-back pose.

He moves, a brush points— 'There!' A dab. He sighs, breathes out, and lays the brush down.

'Rest, rest.'

In a pantomime performance, as of someone who has posed the live-long day, she slowly breathes in, inhaling deep so her lungs must break, as her arms stretch wide in a living crucifixion. Her spine goes concave in luxurious stretching.

Naked, she approaches, and stands hands on hips in tall inspection. 'Was that it, the great stroke? That dab? That smudge?'

'Don't tease me, Mae. That smudge means very much to me.'

'What does it mean?' Here, indignant, is the true wide smile, the gate of teeth.

'It means we've started. OK, let's go on.'

She deposits on his face the kiss of loving mockery, and returns to take her pose again.

~

Let's say he is working late one night, when there comes a loud knock at his studio door. Crack! Strange, but he goes to open. It isn't Mae. It's Rubens, Gerbier, and Cardinal Richelieu. Without ceremony they step across his threshold.

'Won't you sit down?' Actually, they have already sat, on the kitchen chairs he has here and there.

Rubens remarks, 'King Charles is outside, in the carriage.'

'Won't you ask him to come in?'

The pop eyes of Gerbier bulge. 'He cannot come *here*. He is a King.'

Richelieu raises supercilious brows, and casts his eyes, wearily, once to the ceiling.

'If you don't mind my asking,' Bloodsmith inquires, 'Where have you come *from*? Have you come from History?'

The three exchange looks, unwilling to speak. Then Rubens says, 'We come from the Furnace.'

'Are you angels?'

'Angels do not come from the Furnace. Angels come from the Bed.'

As he sat, Rubens looked round the room. 'Are those your pictures?'

'Yes, *Maitre*. This is a new one, just begun. My big painting of Mae. If you would look at it . . . '

'I know Mae,' Rubens said. 'I would travel with her to both ends of

261

Time.' But when he studied the canvas, his face stayed opaque.

He turned from it. 'He who would paint Peace through the world must include the Princess of Africa. She wears a blood ruby on her brow.'

Leaning forward, Gerbier added, 'And mind thou this! A National Bank will save the polity from the whim of ravenous avarice'.

Slowly then, with state, Richelieu got to his feet. He lifted one hand high, and began to chant. It seemed to Bloodsmith that he had never heard a sound so beautiful as this rising baritone which swelled as though Richelieu stood within the crossing of a cathedral.

'The goddess Europa is turned to a tree

Of dogs' heads barking endlessly.'

Richelieu looked round as though he had silenced them all.

There was a pause, then Rubens and Gerbier rose.

Bloodsmith asked, 'Are you leaving?'

Gerbier said scoffingly, 'And would his Eminence stay?'

'Well . . . no . . . '

Rubens held out his hand, and kindly said, 'Such a visit as this comes only once in a life.' He smiled. 'Good night, then.' They shook.

Gerbier also held out his hand, 'Good night, Sir Stephen.'

Even Richelieu briefly extended two fingers, perhaps for him to kiss but he did not do so. Loftily Richelieu stalked from the room.

He hurried after them to the doorway. And it was true, a carriage stood in the street, with a team of horses. Inside the carriage, he could see King Charles, looking straight ahead with his long hair behind him. He seemed aware he was looked at: the shy fingers of one hand played lightly at his neck. Then he called out clearly to them all,

'There is a table set for the feast of love that is m-m-made for man by the morning star.'

The others joined him in the carriage. From the window Rubens gave a wave. Then the carriage started, but instead of moving forward, the horses pulled it round where it was. It rotated in front of him. As it turned, it vanished.

They had returned to the Furnace and he went back into his studio, scratching his head but with an odd sense of blessing.

11

And I shall catch up with Rubens, he thought, etching needle in hand. For they must be careful, no way can Mae come every day. Things must be spaced.

Both within 'Rubens in London', and within *Chess with Kings*, Rubens is approaching the final crisis. He is gnawed by a hidden private wound – how may that ever be assuaged? He worries for the uncertainty of his Mission of Peace; time surely is running out? Also he worries for the great picture he planned. That noble allegory he had projected for King Charles, the great painting of Peace and War, it is not yet clear. One change he has made. Hispania and Britannia are swept away, and in their place, in the centre, will be Pax herself, the Goddess of Peace. That must be the best. So she stands not for one Peace only, but for Peace in all the Nations. Minerva still stands at her back, pushing Mars further off. Nor is Mars to be simply shut in a temple, rather the hideous Fury Alecto, green-skinned and shrieking, brandishes her torch and calls him to war.

The loss of Hispania has saddened him, but the Indian Maid is far removed. And Britannia, there had been a danger there, if she came to resemble Deborah Kip. At least he has found his great model for Pax, away from the unease of the Gerbier house. She is a corset-maker's daughter called Bet, who, he has been told, will pose for artists. Her home is in the small streets behind Charing Cross, and he is able to visit and work freely there. Bet herself is in charge of the home, her parents being dead. He must make his oil-studies in her own chamber, since she has a baby, who may only at certain times be left with her great-aunt. Bet has stood, holding a wash-basket against her hip, in the posture of the woman who will bear a great basin of gold towards Pax. Now she must stand for Pax herself.

With all his troubles and fears, it is a relief to make his way to her house. So today, on a keen morning of birdsong and sun, he has threaded the crush and arrived. At moments he feels stabs of pain in his joints – let it not be the gout, returning to plague him. But he is panting and pale, he has loosened his shirt-strings to be free in his work. While she is busy with her baby, he has kneaded freshly the paints he mixed yesterday. He is ready, and the baby has been laid down, contentedly snuffling in its sleep. The three of them are like a small family. He bids her be naked.

'Bet, you stand with the sweetest grace.'

'In course I do. I have watched how the ladies do stand in the park.'

'There is sweetness also in thy speech.'

'Music to thy ear-holes, is it?'

She stands, head turned, one hand to her breast. Her plump flesh puckers at the base of her neck: she is full of cream, she is cream itself. The poor room has daub on its walls, which in places has cracked to show lathes of grey wood. Her fair hair is newly washed. She is a vigorous fat young mother. She is so much the beauty he loves to paint, that almost his heart is filled with sadness. But this is home now.

The room goes quiet while he sinks to his work. The fresh sun falls on her and on him, while the soft snoring of the baby continues.

She asks, brusquely, 'How's yer old embassy getting on, then?'

'Ah, Bet, I have news. Some say at Court that the King may name Sir Francis Cottington as Ambassador to Madrid. It is not done, though. Nor is it known just how the King turns. When I wake in the night, I worry how the French may undo all my schemes. They have sent a new Ambassador, whom I greatly fear.'

Bet's face is serious.

'Nor are the French my only worries. For also I am exercised as to whom the Spanish will send to London. I have sent many letters to the great Count-Duke, who is my master. I have said I need the name of the Spanish Ambassador. And that he has not provided me.'

'Ah, 'twill come,' she says lightly.

Rubens smiles. 'You are sure of that?'

'In *course* it will come. But 'twill not come soon.'

'No?'

'Why, you know what they say of Spain.'

'What do they say?'

'They say "Ah, if Death only came from Spain . . . " So I say, worry not, Sieur Peter, on any of these accounts.'

'And yet I worry.'

'Worry then, if you will, dear Sieur Peter. You are a gentle painter and a gentle man.'

'Thank you, Bet. Your counsel is precious to me.'

She makes big eyes. 'Honoured indeed!'

They fall quiet, as the work of painting resumes

Till he pauses. Perhaps he has spoken, for she seems not disturbed as he puts down his palette, and crosses to her and kneels on the floor, and rests his fingers on the sacks of her breasts, which, though she has just fed her baby, look still as though they ache from fullness. The blue veins, spidering towards the nipple, seem themselves burdened. Exchanging with her a light loving look, he bends so close his mustachios graze the brown halo round her teat. Tender hands press till, in a spurt, a white arc of fresh milk, clear like water, travels through sunlight into his mouth: in the warm room that has grown deeply still. Hot sun blesses the pink-white body of the fair-haired young mother, and blesses too the balding, hazel-haired man, sunk on his knees in reverent love, like a communicant.

~

It was with difficulty that Rubens made his way back to the Gerbiers. The big toe of his right foot hurt more than before, as if he had a razor inside his shoe.

He limped precautiously into the house, making slow steps towards their noise. At the doorway of the hall he came to a stop. Except for Balthazar, they all were there. Nearest the door was little Susan, in the act of looking up, startled by his arrival but pleased to recognize him. The other Gerbier children had not seen him yet. Behind Susan, Elizabeth laid a dish on the table: the white light lit her pale face and gold hair. Beyond her, her brother George spoke in her ear, and next to George, Deborah Kip reached a hand to the fruit-bowl, quietly smiling at something they said; next to Deborah, on the other side, was Agnes the cook, giving her views. On the floor, the cat sprawled on its back, stretching its limbs towards the doorway.

Then the whole picture changed, broken by his own arrival.

'Sieur Peter Paul', 'Sieur Rubens'. All their eyes (including the cat's), were turned like lamps on him. Thus they pulled him into the picture; he could not see it because he was in it. He hid the discomfort in his limbs.

But when, after the meal, he limped to his room, it was the first scene that came in his mind. Holding a chalk lightly, he sketched the way they had been arranged, with Susan's face turned in his direction.

His wrist stabbed now, he had to stop. He turned his hand slowly: it was reddened and swollen. His thumb was ready to hurt if he moved it.

'Hand, you will not draw again.'

He sat back closing his smarting eyes. The agony approached. It was good he got down this sketch, before his powers were cancelled. His great grief was that if the gout, returning, took his hand, then the great work could not be finished. Not in time to present it to King Charles, where it could help his bargaining. His hopes were failing.

'Father.'

He looked quickly round the room, but his father's presence was faint or absent. The walls were plain and bare.

Only, when he lies back to rest, a quick picture comes, small but clear as a hallucination: Jan Rubens in black, and draped in chains, stands before Prince William, husband of the lame princess, who is seated up on a dais.

'*Something* you must say, Sieur Rubens.' William's voice is clear and dry. 'Do you *deny* you were the lover of the Princess Ann?'

As ever, Jan Rubens says nothing. His fingers flutter. Finally he draws a great breath, meets the eyes of Prince William, and, for all the weight of the chains, stands upright.

'Great highness, one thing only shall I beg from you – that I be killed with a sword and not with a rope. For I am in my condition a gentleman.'

There is a kind of swallowed growl from William, then he mutters to the guard,

'Get his carcass from my sight!'

This is the moment, which the son of Jan Rubens sees before him. But for the disgrace, he could make it a painting, that moment when, before the contemptuous eyes of the wronged Prince of Orange, his trembling father pulled his frame together, stood tall, and begged for a gentle death.

As Bloodsmith reflects, Do I etch with acid this scene I have drawn? Or, as with Rubens on his knees before Bet, do I put it on the back-burner, from tact and discretion, and leave just my sketches, for whoever may find them… if anyone does?

12

In the Art School he saw Grieve in the distance; a match-stick man at the corridor's end. He turned aside. Sooner or later the confrontation would come.

He almost collided with his colleague Ollie, whose hair was wild. His beard spread in tongues like flame below his chin.

'He's done it, Stephen!'

'Done what?'

'He's cut me.'

'You mean Attila? He can't cut you, Ollie.'

'He bloody can. He bloody has.'

'He can't cut Fine Art. What'd be left?'

'No, don't you see? He's streamlining Fine Art. He's cutting the Foundation Course. They can do that down the road, and come here after.'

It rang true. Bloodsmith lost colour.

'We'll fight it,' he said.

'Fight it?' said Ollie. 'By Christ, we'll fight it!' As he lifted his head in resolution, the whole wide plate of his beard lifted high. 'We'll grind him to powder.'

'A united front.'

'Absolutely.'

They looked each other in the eye.

'Will there be a handshake?'

'What, a Golden Parachute? I should bloody hope so. He can't put us out in the street with nothing.'

'The problem is we're part-time. If we were full-time . . . .'

'He has to give us *something*. I've got homes to maintain. And what about you? Are you sure he's going to keep Printmaking on? It's hardly high-tech.' He had evidently grown irritated that Bloodsmith did not worry more for himself.

'You're right. I haven't a clue how Printmaking stands.'

'We'd all better worry.'

'We will.' They parted.

Though Bloodsmith's worry had a different twist. If he were somehow safe because Grieve had had an affair with his wife, that was a mangy situation. And was it true, that Grieve would spare him? Who could say what Grieve would do?

In the meantime life at home grows more difficult. For though he sees Mae again at intervals they both can manage, Robyn is only more tender. She understands his outbursts. She will work, to make their marriage work.

'Yes love,' she says with love in her voice. With gentleness, loveliness in her face. Which is unease, confusion and guilt for him. Much better a distant, ironic marriage, that leaves a space for secret love.

In the middle of the night, wide awake, he lay in the pitch-dark, listening. Robyn, beside him, whimpered. Her moans were no words that he could tell, except that she was deep in misery.

Do I wake her, to save her from the nightmare? Do I let her sleep, so she forgets it?

She did not wake. The sighs tailed away and her limbs stopped moving. Her breathing grew calm. He lay beside her, a dismal spectre miles from sleep.

In the daytime too he must be concerned. Robyn knew in her unconscious that something went on. She had started to tap towards Mae and him, like a blind person creeping tap tap with their stick, listening for sounds from people who are seeking to keep very quiet.

Yet on an evening before he saw Mae, he was surprised at the calm he had achieved. He was in the kitchen peeling onions, discussing once more the lottery bid.

'Can I have the onions, Stephen?'

He came over, carrying the chopping board.

In an extraordinary voice Robyn said, 'Where's your head, Stephen?'

He woke to what he'd done. He'd thrown the chopped onions in the bin, and kept the skins to put in the cooking.

'I don't know what's wrong with me.'

'There's something wrong,' Robyn said grimly. 'Go and sit down.'

He stayed where he was, but still was distracted, while Robyn was angry but also bewildered, and glanced at him as if Alzheimer's began.

He thought, Mm, this is not so easy. Really there is a huge issue here. Robyn had found cheating ever more difficult, the longer it went on. So it was going to be with him. But choices, decisions, I won't face those now. Because with Rubens, the Rubens Suite, I'm arriving at the crucial point. The key picture, the key pictures... nothing must interrupt that scene. It will take me days. I'll sort my life when the art is done.

13

Rubens' crisis in London, laid flat on his back, is described by Gotthelf and dramatized by Jens Claeys. Their books are beside Bloodsmith, though he hardly now needs their pages. Full with Rubens, he will imagine (he will live) those tribulations through in art. In the process he will fill in certain lacunae, marked with small stars in the printed text, which interrupt *Chess with Kings*. For Bloodsmith has guessed the whole story now.

Late in 'Rubens in London' we find a positively lurid relief-etching. It looks like a giant hand-print, as if a titan pressed his fingers into inks then onto paper. Except that he would need to be a wounded, even, a crucified titan. For those jagging lines round the break in the hand – are they *sensations*? Such as a hand would have, if held against a wooden beam, under the spike of a square-sided nail as the mallet comes down and the nail in one jab is through the frail flesh and into the wood.

But already we are tumbling (the whorled lines wheel) towards the stretched-out man alone, in his sunlit wood-and-plaster room, in the London house of the Gerbiers. Is it his punishment for hob-nobbing with high life, that he suffers the disease of the great, not the good? His right hand we cannot even see, it is so hidden in fat bandages (enclosing a poultice of hog's fat with witch-hazel). Could we see it, we would more than wince at the hard, tight-skinned shining red swellings on his fingers and his knuckles. His moan we hear,

'Here I lie, Peter Paul Rubens styled the Prince of Painters, fetched low in the pit of that ignoble pain, Gout, a disease I do not merit, who am moderate in my appetites. Ooooh! It is a hurt like none other I have ever known. If I had but fair thoughts . . . But my thoughts too are scimitars. The shame I bear now, the stain, the dishonour! God's wounds! Ooooh! My great toe! In truth, I sinned as much as any; but men are beasts. My Isabella, I laboured to think you the best of women, and noble (nearly) as my mother, Maria Pipelynx. Turn and turn your eyes, blind eyes, to see me in my plight today! And my bladder... I shall crack... I can lie still no more. Joachim! I have need of you. It shames me to ask it. Good Joachim, I pray, help me please to the jordan.'

So Joachim helps his master lift up his bed-shirt, and aim his penis with his hurting hand, while Joachim holds the jordan to receive the steaming piss.

'I thank you, Joachim, for doing what no man should do for me.'

'Will you drink more, master? They have brought a new pitcher.'

'*More* water, Joachim? I feel I have drunk the whole river of Thames. Can that really be all the physician will say? Water and water and yet more water.'

'Why, master, it is not only water he gives. You have already had a plenty of his juleps, syrups and elixirs.'

'Remind me not of his elixirs. But who comes now? Why, Mistress Susan. I see you have brought your children also. Thank you, good Joachim, I shall talk with Susan.'

She sets her dolls on the bed all round him. 'They are grieved that you are ill, Sieur Peter.'

'I thank them. But I do not see Pleasance. Is Pleasance ill also?'

'We do not love Pleasance.'

'Oh. Has Pleasance been naughty?'

'She has not been naughty. But she is ugly. Sieur Peter, I am come to ask if you desire a dish of tarts.'

'Why, yes, if you will, Susan – if your children will but help me to eat them. For I do not know if tarts will heal my affliction.'

But she was gone. He heard her voice call, 'Marilian! Sieur Peter says he must have tarts.' He heard the clear voice of Deborah intervene, 'Are you sure, Susan, it is Sieur Peter who said he must have tarts?'

'He did, he did. His brother-in-law told him, we made tarts today.'

She did not come however, and presently he heard feet trip in the passage. George Gerbier had brought a visitor to him. He blinked as if his sight had clouded, then he saw the corset-maker's daughter.

'Why, Bet. I am joyed you came, I did not look to see you.'

''Twas but a step.'

'You are good to come, to a poor man on his sick-bed.'

'I worried, for you came not when you said, as always you had done before.'

'How doth Philip?'

'My great aunt guards him. And she is better likewise. The specific that I bought, with the money that you gave me, hath done her good. She is up from her bed, and you are lain down.'

'Truly, and that is most grievous. I needs must be up, and make haste to the Court. I am filled with fear, for the words which de Châteauneuf and the French may spread. And the Dutch likewise. I must fight in words for the Peace I would see – and here you see me, laid low in hurt and bandaged round. I cannot finish the painting I had a mind to give the King. I cannot even step. I can do nothing at all.'

'Maybe you have already done all that was wanted, and all that you could.'

He slightly shook his head, his face knit tight.

'God help me! The matter must be as He wills. But Bet, I pray you, sit here please on the side of the bed. Your carriage is more graceful than a Maid of Honour. I do not know how you have come by such art.'

''Tis true I have watched many ladies closely, that did visit our house for their privy garments, but I came not here, to hear my praises.'

'Nay, tell me, were you much in your father's shop?'

'I was tied by his ribbons to the bench, and thus knew people of the noblest kidney. For none had the skill my father had, in shaping a strong yet slender busk. My father made the Lord Chancellor, his corset. Also he made the truss, that held the mighty hernia which the Bishop of Worcester bore. 'Twas rumoured he would be sent for by the Sultan of

Constantinople, to assist certain matrons, the mothers of princes, who held high sway in his Seraglio. In truth it did not come to pass.'

'Yet he had good custom, for sure.'

'Good, and, as we say, not good likewise. For he also made such integuments as those men wear, who crave constraint. He was called to set free the Alderman of Cheap, that day his bumboy ran away with the keys.'

'Was he so? Well. I trust you were not tied too tight to his bench?'

'Nay good Sieur Peter, I had extension to roam, and have fallen in plight among the bobbins. I once did eat my mother's needle. My boyhood friend was a little blackamoor boy. They had dressed him in silks, so he looked a prince. We have made frolic among the bolts.'

'Do you know him still?'

'Nay, he was lost to me long whiles ago. Since then I have been behind the counter with others, as you do know, for I have told you my story.'

'But always I think you were called by Love, who is a most powerful and blessed god.'

'Yet I know not if I loved the others, as I loved my Indian Prince. One thing I know, I shall not wed unless I love. And this is within my power to choose, for the house is mine, and the yard behind, and the stable that stands at the end of the yard. Sadly and early I became a mistress of property, and I shall live as I do choose.'

'Sweet Bet, you are as wise as lovely.'

'I am a London maid, tis the long and the short of it. Your gifts, Sieur Peter, have been a stay and a help. I like thee much.'

'Lady Bet, I would kiss both thy hands and thy feet. Ooooh!'

'Be still, dear sir. You are not for kissing today.' Her eyes grew warmly serious. 'But wait in patience on thy hope.'

She smiled again, with lowered eyes, a quiet luminous smile. The house was still, and family voices far removed. Softly she lifted back the covers and the sheet, and lifted his bed-shirt and folded it up, as he lay scarcely breathing.

'My dear kind painter.'

Her face sank from his sight, so all he saw was the top of her cap. He felt her mouth.

With ease he lay stretched out in stillness.

He said, 'Most dear most beauteous dear sweet heart. I thank God you came today. It was a blessing like no other.'

'Nay, you are a sweet man, Peter Paul, and I do like you that you are kind. Well, I think that I will go now.'

She left, he lay in transformation.

'I know not if this be your gift, dear God, I will not believe it was sent of darkness. The treasures of your love are beyond all guessing. But who can know thy hid intent, who have given us to dwell in this house of flesh, which is a den of temptation, and a nest of delight.'

He lay in reverie through the warm afternoon, as the light from the casement approached the bed-clothes. The pain returned, and with it his hurt from Isabella; at moments the anguish in his joints *was* the pain of cuckoldry. For that hurt, there is no cure. Except that in some way matters had changed, and he found there was something he needed to do. But what it was he could not guess.

He looked in the corner of the room, where sometimes the spirit of his father stood. Today there were few shadows, but those that were there, stirred. Like a crinkle or crackle in the air, the far-off voice he had heard before whispered close inside his ear, 'Think, my son, on what your mother did for me.'

He started, but no more words came. The shadows settled, like a breeze that has moved fallen leaves then dies. His father had spoken, and gone.

But what his mother did to save his father . . . He had been told, but all that was so very long ago. He was half asleep, but already he had begun to dream, a waking dream, that came and went with the waves of pain. He knew he was both in the Gerbier house, and in the high tower of Dillenberg Castle. A short dark figure stooped beside him and turning he saw it was his mother, Maria Pypelinx, dressed in black, and kneeling as in prayer on the large, cold black-and-white tiles. Her face was younger than he remembered, and pretty though plain from grief.

She did not see him, and in front of them both, high up on a dais, was Prince William himself, with his blank grey face and small, dry, heavy-lidded eyes. He spoke,

'Had his cousins come, to plead for his dishonoured life, that is but what I should expect. But that *you* come – I am astonished.'

Softly, clearly his mother answered, 'Gracious lord, he was a most dear husband once. I doubt not he will be a good husband again.'

'You have forgiven him his trespass?'

'That I did long time ago. I forgave him, and with all my heart. It is many months you have held him in your dungeon.'

Rubens lay back on the bed, with his eyes tight shut, drifting between waking dream and delirium. When he opened his eyes and looked about him again, not knowing how much time had passed, everything was where it had been before. His mother still knelt on the black-and-white tiles, and Prince William gazed at them both; abruptly he called to a man in livery who had appeared in the room,

'You, sirrah, fetch here a chair!'

Clearly Rubens saw the man's legs, in hose, below the heavy, carved, wooden chair, which advanced through the air towards them.

'Good madam, you must be tired with kneeling.'

His mother stayed down on her knees. 'Merciful prince, I thank you for your courtesy. But I shall not rise from these cold stones while my husband languishes. Yet again I beg humbly that you award me his life.'

'Good lady, I urge you to understand me. That you have forgiven him, and now beg for his life, for that I honour you to the heights. But pray understand, I cannot merely release the man, who hath so injured my house and mine honour. It may not be.'

He said it firmly, even regretfully. But so it is: the honour of a princely house.

His mother nodded. She swallowed. With lowered head, with downcast eyes, she began to speak. He heard her words, though at times it was not clear whether her words were outside or inside his head.

'Then, most worshipful and gracious, I have no choice but to say one thing more, which I would fain have left unspoken. But as to the honour of your noble house, there are few if any who know ought of this matter. Some style you "The Silent", and your people have been skillful, in keeping this thing hid. But to win my husband's freedom, you must know I am willing that all the world shall hear my story.'

He saw the Prince start, while his mother's voice strengthened like a music.

'Were I to complain aloud, I believe word would travel like fire in straw. News sheets would shout it, from France to Russia, from Sweden to Italy. I have letters lodged with others now, which may bring this thing to pass, should I not be seen again.'

William's brow had knit tight but she did not stop, and he drew closer to his mother. He was kneeling on the stones himself, which were icy and hurt his knees. He *was* his mother, as he heard her say, in a whisper that also filled the chamber,

'Were our shame to be known, I would be shunned and destroyed, I would be less than dust, and my children likewise— but also it would hurt your house. In my deepest grief I say this, here on my knees and at your mercy.'

He gazed rapt at the whitened face of the Prince.

'Yet still, in all humility, I prostrate myself and kiss your shoes in pleading that, with the mercy and charity for which your name is known, you take pity on my sufferings, and release unto me my long-imprisoned husband, Jan Rubens, who has suffered much. Of what has passed heretofore no word will, to anyone, be ever said.'

The light had changed. The Prince now sat close to the foot of the bed and seemed no longer to be up on a dais. His face was steady, then he called aloud,

'Sirrah, the chair! Good madam, I pray you rise and sit. I do remember that in your first words, you made mention of a worthy fine, which might buy your husband's release into honourable detention.'

'Most elevated, blest and merciful prince, I kiss the ground beneath your feet.'

Instead of kissing the ground, however, his mother got up stiffly, and, with a deeply solemn bow of her head, sat back in the large carved chair.

He hardly listened to their bargaining, for bargaining was a skill his mother had, as needs must a wife who had married Jan Rubens. A figure was found, which would allow Jan Rubens' release, on condition that he reside always in the town of Seigen.

His mother said again, 'Most worshipful, from my heart I thank you.'

The scene was receding from him, and fading. Dimly he saw Maria Pypelinx take her leave, retiring backwards with bows and curtseys to the Silent Prince who himself was distant and shrank away.

Only after they had gone he thought, I did not see my mother's eyes. She had not once looked to him, whereas his father's eyes were always on him.

He remembered his mother was close to Isabella, as husbands' mothers are often not. She once said, when he had been impatient, 'You will lose that girl.'

Why had his mother kept her eyes from him?

~

As the bronze light crept across the sheet, he thought of Jesus, and how he is never alone on the Cross, for his friends are gathered tenderly by. But she that is always closest to him is the maid with the long blond silk straight hair, who weeps as she bites her lip, and ever a yellow strand of her hair will rise and curl about His feet. Always, in his Crucifixions, Mary Magdalene was close by Jesus. For she it was who loved Christ best, and of all us sinners He loved her best. She was forgiven her sins because of her love.

He drifted into sleep and out. When he next came to, Deborah Kip sat beside him, with a pottage of millet with potatoes and onion, and a spoon to feed him.

'Mistress Deborah, I am a burden to all who know me.'

'No burden, poor Peter Paul. Will you eat? I have also a decoction for you to drink. It has celery seed and burdock, autumn crocus and meadowsweet, all as the apothecary gave direction, and most potent he assured me for the curing of gout.'

'I thank thee,' he said, as Deborah brought the wooden spoon to his mouth.

He was quiet when he had eaten. Then he said, 'Mistress Deborah, I have told you of our Clara Serena that died.'

Deborah nodded.

'And I have told you of Isabella's grief, which to my shame was greater than mine, so I grew impatient, and reproached her for it.'

Deborah face was serious.

'When Isabella was close to death, she said to me, "Peter Paul, you will miss me, I know. But I am not sad to die. Because I am going where Clara Serena is. I know not if it be Heaven, or Hell, or dark wet earth, but where she is, there I shall be. That is my home, I want no other.'

Deborah waited till he spoke again.

'Two nights later, and in the darkest time of night, she sank into the arms of death as though her lover after all were neither me, nor any other, but only Death himself.'

He gazed into the thought before him. Deborah saw she still must wait.

'Isabella had a need of love. After Clara Serena died, her need was great as the firmament. I did not give that love. My heart was small when hers was great. I failed her.'

For a moment his bandage touched Deborah's hand. 'I drew her once, and I carry that drawing in my head. You see it is a woman, with a grief in her soul. You see... perplexity. You may guess she feels a want of love.' He frowned, his breathing was a kind of panting. 'In truth, I do not know for sure what Isabella did or did not do. But if she sought another's love, the greater fault in that was mine.'

Deborah found she was not sure whether still he knew that she was there. His lips moved as though he spoke, then he turned to her.

'Mistress Deborah, will you pray with me?'

'Gladly, Sieur Peter.'

She joined her hands, as he held close his bandaged hands. Then she heard, or overheard, him say,

'Dear loving father, I humbly pray you forgive my sins. For I have sinned, and with so many. My guilt is greater than I dared to think. I know not if I merit forgiveness or flames. But if there is ought in my Isabella that may be forgiven, I do forgive it, and that with all my heart. All else I may do, and I do this now, is to pray from the true depths of my soul, that you bestow your fullness of gracious blessing on the soul of my wife, Isabella Brant, and on the soul of our daughter, our Clara Serena.'

To Deborah he said, 'I thank you, mistress Deborah. Pardon me if I ask, that you leave me now. I mean to weep, but with discretion. I shall not bawl, to wake the house.'

Deborah quickly bent and kissed his brow, and with no sound slipped from the room.

He abandoned himself to the grief that came, and wept more simply than he had before. The only thing that was not clear, was just for whom it was he wept. Because now he wept for Isabella, and now for Clara Serena (he saw them both) and now for both them and himself together, and again for each and both of them.

When the weeping calmed he sank in slumber, and slept on as the night came down.

~

It may be, at last, his trials were ending, for in the morning Balthazar came in quickly.

'Friend Peter Paul! Word is come!'

'What word?' he murmured.

'Why of the naming of the Ambassador from Spain. Or so the courier saith. The Count Duke hath sent letters, and this to thee, which, if you will, I shall break the seal and read.'

Which at Rubens's request he did. So was confirmed the naming of Don Francisco Coloma, as the Ambassador of Madrid in England.

'But what of the English? I know not what trick they may play now.'

'Nay, it is as you had heard before. Sir Francis Cottington is named aloud, to be sent as Ambassador to Spain.'

Rubens nodded. 'I am relieved. I had feared that plan would be undone, by the schemes of the Cardinal and the words of de Châteauneuf.'

'So it nearly was. But that Cardinal, at last, was too clever by half. De Châteauneuf was adroit in the words that he spoke to the King, and more adroit in those he spoke to the Queen. You knew not, Peter Paul, as you lay sick, how near your mission came to failing. But de Châteauneuf overstepped himself. For he was followed to his meetings with the Puritan great, those most known for their hatred of Spain, meetings which he tried hard to hide. He even met in the greatest secrecy with those who would end the rule of kings. The words he spoke there were sometimes heard. Thus he overreached himself, and both he and the Cardinal were undone. He hath returned to France with great dispatch.'

Rubens crossed himself. 'How was he heard? The French are skilled in secrecy.'

'Yes, but he was followed by the chief spy of Lord Weston. A most curious man, and overly hirsuit, so you could think he had the head of a lion. He is easy to see, yet most adroit when he would not be seen.'

'Maybe I have glimpsed that man.'

'They say if he but close his eyes, you cannot find him anywhere. None but Weston know his name.'

Rubens nodded. 'There are many spies. There is one, dressed like a Puritan . . .'

'Not always – but I have heard of him. Some hold him for a Rosicrucian and others for a British Israelite, but for all I know he may serve the Dutch. For my part, I suspect the Swedes, they are busy now. Or both or neither, depending on the day of the week.'

'And others— but let them be. They will not tell us who they are.'

Balthazar gave an aged smile. 'This is the world of politics, where no man speaks his own true mind... except yourself, dear Peter Paul.'

'I too can speak to please, if need be. But it is true I serve no other cause, except the peace of nations.'

'And of peace between their warring faiths. I honour you for that the most. I rejoice that your labour has borne fruit.'

Already matters were arranged. Sir Francis Cottington would make his way to Madrid, timing his arrival for that same day, on which Don Francisco Coloma would arrive in London. And thus the Peace would be made real.

Rubens and Balthazar gazed to each other, with an open friendliness not shown before. Then Rubens closed his eyes and sighed. 'I thank thee God, it is Thy grace that brought this Peace to pass. And so I pray we make an end to wars.'

'Amen,' said Balthazar, and left Rubens to rest.

The twilight thickened as Rubens rested. In the deeps of the night his father's voice spoke one final time. 'My son, you did well. Therefore it will be given to you, to journey to the ends of time and space, even to the ramparts of Heaven and Hell. Close by you will be your Indian Maid, whom others know as Lady Rawlings. You will love her yet you will not love, so honour is saved.'

Whether or not he had dreamt, he was clear awake now. But no further word came in explanation.

~

When Deborah next came, with her bowl of pottage, he found he could hold the spoon himself.

'Mistress Deborah, something came to my mind this morning... I wonder, will it displease you, if I place your children in the painting I meditate, which I purpose to call "Peace and War"?'

'Why no, Sieur Peter. But would they not make a troublesome baggage, and undo all thy allegory?'

'Rather, I shall make them the core of my allegory. But you will see.'

'Pray do thy will, Sieur Peter.'

14

Rubens' crisis, then. The drawings had occupied Bloodsmith for days: in charcoal, in water-colour, in soft pencil and stump. Rubens with Bet, with Deborah, with Susan, with Joachim. From the sketches he would make as many prints as he liked. Though the effect of drawing Rubens in his grief and contrition was to make him say to himself, Should *I* be honest about *my* dishonesty?

But once you do start, even honesty is easy, and the tongue will run on – as both Robyn, and Geoffrey too had shown, when they once started to confess. No way will I tell all, he thought. Nor will Mae, I'm sure of that. Actually it isn't necessary. There's tact and good sense, after all.

I fell in love with Mae as man and as artist. There's nothing dishonest in falling in love. Yet I hid it from Robyn, and that was dishonest. I meant it for the good, to protect her and our marriage, our home and Sally. Or maybe I just lied for my own convenience. In any case Robyn felt it – of course – and went somewhere else. Adrian gave her what I did not. Then I felt that, and flung back to Mae, whom I loved and love with honest love. Though I live a huge lie now. And so does Mae. As Robyn did. She doesn't now. So what to do? Do Mae and I tell all and smash two homes? Because love is love. For all my lies, my love is real. Does that mean I don't love Robyn? It's not so clear. Because I both hate her for screwing with Grieve. And I love her as well, deep down as they say. That just is... the contradiction.

So what should I have done? It's true I could have tried harder to have it all out with Robyn right back at the start. Then I might not have had the affair with Mae. I can't wish for that. It would be like wishing you had had an abortion when the baby is your growing child. Should I have tried to take off with Mae the first time I knew her? That wasn't on at all – *and,* if it had been, it might not have been the answer. I wouldn't do that to Robyn. What is the answer? Polygamy isn't for us. Ménage à trois is not for us. 'Open marriage' is not for us. And honesty is not for us. Nothing is for us, and there isn't an answer. So I've got nowhere. We're nowhere lovers. While the loving, the lying and the cheating go on and, in honesty, I don't see how they will stop.

~

He spoke too soon. In the red studio, the following day, the inevitable occurred.

It had begun as a low-key day. Soon after Mae came, they went to canvas. Low cloud pressed pale-grey on the roof-window, almost you could think it leaned its belly on the glass. In the cold light (he didn't want electric) Mae paused by his board of reproductions.

'That's a new picture.'

'I looked it out. It says on the back it's by Van Dyck.'

She goes in close. 'But is that Rubens by the coffin?'

'Yes. It's called "Rubens mourns the death of his wife". And there is Rubens, with his thinning hair and with his children, kneeling by Isabella's coffin. You can just see her face. The only thing is, who's the young man at Rubens' back? He gets as much attention as Rubens.'

'Is he one of the artists from the studio? He's holding a portfolio.'

'He's old for an apprentice, and obviously a gentleman, with those crimson hose and that gold hat-band.'

'And so?'

'He's got Van Dyck's nose, sharply pointed at the end.'

'What? You think Van Dyck painted himself into the scene?'

'Or someone else put Van Dyck "in the picture".'

'Maybe Van Dyck was there then.'

'He was in Italy when Isabella died. But look at the eyes! Rubens' eyes are dull with sadness and this chap's eyes are keen -- fierce. He looks consumed. The death of Isabella is a hard fact for him.'

She gazes at the painting. 'You think someone is telling us something?'

He shrugs. 'Painting's are -- ambiguous.'

'OK.' She stood. 'To work.' She stripped.

'There. No ambiguity now.'

'I wouldn't say that. I like you ambiguous.'

The pose, for this painting, has changed since they began. She stands simply, her arms to her side, with the slight tilt of standing at ease. There is a reserved smile, except that in her forward mouth her strong white teeth show. Do her eyes seem to have a veil upon them? Though she is watched, she also watches, a lean sentinel on the horizon.

He was bent to his canvas when he heard the door click. Looking up, he saw Mae's face turned in profile. Her eyes, nose and chin had gone sharp alert. He was startled, even shocked, to see her so keen-edged.

Yet not so startled as he was the next instant, by the clear-voiced 'Stephen, hello.'

He turned, and saw Robyn framed in the door, at just that moment when her face changed too. She had entered with something flushed and brave in her look, surprising him, roguish, arriving unexpectedly. Her face, as he watched, went tombstone-grim, as she took in the room, and said 'Oh.'

'Robyn! Come in!' The false effusiveness sprang to his lips.

'I'm sorry, I'm interrupting. Excuse me. I'll go.'

She did not go. She stood looking stunned, pale as if her blood were transfused away.

'We'll stop.' He had laid down his palette, and Mae was stepping from her pose.

'Stephen, no. I don't want to interrupt. Please carry on. We can talk later.'

He knew that English voice, metallic and hard-edged. Still he said, 'I'll make some coffee.'

'No! Then I'll go at once. Please. Go on, Stephen.' It was Robyn's school-prefect voice; with a catch in it that moved him.

'Robyn, this is Mae. Mae, Robyn.'

The women smiled shortly.

Words died, they all were tongue-tied. He could do no other but pick up his brush again. It trembled in his hand, as though ready, on its own account, to flick paint round the room.

'You don't mind my watching, Stephen?'

He shook his head.

In that same clear voice, but more brittle-sounding, she said to Mae, 'Do you mind my being here?'

'Of course not,' Mae said, equally clearly. It seemed all her figure had contracted inwards and she stood like a staff, rigid with dignity.

Robyn stood with her straight profile lifted: her yellow hair streamed as if a wind blew in her face. And Mae stood naked but self-possessed, precipitously slim, her woman's body tightened to sinew. He, in comparison, felt like nothing: not their bigamous man, but a beetle or dog that would scuttle to hide.

'Stephen, please go on.'

Mae's face was mask-like, her eyebrows hoisted in quizzical arcs. She stepped back into pose, Bloodsmith dabbled his brush. He tried to smile in Robyn's direction – but what a ghastly smile this was, a rictus cranked up by primitive derricks. She stared back at him with searchlight eyes, so he looked away. She moved behind him, where he could not see her.

Mae's easy pose had turned menacing, like someone waiting dangerously on the opposite pavement. No way could he paint like this. He shivered the brush towards the canvas, and at the last moment closed his eyes.

Perhaps Robyn had stepped out of sight behind him, in order not to distract his painting. But it was worse now he could not see her. Her breathing was restrained, but sounded like panting; his shoulders flinched. The temperature in the room was rising. His skin prickled, he must be blushing all over just as, once, he saw Robyn blush. And the blush was heating like a rash, an inflammation calling for calamine. Previously, he had hardly felt shame, but chagrin it seemed was cooped inside him; in instants he inherited the guilt of a year. It made him indignant, why should *he* feel guilt? What had happened between Mae and himself was unwinding bright-lit on the studio floor, and against all reason it looked like guilt. It was not guilt before goodness, or guilt before God, it was guilt before Robyn… and all because he had opted for secrets.

He fumbled his colours. The corner of his eye saw the white of her coat. He could no longer hear her breathe, it seemed she had ceased to breath entirely. He saw Mae grow steadily more unhappy, but still for now he continued to paint. They must not be tripped into open war, and all by surprise with no one ready. He kept his movements cool, the picture of care and concentration. But his sight was failing, the studio blurred. They three were set in burning ice, just as in the old-fashioned Hell. They were in the red furnace. This was the firebox where love burned to dust.

'Rest'. He put brush and palette down.

'Thank you very much, Mae.'

She sighed and, deliberately, relaxed.

Robyn said, 'Stephen, we have to talk.'

He nodded, putting his paints away. They all were in motion. Mae reached for the kimono and slipped inside it. He tried to read her face, but that face was sealed. Grim, grim, grim, that closed set mouth and contracted nose.

To Mae, Robyn said, 'You must ache!'

Mae rubbed her neck, almost pulling her back-skin round to the front.

'I'm supposed to stand relaxed, but that's not easy to do.'

'He doesn't think how the model feels. And it's cold in here. How can you stand it?'

'I wasn't cold, but I am stiff.'

He listened as the women made a chatter, cold-voiced and hard-voiced, leaving him out of it.

'Would you like coffee?' he asked the room.

'I don't want coffee,' Robyn said sharply.

'I must go,' Mae said, 'I'm late for Gavin.'

'And we must talk, Stephen,' Robyn said firmly.

'Right,' he nodded, 'yes.'

'We must talk about Sally.'

'Sally?'

Only now he saw, Robyn had a reason for coming, a reason different from catching him *in flagrante*.

'Sally's all right?'

'All right? In a sense, she's all too well.'

Mae emerged from the screen, dressed. She did not look his way.

'Goodbye.' She threw one word to both of them, polite as a stranger. In grief and desolation, he watched her step quickly towards the door. Robyn firmly stood her ground, frankly staring as the other woman departed the territory.

So, he was alone with Robyn. The affable front she had put on for Mae disappeared.

'What about Sally?'

But Robyn, with Mae gone, put Sally on hold. She went up, too close, to stare at his canvas. He heard her breathing come in quick snuffs.

When she turned to face him, he saw the white of her eyes all round the iris.

'What's going on here, Stephen?'

'Oh, I'm just keeping my hand in, painting the figure, you know.'

'*Keeping you hand in!* It's more than that. I know who she is. You told me you were doing Rubens. Rubens in London. This doesn't look much like Rubens to me.'

'I am doing Rubens. Look at that print, that hand there is Rubens' hand. If you look close, you'll see him in bits, Rubens in bed, tormented by gout. And *that's* Rubens, the picture strip, though you wouldn't think it.'

'But *she* isn't in the Rubens series. Is she?'

'In a funny sort of way she is. She's one of our models, for the Life Class – ask at the School. Maybe she's the best model. I thought I'd paint her again. So I didn't tell you. I ought to have done. I know that.'

She stood with arms folded in the room's dead-centre. Should he say, 'Robyn, I love her. I'm sorry, but it has happened. I can't change it now.' This was the absolute chance to speak. How could he hesitate?

'Sometimes I need to paint. I can't do print-making all day long.' That was all he would say, Robyn must make the best of it.

She turned from him, and slightly buckled. To herself she said quietly, so he just heard,

'You used to paint me.'

'I did. I will.'

She looked again at the painting. She turned to look at him, with the same examining eyes. She stepped from it, shaking her head. 'It's my fault, after all. I can't blame you.'

'Tell me about Sally.'

'I'll tell you at home. I can't talk here.'

They left the studio, and walked side by side, not speaking. She strode energetically, as though she were by herself. Till he stopped in the public pavement and said,

'Please, Robyn. Tell me about Sally.'

'What's to tell?'

'You came today because of Sally.'

'Of course I did. A lot of good it did me.'

'What's new? Tell me.'

'Only she's not coming back tonight.'

'Is it a rave?'

'A rave? You've no idea, Stephen, have you?'

'She's stayed out at parties before.'

'This is not a party.'

She turned heel and strode briskly up the street, her yellow hair whipping as she walked. He caught up and walked beside her again.

'Where is she going?'

'She's spending the night with Mark.'

Bloodsmith thought. Yes, there was a Mark. But he didn't remember well.

'Did you say she could?'

Again, the blue-white raving stare. 'Yes, Stephen, I did. She had been going on about it. One night and one night. She asked me not to tell you. It was between women. And I said no and no. But this morning I said yes. The weekend's coming... somehow I gave in. And I wish I didn't. I couldn't go to work. That's why I came to you. And I wish I hadn't done that either.'

'You should have told me before.'

'Tell you, Stephen?'

He took offence, but it did him no good. 'Do you care about Sally, Stephen? You care about what you do in your studio, whether it's "art" or not. And whoever you do it with.'

So she brought him back to Mae. The issue, even so, was Sally.

He said, 'You're right, it shouldn't happen. Well, it's one night. She'll be back tomorrow.'

'I shouldn't have said one night. If one night, why not lots of nights? I feel I've said it's all right if she leaves home.'

'We'll draw the line just here, after tonight. We'll make it clear, that's it. It shouldn't have happened now and it doesn't happen again.'

'OK, yes. But I don't know if she *will* come back.'

'*If?* We'll go there. We'll drag her back. Do you know the address?'

'Yes, Stephen. I know the address.'

Here they paused, at their own address.

Inside, they felt the absence of Sally, as though she had left for good. It was a dead and empty house. It was their house.

They fetched up in the kitchen, and eventually, together, set to make a meal. He peeled, she chopped.

Ending the silence, he said 'Do you want to talk about my painting Mae?'

'No I don't.'

'You seem very fed up about it.'

Here she paused, and put the knife down. She raised a hand to push her hair back, as she examined him and said, 'Is painting the issue, Stephen? I'll tell you something about that "painting": I don't think it's great. I think it stinks.'

'Why?'

She did not answer. Then abruptly she said, 'Paint what you like, Stephen!' With a shrug she flung back to the chopping board. Clap clap clap came the blade on the wood.

'Oh bugger!' She had cut herself. They saw the line across the back of her finger: fine, a hair line, just like nothing. Then the blood pushed crimson, glistening, scarlet fingers across her finger.

'Bugger! Bugger!'

'Come under the cold tap.'

They were both at the tap, which fizzed ice froth at mains pressure. He squeezed the finger, so it looked white with no blood at all. But each time she drew it from the water, the blood poured again, diluting, spreading rapidly over her hand.

'Sit down.' He got plasters, antiseptic. After more washings he dried it quickly, poured on germ-killer, slapped on lint, and attached a plaster tightly.

They waited to see if the bleeding stopped. Her face was colourless.

'It's stopped.' He was glad he'd had this thing to do.

She sat, gazing at her finger.

He did what remained of the cooking. As they ate, they talked of Mark.

'Do you know him?'

'I've seen him is all.'

'Do you know anything about him?'

'Sally won't say anything.'

'That isn't much good.'

'Now you say it, Stephen.'

'Tomorrow she comes back. That's it.'

Robyn said no more about Mae. Eventually they went to bed, though it was not possible they could sleep.

He woke in the night. Robyn was not in the bed. He heard her moving about in the house. He got up, and found her in her dressing-gown in the living room. There was a late-night show on that she was not watching.

He sat, in case she wanted to talk.

She didn't talk. He went and made Ovaltine and brought it to them.

Finally they went up again. Again Robyn started to sleep before him. To him sleep did not come now. Sally came. He remembered the small girl in the Rubens painting, who reminded him of Sally when little. He remembered Robyn saying they had lost the plot. But was it Robyn who had lost it? Robyn was on the case. Slowly, unwillingly, the words grew clearer in the darkness. Robyn was on the case more than me. No. Robyn was on the case, and I was not.

He thought, Rubens had a daughter who died. Sally's alive but she's off the rails. And I was not on the case.

~

'If she doesn't come home,' he said in the morning, 'we'll go round and get her.'

'We'll see if she comes. She said she would.'

'Right.' He clattered nervously through his breakfast.

'I'll be off,' he said finally.

'What?'

'I have to go in.'

'Oh, you're going to your "studio". *Of* course.'

'I'm *not* going to the studio, I'm going to the Art School.'

'But it's Saturday!'

'No, but there's Degree Day coming. We're all going in. I've got the print students coming, to do extra stuff for the show. I'll ring to know if Sally's back. And you ring me, whenever there's news.'

'At the School?'

'The phone's near the Print Room.'

'You weren't in the Print Room yesterday.'

'They had lectures yesterday.'

Did she believe him? Her eyes were narrowed tiny.

At the first payphone he saw, he stopped to ring. Were he and Mae ruined? What if Geoffrey answered the phone? Too bad.

In the event Mae answered: Geoffrey was away at a managers' conference.

He apologized as though it was his fault that Robyn came, 'So sorry, no idea, so difficult— '

Coolly she said, 'I'm coming into town today.' It would be in the afternoon.

'We must talk.'

'Yes.'

They agreed to meet at a café with a roof-garden near the Art School.

In the Print Room itself there was a curious calm, which came from the students' concentration. Now the Degree Show had risen above the horizon, they worked in a patient, focused way. As often happened, in their very last months, their style came together where they floundered before.

'Oh that's *good*, Imogen. *Really* good!' It was the print of the rave, which always had been simply pretty. Now it jagged in lime-green and violet, with an acidity that made the eye leap. He pondered. 'But, do you know what? I'd make the third colour black.' The outlines were deep blue at present. 'Black will pull it together.'

They discussed, he circled among the others, and came to Laurie ('Lorry') Park, who looked punk-rock and menacing.

'Oh!' he said, surprised and pleased. It was a plate that had worried him, a straight-ahead abstract, just a square in a square in a square, each balanced against the others off-centre. But now instead of three colours, there were only two: deep grey and deep purple. The third square was simply white, deep-embossed into the paper. The two colours married, sharp-set against the white.

He nodded and Laurie's pierced face beamed. The simple, subtle print was right beyond words.

The room was quiet, the students busy. He was absorbed in the Print Room, while his life, in another world, blew apart.

Late in the morning he rang Robyn, but there was no news of Sally yet.

He lunched in the student bar with his students. They talked acids and inks. Balancing plastic cups of coffee, they walked back to the Print Room and resumed.

'Mr Bloodsmith!' He was called to the phone.

As he hurried to take it, he knew it was Mae. Saying what? She wouldn't come after all? Not ever again?

'Hello!' he said, in warmth and anxiety.

'Stephen?'

'Robyn!' He swallowed. 'Is Sally back? How are things?'

'Not good. She came and went.' A pause. 'I would be very grateful if you came home.'

It was the courtesy that chilled.

'I'm coming.'

Before he went, he faced the question, what about his rendez-vous with Mae? He *should* be back in time to see her. And if he wasn't? He didn't want to ring again.

The grey sky outside his house was white.

'Robyn?'

The hall was empty and dim.

He heard Robyn's voice, oddly quiet. 'I'm here, Stephen.' She was very near, in the living-room. He shot off a prayer, 'Let nothing terrible have happened here!'

Robyn sat in an armchair, her legs curled under her. Her eyes were red, her fair-skinned face blotched white and red.

'What happened?'

'Sally's gone.'

'What do you mean gone?'

'She's moved out.'

He could only stare, drop-jawed – a cartoon gawper.

'Where's she gone?'

'Where do you think?'

He sat down in the other armchair. 'But she came back?'

'She came to get her things. We had a fight, Stephen.'

'Are you all right?'

'I'm not hurt in that way.'

'We'll go and get her.'

'She won't come. I don't know if I want her back.'

He heaved a big sigh. 'How did things get to this?'

'I always said, we should set firm boundaries.'

'You were right. But she was difficult all the way. Because of her "friends".'

'No, Stephen. She was difficult because *we* weren't firm. Because we were liberal, arty types. Denouncing "authority". And as for our own "authority'? We blew it. Other people's children don't leave home.'

'Don't they?' He knew they did.

Robyn gave a kind of stifled gasp. 'I'm a lot to blame, I know.'

'*You're* not to blame, Robyn.'

'Don't say that, Stephen. It doesn't help. *And it isn't true*. I know I'm to blame. I was – away. But so were you, very much, in a way that goes back years.' Her gaze set. 'We fucked up.'

Things were too grim for self-defence. He nodded. He said, 'Yes.'

They were sitting dead-faced, more like chairs than like people in chairs. Still a part of him thought, If I'm here for hours, how do I get a message to Mae? How do I say I won't be at the café?

He heard a swallowed cough, and realized Robyn was crying. He went and knelt beside her chair, and found a way of leaning across, so his arm held her close.

She let herself be comforted. They held each other.

He stood. 'We'll go and get her.'

'I don't think she'll come.'

But she got up, bedraggled.

He walked round to the rented garage. With difficulty he started the neglected car. He scooped up Robyn, standing on the pavement, and drove in the direction of Mark's. Robyn sat like an ice-queen beside him. Still he thought of Mae, she'll come to the roof-café, and I won't be there. Then a spark struck in him, as if off a stone. So *let* Mae come, and not find me! It was like a flash of spite for her.

That was bad but he had other work now. From the urban freeway they branched off into back-streets, and fetched up in an alley with a rope-factory at its end. The workshops had curved rooves like Nissen huts, painted black as if with old pitch. There was some overgrown waste ground fenced in with chicken-wire, where supermarket trolleys lay woven with nettles. And a small terrace of gardenless houses, with motor-bike engines and dead TV sets piled in tiny yards.

They parked in front of the locked works gate, and walked down the terrace making out numbers.

'What will we say?'

'We'll tell her to come home.'

'We must be careful, we must say it the right way.'

'This is the place.'

They hesitated outside a house, which had started to shed its false-stone cladding. Its inch of frontage was mud and weeds, and a fallen wheely bin without its lid. The windows were as dark as though the walls inside were painted black.

From within the house, savage barking began. A wolf, wolves?

Their pale faces looked to each other. They picked their way up the skew cement pavings. Their state was: horror; worry; love; grief; alarm; anxiety; fear.

The bell made no sound. With the metal of his car-keys, Bloodsmith tapped on the frosted glass—

To awaken racket. There was scuffling and slithering, paws sliding on lino, and new barking, sudden, deafening, right in front of them. Was it a Rottweiler? The baying was hectic, furiously impatient to maul and murder.

Bloodsmith pushed the letter-box open. He was gazing directly in the open maw, pink-grey, dripping strings of spit, fanged with elongated canines. He saw the rolling, infuriate dog-eye. For a moment he wondered, is the dog frightened? Then again came the spittling dog-gob, frothing death an inch from his eye.

'Christ!'

'Come away, Stephen.'

But he stayed. Through the letter-flap he roared, down the gaping throat, 'Sally! Sal! Are you there?' The wolf-dog stopped barking. It gazed at him, surprised.

But no Sal came, and no one else. The dog had come, and would not go.

They looked at each other, helpless.

'Shall we leave a note? Telling her to ring?'

'Better to come back when she's here.'

Abashed, they retreated to the road. His heart, like hers, had sunk beneath the ground they stood on, and on down through the clay.

By the car they discussed.

'We'll go home,' he said, 'I'll come back with you.'

'It's all right, Stephen.'

'What's all right?'

'We can't do anything now. We'll come back tonight. Go back to your Art School. I took you from the students.'

'Forget the Art School.' He was geared to domestics.

'No, Stephen. That's not right. Go back. I won't go home now, I don't want to. I'll go to Print Positive. Drop me off there. We'll come back to all this tonight.'

'Are you sure?'

She was. And yet it was not to his students he would go. For, all unexpectedly, he was free to keep his appointment with Mae. Even, he was dispatched towards her, and on four wheels for greater speed.

~

He arrived before Mae at the cloud-blown roof-garden. He wondered, how will I handle this now?

But, 'Hello, Stephen!' She had come, weaving narrowly between the tables. Her face was serious and sad as Robyn's.

They kissed on the cheek like friends.

'Please sit, I'll fetch. What will you have?'

He went and got coffees. Then they both were sitting, she well wrapped up in her yellow coat. He held her hand, that rested on the table, long thin hand with twig-thin fingers, coffee-brown on top. The hand was cold, he clasped and soothed it, gazing up at her face. The lines of her cheek-bones, continuing down, made an indentation either side of her mouth.

She said, 'When the door opened— oh, I never wanted to be in a situation like that.'

'It was terrible. It was the worst that could happen.'

'No,' she said, 'Not quite the worst.' Perhaps a little she smiled.

'I just wish it hadn't happened.'

She said sweetly, 'It wasn't your fault.'

'I didn't do right – not by you – not by Robyn . . . '

'Well, it's happened.' The cold hand woke and squeezed him back. 'How was it at home?'

He saw that in her mind, the great trouble was his.

'Not good. But the reason Robyn came, was Sally.'

'Sally?'

He said.

'I'm so sorry, Stephen.'

He nodded seriously.

She said, 'It may be the best thing.'

'What do you mean?'

'Maybe Sally needs to get out. Your house seems like a bomb. Maybe you'd both get on better with her, if she did live somewhere else.'

'You don't mean, with the bloke.'

'No. But have you thought? Maybe the bloke is not the main thing. Maybe the main thing is leaving home, and the bloke is just a way to do that.'

He looked at her doubtfully.

'Maybe I say that, because I'm a more alone person than you.'

They talked about his family life. Mae sounded like a best-friend not a lover.

They came back to Robyn's call at the studio.

'I'm so sorry it happened.'

'Don't keep saying sorry. She had a reason to come.'

'But it's painful for everyone.'

'That's true. That is true. That is very true.' It seemed that as she took in her own words, she sat more upright, like a person drawing themselves to a height.

'I never thought— I *never* thought that I would be "the other woman".'

'You're not "the other woman". You're not the "other" anything.'

'No, that's not true. I'm very "other".'

'Not to me. Not now. No.'

Her head came forward, chinning her hands that were clasped up in an 'A'. Her eyes had gone un-seeing. They sat and sipped. It was his hope that though they had had a colossal knock, still, just by being together, the broken bones of their love would knit. The coffee had chilled. He asked the long-postponed question.

'When shall we carry on?'

She looked then surprised – even, shocked.

'Carry on?'

'With the painting.'

Her grave, almost frightened eyes. 'I won't come to your studio again.'

'We can meet somewhere else.'

'We *are* meeting somewhere else.'

'I don't mean like this.'

'You mean what? Like motels? Like someone's flat?'

He wouldn't press for motels now. 'I want to finish my painting of you.'

'Your wife will come again.' There was something cold in the words 'your wife', not only to Robyn but to him as well, as if he betrayed her by having a wife, for all that she too had a husband.

'She won't come again.'

'I think she will.'

She was gazing out over the battlements, beyond the works and through the cranes, and on into the empty whiteness. She made a wry face. 'She knows about us now. Soon she'll work out everything.'

Abruptly she stood. He looked at the vertical figure above him, elegant in the yellow coat. She impressed him as much as when he first saw her in the life class. But to see her the same, and to like her just the same, was a knife that cut him through.

He stood too; they were leaving. Carefully they wound between the tables, threading the backs of chairs and humans. He looked with love at her slender neck, between the coat and frizz-banged hair. Beyond her, beyond the concrete balustrade, were lines of tiles and other rooves, there were square tops of buildings with square blocks on them, and beyond them feathery tops of trees. Further in the distance was an old gasometer, telescoped empty, and the chimney of the hospital incinerator. She looked so noble seen from behind that she might have been a girl-Christ grieving for Jerusalem. Except at this moment she turned sharp left, and swiftly climbed downstairs.

At this moment, he had a vision. It was something half-seen, in the corner of the eye, but enormous. A giant flying creature, making over the rooves towards him. It was either transparent or made of shadow, shaped like a gigantic sting-ray, with featherless wings which had no bones. It was far off, over the goods yards, but coming in low. He knew its nature: it was the bird of sadness, it was sadness itself, growing towards him on slow-beating wings.

It was part of this vision, it seemed to him afterwards, that at the moment he turned to follow downstairs a sigh rose from the extended city, which was both a gasp torn from the roof of his lungs, and a moan like that which went up over Memphis, when the dearest of Egypt died in one night.

Outside he said, 'See you'.

She looked at him then, her smile was wan.

'See you?'

It was like a question. So they parted.

~

He patrolled their streets, looking for a parking slot. He let himself in the house.

'Robyn?'

No answer. He was early, after all.

He wandered through their home. In Sally's room, his eye caught on 'Superhog', an embroidered winged pig flying over skyscrapers. He drifted from room to room, feeling like a double of himself. With luck, he would meet the real Bloodsmith downstairs.

He was relieved when he heard the Yale key turn in the lock. Sally?

'Stephen?'

Robyn looked exhausted but flushed: evidently she had spent a good time walking.

'Nothing from Sally?'

'I've not been back long.'

'I'm so angry with her. I'm furious.' Robyn sat down. 'She's throwing her life away. Junking it. Trashing it. I could rend her limb from limb.'

'We'll go and get her.'

Robyn glared. 'She won't come back.'

'We'll see.'

They had a bite, desultorily. The television showed a population streaming from a town, with close-ups of a man in loose white baggy trousers. He was laden with bags and sacks, and ran with a square bundle made up of layers of eggs, tied in corrugated paper.

They went to the car, and drove to the house. As before, he parked by the rope-factory gate. It had grown dark, but the house was brightly lit.

He knocked. Again, the hectic scampering paws slipping and a-sliding on the lino, and barking in the last paroxysm of fury.

The door opened. A man stood in the space. He was tall and broadbuilt, swarthy, unshaven. In Bloodsmith's eyes his skin looked scarred: pockmarked, cratered, hideous.

Bloodsmith said, 'We'd like to see Sally.'

Robyn said in his ear, 'Just say, send her here.'

The hideous man looked at them. Was he truculent, sneering?

'I'll see.'

He half turned away, then turned back.

'Do you want to come in?'

'No thank you,' he said.

'No,' said Robyn.

He smiled or leered, and left. The wolf-dog stood on the threshhold panting, its useless long tongue hung out from its fangs. It gazed at them with an aged look, and seemed to have forgotten its fury.

Sally came to the door. Her face was red, her eyes sparkled. Was it tears, was it hash? She wore a loose shirt hanging out.

'Hello,' she said, in a low voice that slunk out of her nose.

'Sally, you're coming home.'

Her face at once went tight-skinned and bright.

'No, I'm not.'

'I'm not arguing in the street, Sally. We'll talk at home.'

'We can talk here.'

'I'm not talking here.'

'Perhaps we can talk,' Robyn put in.

'No,' he said, 'We're not talking here. We'll talk at home.'

'There's nothing to talk about.'

'What do you mean, there's nothing to talk about? There's a hell of a bloody lot to talk about.'

'The only thing to talk about, dad, is whether I live at home, or whether I live here. And I'm not living at home. I'm not your property, you can't make me.'

'Whatever, Sally. Even so. We will talk at home.'

The man came up, towering over Sally. 'Would you like a cup of tea?' He held high a mug the size of a tankard, and pointed at it with the finger of his other hand.

Robyn thrust forward. 'Sally, I've something to say to you. You're behaving like a bloody slut.'

Sally shrieked, 'I'm not a slut!'

She slammed the door.

Robyn's head recoiled. A moment's pause and she shouted furiously, 'Open this door, Sally! Now!'

On the other side, the dog exploded: nuclear barking, terminal rage.

They made out other voices, inside the house.

'Open this door, Sally!'

Above the barks, they heard Sally's voice, rising high as if she were crying.

'I'm not talking to you, mum.'

'Tell her, Stephen.'

'Will you let me?'

He went to the door. When the dog was quiet, he shouted 'Sally!' The dog erupted. He waited till it stopped, and called 'Sally!'

Her voice came, tearful, indignant, annoyed. 'What is it, dad?'

'Sally, we'll talk about this at home.'

Her voice swung high, 'Dad, I'm not coming home!' The dog supported her.

He struck the door. 'You must come, to talk.'

They waited only a little time on the doorstep. They went round the end of the terrace, and came at the house from the back. From the garden fence, he bellowed 'Sally!'

They came round the front of the house again. He would learn from the dog, he sharpened his call to a knife-shout, 'Sally!'

Other doors opened. All down the short terrace, people were emerging, alarmed and flustered. He called again, blade-voiced, 'Sally!'

His neck hurt as if he'd cut his throat, but he called once more. The dog barked back. The night was dark. What a sight, if anyone who knew them saw them!

The door opened again. The man stood in it.

'Sally's coming. Talk to her at home.'

Sally appeared, with a parka round her. Her face was white and red from crying.

The parents stood grim-faced, watching her come.

'Let's go,' he said.

As they walked towards the car, they were aware Sally stayed to kiss the man. She followed them to the car. She got in the back seat, they in the front. They drove back in silence, except that at intervals Sally burst out, 'I won't stay at home!'

They gazed ahead. When Bloodsmith glanced sideways, he saw the stark face of Robyn, facing forward resolved.

At home they negotiated.

'I'm not living here.'

They insisted, urged, argued, pleaded; talked, shouted, paused, cried. In the end they settled, like politicians, for compromise. Sally would stay at home weekdays, and spend one weekend night at the other house.

By the time they finished, they had settled for this.

'Look,' he said, '*Unto Death* is on.'

Sally said nothing, they all watched it gloomily.

In the serial itself, matters have grown serious. Fat Mustafa mourns his pole-dancer, who gave him up when she found he was helplessly ticklish. Though it was a forbidden, a sinful, love, he has never loved anyone as he loved her and her pole. He weeps on Broadway and he weeps in Times Square. He weeps as he lolls the rolls of himself, cataracting sweat in the near-solid steam of a New York Turkish Bath. Also we see more of the New York police, bewildered by rumours of a deadly threat. Beautiful Mohammed steps from a cloud of New York steam, materializing to his Polish-Jewish girl-friend with a face grey-green like the living dead. Weeping he begs her to leave the city, she must be gone by a certain date, before the city is bitten by the Teeth of God. She sees they face death but she won't go without him, and he will not come with her.

They went to bed. 'It's terrible,' Robyn said.

'It's better than nothing.'

They sighed, and settled to try to sleep. They had patched up an arrangement. How long would it last? The house was on the rim of disintegration. At least Sally slept at home that night.

They held hands as they lay in bed.

'She's back,' Robyn said, 'But *where* will it end? You saw him, he's dreadful.'

'But she's here. For now, at least.'

Robyn's hand tightened on his, his on hers. They lay side by side, gazing at a ceiling they could not see.

When Robyn slept he thought of Mae. For Sally was home. And surely it was not possible that his love for Mae – their bond, their passion – could, just suddenly, be stopped in its tracks?

15

However the crisis of his life blew up, 'Rubens in London' would not stop now. As Bloodsmith's studio was invaded, so too will be now the studio of Rubens. The event is imagined in *Chess with Kings,* and in a large print, late in Bloodsmith's series, we see the invasion. The door has opened just as Rubens is telling the Gerbiers' eldest daughter, Elizabeth, how she must pose within that great canvas which he will give to King Charles.

'I fear we disturb you, Sieur Peter.'

'By no means, Mistress Deborah, I am glad to see you. And little Mistress Susan. Pray be seated, and permit me to paint while I talk.'

'Should we not be silent?'

'No, I have the wit to talk and paint together. You see I am advanced in painting Mistress Elizabeth. Ah, but Elizabeth, pray hold up the hem of your dress. You can rest your hand on the table's edge.'

'It hurts to stand like this, Sieur Peter. I wish you would paint me standing straight.'

'Forgive me, but I need you to lean forward. Others in the painting are standing straight, if all stood so it would make a fence. And your leaning is of moment to me. It is one side of the pyramid that sustains this painting.'

Elizabeth sighed, and stayed as she was (half-seated on a stool, one hand on a chair-back).

He continued to work, till the voice of Susan reached them, making a whisper of complaint to her dolls,

'He is taking a long time painting Lizzie.'

'Susan!' said Deborah.

'Patience, sweet Susan. I shall come to thee. Elizabeth, hold still one minute more.'

Rubens touched the point of his brush in his white, then placed a speck in the cavity where her eye was set, where the white skin was waxy and caught the light. He put another white speck in the shell of her nostril, where the pink skin was slightly moist. And a white dot on her bottom lip.

'Ah!' said Deborah, 'Now the whole face doth shine the more. It is Lizzie exact to the life.'

'Rest,' said Rubens.

'Hooooh!' said Elizabeth, standing tall. She worked her shoulders and swung her head.

Rubens screwed his eyes tight. 'I will rest too.'

They were now in a line before the canvas which, supported by a brace of easels, almost filled Rubens's chamber. Many of the figures were still to be painted, and existed only as drawings in chalk. But in the centre it appeared there was a naked woman, with a squatting satyr before her. She will be Pax, and the woman and man behind her in armour will be Minerva and the war-god Mars. But in the foreground, where once Rubens planned to show an architect, and a woman with a lyre, he now has children. George Gerbier is already painted, holding a torch and a wreath. In front of him leans Lizzie, just completed. The wet paint shines in her cloth-of-gold dress, as if it were a marriage of sunlight and water. In front of Lizzie is the outline of Susan, sketched in chalk.

They heard the landing timbers creak.

'What goes on here?'

'It's father!' Lizzie made wide eyes to Susan.

'You are home, dear heart,' Deborah said.

'Good day, friend Balthazar.'

'To thee good day, friend Peter Paul. But can you work with my brood all about you?'

'But it is your brood, as you call it, that I am painting.'

'Father, he is going to paint me now. Aren't you, Sieur Peter?'

Balthazar said, 'What, a little thing like you, Susan? You're much too small. I don't think I'll let him.'

'But father, I am wearing my best black bodice. And my finest muslin blouse. I made our Lizzie put pearls in my hair. And look, I am wearing my new white apron.'

'Susan!' cried Lizzie, 'You *don't* wear your apron, not with your black bodice and muslin and pearls. What say you, Sieur Peter? Should not Susan take off her apron?'

Susan looked at Rubens with a lower lip that shivered.

'In the art of painting, Mistress Elizabeth, one should do those things that awake most wonder. And thus I think Susan may wear her apron, as she would not were she going to Court. For also it is fine-stitched apron, and white like the untouched snows of Atlas. And linen too is a fruit of Peace.'

Susan went and stood where he bid her.

He dabbled colours.

'Look at me, Susan, I beg of your grace, not at Balthazar just now.'

Their talking stopped, for Rubens's hand moved quickly now. His not long nose tautened, he seemed to breathe through his mouth. He held in one hand both his palette, and several fine brushes. With one or other of these, he would dab his colours, with fine light pecks like a bird picking grain.

They had passed into a trance where they could not talk, infected with Rubens's concentration. The brush at last they scarcely saw, as they watched the face of Susan grow to life before their eyes. Where some of her hair fell over her brow, they saw her white forehead through the finest gold threads.

'Oh, look mother, that's Susan's nose exactly! Why mother!'

They all turned.

'Your pardon, forgive me. But it so much is Susan. Don't look at me, please. Sieur Peter, I did not know till now what a painter you are. All my babes, to the life! Come, Balthazar. Hold my hand and stand by me. Forgive me, I am unprovided.'

'I want to see! Sieur Peter, may I go?'

'Wait, Susan, I beg, one instant more. One spot of white, to the white of your eye. And... there. I have finished. I thank thee, for thy grace and patience.'

As Susan trotted round to see, Rubens rested his palette down. With a finger-nail he scratched his eyebrow, and surveyed his painting.

'What say you, Susan? Do I have thee?'

But all that happened, as all of them looked, was that Susan's face puckered and withered.

'He's made me fat! I don't think he's a very good painter!' Tears splashed zigzag on her turning red face.

Consternation has entered this room. An artist and a family are fallen in a strange despair.

Rubens indeed has put his hand to his head, as one who might say: Have I done it again!

'Go back, Susan, I pray. I will labour to mend what I have marred.'

But Susan stood planted. She said to her father, 'I don't know if he can.'

'Susan!' cried Deborah, 'Sieur Rubens is called the Prince of Painters. He is the master painter of the world.'

'I don't think so.'

Rubens, at this point, lost his indulgence.

'Susan, I purpose to give the King this picture. If you would have him see thee fair, you must step back and take thy pose. The choice it is entirely thine.'

In dudgeon, Susan returned to her pose.

He took his brushes, the family's noses were at his elbow. He added an extra white fold to the apron, so it hid more of Susan's plump right arm, and he strengthened the shadows.

'Come and see, Susan. I can no more.'

Sturdily she came, and stood with her hands on her hips. So quietly they could hardly hear, she murmured 'Tis better.' Cold thanks. But all at once she turned to Rubens, and elegantly, even with dignity, dropped him a curtsey.

'That's nicely done, Susan,' Deborah said quietly.

'Susan, you have made a great nuisance,' said Lizzie.

While Deborah attended to her children, Rubens talked man to man with their father.

'You have a painter's eye, Balthazar. Think you this a likeness to your brood?'

'It is a work of great competence, and a true likeness surely.'

Rubens's brow fluttered but he murmured suavely, 'I thank thee for those gracious words, my brother of the brush.'

Balthazar continued. 'One question only detains me. That satyr that kneels before Peace – it is a *satyr*! I am not sure I have grasped thy fullness of allegory.'

'Why, it is one we both may know. For this grizzled satyr, I mean his face to resemble a kindly father, yet also he is the lusty great seed-power of Nature. And both the leopard that rolls on the floor, and the cornucopia he doth hold forth – why, both may be seen to spring from his loins. He is the opposite man to Mars, and all his force but makes a Peace, in which the fiercest powers but play. And all the fruit of his cornucopia is children, even thine own, whom I do love.'

'It is brave allegory, friend Peter Paul, with more of fire than I first had supposed, when I heard tell of an Allegory of Peace.'

'It must be a virile and potent Peace, else it hath not power to abide.'

The clear voice of Deborah has called, 'Come Lizzie, come Susan, and bring your children. We must leave Sieur Peter to his works.'

Still Gerbier, beside the painting, frowned. 'Forgive me, but had you not once the pretty conceit, to show Mars pressed by Minerva within the Temple of Janus?'

'Oh, I gave that conceit over, as being too curious.'

'I am sorry for that. The learned will be much dismayed.'

Rubens raised his brows ruefully. 'Another day then, I must amuse the learned.'

Balthazar, having complained, was happy. 'Let us drink wine, friend Peter Paul, to ease you from your toil.'

Rubens has flexed his hand again.

'I thank God the gout has left me.'

'Come then. For the wine will be the best wine, to drive the gout from all of us.'

The men follow Deborah and the children from the room: one might trace the deep timbre of their voices, following the singing voices of the others, as they clatter down the staircase, and are lost in passages.

The half-finished canvas rests alone in the room, where the pensive girl, with a slightly lisping expression, leans forward in profile, holding the hem of her cloth-of-gold dress, so as nearly to enclose the younger plump-faced girl, in the black velvet bodice and whiter-than-white apron, who gazes towards us, with hesitant interrogation, from within the gentle embrace of Lizzie. Behind them again stands the tall war-god Mars, looking back and down to see them, while Minerva shoes him off, and the Fury Alecto calls him to battle. Near to the children, the cream-fleshed Goddess Pax is seated, squeezing her breast so milk arcs into an infant's mouth. In front of her is the vigorous kneeling satyr, who holds forth his lightly sketched horn of fruit as if he would say, across the picture, 'Susan and Lizzie, have a grape!' From between his haunches, the leopard emerges, rolled on its back and showing a pink tongue. Both the rich bright colours, and the white canvas where unpainted, shine in white and gold and red as the dusk thickens to veil it from us, in the panelled upstairs room of the old house of the Gerbiers beside the Thames near Charing Cross.

16

He had to notice that Robyn made no mention of Mae. Everything she said was controlled, she would not show even curiosity. If they were together in concern for Sally, still, in the next days, the glaciers arrived, their Ice Age came down from the whited-out sky. Resolutely and grimly Robyn managed her life, both her gallery, about which she no longer spoke, and also their home. To Bloodsmith she was carefully polite, in a way that applied a pressure on him.

Sometimes he found her, in corners of the house, come to a standstill with a bitter depressed look. Ages since, it was he who hurt from faithlessness. Now it was Robyn. I have come where she was. It's a sort of Purgatory, living like this.

Nor was he seeing Mae. They had sad desultory phone-calls, but they had not yet found another place to meet. Also he needed for her to come to his studio, so he finished the Mae-painting he had begun. Eventually she did come, on a day that seemed safe.

'Hello, Stephen.'

The room stayed cold however he heated it. Their faces were peaked, even aged. It was like standing on the edge of a lunar crater, where a meteor burst a millennium ago. Mae's face was defiant and gaunt when she posed, nor could she stand quite still as she used to.

Nor he. 'Don't keep turning round,' she said.

'What? I'm sorry, I didn't realize.'

'No. It's OK. I know why you do it. I'm looking at the same place.'

She was, she was looking behind his shoulder. He knew whom she saw, and he himself turned also. The living have ghosts, and Robyn's was there. Mae felt it and he felt it, the burning vibration in the light was Robyn.

Even so he painted. There was a flutter of shadow. Perhaps a thicker cloud passed over the roof-light— he did not look up, but there was a throb in the air, as if big wings beat once in space.

'May I rest?'

'Please rest.'

His eyes met hers. There were tears in her eyes and her eyes were burning. When he took hard hold she only half resisted: she did not give but she was not closed. Her mouth was obstinate, or angry; her kiss was hard. The acrid redness stepped out from his walls, it was round them and in them. When he shut his eyes he saw boiling crimson.

They loved on the floor. This must be last love (except that the embers were not dying but heating). They had not met for too long. There was an absence, a deficit to be made up. In the low light her shining skin was darker. In a fever they clasped caressing harder.

'We mustn't make marks!' she said. Tooth-marks, claw-marks, marks of the lust-beast.

She was burning hot and the heat was in him. He looked down on her perfect black slenderness. Her eyes were ravenous. Like his own they were fire and desire. More than torrid, more than tropical: they two were riding the Equator. They embraced as if with violent holding they could weld the two of them one.

Or you could say it was love in the oven, in Daniel's furnace, until all gave and melted, she cried, his life poured into her.

They lay back, collecting. In silence they washed, he disposed of his precaution. In concert they dressed. The red in the walls had gone hard and cold. His genitals ached as though they were emptied forever.

With few words she left. You could wonder, had they done with each other?

After she had gone he sat facing his painting, at a standstill. He was facing a cruelty: was it possible he would paint his Vision of Mae only exactly as he lost her?

17

Full summer has come, with Degree Day less than a week away. The air is humid and ominously laden, as if giant feet are treading nearer. Catastrophes are on him, he can be heading for the all-time smash. Has he lost Mae, however he loves her? Does his marriage hang by a thread or by a hawser?

Perhaps in reaction to these strains, in an odd space of time one afternoon, he is smitten with caprice. He thinks, But I've no pictures of Joachim and Willem, Rubens' man and Hendrik's man! I'll remedy that. There is that odd late chapter in *Chess with Kings*... He takes a big pad, and a pack of coloured crayons he borrowed once from Sally.

Joachim and Willem: they are rivals in love for plump Marilian, together they will take her out. Each has a large basket and so has she. They hire a rowboat upstream of London. In his cartoonish sketch broad Joachim and sinewy Willem sit side by side, each with an oar, watching black-eyed Marilian lounge in the stern in all her white and gold-pink beauty. Let the water be motionless, a mirror, as they advance into a summer's day breathless with beauty! Pollen hangs in the air, turquoise damsel-flies flicker through the dapple. As the river bank rises, they watch a rabbit in silhouette scamper round the next bend.

Having landed they spread a cloth in a meadow of sumptuous grass. Marilian lays out a pigeon pie she has made, a loaf, grapes and peaches, flagons of French wine and sweet Malmsey (all from the Gerbiers' kitchen). Joachim lays out strawberries and pears (from the Gerbiers' walled garden), Willem giant mulberries gathered in a dock leaf (from a tree only he knows). Each will proffer to Marilian a nosegay, a lily from Joachim and carnations from Willem, each rewarded with a ripe-lipped kiss. Let summer time in all her splendour bestow her blessings on this day! Far off a cow rests, chewing. A joyous scene.

Too peaceful, though. For soon the men, inflamed with wine, will compete. Willem serenades Marilian to a small bagpipe, clearly handmade from a pig's bladder. Which provokes Joachim to warble, plying his bow on a plank of wood with a single string. Presently they rear up, arguing whose song Marilian likes the best— regardless of anything she may say. Then whose bouquet smells the sweetest, then whose fruit is ripest, and so they come to blows, hurling peaches and over-ripe pears. Ah, but Joachim spies a cow-pat, sun-dried and crisp, and send it spinning like a discus into the boney head of Willem, who slams his own gigantic cow-crap onto Joachim's head, where the crust remains aslant like the cap of a king's councillor. All this Bloodsmith cartoons.

'Stop it!' Marilian's furious voice gets through at last. 'Into the river, boys!'

We'll draw all three of them bathing naked, the men furiously scrubbing their bodies and clothes, while snatching eyefuls of Marilian's gold creaminess. Till they emerge, clean and glowing like the newly baptized freshly washed from the shit of sin. The men hang their clothes on branches to dry, while Marilian lounges luxuriously back. Her black eyes flutter.

'Come to me, Joachim'.

See Willem gape as though the sky fell down, till her smile says to him, *Just you wait*. And when Joachim, having loved her, rolls sighing deeply onto his back, she says with her darkest gleaming gaze, 'Come to me, Willem.' So Willem comes and loves her too.

Which gives Bloodsmith his comedy print of the trio, the fat and thin naked man lying back, each resting his head on a generous breast, while the lightest of breezes and Marilian's finger-tips softly ruffle their hair. In turn all three sip the sweet Malmsey to the end, while the day in its pleasantness grows only riper. A fête champêtre à la Brueghel.. A pair of cabbage whites flutter nearby, while quietly they watch the skylark above them climb and climb then dive.

When dusk begins they will stand, and put on their dried clothes. Joachim and Willem mutter quietly, looking at the cow that has now drawn close. Both suddenly sprint, and scramble and tumble onto her back.

'Ga op!' shouts Joachim.

'Snel!' calls Willem, slapping the cow's rump.

'Soho!' cries Marilian.

There is a shortest bucking rollicking run, and both crash off. To gather their picnic, get back in their boat, and make their way home with no effort at all since the clean beautiful river bears quietly forward their warm sated restfulness.

These things he has sketched, the more happily the more disreputable they were, as he wistfully dreamed love is big, love gives, love likes a laugh.

~

In truth, days later, love caught him again. Returning home, relaxed from a good day with the students all working full-pelt for the annual show, he called through the house, 'Robyn!'

'Stephen,' she answered, 'Come up!' He was startled by her cheerful voice.

He climbed the stairs, to meet on the landing a naked Robyn, who wore only a head-towel, folded up on her wet hair like a Pharaoh's hat.

'I had a bath, and a drink in the bath.'

'I'm very glad. *What* are you celebrating?'

'Great news! It's all coming right.'

'That's great! What is coming right?'

'We've *got* the funding for the Feasibility Study. And beyond that, things look *very* good.'

'You've heard something extra.'

'Well, there was the letter at the Gallery. And then— I had a phone call.'

Even then he thought, from whom came this phone-call?

But the call was from a safe soul. It amounted to saying, Robyn's case for expansion was thought by the knowing to be very strong. In sum, it would happen.

'That's great! No, it's wonderful.'

She towelled her hair. 'You can have a drink, Stephen.'

'Thanks. Is that bubbly?'

'No, it's bloody sherry. You can buy me champagne later.'

Good news plus happiness made the aphrodisiac. She was for kissing, they kissed. She sat down naked in a bedroom chair.

'Of course, there are complications.'

It turned out that the city-centre plot, which she had her eye on, was no longer good. But she had found somewhere better, beside the river: it had been a small power-station, from the times when cities made their own power. It was fed by coke, that came up the river by barge.

'Of course I'll only have a part of it. The Arthouse Cinema is coming in too. And I'll join up with the multi-media centre.' The Council had decided it was right for an Arts Complex.

'That's wonderful, Robyn. Congratulations!'

'We'll see it soon, it's all arranged.'

Naked, she relaxed, exalting. From the mental cavern where he had crouched estranged, he looked out at her on the wicker chair. Her pink-white body glowed, full and soft, mature, at ease, glistening where it was polished by toweling. Her fair hair was yellow-brown from wetness, damp locks attaching to her forehead. He caressed her, they kissed. As she stood from the chair their old love and desire tottered back up from the pit of the past. Damp and warm, she shone with cleanness. Like a breath, like teleporting, they slid onto the bed and lovingly caressed and at leisure made ample love.

They lay quietly afterwards.

'It's *very* good news,' he said again. 'I'll go for champagne.'

'Stephen.'

'Yes.'

'Before you go— give us a kiss.'

Another? He did.

It was only as he left the house for the off-licence that the knowledge broke clear in his head. This might have been love, but it was also betrayal, betrayal of his love for Mae. The betrayal was in the *ease* with which he made love to Robyn. Though how odd that was too! Would he feel guilt for making love to his wife?

As he came up the road with the sparkling, Sally converged on him. Her face was sour, from having to hurry home.

Her look changed as he told her the news.

'WOOOOOoooooo!' she cried out loud in the street. 'That's GREAT! That's great for mum!'

She banged into the house, so he heard her from outside it, 'Mum, that's absolutely fantastic!'

That evening the family caroused. Whatever the damage to his love for Mae, he found he could not help forgiving himself. Together they watched *Unto Death*, where attention had shifted to Lieutenant Solomon, a stout African American cop, with his boney sidekick Victor O'Hilligan. Though the NYPD has been sceptical, these two follow clues up fast, till the only problem they have is the multitude of leads they find to disaffected types and groups, from the subways to the suburbs. As they pass from cellars with suspicious amounts of fertilizer in apartment blocks that have no gardens to lilac coloured wardrobes bursting with every kind of firearm from handguns to assault rifles and semi-automatics, their heads reel. For how many suspects may you not find, if you start to target those individuals who want to blow up everything?

18

And now it was here, Degree Day itself, the convulsion of the year; an end to the hectic late-night hammering, the hurried repaintings. Even the mountains of detritus – hessian, paint-pots, nails, strips of canvas, blue-tac, pins – were all replaced by an ordered space, swept and neat as a young couple's home. The usual population had disappeared, and instead of people with slashed jeans and hair like birdsnests, laughing and hooting, a new race had appeared. The average age was older, for the students had parents one could not have guessed. So there were middle-aged men in suits, and younger men in new-washed shirts; older women in frocks and dresses, and younger women in combos and outfits. Bloodsmith recognized his own students returned to the demureness of sons and daughters. On everyone, on powdered faces, close-cut hair, on shaven cheeks, was the shine of celebration.

In a packed hall, a pop channel disc jockey gave out the scrolls, to art students who looked suddenly like students at a university, all gowned (though the gowns were art-school colours). He was struck by the way the shafts of light fell. One landed where a hand received a scroll, as though the scroll carried a blessing into the hand that made the art. Then the ceremony was over and in the clean spaces, he moved among parents and was buttonholed by students. The social person in him rose, to meet these affable machinists and teachers, business men and lawyers and even artists, from whom the students he knew had emerged. Then Grieve passed in the distance, gleaming in a neat-cut aluminiumish suit. He thought, that man can't get off free... and I've done nothing about it. His heart banged like an elephant's heart, clunk pause clunk. Normally Robyn was beside him on Degree Day. Without words they had agreed she would not come this year.

He was cheerfully accosted by the parents of Imogen, who already had a place to do an MA at Goldsmith's. They chatted about her prospects, as Imogen herself came and went, then drew her parents away. 'There's an installation you have to see. Everyone says. It's called "The Garden of Hieronymus", it's based on Bosch.'

He did not hurry, but presently he came to the room of installations. There was a wash-basin made of coarse matting. A kitchen chair bore a softening spire of hard-set honey. A robotic superhero reeled like a drunk. He headed to a structure at the end of the room, which issued unending moans. He knew this must be 'The Garden of Hieronymus', but immediately it looked like a gigantic strawberry, made out of scarlet pvc.

The entrance, he saw, resembled a rectum, but still he went in. Evidently the wave of interest had passed, for hardly anyone was there. In low light he saw gigantic melons of papier maché with jagged Halloween mouths across them, from which the bottom halves of dolls (stripped naked) projected. Legs waved, sometimes a head and arms. An inflated plastic globe rolled loose on the floor, with two life-size naked inflated figures inside it, arranged to look as though copulating. On the end wall a projection-screen showed blown-up shots from Bosch. A woman upside down in water had a fruit between her legs which cracked like an egg to release a songbird; a black man and a white woman loved. Between these shots came snaps of video, where a woman's head crooned night-club numbers. Below the screen was a bedstead of the simplest kind, an iron frame criss-crossed with metal strips. On it lay two life-size figures cut out of cartridge paper, a starkly semi-abstract naked man and woman, or boy and girl, who lay hand in hand and goggled at the screen. The man had a big 'A' on his chest and the girl a big 'E', while the paper banner between the bed-posts said in big letters 'A and E'. Over this scene another projector played, so the whole interior seemed to stream with turbid liquid, and Bloodsmith recalled the rain-shadows falling on Robyn. Then he saw there was someone there he knew. Through the pouring images the man was hard to make out, but he saw this was no parent. This was Adrian Grieve in his shimmering suit.

He had not noticed Bloodsmith, and seemed abstracted, staring up at the screen, where naked figures in water gnawed a giant blackberry. Then the video cut in, with artillery firing, and – gross – a penis ejaculating to camera. The sound-track turned to Father Christmas laughing, yo-ho-ho.

Any moment, he thought, the man will turn round. For weeks he'd said, I'll cut his balls off. Obviously he wouldn't. Women are free, you don't fight over them like a Neanderthal.

Instead of turning, Grieve bent down to examine a photo bluetacked to the wall. So, when he sees me, do I eyeball him with a killer eye? That's not much.

Grieve stood straight and scratched his head, evidently in thought. And then, I am loving another man's wife. I can't hit Grieve for doing what I'm doing. But to turn round and walk away, like I'm pissing in my pants!

Too late, in any case. Grieve did turn now, just as the lighting changed to strobe. In jagged shots he saw Grieve look up: Grieve's face surprised; Grieve's mouth half open.

'Stephen,' he said, breathlessly. Bloodsmith felt his own hair stand up like a cat's.

'You should have kept clear of us.' The words were out, he heard their menace.

Grieve made an odd sound, like a laugh without breath. 'By Christ you're right. I wish I had.'

Red-hot boomed through him – the bastard Grieve had insulted Robyn! His shoulders hulked to block the space. In truth, he loathed Grieve from the moment he first saw him.

'Let me through, please.' Grieve stepped sharply forward.

He did not move. Grieve was standing too close to him. Let him back off and go round the back way.

'If you please,' Grieve repeated, the Principal insisting. In some way he loomed closer.

But — stand your ground, Grieve shall not pass! It must have been then that they saw they would fight. Men fight, there's testosterone. Rubens and Lucas Vorsterman fought. Even Peace must be fought for. A hot tingling poured upwards through Bloodsmith.

And perhaps it was not about Robyn at all. Grieve was the power-figure standing high over him. For months Grieve let him fear for his job — would he scrap Printmaking? Nor can it happen, that you sit quiet while your boss screws your wife. Are you man or mouse? Time for the slaves' revolt. Time to hack power in the kisser, boot it in the kidney. Let his job go to hell.

But they were artists, both. How do artists get to strike a blow? Through the strobe-flashes they were humping and heaving towards each other, grunting and snoring. Grieve's face was all circles, round eyes, round nostrils, round ring of lips. His own fingers were flexing, opening and closing.

'I wasn't unwelcome, you know.' There was truculence, a sneer, in Grieve's voice. 'You ask Robyn.'

Thank God he said that! Grieve's face was so stupidly pumpkin-shaped, it bobbed sideways like a head on a spring at the instant Bloodsmith's fist whacked into it.

Events moved slowly at breakneck speed. What most surprised Bloodsmith, for the man had no right, was the sight of knuckles growing in strobe-jerks at his eye. Would his eyeball burst? He was shocked how it hurt.

Still Grieve, with his scarlet cheek, came on. A voice in his ear said, Live up to your name, Bloodsmith! Aggression seized him. As the strobe turned green, and the woman's voice groaned sweetly, he brought his knee like a piston up through Grieve's abdomen, and as Grieve bent double croaking Bloodsmith punched his ear so his head jiggled now like a fruit on a stalk. Then he flapped his fingers, which hurt as if he'd broken them off.

Grieve was back, and punched him in his own solar plexus, so hard that, cartoon-like, he imagined a fist-shape sticking out of his back. In blinding agony he thought of ruptures and hernias. He staggered upright.

On the screen a man inside a pink fruit watched a black mouse start down a glass tube towards his face. For a moment the two of them oddly hugged each other, restricting arms, then they lost balance, somersaulting sideways into the bed-frame. The paper Adam and Eve were ripped in shreds, and taut wires snapped, while the bed-frame gave a diatonic cluster of twangs.

The strobe stopped. They were back in the still, dim light of the start, but caught in a strange entrapment. For they stood within the iron bed-frame, broken bed-wires and snapped metal strips jostling round their knees. If either bent down to release his legs, the other would hack him. Grieve's hair had fallen across his face.

'You're in the street, Bloodsmith. Get your cards.'

'My job? I don't give a damn.' He made to slug him freely, but Grieve's arm came up to parry, so they bluntly banged each other's chests. Their feet shuffled, the bed slipped with them. It grated and squeaked shrilly on the floor as if they were lurching in a misconceived vehicle. The woman's voice sang huskily, the screen showed a blue porcupine. Then a different sound made both stop and turn—

—to see they were no longer alone. When had they arrived, these stupefied watchers? Young faces gawped, old faces showed bewildered. Perhaps they thought this was a 'happening'. Performance art at the cutting edge, real blood too. The sound-track crooned softly, pulsing erotically below the floor.

'Excuse me . . . ' someone began.

Bloodsmith had stopped, thinking Grieve, as Principal, could not strike in front of parents. He was wrong. Grieve looked at them, drew breath, then his fist hit Bloodsmith's side so hard, he thought, 'There's my liver burst.' He stooped down, winded, then called out,

'Hey, Adrian. There's a hole in your leg.'

'What!' Grieve bawled in fury.

'There's a hole in your leg.'

He pointed down, and Grieve looked too. Within the tear in his trouser leg you saw a jagged gash the length of his calf, where his skin had been ripped by some jag of the bed. They both bent down, and stared deep inside the wound where the glistening sinews slid over each other in a light red wash. Almost you saw the bone but no blood gushed.

'Hold it shut,' Bloodsmith said, bending to close it, but instead of helping Grieve swung a wild punch, then stared, as if hypnotized, at his wound. Abruptly he fainted, so his head flopped across Bloodsmith's chest.

'Does he need a tourniquet?' someone called.

'Yes, round the neck,' Bloodsmith answered. 'Call a bloody ambulance!'

The parents moved in and supported Grieve, while their student children hurried to turn off the electrics. But they must have pressed the wrong switches, for while Grieve was carefully extracted from the bed-frame the strobe-light went into overdrive, the woman on the soundtrack sang backwards in rewind, while the screen froze on an oyster shell with four naked legs protruding.

As he came to, Grieve softly growled, 'Bloodsmith, you're a dead man.'

'Thanks for that.'

Grieve passed out again, briefly.

At the installation's gate a greater audience waited, more parents streaming in, who watched the shaken figures emerge, and among them two men with wounds and bruises, and – what was most strange – both wearing what had been the smartest of suits, which they had splashed with red paint, and slashed at the knees like any torn pair of student jeans.

19

Among the last prints in 'Rubens in London' (which Bloodsmith made through thick and thin in his time of stress) is a lavishly coloured, hugely crowded design. It shows a climactic public occasion: the arrival in London of the Spanish Ambassador, Don Carlos Coloma. By exchange of couriers, the dates have been synchronized. At a stately pace, passing at a distance, Sir Francis Cottington and Don Carlos have proceeded across Europe. But still it is January, in the new year 1630, when they arrive at Madrid and at London. Looking up from Bloodsmith's print we may picture for ourselves the new-built – but seven years finished – Banqueting House of Inigo Jones, with its white fluted columns and white pilasters. The gilt ceiling is oddly blank, for the great allegorical paintings of figures winged and wreathed, representing the Peaceful Reign of James I, have not yet been attached – they are not yet painted, though they have been commissioned, and indeed the artist whose hand will paint them, one Peter Paul Rubens, should be in the room. Surely? Though where is he? A quick glance has failed to find him, nor can we look longer for him. For all eyes turn now to two figures who have sat on the dais at the end, crowned with a crimson canopy that bears the British Arms. Of whom one, from his short legs, we know is Charles I. His eyelids seem reddened and slightly swollen, the lids have a heavy, horny surface. His nose is straight and somewhat fleshy; as we look, he pulls it, then gives a curl to his fox-coloured moustaches. We may see he is not completely pleased. But maybe we have gazed too long, for the royal eye twice has turned our way, with a marked cold hardness, as if he would say, 'Do you look at *me*, Sir/Madam?'

So let us lower our eyes, and raise them to the lady throned beside him. And this is the *real* Henrietta Maria, not an elegant pert-nosed film-star, but a short plump lady almost like a fat child. She has a fold to the skin at her eye, which makes it small but also sharp, the more so when she meets our irreverant stare. She can evidently tell we may not be good Catholics. A lady beside her holds the white fluffy dog, which otherwise Henrietta Maria would hold, which turns its pug eyes full upon us, detecting strangers from another age and impatient, if we approach, to snap.

We beat our retreat, and thus we notice how the hall is arranged. Down the length of the Banqueting House, and out through the door at the end, there stand on the King's side of the Hall the lords and knights and gentlemen attending. Down the opposite side, the Queen's side, stand their ladies; all awaiting the arrival of the Ambassador from Spain.

Who surely approaches, for there is a noise of hooves outside. A quietness spreads back from the doors of the hall. There are tramping feet, clinkings, rustlings. The doorway darkens with a gaggle of attendants, till a man enters, sturdily built, with a weathered face. About his neck he wears a gold chain, and about his torso a blue satin slash. He carries a truncheon. His mien is grave. He is Don Carlos Coloma.

Nor is he alone. For at his side, before the other attendants, steps the man who has brought this Peace to pass, the Sieur Peter Paul Rubens of Antwerp. Grand himself in black satin and velvet and with the richest white lace, you could not think him a mere artisan. Nor does his face show humility, rather there is a dignity.

The only disturbance, as they draw near to the thrones, is a whispered commotion at the end of the hall where those ladies who stood outside, in pressing to get in, have crowded so close that their cartwheel ruffs, so finely starched, have collided and crumpled, and got dented and busted, so they seem ladies escaped from an upset, and a rustled muttering is heard down the hall. But all is stilled, as Don Carlos begins to speak

Rubens listens with a grave attention, though no words here are new to him. All unwished-for, he remembers Van Dyck. Because he must soon return to Antwerp. Will he strike the adulterer? Or call him out, as a gentleman would? What does honour demand?

Away with such thoughts, they have no place here. Stately words fill the space of the hall. Till he sees, high in the line of ladies, her he calls the Indian Maid. Just as she sees him. Their eyes lock. He knows at once, it is love's duel.

She has looked away but her skin has darkened. That must be how she shows her blush. He knows their eyes may not meet again, still his heart makes slow beats like the Angelus bell.

But the King speaks further, even his own name is said. At this instant he is the axis of space.

20

It was odd, after the fight, how little was said about it. Of course, term was ending and people dispersing. When he saw his colleagues again, it would be old news. Presumably there was *sotto voce* gossiping, but to him they were discreet. Did it mean they all knew about Robyn and Grieve? Anyone with a brain could work that out. Yet no one made allusions, or asked him how he was with inquisitive solicitude. Ollie looked at him frowningly but said nothing, and Bloodsmith said nothing to Ollie. Perhaps they thought the fight was to do with Grieve's cuts.

He had bruises and a classic, dark-purple black eye, so he went to the Art School as little as possible. He wondered whether he was sacked, as Grieve had said, but no letter of dismissal or redundancy came. Grieve was not in evidence. He would be confined to his home for some weeks or more, with his leg, lined with stitches, rested up on a chair. When the Art School heard he had applied for a prestigious art-headship in London, this too was passed on as though it had no bearing on Bloodsmith. Perhaps it did not, for Grieve never denied he was the sort of person who puts a place to rights, then moves on to higher things.

Even with Robyn the topic did not arise. She gasped when she saw him, but he gave her only a cursory account, and she did not press for more. Did she and Grieve discuss it on the phone while he was out? He doubted it; he would not know.

It became clear that the fight, and all the scandal round it, would fall into place like a car-crash in the past, to be hidden by time, as a white polished scar might sit on your body, out of sight under clothing and never mentioned. He could not feel good about it. In truth, he was no better than Grieve. He had made a public show of what should be kept dark. Nor could he say, he fought with Grieve because he loved Robyn so much.

It was clear by now there was not a lot in his whole story that he could feel good about. He was cheating and lying onwards daily, while he was liable still to try and lay down the law.

In some way all the Art School knew that with Grieve's possible departure his reform plans were stopped. Printmaking would be safe after all. Fine Art would not be streamlined. The Foundation Course would stay. In the larger world too, there was change in the air: a relaxation in the terms of occupation, a transition from invasion to mere policing, announced like a new, benign social service.

Ollie at this time was much seen in the corridors, large as a monument, his soft chest expanded as his soft voice repeated,

'Attila? Oh, we saw him off.'

~

For several reasons together it was hard now for him and Mae to meet. But you can't switch off love as you switch off a light, and in the end they fixed for a motel. It was away from town and near the motorway, the people staying there would be long-haul. You would not be surprised by someone you knew.

'But what to say?' he wondered, ringing to book. Would he pretend they had been driving all night, and needed to crash at mid-day?

'That's OK, honey-bunch,' the middle-aged voice said on the phone. Nothing needed explaining, he was told the price.

From the car he saw Mae waiting on a pavement, in a brightly pink two-piece: she looked vulnerable, so slender, he was filled with a love that was tender with pity; for her, them, for their vulnerable love.

'My love' and 'My love'.

His free hand holding hers, they drove till they found a terrace of bungalows, with high pitched rooves like witches' hats. They were set within a horseshoe of trees. In the yard one or two of the saloon cars had fluffy toys in the back window, and what looked like local registrations; there was only one large articulated lorry. He mused, was this the city's love-hotel?

The office was not old and not dirty. It was as anonymous as they could wish. The blonde at the desk twinkled brightly through her middle-aged horn-rims, so he recognized her from his phone-call. Her eyes said she knew their game. She didn't know who they were, but she was on their side.

'There you are, my love.' She gave him a plastic card for a key. 'Ring if you want anything.' Clearly she knew they had what they wanted.

The room was clean, with a bright red chair and a bright-coloured stripe from side to side of the bed-cover. On the wall was a meaningless red-and-blue abstract, which perhaps hung in all the other rooms also.

So they had what they never had before, a clean-sheeted fresh-made bed all their own, for as long as ever they could wish to be there. Kissing, they undressed and climbed between the crisp sheets.

She said, 'Things have got sad and difficult.'

He, 'You think we're on borrowed time?'

'We are. Let's do something with it.'

They talked on love, till they came to the dark side. They had hardly been there before. Her eyes gleamed.

'Shall I tie you up?' It was a theory-question, he had nothing to tie her with.

She glowed more darkly.

'I *am* tied, in my head.'

She lay with her slim arms so tightly held in close beside her that he saw he was loving an armless black and beautiful Venus de Milo, reed-slender.

She shone to him, he fell upon her, clasping and caressing, while only her head moved, turning with her eyes closed in an endless deep sigh. As her breathing changed he kissed her more fervently, till she whispered in his ear,

'I want you to tell me something.'

'I will.'

She held him with burning fever-eyes.

'Tell me I have cancer.'

It must be his eyes opened wide – but he had promised. He took breath, then whispered the diagnosis.

'Mae... I must tell you... I am so sorry... you have cancer.'

She gave a yet deeper, moaning sigh. Like breathing in he saw the word he had said shiver and expand inside her. Her arms moved now, and flexed: out of here, Venus de Milo. He watched the death-life fill her growingly. She grabbed and caressed him with more muscle, more zest, than ever before. Her long lean arms were spider arms, while her kisses roved and dug.

'I see it,' he said. 'You are the female praying mantis, devouring her mate.'

'I am. You are. I shall eat every shred of you.'

'Mouthful by mouthful.'

'Exactly. Ah. But boy, you taste good.' She licked her lips, and pulled him close, but now he was clasping too. It was a kind of slow wrestling, they were knitting each other into a loose slipping knot. He was upside down over her, loving her bush and lick-kissing like eating her inner thighs. Till at last they loved fully and later lay back. She did not chatter. Their arms stirred in a luxurious desultory twining.

As he lay with her, and glanced to her, a knowledge came. She had given him a secret, it was the final trust. He loved her utterly and absolutely. He loved her straight soul whatever its twists and he loved her slim energetic dark flame. It was love, nothing else, that was it. He saw this. Still he knew there was another Stephen (off-duty today) who was tied, deep down, to Robyn as well. There just were two Stephens, tied to different women absolutely. Maybe Rubens knew this, that you can love different people who are the opposite of each other.

He lay beside her and looked towards her. He loved her more than ever but the doors of life were closing on them. As he leaned up from the pillow, so did she at the same moment, and their mouths and faces and then arms and bodies joined in a new long, longing kiss of extreme desire-full tender love.

When they left, dressed and in order, there was a brief blur behind him. What? A head had popped out momentarily from a door down the hall: it had seen them for a second then shot back in. He still piecing together the blurred bits of glimpse. He was not even sure if it was man or woman.

He did not say to Mae. He did not know if she caught anything. But he said to himself, as they crossed the yard, Someone saw us who knows us. Someone who knows me. Or someone who knows Mae. Who will they tell? The whole bright day glared danger.

He opened the car-door. But that head had shot back at once – because they were afraid if *we* saw *them*. Who though? What'll they do?

There was no knowing.

~

He had seen a message in Rubens' story and in his. There is a contradiction in the invention, marriage. You want your partner to be loyal for ever. But you, for yourself, cannot be loyal for ever. The tree of life is not so still.

Even so he had not found that image in which his thoughts came all in one. But as he sat in his studio, cogitating, that tingling he knew began in his head. He laid by his pencil. Since he started on Rubens he had begun to see head-films. This would be the biggest of all waking dreams. Come to me, hallucination! He saw a green hill.

People appear— but alas, they are illicit lovers! Down the green hillside clumps the lame princess of Germany (her upturned buttocks wag cheekily) with tall Jan Rubens stooping close. At an easy pace plump Rubens strolls in with a richly dark woman from his travels in Italy. His good wife Isabella Brant follows, with a bending, fawning young Antony Van Dyck. Then yellow-haired Robyn arrives, slimmer and better-exercised than any Rubens girl, with her exquisite boy-man Adrian Grieve. Finally he himself trips in with Mae. He is lightly built with a bit of a blunt boy-face. Mae is naked as in so very many pictures, slender, erect, with tender sweet lovely breasts.

But what shall I do with this sorry crew? Have them frolic in an orgy in synchronized sex? The adulterers' picnic? But that is not what he wants on this day now. Give me the opposite! The utterly different! Away with actuality, I'll hit them with The Impossible Dream, which actuality makes us yearn to see.

Still he has not made a mark on paper, but he takes now a large roll and unwinds its paper across his table-top so it falls to the floor on either side. He starts to work quickly with a greasy black crayon, sliding the paper on as the scenes and figures multiply. Let the Unimaginable present! Look, the lame princess gossips with Maria Pypelinx, while William the Silent, in robes and a linen apron, bears flagons of ale to share across the hill. The haggard King of Spain nods smiling to him, while he chuckles at a ribald aside which Jan Rubens whispers in his ear. Especially, in the foreground Mae and Robyn squat chatting on a tartan rug, then dissolve in laughter as they clutch each other like sisters. He understands (it's in the picture) that they are laughing fit to bust at him, as he dangles ruefully in front of them: he has become a joke, but they are not bad-mooded. Beside them, on the rug, Rubens lounges comfortably, fanning his balding head with his wide-brimmed felt hat. Isabella and the dashing young Antony Van Dyck sit like girl- and boy-friend before him. The three chat easily while Rubens calls a plump teenager to join them. 'Helen! Come here – have a seabream sandwich!' Oh, and over there his own daughter Sally is walking on her hands. Beside her, and certainly darker than Mae, is a fully African girl who flexes her fingers with pleased amazement, though only Bloodsmith can know she is the girl in Sierra Leone whose hands were cut off by a bold soldier of those years, and are now miraculously restored.

For drums roll and down the hill come soldiers, even the Grand Old Duke of York, flicking his hawk-head to opposite sides. Rubens and the picnickers lean back to watch. There are squadrons, even regiments, in turbans and bearskins and helmets with visors, and as they come they chuck down in front of Rubens mace, pike and assault rifle. A patch of snow blooms, where khaki greatcoats open arms to each other. It must be Fritz and Tommy, in the Christmas truce of the First World War. They toss their tin hats in the air and arm in arm, sipping gin and schnapps, bawl carols, 'It came upon the heilige Nacht where Tannenbaums watched by night . . .' All down their Line there is quaffing and joking. A bearded soldier in a breastplate, in a helmet with a knife-edged iron crest, sledge-hammers his cutlass into a ploughshare. For every inconceivable is here today. Jesus Christ, with bandaged hands and feet, leans his elbows back on the grass, chatting with the young plump straight-nosed Mary Magdalene of Rubens. Her long hair is spun platinum shiny as silk. They share a sardine from a cardboard plate and clink plastic cups which forever fill miraculously with slightly sweet red wine. In a deeper hollow Adolf Hitler hunches cross-legged, faced away from everyone in agonized weeping. Often he hurls and writhes his head and hoarsely croaks like the brays of a donkey, then again his black quiff flings at the earth while his tears pour without end for the evil he has made. These tears are black as tar but matt, they fill a reservoir that has no ripple, it is liquid death. Further back anomalous creatures graze, and in the sky overhead an ungainly monster, half lobster half rhinoceros, lurches through the air on iridescent gossamer butterfly-wings.

He sat back. By now the unrolled sheet of paper was at least half the length of his studio wall, he could tape it there like a Bayeux Tapestry. It showed what was not. But Rubens was in it and he was in it. On the skyline was the Tower of Old St Pauls, that burned in 1666. In the river an upside down boat broke surface.

He let himself catch breath. It was his vision, of lust and war transformed to peace. He would compress it to a print and name it, 'The Impossible Feast'.

~

When he next rang Mae, he was startled to hear her high voice. As soon as she spoke, she interrupted herself. 'Marjorie saw us at the motel.'

Marjorie? He knew no Marjorie. 'Will she say?'

'I hope not,' she said curtly. Then, 'She knows Geoffrey.'

'But you talked to her.'

'I said it was a one-off. And it didn't work, nothing happened.'

'Mm.' He didn't like that.

'I don't know what she will do. She said she wouldn't say anything.'

'Good.'

'You don't know her, Stephen. Marjorie had a thing for Geoffrey.' A pause. 'I'm terrified. That would be my nightmare.'

His too? Or his dream? Was this the cataclysm? All the future was up for grabs. Abruptly the road ahead was two roads; or more.

She said, 'We *must* stop. We're on a cliff-edge.'

But nor are these words that full stop. And the future is an open door.

21

They drove to the site of the art-complex to be, in which Robyn's new gallery would have a place. They passed old warehouses near the river, and got out in a courtyard with walls of yellow brick, and windows at odd heights.

'So this was a mini power-station,' he mused. 'I never knew what it was.'

'I think this will work out,' said Sally.

'Why do you think that?' Robyn asked.

'I like that tall doorway. People will want to go up through it.'

Robyn explained, 'That's so you come in at the right height for the Control Room'.

They climbed up the steps, and tried the key, which was stiff. He brought the WD-40 from the car and worked the lock open.

The floor inside had a fluff of dust, which shifted in the draughts from the broken windows. In it they made out recent footprints, other inspectors like themselves.

'Well, Robyn,' he said, 'This *is* a space.'

She smiled, 'It's great, isn't it?'

In the centre, a curved machine rose gigantically, like some beetle-creature the Egyptians adored. Within it he made out turbine-shapes, but it was all disconnected, no cables or ductings ran from it.

'Sally, come off it!' he shouted.

She was clambering up its shoulder. 'I won't get a shock, dad.'

'You don't know what may happen. GET DOWN!'

Instead she gingerly stood tall on the hump-backed summit. Then chanted, 'I'm the King of the Generators!' She looked as though she rode a whale that ploughed the glimmering dusk of the room.

'Sally, come down!' Robyn bawled also.

Slowly, she did. And, shclrank!— as she clambered, her foot went through a metal cover, which broke in brittle flakes of rust.

'Dad!'

'Stop! Don't move!'

Carefully he climbed. He helped her extricate her leg and carefully they worked their way down again.

'Oh fuck fuck fuck!' said Sally.

'Are you cut? We should get a shot!' said her parents.

She was not cut, but the leg of her jeans was ripped.

'Oh!' she wailed, 'I only took them in last week! I sat hours in the bath, to make them fit!'

They continued their explorations, and in their talk the building was rapidly refurbished: old pieces of derrick were painted olive-green, the walls pure white. But the white must have a dash of black in it, he reminded them, or it would be blinding.

'We'll see what happens,' Robyn said quietly.

They closed the door and locked it, then drove out of town and had a pub lunch. Afterwards, at the edge of a field, they lay in the sun to digest. Sally tuned the car-radio to unknown stations, and presently started to dance. They looked with pleasure at her fit young figure, then Robyn got up and danced also. Sally did not welcome her, especially as she swung her arms in different, not-quite-right orbits from Sally's, but presently they fell into a rhythm, and borrowed from each other's movements.

'Come on, dad,' 'Come on, Stephen,' they called. They knew he wouldn't. They looked like giants from where he lay, he saw far-off churches between their ankles. It seemed he was both with them, and light-years distant, viewing them through some optical instrument. He asked, what do I feel? Everything? Nothing? Things were shaping for Robyn, she was on course to be a paragon of the community. But their marriage was... What, an empty space? Can you make a loving marriage all over again, or will it be at best – a convenient arrangement? A sort-of peace, not a good peace. Come to think of it, what peace had Rubens got? Was *that* a true peace, or just armed neutrality like when kids say 'Pax!'. While they all stockpiled arms?

He was hurting, his eyes pricked sharply, while the women still danced on the grass. The love-world with Mae filled the sky like a planet, and enormous sadness hovered nearby. A huge loss was coming, of Mae or of Robyn or both. Also there was Marjorie. Would she start Geoffrey on their track? There was no solid ground to stand on. In the meantime he lived split in two.

Tired from the sun, they climbed in the car. Sally napped in the back, but as they came indoors, she shot into the living room. Theme-music jazzed.

'It's the last episode,' she called; they stayed in the kitchen.

In the last episode of *Unto Death,* fat Mustafa, elegant Mohammed, serious Ahmed and toothy Iskander meet in a room in the Empire State. They are haggard, whey-faced, hardly able to move. But they open the four green attaché cases, all four of which contain, within armour, weapons-grade nuclear material. All will fit now into a single cylinder. Mohammed we can see is praying and weeping for his Polish-Jewish girl: pray Allah that she *has* left the city. Mustafa bites with relish a giant burning chile, which his doctor has forbidden to him. Ahmed says a solemn prayer, we see his glasses mist. Iskander catches all their eyes, and presses the switch from which those wires lead, which will detonate the secondary explosion and collide the nuclear material.

The special surprise of the last episode, however, was to reveal that in other cities also, there had been other groups of four Mujahadeen, all working to the self-same schedule, so that with perfect synchronization not only New York was vaporized in an instant, but London, Sidney and Moscow too. The meaning of 'the bites of God' became clear. For, as Sally had surmised, the weapons were a new form of super-bomb. Where the cities had been there were cavities which you could see from space, between the fluorescent clouds.

It was a shell-shocked Sally who came in the kitchen.
'Was it great?' he asked.
She gazed as though he spoke a monster, and sat.
'Wicked.'

22

Rubens stayed two more months in England after the arrival of Don Carlos Coloma, awaiting permission from the Count-Duke to leave.

Bloodsmith speculates on how Rubens' thoughts may have turned on the subject of Van Dyck. For they were certain to meet, sooner or later, in Antwerp. Probably it grew clear that Rubens would not call him out, or hire ruffians to break him. After all he had only Balthazar's word for what Antony had said, and even then it could have been an idle brag – or simply Balthazar's malice. And supposing Antony and Isabella had been together, who knew of it or even cared now? It was wiser to show no sign that anything could have been amiss. Nor would he give Antony the satisfaction of seeing that he, Rubens, knew he had been humbled. All he would show Antony would be a certain coldness, as if he looked down at him, not unkindly, from an extreme height. Surely that was fair, whatever had happened or had not happened.

Also if you treat a thing as though it never happened, slowly time changes things as though, indeed, that event was not.

What he would do, when he was home, was to find a fair bride, young, ripe and sweet. He could not make his first marriage good, so he would make a new good marriage. He would not travel away and leave her, he would buy some big old grange in the country, and stay there with her, and be uxorious. He would paint her and love her and father her children. She and no other would be his model, and if he painted three goddesses, they would all be her.

This might be his dream. But he was not at home yet. Nor was he betrothed, he was still a free man.

Also Bloodsmith has before him the final scene – scenes, rather – from *Chess with Kings*. Throughout the book, Claeys has seemed unsure what may or may not have happened between Rubens and Lady Rawlings, whom he also calls The Indian Maid. Maybe more was hinted within 'the missing chapter'. In any event, he ends his book with an episode that he calls 'an imagining', and which, more than any other, has been a lure to Bloodsmith.

We are told that Rubens woke one night from a deep trench of sleep, and crept stealthily downstairs. In an alcove which he did not remember he found a car of brass. It was like a chariot from his paintings, decorated with lion-heads and swags. It did not have wheels and was the shape of half-barrel, cut lower at the back so you could step into it. He saw that it was fashioned by Cornelis Drebbel. He knew it was the Car of Art because in front of him, once he got in, was a panel somewhat like a palette, with jewels of different colours. He played on these jewels, and the walls about him, of wood and lime-plaster, wavered and vanished. Then it was hard to tell whether the car was still and the world dashed past, or whether the car sped clear of the world. Dark woodlands and heath wheeled beneath him.

With another touch on a jewel he landed the car in the grounds of a wide-winged country house. Small figures came and went with torches. He could hear a harpsichord and bass-viol, and the calls of people dancing.

He slipped inside, and presently found the person he sought: her ruff was of the lightest airy tracery, so her dark fine-boned head seemed to float in space.

'Lady Rawlings, I am ever your servant.'

The Indian Maid dipped her head. 'Sir Pietro Paulo. My lord is gone overseas.'

Courteously he led her through the hedges and walks. Beyond the trees to the north, they saw a glimmer of light like a furling curtain. He said, 'This island is far to the north'.

'But those lights are no mystery to me. Each year my people cross the wastes and see them. But most we follow the morning star.'

'Who is the morning star?'

'The morning star is Venus and Satan and Jesus.'

Rubens frowned, then nodded. 'Let us visit the stars. Will you join me?'

Her eyes were vigorous and black. She sucked her lip, then siezed his hand, and stepped into the car. With a touch on the panel they swept to the sky; the air blew hard in both their faces. Then all wind stopped. She gazed astonished while it filled him with youthfulness to see the stars blaze in the jet wall of Space. A great distance away a majestic woman leaned across the sky, she squeezed her breast so that her milk made arcs in the air. Some found their way into her child's mouth, the others turned to stars. Elsewhere was a beast half goat, half nautilus shell, and it bucked its horns as a meteor passed.

With a touch on the panel the car swerved forward, so they sped through the wall of stars, and emerged beyond Space in even light. Ahead was a vast high mountain in air, with ramparts and walls, circle on circle, while the upper levels shone with mists and rainbows where figures flew with many-coloured wings. They knew this was Heaven. On a throne at the peak sat a bearded man, who raised his hand like a blessing— or was he waving to them? Rubens thought He looked straight through them, though he knew He looked at all men so.

When they peered over the side of the car, they saw far below them that the light grew turbulent. At the bottom of space there was darkness and smoke, and sparks of fire. As their gaze travelled down they heard faint sounds rising, cries and shrieks maybe of uncountable souls, but faint and fading as a breeze.

They turned back to Heaven but Rubens must, nervously, have touched the wrong stone. For the car gave a jerk, even though they stayed just where they were. He had caused the car to fall backwards through time. In moments centuries fell away: the mists round Heaven converged, and a gold light grew. Then the high walls were rent, there was smoke and din, the angels fought in savage war. One angel was split from neck to waist, and red fire roared from his eye-sockets. The top of Heaven's mountain was a torment of cloud.

He pressed again, so they thrust yet faster back through time. The warfare stopped, and the music and song that came to them now made them close their weeping eyes. The dazzle brightened to blinding, for Heaven was being unmade. Its enormous cedars were shrinking, the high towers and walls unbuilding, while winged throngs joined in the centre of light.

They emerged in darkness. The space was close, the car was still. It was the thickest night, where the hot air pulsed as if inside a heart. He knew he had come to the source of creation. They were inside God in the centre of fire, before there were space and motion and time. There was no further the car could go.

Nor could they stay. Together as one they pressed the panel, and knew they flew at yet faster speeds while seeming to hover in one place. White mist pelted past: it was the texture of Time, as they raced pell-mell to Time's other end. They saw stars die, then the globe of Creation split asunder, where a young man in a red cloth sat on a cloud-throne. New armies of angels descended from Heaven in a golden locust-swarm.

Even past this the car drove on, through endless singing, but they came at last to the shore of a sea. There an elderly bearded man walked on the sand, while the man in the red cloth sat on a dune. There was a further figure they could not see clear, like a woman clothed in large white robes. The sea lapped quietly, an impossibly large red sun was setting. In some way he knew there was everyone here. He said, 'We have arrived at Eternity's edge'.

Her eyes gave a sweetly tired smile. 'Will you take me home now?'

Weary himself, he steered the car back to earth, and landed beside a thicket of trees, from which they could see the bright-lit country house. He helped her to alight.

'I thank you for the ride,' she said.

His voice went hoarse, he had gone young as a boy. 'Will you walk a space with me?' The words felt like his most desperate prayer.

She gazed at him gravely, then took his hand. She led him through trees, to a small pavillion. The door was open. There were logs in a basket, and twigs for kindling. On a shelf they found a tinder-box.

Rubens arranged the logs. She was skilful with the flint, and soon a small log fire was burning.

He caressed her clothed arms, feeling their firmness through the satin and velvet. Carefully he unfastened catches and laces, till she gave her husky deep-toned laugh, breathed in quickly, and the last strings slipped so dress, bodice and petticoat fell to her knees. He watched the firelight play all over her. She undid her hair, which was utterly black. Naked he stood in his middle-aged fleshiness, embarrassed at the fall of his stomach, which he had small power to tauten. His face had come to a serious focus, intelligent with longing.

They have lain down before the fire. She bends close, and with a kind of sniffing and snuffling proceeds at her leisure to smell him all over.

'There is something in the scent of your body I like.'

The firelight has married with her dark-brown skin. From within her helmet of black oiled hair, her eyes burn like pitchballs.

They have fallen on each other in the fury of love.

Rubens and the Indian Maid have met. Where they lie, side by side, is the peace of flames, and the home of love.

Only after he bade her farewell, and left the pavillion behind him, he shuddered and felt the strain of his travelling. He pressed on into the darkening heart of the wood, as if it were the place he came from. The branches bent down as though to enclose him, as though he could turn to a tree like them. For a moment he was unsure who he was, whether Rubens, or one who acted Rubens, or a painter in another age, or another man he could not see, or no man but a spirit at loose. The Northern Lights in the sky extended, like a visible form of organ music. He disappeared, reabsorbed into invisible flame.

23

Finally it was clear what had to be. Also that it would happen today. She would come to his studio one more time, so he would finish the painting he was making.

'Stephen – how are you?' She spoke with a deep-toned, worn affection.

'Marjorie – is discreet?' he asked.

'I think. I hope.' Nothing was sure.

A little they chatted, but it was like friends. The word 'over' did not need to be said. The dry white light from the roof-light said it. The closed air in the room endorsed it, birds-feet on the roof-window tapped it in morse. He looked at her with tender eyes, thinking, I am seeing someone that I know *very* well.

They had coffee then she stripped behind the screen, and came and posed as she had before. He saw the slim, dark-skinned body, standing in the pale fall of light. He looked with growing hurt and yearning.

'What are you thinking, Stephen?'

Startled, he came to. 'Nothing.' He inspected and dabbed, working on particulars of light and shadow, details that had worried him, when he did not have her in front of him. But after all there were not many of these. He stopped and gazed. For it was as he feared. The picture needed only a few strokes more, and then it would be done. He was like a person who turns a corner, and there it is, the road stops dead. There is a time to stop.

King Charles I of England ended his life in a way that Rubens could not have guessed. He was led through the Banqueting House in

Whitehall which had by then, on its gilded ceilings, the paintings that Rubens and his pupils had made, of The Union of the Crowns, The Apotheosis of James I, and The Peaceful Reign of King James I. A window in the north wall had been taken out, so Charles could walk directly from the hall onto the scaffold. To one side of the platform, he saw the block, which, like any butcher's, was simply a section of the trunk of a tree. Kneeling, he rested his head on the cloth, that lay on the resinous new-sawn wood. But before the beheading, he was allowed, like all condemned men, to say a final prayer.

Though the platform is in the open, it is hidden from common view by a screen of black drapery. In the windows opposite, and on the rooftops, people have crowded. The King has pardoned the masked man, who rests the head of his axe on the ground while his hands quietly try the haft. The busy rooftops and the street grow quiet. A slight breeze stirs the hem of the Bishop's gown, and stirs the grey locks about his ears (the King's hair has been cut short).

The kneeling man continues his prayer. Already he is in position for the blade to sever him, but the prayer can continue as long as he wishes. There is no hurry. He can, if he will, pause and simply listen to a bird's call, to the neigh of horses a distance off, to creakings and splashes from the Thames. Till the thought returns, that though he is alive, he has nowhere to go. He is imprisoned in this prayer. If he delayed longer, nothing would change. Does he start to *want* this prayer to end? In a single movement, he spreads his arms wide and the lifting axe wheels and descends to his neck.

So with his painting. Saying it is done is goodbye to Mae. I can't stretch it longer. Like a freeze-frame starting to move, he dabbed the palette and marked the canvas. Presently he stopped, he was adding nothing.

'Stephen?'

'It's done.'

'What?'

He rested the glass palette down.

'It's finished. I don't want to do any more to it.'

'Let me see.'

She came and gazed at the enormous painting. In the centre stood the tall figure of herself. Out to either side there was much scraped canvas — how could it be finished? In some places, unadulterated colour made a flash like coloured lightning. Hovering in space were pieces of cartography, snaking short stretches of the outlines of continents: America? Africa? Eurasia? Here and there names were written, place-names, historical dates. Stretches of canvas were just space or colour, but in other places the small crammed strokes were at once like close writing, and like small jammed figures. You could guess prisons; rape among the baobab trees. A burdened galleon sheds its human cargo in the sea; work-forces bend in the fast-growing cane. A tiny flash is the snap of a lash. Though there were green-blue liquid areas, still there was pain, you saw fire and destruction, in places tall flames arced over in wheels. But most she gazed at herself. He had gone in very close, to parts of her body she did not think about, so not only her breasts were there, but the area underneath her breasts, where you saw how the flesh was shaped by her ribs, and by the boundary where her ribs stopped. He had tried to be both exact, and unemphatic, for such items as knees and ankles. But her softnesses were soft. There was a kind of courteous care to their glow. And he had made her preternaturally tall. Was it the scale, the angle he chose? She looked as though she banged her head on the sky. Her face had a look, tender, searching, penetrating. Had he imposed it? Had he imposed?

That look advanced like a slow spear through you, uncovering to the centre. She was impressed and uneasy, like a person paid too big a compliment. There was a gentleness in the painting, for this naked power who stood relaxed, her weight on one hip, but who seemed also on the verge of movement. Especially he had done something, up at her shoulder-level, so you could wonder whether the odd shapes behind her were also wings grown from her. He had made her skin darker again than it was. She was standing but she was flying as well. She moves towards us *from* the picture. She is a figure standing in a conflagration, like the angel in the sun.

'What do you think?'

'I don't know. There's a lot there.'

They scanned the big picture together. They leaned towards it as if a wind blew from it.

He waited, till she turned, with warm eyes; wet eyes.

'What I make out, I like.'

With bravura he said, 'Let's have a drink.'

He had a bottle of red wine in a cupboard, lying flat and well matured. While she put on the kimono he opened it. She raised her coffee-cup of wine, 'Success to our picture!'

'Our picture!'

They sipped, they surveyed, he mentioned his dealer.

'Is it a companion piece?' she asked. 'I mean, it's like, and different from, the painting you were doing, of Robyn and Europe.'

'It's true. I didn't think of that.'

She laughed. 'Perhaps you should hang them back to back.'

They fell quiet. He looked at her, face down in thoughtfulness. Her eyes kept making small quick blinks. He raised his cup again.

'To our next one.' He had decided this was what he would say.

Her jaw-edge tightened.

'Stephen.'

The roof-window clouded.

'Mae.'

'I meant what I said. We won't meet again. There's just no other way.'

He slightly nodded. They sat. They had got there.

The room was black and hot and red, the blood banged through his head.

Abruptly he said, in spite of all his plan, '*Let's* go public so we stay together.'

'I won't do that.'

They were still.

'I am where I am, Stephen.' She meant, in her marriage.

'People leave their marriages.'

'Yes, they do. But we did not. A person leaves their marriage when they know for sure that it is sunk.'

'Not always.'

He had stood and come close. He moved to hold her, and—

'No, Stephen.'

She pushed hard with her arms to heave him away. So long he had admired her sinews, the warrior maiden lean but powerful, and now he was given to feel this strength. She meant business. He must say too, this is the best way. This is how we will do it.

The hot atmosphere crowded. All the other Maes, from his pictures about the room, stepped forward and stood watching, arms folded or akimbo.

She had gone to dress, she came back dressed. Her face was grey, it was tired and sad. She looked exactly as she had looked long ago. As she looked at him seriously, he saw her eyes again brim with tears.

'You'll write and tell me what happens with your painting.'

'Of course.'

As he watched, she flared in soaring light. Her hair is wild, a bush of fire. She was love and passion. He was letting her go.

She was crying, the tears ran down her face. She stepped forward, 'Goodbye, Stephen.'

They kissed, she kissed him. But what sort of kiss? A peck? It was too quick. She was walking through the studio towards the door.

He watched, and round him others watched. The floor tipped over, the walls swung down. The room filled with people: not pictures of people, but the people themselves. A sly Cardinal stood on watch. Rubens was near, with his steady cool eye. The Count-Duke of Olivarez, with his down-flattened nose, stepped forward from the shadows with a nervous haughtiness. Further back, on a lifted throne, a gloomy white-faced sombre king watched him with a meditative face. Balthazar Gerbier stood in the corner, tensely staring, with his wife and children.

Turn, he was praying. And at the door she turned. She gave her quick smile, even in tears.

The moment the door closed, he felt a crisis of tearing. In hallucination, the Mae in his painting shot up huge. Walls dissolved; the roof-window opened; her vast bright figure stood in vision above him.

The room was crowded, then the room was empty. He was sitting on a chair in front of his canvas. He was studying the finished face of Mae. It had the look with which she had gazed at him, many and many a time. He realized what it was that this look said. It was a look of recognizing. It was a look of seeking and finding. It was a woman finding the person she could truly love.

As he sat before the picture they had made, the shadows swooped and closed towards him. The roof descended, the roof-window darkened, for what arrived as the air turned thick was a misery that he had not guessed. It filled him with lead and bore him down into the earth.

Later he stood and said, 'No!' But there was no one there to hear it.

~

If we visit him after a time of hours – maybe days – we shall find him sitting, a drawing board in his lap. His pencil taps his lip, then moves to the empty, waiting sheet. It hovers.

Behind him, on canvas, a dark, tall, wide-winged figure faces with veiled, tender eyes the blank unknowable future.

24

It is another eight months before Gallery Hearn opens its doors to the Private View of *Rubens in London*. The large, strongly coloured prints, often crowded with figures in a steep perspective, and with something surreal in them, run in a line round the available walls. There, between heads and effervescing glasses, one may glimpse plump Rubens on the threshold of the nightmare Court of Madrid; a giant Rubens and King Charles face to face, inside a Queen's House at Greenwich cut open like a doll's house; Rubens and a dark lady flying through the Heavens in a tub made of brass. The whole set can be bought as a loose-leaf 'livre d'artiste', with a short text by a writer friend set large in elegant type on deckle-edged paper. There are quotations from Rubens' letters and from Jens Claeys, Hans Gotthelf, C.V. Wedgwood and others, and Bloodsmith's debt to *Chess with Kings* is generously acknowledged. A copy that one may leaf through rests, brightly lit, on a table. Here and there large racks stand, where you may pull back, one by one, the preparatory drawings Bloodsmith made, in see-through plastic envelopes: sheets crowded with tiny sketches, some in sequence like a strip cartoon. It appears Bloodsmith has visualized every detail in the chains of event in which each scene arose, down to things people said, which are set out in tiny writing in almost illegible speech-balloons.

Critics jot in corners, while the rooms otherwise are voluble with acquaintances, friends and relatives. Former students examine the technical effects; artist friends discuss their own work. Between these conversations Miles Hearn suaves, allowing the rumbling timbres of his voice to dredge subterranean registers that no other voice can plumb. Well, this way Hearn's views creep inside every ear, and Bloodsmith wants this to occur.

True to his exuberant nature, Hearn has hired two waiters in the dress of the 1620s, to pass round the sparkling while wearing fat slashed sleeves and velvet caps. And in the few words Bloodsmith himself says following Hearn's intro he recalls a conversation with Hearn, where they wondered whether to publicize the show by having flying Rubenses, in cartwheel ruffs and luminous doublets, wheel sky-diving through the London's air, on the model of the Flying Elvises in Vegas. Rubens' mission itself is not for joking, and Bloodsmith turns his talk to War and Peace and Art and Peace and Rubens' ambition for the peaceful union of the nations of Europe.

It is noticeable that as he speaks, Bloodsmith glances every so often to Robyn. Evidently he has tested his 'few words' on her. Her blue eyes quietly rest on him, with only momentary flicks to either side, acknowledging acquaintances. We can see they are old hands in managing a Private View. Not forgetting Sally – for both Bloodsmiths turn smiling, at good moments, to her. If in any way the relations of Stephen and Robyn are less than completely warm and cooperative, we cannot tell this by watching them. It may even be that Robyn, more than Miles Hearn, is responsible for those interviews with press, radio and telly, which, through the day, have drawn Bloodsmith into quiet corners, where he mentions, among other things, the love of Van Dyck and Isabella. He hints that all secrets will be revealed, when the 'missing chapter' of Jens Claeys is found at last.

By the time all words are over enough red dots have appeared on the corners of frames, and the Victoria and Albert Museum has ordered a complete copy of the 'livre'. With most of the visitors gone, Hearn, the Bloodsmiths and certain relatives and friends troop off to eat convivially.

A week or two later someone else visits the exhibition, during a day-trip to London. She is tall and slender and elegant and dark-skinned. She works her way round the prints, studying each closely, also the livre, and the racks of drawings. Afterwards she stands in thought near the door. Her face is grave, and at one point she touches her eyes with a tissue. Then she realizes that Miles Hearn is inspecting her with increasing interest, and is preparing to introduce himself.

A shiver passes through her; it is perhaps also a sigh. She steps outside and begins to walk slowly up New Bond Street. Looking up, she sees herself reflected in another dealer's plate-glass window. Abruptly she smiles, and the elegant dark woman there returns a wide, white smile. She quickens her pace, her lean legs grow brisk. Maybe she is joining her husband for lunch, with plans for the afternoon and a theatre in the evening?

~

In February 1630, shortly before Ruben returned to Flanders, King Charles conferred a knighthood on him. The King gave him the sword with which he dubbed him, the sword itself being enriched with diamonds. Rubens in turn presented to the King the great painting representing Peace and War, which he had made in the Gerbiers' house.

Rubens finally left London on 6 March. We may imagine the small cavalcade winding through the orchards and vineyards of Kent, perhaps with a wagon following, bearing their trunks of apparel and souvenirs.

After reporting to the Spanish court, Rubens returned to his two sons, and to his life and his painting, at Antwerp. In December 1630 he married the pretty, plump, blond-haired Helena Fourment, then sixteen. He painted her many times and she bore him five children. He suffered increasingly from the gout, and died in 1640.

His English expedition was not his last diplomatic mission, but it was his most successful. The Peace he made with England endured for some years in a Europe that itself was increasingly embattled, in the period known now as the Thirty Years' War, which began in 1618 and ended in 1648. It was not one war, but many wars tied together, and when it ended other wars began. For war continues and through history the death-toll and the atrocities worsen.

Balthazar Gerbier became for a short time the English Resident in

Brussels, where he was party to conspiracies and then, being short of money, sold his knowledge to the Archduchess. Back in London he opened an Academy of the Muses at Bethnal Green, where he taught astronomy, navigation, fireworks, fortification and riding the great horse. He died in 1667. His proposal for a national bank, which he had pressed on Charles I and others, was realized when the Bank of England was founded in 1694.

His daughters Elizabeth and Susan escaped their family, in the 1640s, by entering the English convent of Sion in Paris. Balthazar published pamphlets appealing for their return, and they did return. Little is known of their later lives.

The later life of Stephen and Robyn is outside this account. But if Marjorie keeps quiet, and if they stay together, they may in time get back to the closeness and intimate love they had once. That can't happen overnight – it could take ten years to get there truly. Hardest for Bloodsmith, in that event, will be those times when he dreams he is still with Mae, or that she has come back to him as she did before, then he wakes to find she is truly gone. Even so the day may finally come when, if he finds an old picture of Mae in a portfolio, he will sigh and turn it over. For he will no longer be in that realm, which will fall slowly into the past like a feather down a mine-shaft.

Over the years he will return to his subject of 'The Impossible Feast'. In all the versions soldiers from several centuries will gossip with half their armour off. Impossible creatures wobble over the sky, some of them flying upside down. Each etching will show what cannot be, like Robyn and a woman dark as Africa sitting engrossed in a tête-à-tête while Rubens, in his slashed doublet, ribs Bloodsmith. His other arm rests lightly round Isabella, and the young Van Dyck warbles, with a lute, to them both. King Charles sits with them, with his head in his hands. His raised eyebrows say, 'I must make the best of this.' In a flying green gondola above their heads Cardinal Richelieu, in all his crimsons, makes a point, with some heat, to Mohammad and God.

If we ask Bloodsmith what *thought* he has on this theme, he will say: there are several kinds of impossible feast; any form of Heaven is an impossible feast; a happy adultery is an impossible feast. World peace is *the* impossible feast. The peace painting that Rubens made is an impossible feast, for leopards do not roll over like kittens simply so children may play with them, nor do world leaders call off a war because they see that tens of thousands will be maimed or killed— And yet the Peace that Rubens wanted occurred. For the impossible may also happen. In love, also, the Impossible may arrive, and the banquet. Then, simply, the impossible feast is Love.

The painting Rubens made in London is known as 'Peace and War.' After the death of Charles I it passed into the possession of the Doria Family in Genoa. Many years later, it was bought by the Marquis of Stafford, first Duke of Sunderland, who, in 1827, presented it to London's National Gallery. It hangs there now, on the red-damasked walls. In it may be seen the bare-breasted goddess Pax, squeezing an arc of milk towards the mouth of a babe, while behind her the armed goddess Minerva pushes away a mature-faced Mars. In the foreground, next to the playful leopard, a grizzled satyr pours his cornucopia towards three children, who are known to be George, Elizabeth and Susan Gerbier. Susan gazes to us out of the picture, with a quick look, direct, as if she knew us already. So she met the eye of Charles I, inspecting his gift, as she had met the eye of Rubens, seeing her and painting her, with that look which Clara Serena earlier had when she was small and caught his eye brightly in the young home he had once with Isabella Brant.

NOVELS by John Harvey

The Plate Shop (Collins/Fontana, 1979)
Winner of the David Higham Prize for Fiction, shortlisted for the Hawthornden Prize and the Yorkshire Post Fiction Prize

'Not merely unusual but also very good – precise, subtle, authoritative and unexpectedly exciting.' HERMIONE LEE, *Observer*

'A prose which is accomplished, poetic, incisive.' A.S. BYATT, *Times*

'The novel's people are alive in a prose of precise passion.' CHRISTOPHER RICKS, *Sunday Times*

'An admirable first novel... pre-eminently a book for the times... one of the best novels about work that I can remember.' THOMAS HINDE, *Sunday Telegraph*

Coup d'Etat (Collins/Fontana, 1985, Athenaeum in USA, Best Seller Bell in Greek translation)

Selected by Chris Patten in the *Sunday Telegraph* as 'the novel which shows the best grasp of political life'.

'What a treat ... stylish, politically interesting and immensely readable.' NINA BAWDEN, *Daily Telegraph*

'Tolstoyan . . . a wide-ranging, detailed and sympathetic portrayal of a whole society.' ANTHONY THWAITE, *Observer*

'Impressive, compelling . . . it is a fine work . . . tense, exciting and significant.' ALLAN MASSIE, *Scotsman*

'One's main feeling in response to this gripping novel is gratitude. John Harvey has shown us what the novel can and should be in our time. He undertook an enormous task, and has constructed a novel of accomplished craftsmanship to carry it out. It is moving and harrowing: and it is sound.' DAVID HOLBROOK, *Authenticity and the Novel*

'Moments of intense suffering and intense tenderness are treated with equal sensitivity by John Harvey in this fine novel.' *Greek Review International*

The Legend of Captain Space (Collins/Fontana, 1990)

'The picture he paints of parenthood is eerie, convincing and, in a perverse way, beautiful.' MAUREEN FREELY, *Independent on Sunday*

'An impeccably spare prose... It is hard to say precisely why this bare narrative is so memorable and haunting. It is partly because of the assurance with which Harvey chooses the details of life we are given. He gives us things in a few lines — a human body, a crying child, a heavy lorry, so that we are made to see them simultaneously as the characters see them, and from some huge distance, as perfected instances of some terrible mystery of human existence.' A.S. BYATT, *Independent*

'Compelling and enjoyable . . . John Harvey writes with consistent authority. The prose is spare, evocative and effective... In his prose, which is at once stylized, rhythmical and unadorned, Mr Harvey recalls

Hemingway; it is a prose which commands attention by its laconic denial of any flourish; a prose which as it were steps modestly back into the limelight.' ALLAN MASSIE, *Scotsman*

The Subject of a Portrait (Polar Books, 2014)

'The novel is so alive, so full of movement and momentum.' ANITA DESAI

'Captivating . . . a discerning and rather sumptuous study of one of history's most infamous love triangles.' *Independent*

'Excellent; I was taken by every page; more, every sentence. It is beautifully and startlingly written, the sudden shifts and turns, impulse and counter-impulse within and from these remarkable people. A very fine love story.' CHRISTOPHER RICKS

'A true page-t`urner . . . it becomes impossible to put down.' *The PreRaphaelite Society Review*

'The characters of Millais and Effie are far from romantic stereotypes; their passion is depicted as convincingly as Heathcliff and Cathy's. But it's the strangely sympathetic portrayal of the monstrous innocent Ruskin, with his angels and demons in constant conflict, that dominates the narrative and lingers in the memory.' *Tredynas Days*

'Powered by lyrical prose of the highest order . . . John Harvey's evocation of Victorian England and its climate of sexual repression will be hard to match. So too will the subtlety and eye for intimate detail with which he brings alive an achingly beautiful love story.' FARZANA SHAIKH